SATURNINE

Dan Abnett

BLACK LIBRARY

A BLACK LIBRARY PUBLICATION

First published in 2020.
This edition published in 2022 by
Black Library,
Games Workshop Ltd.,
Willow Road,
Nottingham, NG7 2WS, UK.

Represented by: Games Workshop Limited – Irish branch,
Unit 3, Lower Liffey Street, Dublin 1,
D01 K199, Ireland.

10 9 8 7 6 5 4

Produced by Games Workshop in Nottingham.
Cover illustration by Neil Roberts.

See Black Library on the internet at

blacklibrary.com

Find out more about Games Workshop
and the world of Warhammer 40,000 at

games-workshop.com

Printed and bound by CPI Group (UK) Ltd, Croydon, CR0 4YY

*For Terrance Dicks, 1935–2019, who showed us all that
there was nothing humble about the humble tie-in.*

THE HORUS HERESY®
SIEGE OF TERRA

It is a time of legend.

The galaxy is in flames. The Emperor's glorious vision for
humanity is in ruins. His favoured son, Horus, has turned from
his father's light and embraced Chaos.

His armies, the mighty and redoubtable Space Marines, are
locked in a brutal civil war. Once, these ultimate warriors fought
side by side as brothers, protecting the galaxy and bringing
mankind back into the Emperor's light. Now they are divided.

Some remain loyal to the Emperor, whilst others have sided
with the Warmaster. Pre-eminent amongst them, the leaders of
their thousands-strong Legions, are the primarchs. Magnificent,
superhuman beings, they are the crowning achievement of
the Emperor's genetic science. Thrust into battle against one
another, victory is uncertain for either side.

Worlds are burning. At Isstvan V, Horus dealt a vicious blow
and three loyal Legions were all but destroyed. War was begun,
a conflict that will engulf all mankind in fire. Treachery and
betrayal have usurped honour and nobility. Assassins lurk in
every shadow. Armies are gathering. All must choose a side or die.

Horus musters his armada, Terra itself the object of his wrath.
Seated upon the Golden Throne, the Emperor waits for his
wayward son to return. But his true enemy is Chaos, a primordial
force that seeks to enslave mankind to its capricious whims.

The screams of the innocent, the pleas of the righteous resound
to the cruel laughter of Dark Gods. Suffering and damnation
await all should the Emperor fail and the war be lost.

The end is here. The skies darken, colossal armies gather. For the
fate of the Throneworld, for the fate of mankind itself...
The Siege of Terra has begun.

DRAMATIS PERSONAE

The Traitor Host of Warmaster Horus Lupercal

FULGRIM	'The Phoenician', Primarch of the III Legion
PERTURABO	'The Lord of Iron', Primarch of the IV Legion
ANGRON	'The Red Angel', Primarch of the XII Legion
MORTARION	'The Pale King', Primarch of the XIV Legion
MAGNUS THE RED	'The Crimson King', Primarch of the XV Legion

The IV Legion 'Iron Warriors'

YZAR CHRONIATES	Lord Captain of the Second Armoured Century
ORMON GUNDAR	Warsmith, Stor-Bezashk
BOGDAN MORTEL	Warsmith, Stor-Bezashk

The XVI Legion 'Sons of Horus'

| KINOR ARGONIS | Equerry to Warmaster Lupercal |

The Mournival

EZEKYLE ABADDON	First Captain
HORUS AXIMAND	'Little Horus', Captain, Fifth Company
TORMAGEDDON	
FALKUS KIBRE	'Widowmaker', Captain, Justaerin Terminator section
LEV GOSHEN	Captain of the 25th Company
TYBALT MARR	Captain of the 18th Company

SERAC LUKASH	Line Captain, Fifth Company, Haemora Destroyer Squad
URRAN GAUK	Line Captain of the Justaerin Terminator section
XAN EKOSA	Assault Captain, Cthonae Reaver Squad, 18th Company
DERALL	Line Captain of the Catulan Reaver section

The XII Legion 'World Eaters'

KHÂRN	Captain, Eighth Assault Company
EKELOT	of the Devourers
KHADAG YDE	of VII Rampager
HERHAK	of the Caedere
SKALDER	
BRI BORET	Centurion
HUK MANOUX	Centurion
BARBIS RED BUTCHER	
MENKELEN BURNING GAZE	
JUROK	of the Devourers
UTTARA KHON	of III Destroyers
SAHVAKARUS THE CULLER	
DRUKUUN	
VORSE	
MALMANOV	of the Caedere
MURATUS ATTVUS	
KHAT KHADDA	of II Triari
RESULKA RED TATTER	

GORET FOULMAW

CISAKA WARHAND   Centurion

MAHOG DEARTH   of VI Destroyers

HASKOR BLOOD
SMOKE

NURTOT   of II Triari

KARAKULL WHITE
BUTCHER

The XV Legion 'Thousand Sons'

AHZEK AHRIMAN   Chief Librarian

The III Legion 'Emperor's Children'

EIDOLON   Lord Champion

VON KALDA   Equerry to Eidolon

LECUS PHODION   Vexillarius

QUINE MYLOSSAR

NUNO DEDONNA

JARKON DAROL

SYMMOMUS

ZENEB ZENAR

JANVAR KELL

The Dark Mechanicum

EYET-ONE-TAG   Speaker of the Epta War-Stead
                                linked unity

The Defenders of Terra

JAGHATAI KHAN   'The Warhawk of Chogoris',
                                Primarch of the V Legion

ROGAL DORN   Praetorian of Terra, Primarch of
                                the VII Legion

| Sanguinius | 'The Great Angel', Primarch of the IX Legion |
| Malcador the Sigillite | Regent of the Imperium |

The Talons of the Emperor

Constantin Valdor	Captain-General of the Legio Custodes
Amon Tauromachian	Custodian
Tsutomu	Custodian, Prefect Warden
Jenetia Krole	Vigil-Commander of the Silent Sisterhood
Aphone	Raptor Guard, Silent Sisterhood

Officers and Seniors Militant of the War Court

Saul Niborran	High Primary Solar General
Clement Brohn	Militant Colonel Auxilia
Sandrine Icaro	Second Mistress Tacticae Terrestria
Katarin Elg	Mistress Tacticae
Niora Su-Kassen	Solar Command Staff, former Admiral of the Jovian Fleets

The VII Legion 'Imperial Fists'

Archamus	Master of the Huscarls
Diamantis	Huscarl
Cadwalder	Huscarl
Vorst	Veteran Captain
Camba Diaz	Lord Castellan of the Fourth Sphere, Siege Master
Fafnir Rann	Lord Seneschal, Captain of the First Assault Cadre

FISK HALEN	Captain of 19th Tactical Company
TARCHOS	Sergeant, 19th Tactical Company
MAXIMUS THANE	Captain, 22nd Company Exemplars
SIGISMUND	First Captain, Marshal of the Templars
BOHEMOND	Venerable Dreadnought
BLEUMEL	
THIJS REUS	
MADIUS	Captain, Wall Master at Oanis
KASK	Sergeant, Wallguard
LEOD BALDWIN	Seconded to kill team duty
GERCAULT	Seconded to kill team duty
MATHANE	Heavy weapons, seconded to kill team duty
ORONTIS	Heavy weapons, seconded to kill team duty

The V Legion 'White Scars'

SHIBAN KHAN	called 'Tachseer'
NARANBAATAR	Stormseer
KHERTA KAL	
YETTO	of the Kharash
QIN FAI	Noyan-Khan

The IX Legion 'Blood Angels'

RALDORON	First Captain, First Chapter
ZEPHON	'The Bringer of Sorrows', Captain
BEL SEPATUS	Captain-Paladin of the Keruvim Host
SATEL AIMERY	

Khoradal Furio
Emhon Lux

The Imperial Army (Excertus, Auxilia and others)

Aldana Agathe	Marshal, Antioch Miles Vesperi
Konas Burr	Militant General, Kimmerine Corps Bellum
Ahlborn	Conroi-Captain, Hort Palatine (Command Prefectus Unit)
Bastian Carlo	Colonel (33rd Pan-Pac Lift Mobile)
Al-Nid Nazira	Captain, Auxilia
Mads Tantane	Captain (16th Arctic Hort)
Willem Kordy	(33rd Pan-Pac Lift Mobile)
Joseph Baako Monday	(18th Regiment, Nordafrik Resistance Army)
Ennie Carnet	(Fourth Australis Mechanised)
Seezar Filipay	(Hiveguard Ischia)
Jen Koder	(22nd Kantium Hort)
Bailee Grosser	(Third Helvet)
Olly Piers	(105th Tercio Upland Grenadiers)
Pasha Cavaner	(11th Heavy Janissar)
Lex Thornal	(77th Europa Max)
Adele Gercault	(55th Midlantik)
Oxana Pell	(Hort Borograd K)
Getty Orheg	(16th Arctic Hort)
And others	

Sindermann's order

Kyril Sindermann	Historian
Ceris Gonn	Historian

Hari Harr	Historian
Therajomas Kanze	Historian
Leeta Tang	Historian
Dinesh	Historian
Mandeep	Historian

Serving the Adeptus Mechanicus

| Arkhan Land | Magos, Technoarchaeologist |

The Chosen of Malcador

Garviel Loken	The Lone Wolf
Helig Gallor	Knight Errant
Endryd Haar	'The Riven Hound', Blackshield
Nathaniel Garro	Knight Errant

At Blackstone

Vaskale	Solar Auxilia veteran, Warden of the Watch
Euphrati Keeler	Former Remembrancer
Edic Aarac	Inmate
Basilio Fo	Inmate
Gaines Burtok	Inmate

Others

John Grammaticus	Logokine
Erda	
Leetu	Her Legionary
Nerie	Pilot, Port Guild

'The Earth has lost its youthfulness; it is gone, like a happy dream. Now every day brings us closer to destruction, to desert...'

– Terran poet Vyasa, circa 850.M1

'I need to fight whole armies alone; I have ten hearts; I have a hundred arms; I feel too strong to war with mortals – bring me gods!'

– the dramaturge Rostand, circa 900.M2

'Immortality, for us, is impossible.'

– Horace, Odes, fl. M1

PART ONE

HELL IS
A CHAINSWORD DEEP

Reiteration

Who knows what He is thinking, or what He was ever thinking? He moves, Kyril Sindermann conceded to himself as he climbed the last of the steps, our beloved Emperor, He moves in mysterious ways.

'Mysterious,' he said aloud, breathing the word like a sigh. The cold echo of the stairwell answered him, the patter of the rain. Sindermann was exhausted. He had come a long way; not just up the thousand steps of the tower, but along the path before that, the long road that had once seemed so promising, but had led him – led them all – into unforgiving disaster.

Kyril Sindermann had walked alongside history as it was being made, and had been appointed to observe and record that process. But history, wilful and cruel, never leads where it is expected. It cannot be anticipated. Sindermann should have known that most basic of professional principles – history only makes sense in hindsight.

Did He know? The beloved Emperor? Did He read history backwards and understand what the end of the book would be? If He did, could He have changed the words? Could He have warned us? Did He try?

Did He know, all along, in His mysterious way, that this would be where it all led to?

Here?

Sindermann unlatched the door and pushed it open. Cold air met his face. The roof garden hissed with rain. Beyond, grey cloud sloped from the upper bastions of the Sanctum Imperialis, cloud-conjured ghosts of the mountains that had been levelled to make way for this citadel. It had once seemed a wonder, a great feat of man, the flattening of a mountain range to make the foundation stone of a city-palace. 'No greater wonder can be imagined,' some witness had written at the time.

No longer. Greater wonders had come since to eclipse it: the war to pacify the heavens; the crusade to crush bestial species; the liberation of lost humanity; the unification of the cosmos.

The revelation of unthinkable horror. The betrayal of all that was.

Now this, here. Mountains had been shaved flat to build a palace, and from that palace, an empire was raised. All that would fail, and the palace would fall, and the rocks that had been planed away to hold it up forever would split, and so too the world beneath that rock.

Sindermann wandered along the garden walk. The Katabat Terrace, a hanging garden, once a paradise. The beds had been left to grow wild, stone tubs and planters split by untended roots. Auto-irrigation and pesticide systems had been shut down to conserve power. The botanical servitors had long since been recoded to serve in the munition vaults. The garden staff had been conscripted to siege labour brigades or sent to the front lines. Other Palace gardens, and there were many, had been turned over to food cultivation.

But not the Katabat. The highest, the loneliest, the Emperor's favourite, near the top of old Widdershin's Tower. It had simply been abandoned. Perhaps He, the beloved Emperor, hoped it could be opened again one day, the gardeners brought home, the precious specimens nurtured back into bloom.

If that was so, thought Sindermann, then hope still existed.

The Katabat had not withered. Rain drummed across its paths, beds and parapets, pooled on uneven flagstones, and overspilled from empty pots. The garden had turned feral, overcome with weeds, untamed creepers and unpruned saplings. Water dripped from the bowed and colourless buds of chemically disfigured flowers. The symbolism was breathtaking.

It wasn't even rain, not natural rain. The entire Inner Palace, the Sanctum Imperialis, of itself a city bigger than old Konstantinopol, had been shut inside its dome of void shields since before the start of Secundus. The shields had never been designed to stay up for so long. All air was recirculated, processed, breathed a trillion times, and artificial weather systems had built under the dome, breeding stained cloud, acid rain and pocket storms that churned and festered beneath the crackling fields. This rain was recycled sweat, body moisture, piss, blood.

It was worse, he had been told, outside the inner voids: toxic smogs and bacterial clouds lifting from the burning sectors and the battlefronts, or artificially engineered; searing firestorms; ash blizzards; epileptic convulsions of lightning spasming from the aftershock of orbital strikes; shrieking tornados, propagated by the concussion of incessant bombardments. The ground shook. Even here, he could feel the constant tremble.

That was just here... Just the vast Palace Zone, the *Zone Imperialis Terra*, a continent wide. Beyond it, global hell, a systematic ravaging of the home planet, a collateral disaster of pollutants, seismic shock and fallout that was harrowing outwards from this monumental focus of attack. He had been told the plume of poison ash and smoke trailing off the Imperial Palace obscured the entire Europa and Pan-Asiatic landmasses.

He had been told…

He didn't need to be told. He could see it. He could see enough. He stepped to the parapet, rain kissing his face, and stood over the thousand-metre drop straight down to the roofs of the West Constant Barracks.

He could see the sprawl of the Sanctum Imperialis Palatine, the scope of the vast city-palace beyond, the Anterior Barbican, the Greater Palace Magnifican, tumbled and laid out like a casualty awaiting death. He could see the vast gates, the spires, the immense forms of the once-majestic ports, the lines of walls that had been built never to fall. Beyond that, in every direction, the belts of flame, the girdling circumference of black smoke banked forty kilometres high. And through the distortion of concentric void shields that blurred the air to soft focus like petroleum jelly on glass, he could see the flash and blink of detonations, the blaze of vast and distant fire-deaths, the streak of energy weapons like lightning light years long. The muffled thunder of existential collapse rumbled on, lagged and softened by the void shields.

No sun, just twilight. Poison grey. Like sight failing.

This, here. Where it began. Where it ends.

Sindermann looked down, down the deep drop. Rain had got under his coat, and into his eyes in place of tears. He saw the toes of his boots projecting slightly over the stone lip.

He had been an iterator, but there was nothing left to say. He had been a historian, but history was dead. He had found faith – not just an intellectual faith in the Emperor's steward-ship of mankind, but something more: a true, shining faith that he had never dreamed possible. He'd clung to that, felt blessed by it for a while, secure against the gathering darkness. He'd even tried to share that word.

But the darkness had thickened. The howls of the Neverborn had drawn closer. His faith had leaked away, frail in the face of pandaemonic horror, as piss-weak as his philosophy and scholarship. No purpose remained for him. Last night, some of his few remaining friends had claimed that there was still some history left to tell: a future that would in turn beget another future that would want to hear, and deserved to hear, what had taken place before its birth. From the Katabat Terrace, Sindermann knew that could not be true.

Others, young Hari, so diligent and dutiful, had insisted that whatever history was left, its dying days should be recorded.

'The death should be marked,' he had said, 'even if no one survives to read of it.'

Untrue, young man. Wrong. Yes, a few days or weeks or even months of history remained, but Kyril Sindermann could see it from where he stood. He could read it in the distant mountain-walls of black smoke that surrounded them, the thickets of unquenchable flames. There was history left, but it was not a history that should be recorded. It was nothing but a litany of pain, of agony, of mutilation, of miserable destruction. No poet ever described the last, involuntary twitches of a corpse, and all historians had more decency than to linger over such things. The history left to write was a night terror of daemons, of abomination, of obscenity, and that should not be set down for anyone to hear.

Even if they tried, there were no words left. No words in any human language could begin to describe the horror of this end.

'I'll speak and write no more,' he had told them.

No one had replied at first. They had all understood what he meant. Kyril Sindermann would not be the first human

soul to step away, to end his witness by choice so he didn't
have to bear the rest of history. Thousands had gone already,
each choosing his or her individual method. To step away
into empty air, a thousand metres above the West Constant
rooftops...

'Don't be a coward,' Ceris had said at last. 'If you won't
speak it or write it, go to the muster. Take a jack-vest and a
rifle. Go to the walls, wherever they point you, and spend your
end there. Don't be a shitting coward. If you don't want your
life, use it for others.'

That had stung. Shame had got him as far as the muster point.
In the queue, the air filled with sobbing and farewells and the
stink of gun oil, he had considered that, quite frankly, he was an
atrocious shot. He would be wasting powercells another could
discharge better than him, using a weapon another could wield
to greater effect. He would be eating rations that could fill other
bellies, breathing air that could fill other lungs.

He wasn't a coward. He was a drain on resources. One made
one's contribution the best way one could.

Besides, he thought, I have seen enough. I was there, the
day... I was there at the start. At the spark, the point of igni-
tion. Right there. I have seen too much, and lived too long.

His toes over the ledge. Rain on his face, tasting of chlorine
and bonemeal. His breathing ragged.

He raised his hands, slow, shaking, from his sides, like a
tumbler balanced on a circus ball, like a fledgling about to
take flight.

'I've seen enough,' said Kyril Sindermann to the rain and
the air and the weeds. 'If He knew that history was going to
eat itself, why didn't He tell us? Our beloved Emperor. If He
had a plan, why didn't He share it? If He had a plan, is this
it? What was He thinking?'

'Were you addressing me?'

Sindermann started. He almost slipped off the wet ledge. He bent down, steadied himself with one hand on the damp stone, and looked around.

'Who's there?' he asked, a halt in his voice.

'I thought I was alone up here. Were you addressing me?'

Sindermann began to climb down. Suddenly the drop terrified him. He clutched the parapet to stop himself toppling.

A figure pushed aside dank vines and tangled branches, and stepped onto the path. The cloth of his mantle was jewelled with raindrops.

'Sindermann? What the hell are you doing?'

'M-my lord, I come here from time to time–'

Rogal Dorn, several times Sindermann's size, took his arm and lifted him off the parapet like a small child. He set him down.

'Were you going to jump?' Dorn asked. His voice, a whisper, was the rumble of an ocean murmuring secrets in its sleep.

'N-no. No. My lord. I came to view the scene. It is… perhaps the best vantage point. So high up… I came to observe, and gain a greater perspective.'

Dorn frowned, nodded. The Praetorian's massive form was unarmoured: a yellow wool tunic, his dead father's old, fur-edged robe, an overcloak of grey.

'Is that… Is that why you are here?' Sindermann asked. He wiped rain from his brow.

'No.'

'Your pardon. I'll leave you to–'

'Sindermann, were you going to jump?'

Sindermann looked up into the giant's eyes. No lie could exist there.

'No,' he said. 'No. I don't think I was, after all.'

Dorn sniffed. 'It's all right to be afraid,' he said.

'Are you afraid?'

Dorn paused. Rain ran down his temples. It appeared he

was actually considering the question, which Sindermann had regretted the moment it came out.

'That's a luxury I'm not permitted,' he said at length.

'Do you wish you were?'

'I don't know. I don't...' Dorn faltered. 'I don't know what it feels like. What does it feel like?'

'Like...' Sindermann shrugged. 'How do you feel?'

'I feel... a biting at my throat. A pounding inflammation of my mind. I feel the limit of my ability, and yet I must give more. And I don't know where that will come from.'

'Then I think, if I may be so audacious as to say so, you are feeling afraid.'

Dorn's eyes widened slightly. He stared into the distance.

'Really? That's a very bold thing to say to me, Sindermann.'

'Agreed,' said Sindermann. 'I apologise. Thirty seconds ago I was intent on flinging myself from the parapet, so speaking truth to a lord primarch is not quite so daunting as perhaps it once might have been... Actually, that's a lie. Now I think on it. Damn me, offending you is... more alarming than the prospect of my own death. I can't believe I said that.'

'Don't apologise,' said Dorn. 'Fear... So that's what it tastes like. Well, well.'

'What are you afraid of?' asked Sindermann.

Dorn looked at him and frowned, as if he didn't understand.

'What are you afraid of?' Sindermann asked. 'What are you really afraid of?'

'Too many things,' said Dorn simply. 'Everything. For now, I'm simply afraid of the idea that I can, after all, know fear.' He paused, then as an afterthought, 'For Throne's sake, don't tell Roboute.'

'I won't, my lord.'

'Good.'

'You should tell him yourself.'

Dorn looked at Sindermann.

'You think I'll get that chance?' he asked. 'That's not the optimism of a man bent on ending his life.'

'Further evidence, lord, that I was just up here enjoying the view,' said Sindermann. 'Is my optimism misplaced? Is your brother close yet? Do we know?'

'We do not. I do not know if Guilliman or the Lion or any other loyal bastard is going to get here in time.'

They fell silent. Rain drizzled around them.

'What were you doing up here, lord?' asked Sindermann. 'Forgive me, but shouldn't you be running this defence? At your post, data arrayed...'

'Yes,' said Dorn. 'Seventy-eight hours straight, last shift, at Bhab Command, watching a thousand feeds scroll, implementing action and reaction. I–' he cleared his throat, 'I find, iterator, as this onslaught wears on, it's fruitful to step away. Just now and then. An hour alone here, or in the Qokang Oasis, to clear my head. To re-see what I have seen. It's all in here...'

He tapped his brow.

'The data. Eidetic recall. I meditate, and process it as well as any strategium's cogitation. Better, perhaps. New forms occur to me, new micro-strategies. I step away to rethink, and recompose. And I try to think, if I can, like my opponent. Like the bastard Lord of Iron, Perturabo. I consider the logic of his processes. In the meantime, the ongoing truth is never far away.'

He showed Sindermann the noospheric-linked dataslate tucked in the pocket of his robe.

'I am sorry I disturbed you, lord.'

'No need. A break or interruption is a healthy tool for thought-breakthrough. Clarity through interruption. One can become too locked in. As in a blade-fight. A rhythm develops, a pattern, hypnotic. You win by breaking the pattern.'

'Then I am glad to be of use,' said Sindermann. 'And glad that I did not find you intent on the same escape that brought me up the stairs.'

Dorn eyed him.

'I apologise for that suggestion too,' said Sindermann.

Dorn glanced at the parapet. 'A thousand metres onto the roof of the West Constant? I doubt that would do the job.'

'What would?'

'One of my brothers, I would expect.'

'Ah,' said Sindermann.

'It was unthinkable,' said Dorn softly. 'We thought... We believed we could not be killed, until Manus fell. But that's just history now.'

They looked out at the burning horizon.

'Have you given up on history?' Dorn asked.

'You heard that part, then?' Sindermann said, embarrassed.

'History eating itself? Yes.'

'The Order of Remembrancers is long dissolved, by Council edict. Its purpose is curtailed. There is no formal program-meme. The late Solomon Voss' great project is abandoned. No more illumination is needed, no more iterators required to articulate the truth of–'

'It was necessary to control the flow of ideas,' said the Praetorian gently. 'Fundamentally necessary, as a measure of security. The word of the enemy can be toxic. The idea of the treason is toxic. It is infectious. You know that.'

'I suppose I do,' said Sindermann.

'Censorship is abhorrent to me,' said Dorn. 'It runs against the principles of the society we were meant to be building. Great Terra, I'm beginning to sound as high-minded as Guilliman. My point, Kyril, my point is... we're not building any more, and we had no idea how words could contaminate everything we hold dear. Remembrancers. Theists. Ideas that, in better times, we might at least have gently humoured. I stand opposed to all that woman Keeler represents, but I would defend her right to say it. In better times. But words and ideas have become dangerous, Sindermann. I don't have to explain that to you, of all people.'

'I understand, I do,' replied Sindermann with a shrug. 'And what is there left to tell anyway? What words left to use?'

'Sindermann,' said Dorn. He paused.

'Lord?'

'Find some.'

'Some... what?'

'Some words, and people to help you use them. The order may be gone, but I feel we need remembrancers now. More than before, maybe, and unofficially, perhaps. I would support the idea. To see the truth, to report it, to write it down.'

'Why, lord?'

Dorn fixed him with a steady gaze.

'Historians toil at the past, but they write for the future. That's the point of them. If I know there are historians still at work, it tells me there will be a future. I think that might strengthen my resolve. The idea of a future, a far future, that will exist and want to remember. It would fortify my purpose, and offer me hope. If the historians give up, then we're admitting an end is coming. Go do the work the Emperor once gave you, and remind me that some future is still a possibility for us.'

'I will, lord,' said Sindermann. He swallowed hard, and pretended that the rain was in his eyes again.

'If we win this,' said Dorn, 'it will be the greatest thing we ever do.'

'It will,' Sindermann agreed. 'Yes, it will. For this is surely the greatest hell we have ever known. I think of the Palace as the solid heart of everything, yet wherever I go, I feel it tremble.'

'Tremble?'

'To the very bedrock. The halls, the walls… I walk the place, you know. Every day, from line to line, within the defences and the bastions. I feel the vibration of the constant bombardment, the deluge of energy quaking the mantle, the sub-shock, the aftershock. I feel it everywhere.'

'I've been told the entire Palace and the crust beneath has shifted eight centimetres west since this began,' said Dorn.

'Extraordinary,' said Sindermann. 'Well then. You see? The tremble is everywhere. I feel it here. At the Hasgard Gate, eight days ago, like an earthquake during that ion barrage. The casements shook. And yesterday, I walked the Saturnine Wall. Even there, a shudder underfoot, like there was palsy in the old stones. Shock, lord, transmitted kilometres through the dirt from the port warzones.'

Dorn nodded. Then he went very still, his mind turning; considering, Sindermann was certain, more memorised data in one second than Sindermann could retain in a year.

'Saturnine?'

'Yes, lord.'

Dorn turned. 'I must return to my post. And so must you. Go down, remembrancer. Do your work so that mine can matter hereafter.'

'I will, lord.'

'Take the stairs, please.'

Sindermann grinned. 'Most amusing, lord.'

'Laughing at this plight, and at ourselves,' said Rogal Dorn, 'may be the last thing we are able to do. When the munitions are all spent and our blood is leaked away, I will look our enemy in the eyes and laugh at his ghastly misunderstanding of the way things are meant to be.'

'I will make a note of that, lord,' said Sindermann.

ONE

After the gate fell
Begin
Oath maker

There's a bond stronger than steel to be found in the calamity of combat.

Willem Kordy (33rd Pan-Pac Lift Mobile) and Joseph Baako Monday (18th Regiment, Nordafrik Resistance Army) had found that out in the span of about a hundred days. They had met on the sixth of Secundus, in the crowds swarming off the Excertus Imperialis troop ships at the Lion's Gate. Everyone tired and confused, lugging kit, gaping at the monumental vista of the Palace, which most had never seen before, except in picts. Officers shouting, frustrated, trying to wrangle troops into line; assembly squares outlined in chalk on the concourse deck, marked with abbreviated unit numbers; adjutants hurrying along the lines, punch-tagging paper labels to collars – code marker, serial, dispersal point – as if they were processing freight.

'I swear I have never seen so many people in one place,' Joseph had remarked.

'Nor me,' Willem had replied, because he'd been standing next to him.

31

Just that simple. A hand offered, shaken. Names exchanged. Willem Kordy (33rd Pan-Pac Lift Mobile) and Joseph Baako Monday (18th Regiment, Nordafrik Resistance Army). The brackets were always there, with everybody. Your name became a sentence, an extension of identity.

'Ennie Carnet (Fourth Australis Mechanised).'

'Seezar Filipay (Hiveguard Ischia).'

'Willem Kordy (Thirty-Third Pan-Pac Lift Mobile). This is Joseph Baako Monday (Eighteenth Regiment, Nordafrik Resistance Army).'

No one stopped doing it. It was too confusing otherwise. No one came from here, no one knew the place, or anybody except the rest of their unit. They brought their birthplaces, regions and affiliations with them, in brackets, like baggage trains after their names. Like comforting mementos. It became second nature. On the eleventh, Kordy found himself saying, as he reported to his own brigade commander, 'Willem Kordy (Thirty-Third Pan-Pac Lift Mobile), sir.'

'Colonel Bastian Carlo, Thirty-Third Pan-Pac Lift Mo– What the shit is wrong with you, soldier?'

They lugged their brackets into the war with them, along with their packs and munition bags and their service weapons, like a little extra load. Then they had to cling to them, because once the fighting started, everything quickly lost definition and the brackets were all they had. Faces and hands got covered in mud and blood, unit badges got caked in dirt. By the twenty-fifth, the long red coats of the 77th Europa Max (Ceremonial) were as thick with filth as the green mail of the Planalto Dracos 6-18 and the silver breastplates of the Nord-Am First Lancers. Everyone became indistinguishable, alive or dead.

Especially after the gate fell.

Lion's Gate space port fell to the enemy on the eleventh of

Quintus. It was a long way from where they were, hundreds of kilometres west. Everything was a long way from everything else, because the Imperial Palace was so immense. But the effects were felt everywhere, like a convulsion, like the Palace had taken a headshot.

They were on the 14th Line by then, out in the north reach of the Greater Palace. The 14th Line was an arbitrary designation, a tactical formation of twenty thousand mixed Excertus and Auxilia units holding positions to guard the western approaches to the Eternity Wall space port. When the Lion's Gate fell, cohesion just went, right across the 14th Line, right across everywhere. A series of heavy voids had failed, soiling the air in the surrounding zone with a lingering sting of raw static and overpressure. The aegis protecting the Palace had ruptured in a cascade, spreading east from the Lion's Gate, and the electro-mag blink of that collapse took down vox and noospheric links with it. No one knew what to do.

Commands from Bhab and the Palatine Tower were not updating. There was a mad scramble, a fall-back, evacuating dugouts and leaving the dead behind. Parts of the Lion's Gate space port were on fire, visible from leagues away. Traitor armies were shoving in from the south-east, emboldened by the news that the port had fallen. They were driving up the Gangetic Way unchecked, piling in across Xigaze Earthworks and the Haldwani Traverse bastions, swarming the enclosures at the Saratine and Karnali Hubs and the agrarian districts west of the Dawn Road. The units of the 14th Line could hear the rumble of approaching armour as they ran, like a metal tide rolling up a beach. The sky was a mass of low smoke, scored through by the ground-attack aircraft making runs on the port-side habitations.

No one could believe that the gate had fallen. It was where they had all arrived, almost a hundred days before, and it had felt so huge and permanent. Joseph Baako Monday (18th Regiment, Nordafrik Resistance Army) had never seen a structure so magnificent. A vertical city that soared into the clouds, even on a clear day. Lion's Gate. One of the principal space ports serving the Imperial Palace.

And the enemy had taken it.

That meant the enemy had surface access inside the Eternity Wall, inside the Anterior Barbican. It had the critical operational capacity to start landing principal assault forces from the orbital fleet: heavy units, mass units, to reinforce the Terran traitor hosts that had begun the outer assaults.

'No,' Willem Kordy (33rd Pan-Pac Lift Mobile) told his friend. 'Not reinforce. Supplant. The first door of the Palace has opened.' An orbital artery had begun to pump. Until then, they'd faced men and machines. Through the yawning hole of the Lion's Gate, other things could now arrive, the way cleared for their advance.

Traitor Astartes. Titan engines. And worse, perhaps.

'How could there be worse?' asked Joseph Baako Monday (18th Regiment, Nordafrik Resistance Army).

They tried to make their way from Southern Freight Quadrant to Angevin Bastion, approaching the top end of the Gangetic Way where it crossed Tancred and the Pons Montagne, in the hope of skirting the traitor armour that was reducing Gold Fane Bastion to rubble. Captain Mads Tantane (16th Arctic Hort) had nominal command, but they didn't need a leader. It was move as one, in support of each other, or die.

Some fled, discipline lost. They were cut down inside two hundred metres, or overtaken by the viral clouds. Others gave up. That was the worst thing to see. Anonymous troopers, their identities lost under a film of grease and mud, no longer able to say their brackets, sitting in doorways, beside broken walls, in the stinking shadows of underpass revetments. A few put pistols in their mouths, or tugged the pins of their last grenades. But most just sat, ruined by despair and sleep deprivation, and refused to get up. They had to be left behind. They sat until death found them, and it never took long.

The rest, the still living, they tried to move. Vox and noospheric links remained dead. The constant flow of updating directives and deployment instructions had been choked off. They had to switch to Emergency and Contingency Orders, which had been issued on paper flimsies to all field officers. They were basic, spartan. For them, the units of the 14th Line, a curt general order written on a curl of paper, like a motto from a fortune cracker: 'In the event of breach or failure at 14th, withdraw to Angevin.'

Angevin Bastion and its six-kilometre line of casemates. Get behind that. That was the hope. A new line. Captain Mads Tantane (16th Arctic Hort) had about seven hundred infantry with him in a long, straggling column that kept breaking into clumps. His seven hundred was just a small part of the eighty-six thousand loyalist Army personnel in retreat from Line 14, Line 15 and Line 18. Packs kept stumbling into each other as they struggled through the ruins, yelling names and brackets frantically to prevent mistaken engagement. Enemy fire was at least only coming from one direction: behind them.

Then it began to come from the flank too. From the north. Close by and heavy, pricking through the colonnades and the gutted buildings, stippling rockcrete, raising puffs of powder-dust from rubble slopes.

And killing people.

Their line, their ragged column, began to crumple. Some scattered and broke for cover, others turned, bewildered. Some fell, as though they were tired of standing up. They dropped heavily, like sacks of meal, and tilted at ungainly angles, their legs bent under them, poses only death could accomplish. Captain Mads Tantane (16th Arctic Hort) started yelling above the chatter of weapons fire, urging them on to Angevin, and a few of the troopers obeyed.

'He's a fool,' said Joseph Baako Monday (18th Regiment, Nordafrik Resistance Army). 'My friend Willem, don't go that way! Look, would you? Look!'

The enemy had emerged. A wide, rolling line of traitor ground troops surged through the ruined fringes of Gold Fane, spilling through broken archways, and across streets, and down spoil heaps, flowing like water through every gap they could find. They were chanting. Willem Kordy (33rd Pan-Pac Lift Mobile) couldn't make out what. There was too much noise. But it was all one thing, voices lifted as one, a sound as ugly as the icons on the banners that wobbled and flapped over their ranks.

The kill-rate increased. Friends were dropping all around them. Willem Kordy (33rd Pan-Pac Lift Mobile) couldn't tell who. A body twisted. Was that Jurgan Thoroff (77th Kanzeer Light) or Uzman Finch (Slovak 14th)? Just a figure caked in mud, identity lost, no longer able to utter its brackets, no face left to wipe clean so that features could be discerned.

Smoke everywhere. Dust. Vaporised blood. Filthy rain. The chanting. The constant crack and rasp of weapons firing. The slap and scorch of impacts on stone and rubble. The hollow thump of impacts on meat. You knew when a body had been hit. A muffled punch came with an exhaled gasp as air was squeezed out of lungs. It came with the sharp stink of burned cloth and exit steam, the burned and atomised innards splitting skin to escape.

You learned the sound fast if you didn't already know it, because it repeated a dozen times a minute.

Willem Kordy grabbed his friend's sleeve and they ran

together. Others ran too. There was no cover. They scrambled up a bank of rubble, rounds slapping the tangled debris around them. Joseph Baako Monday made the mistake of looking back. He saw–

He saw that Captain Tantane had definitely gone the wrong way, and taken two hundred or more people with him. The traitor multitude had boxed them. He saw–

He saw taller figures pushing through the marching traitor files. Beast-giants armoured in black. He knew they were Astartes. War-horns bellowed through the smoke-fog. More now, more giants. He saw–

He saw these Astartes wore armour of dirty white, like spoiled cream. Their pauldrons were black. Some had great horns. Some had cloth tied around their armour like smocks or aprons. He saw–

He saw the dirt was caked blood. He saw the aprons were human hides. The Astartes in black slowed their advance. They let the Astartes in white rush ahead. They surged like dogs, charged like bulls. They weren't men, or even like men. The Astartes in black were upright, like handlers. The Astartes in white galloped, almost on all fours. They shrieked in berserk pain. They swung chainblades and war-axes that Joseph Baako Monday knew he could not have lifted. He saw–

He saw them reach Captain Tantane's group. He saw Tantane and those around him screaming and firing to hold them at bay. And failing. The Astartes in white ploughed into the mass of them, through them, running them down like trains hitting livestock. Slaughter. Butchery. A huge cloud of blood-vapour billowed up the slope, coating stones like tar. The Astartes in black stood and watched, as if entertained. He saw–

A hand on his arm.

'Come on!' Willem yelled into his face. 'Just come on!'

Up the slope, sixty, seventy of them, scrabbling up the

rubble incline, sixty or seventy that had not made the mistake of following Captain Tantane. Up the slope, dragging
each other when feet slipped, up the slope and onto what
had once been the roofs of habitats. The horror below them.
The war-horns booming. The grinding squeal of chainblades.
Billowing clouds of clotting fog.

The roofs ran out. A huge structure had collapsed, leaving
nothing but its frame of girders and spars rising from a sea
of shattered masonry. A twenty-metre drop. They started to
clamber out along the girders, the sixty or seventy of them,
single file, walking or crawling along girders half a metre wide.
Men slipped and fell, or were knocked off by shots from below.
Some took others with them as they clawed to stay on. They
had all passed through fear. Fear was redundant and forgotten.
So was humanity. They were deaf from the noise and numb
from the constant shock. They had entered a state of feral
humiliation, of degradation, mobbing like animals, wide-eyed
and mindless, trying to escape a forest fire.

Willem nearly fell, but Joseph clung to him and got him
to the far side, the roof of an artisan hall. They were among
the first to make it. They looked back at their friends, men
and women clinging like swarming ants to the narrow girders.
They reached out, grabbed hands, brought a few to safety. Jen
Koder (22nd Kantium Hort), Bailee Grosser (Third Helvet),
Pasha Cavaner (11th Heavy Janissar)…

War-horns boomed. Bigger horns. Deeper, howling sounds
that shook the breastbone. Two dozen streets away, true giants
loomed out of the haze. Titan engines, glimpsed between the
soaring towers as they strode along, demolishing walls and
whole buildings, black, gold, copper, crimson, infernal banners
displayed on the masts of their backs. Each was like a walking
city, too big to properly comprehend. Their vast limb-weapons
pulsed and fired: flashes that scorched the retina, static shock

that lifted the hair, heat-wash that seared the skin like sun-burn even from two dozen streets away.

And the noise. The noise so loud, each shot so loud, it felt as though the noise alone could kill. At each discharge, every-thing shivered.

We will die now, thought Joseph, and then laughed out loud at his own arrogance. The giant engines weren't coming for him. They didn't know he even existed. They were striding west, parallel to him, driving through the harrowed streets to find something they could kill or destroy that was worth their titanic effort.

The sixty or seventy of them had become thirty or forty. They slithered down slopes of scree and broken glass. No one had a clue where they were going. No one knew if there was any-where left that could be gone to. Buildings around them were burning or blown out, the streets buried in a blanket of debris.

'We should fight,' said Joseph.

'What?' asked Willem.

'Fight,' Joseph repeated. 'Turn around, and fight.'

'We'll die.'

'Isn't this already death?' asked Joseph. 'What else are we going to do? There's nowhere to go.'

Willem Kordy wiped his mouth and spat out dirt and bone dust.

'But what good can we do?' asked Bailee Grosser. 'We saw what–'

'We did see,' said Joseph. 'I saw.'

'We won't measure it,' said Willem.

'Measure what?' asked Jen Koder. Her helmet was so badly dented, she couldn't take it off. Under the crumpled rim, blood ran down her neck.

'Whatever we are able to do,' said Willem. 'We'll die. We won't know. Whatever we do, however little, we won't know. That doesn't matter.'

'Yes,' said Joseph. He looked at their faces. 'It doesn't matter. We came here to fight. Fight for Him, in His name. Fight for this place. You saw how many people came. At the space port, when we arrived. So many people. Did anyone actually think they would do something significant? In person?'

Willem nodded. 'Collective effort. That's the point. If I break, or you break, then everyone will break, one by one. If I stand, and you stand, we die, but we are standing. We don't have to know what we do, or how little it is. That's why we came here. That's what He needs from us.'

No one said anything. One by one they got up, picked up their weapons, and followed Joseph and Willem down the street, picking their way over rubble, heading back the way they had come.

The Space Marine was in their path, hazed by a draw of thick smoke. Scarred siege shield propped in one hand, long-sword resting across a huge shoulder guard. Plate dented and scored, even the ornate laurels on the breast. Eyes, slits of amber throbbing in the mauled visor.

Their weapons came up.

'Where are you going?' it asked.

'Back. To fight,' said Joseph.

'Correct,' it said. 'That's what He needs from us.'

'You... heard me?'

'Of course. I can hear a heart beating at a thousand metres. Follow me.'

The legionary turned. Its armour and siege shield were yellow.

'I am Joseph Baako Monday (Eighteenth Regiment, Nord-afrik Resistance Army),' Joseph called out.

'I don't need to know,' the legionary replied, without glancing back. 'And show some damn noise discipline.'

'I need you to know,' said Joseph.

The legionary halted, and looked back. 'That doesn't matter–'

'It matters to me,' said Joseph. 'It's all we have. I am Joseph Baako Monday (Eighteenth Regiment, Nordafrik Resistance Army).'

'I am Willem Kordy (Thirty-Third Pan-Pac Lift Mobile),' said Willem.

'Adele Gercault (Fifty-Fifth Midlantik).'

'Jen Koder (Twenty-Second Kantium Hort).'

The Space Marine let them all speak. Then it nodded.

'I am Camba Diaz (Imperial Fists). Follow me.'

'Wait,' said Archamus, seeing them approach, but not looking up, one finger raised for patience.

Niborran, Brohn and Icaro waited. They watched the master of Dorn's Huscarls work at his station, carefully reviewing the data-feed. His eyes didn't blink. They waited. The constant motion and noise of the Grand Borealis encircled them. It was the first time any of them had not spoken in over a day. Waiting seemed wrong. High Primary Solar General Saul Niborran, Militant Colonel Auxilia Clement Brohn, Second Mistress Tacticae Terrestria Sandrine Icaro of the War Courts… They were people you did not keep waiting, not at this time, not in this extremity.

Unless you were in command of the warzone, running it from Bhab Bastion in the Sanctum Imperialis, the chosen proxy of the Lord Praetorian, and thus carrying, temporarily, the ultimate authority of Dorn.

Archamus, Imperial Fists, Master of the Huscarls, Second Of That Name, finished his review and sat back slightly. He looked at them. They were the senior duty officers of the Day Hundred rotation.

'Begin,' he invited.

'Where is Dorn?' asked Niborran immediately.

Archamus' eyes narrowed very slightly. At a nearby station, Captain Vorst looked up with a frown. Archamus saw the look, dismissed it with a small gesture. *Keep your seat.*

Niborran breathed deeply. He was tired.

'Your forgiveness, sir,' he said. 'Let me amend. Where is the Lord Praetorian?'

'Occupied elsewhere,' said Archamus. 'Begin.'

Niborran winced. He rubbed his augmetic eyes quickly with a knuckle. The silver socket frames gleamed against his dark skin, but the eyes within seemed dull. He took out his slate.

'We have run analysis of–'

'How is he occupied?' asked Brohn.

'What?' asked Archamus.

'Leave it, Clem,' Niborran murmured.

'I won't. How is he occupied? Right now? One hundred and more days of this, and the deepest shit yet, drowning in our own blood, and he's *occupied*?'

Archamus' face was expressionless. 'Consider your tone please, colonel,' he suggested.

'Screw my bastard tone, lord.'

Archamus rose. Vorst had risen too, heaving his yellow-plated bulk out of his seat. Again, Archamus signalled him to return to work with a brief gesture.

'We are all very tired,' said Niborran quickly. 'Very tired. Tempers fray and–'

'You don't look tired,' Brohn said to Archamus. 'Not at all.'

'Bred that way,' said Archamus. In the first hundred days he'd stood three tours on the lines. The grazes and dents on his yellow plate hadn't been finished out and were there for all to see. But no, he didn't look tired. He looked Astartes, the way he always did. Unmoving, as solid as a statue. He didn't look tired the way these three humans did, with their hollow eyes and drawn cheeks and shaking hands.

'I will allow you some latitude, colonel,' he said. 'The circumstances–'

'The circumstances are shit, and getting shittier by the second, and Dorn is absent. He is supposed to be running this. He's supposed to be the bastard genius–'

'That is now enough,' said Archamus.

'The Praetorian's absence is concerning,' said Niborran. 'Brohn is out of line, but his sentiment is–'

'We're screwed,' snapped Brohn. 'His plan is splitting at the seams. Lion's Gate is done. They're in. Inside Anterior. The aegis is blown in eight places. They've got engines on the ground and they're walking. Our plan is on fire. It's gone to shit–'

'Get out.'

The words were a whisper, a hiss, but they cut like acid through metal. Everyone in the Bhab strategium fell silent. No voices, just the chatter and babble of cogitators and the crackle of vox monitor stations. Eyes averted.

Jaghatai Khan stepped up onto the central platform. How anyone or anything so big could have entered the Grand Borealis without being heard, or could have walked silently from the chamber arch across the plasteel deck, in full, fur-draped armour plate…

He towered over them. There was blood on his cheek, beard, gorget, left pauldron, breastplate. It matted his cinched-back mane, freckled his ermyet furs, and ran down his left thigh-guard. It wasn't his. His left hip was scorched back to bare metal from a melta burn.

'Get out,' he repeated, looking down at Brohn.

'Colonel Brohn is tired, lord, and spoke poorly,' Niborran began.

'I don't give a shit,' said the Great Khan.

'My lord,' Niborran pressed. 'Colonel Brohn is a senior and decorated Army officer, and an essential part of the–'

'Not a single shit,' said the Great Khan.

Niborran glanced at the deck. He sighed.

'His question was insolently framed,' said Niborran flatly, 'but his point was valid.'

He looked the primarch in the eyes. He did not waver.

'My lord,' he added.

'You too,' said the Great Khan. 'Get out.'

Brohn glanced at Niborran. Niborran shook his head. He tossed his slate onto the desk, turned and walked out. Brohn followed.

The Great Khan didn't even watch them leave.

'Which seniors are on the next rotation?' he called out to the chamber. 'Find them. Wake them. Get them here.'

Several adjutants jumped up and hurried out. The Great Khan turned to Archamus.

'Where's Dorn?' he asked.

'In council with the Sigillite and the Council.'

'Get him here,' he said. He glanced at Icaro. 'You. Icaro. Begin.'

Icaro cleared her throat. 'Aegis failure in eight sectors,' she said. She swept her hand across the face of her dataslate like a sower scattering seed, and threw the data up onto the display. Ugly blobs blossomed across the northern and central areas of the vast Palace map.

'Repairs?' asked the Great Khan.

'Pending. Voids sixty-one and sixty-two are beyond salvation. Lion's Gate Port remains wide open. Bulk landers are setting down along the northern upper platforms at a rate of sixty an hour. Vox and noospherics are interrupted in those sectors and adjacent zones.'

She cast more blobs onto the holofield.

'Multi-point auspex confirms engines walking here, here and here. Legio Tempestus. Legio Vulpa. Perhaps Legio Ursa too. Progressing to Ultimate Wall, Anterior Wall, and into Magnifican.'

'They have one, they want another,' said the Great Khan. Archamus nodded.

'I believe so, lord,' he said.

'Army lines are fracturing across the northern reaches,' said Icaro. 'Assault is a primary factor, traitor hosts driving up from the south. They have Astartes support.'

'On the ground?' asked the Great Khan.

'On the ground, in force,' she confirmed. 'World Eaters, Iron Warriors, Thousand Sons, Luna Wolves–'

'They're not called that any more,' said the Khan.

'My apologies, lord. But I won't use his name,' she replied.

'Just use numbers,' said Archamus gently.

'Yes, lord. Fifteenth, Seventeenth, Fourth, Sixteenth, Third. Perhaps others. Assault pressure is the primary factor, but Army cohesion is disrupted by the loss of vox and comm-channels. We can't issue orders to the places where orders are most needed.'

She looked at the primarch.

'The merits or demerits of the Praetorian's defence plan are moot all the while said plan cannot be implemented,' she said.

The Great Khan nodded, and tried to comb dried blood out of his moustache with his fingers. 'And daemons?' he asked.

'Probably very many,' she said. There was a tiny wobble in her voice. 'Probably the most significant threat to the Sanctum Imperialis Palatine. But they are not detectable by our systems.'

'That assessment is confirmed,' said Archamus.

'We are relying on sighting reports,' she said, 'which are… unreliable and confused. And dependent on vox. We must trust, I suppose, in our lord the Emperor's will to keep them at bay.'

'That trust is never unfounded,' said the Great Khan. He

looked at the shimmering, updating chart. 'They're coming to our doors. Right to our doors. Lion's Gate, Ultimate Wall. But they want that too.'

He pointed to the icon that represented the Eternity Wall space port.

'Agreed,' said Archamus.

'If they take that, they have both principal space ports in the northern reaches. Double the landing capacity.'

'Surely they'll concentrate on the Sanctum now?' Icaro asked. 'The added capacity is useful, but Lion's Gate is closer, its landing volume is immense, and they're at our throats already.'

'No, they want it,' said the Great Khan. 'Get as much on the ground as they can to knock us down. It's what I'd do.'

'And it's what I'd do,' said Dorn. He stood at the foot of the platform steps looking up at them. 'And it's what I know our brother Perturabo would do. Maximise landing capacity. Deprive us of orbital access. I am sure this is as Horus has instructed.'

'They want them both,' said Jaghatai Khan.

'They want them both. They want everything,' said Dorn.

The Great Khan nodded. He looked at Dorn.

'So, there you are,' he said.

'Here I am,' said Dorn. 'I had business elsewhere. Ironic... it's usually you who slips away and can't be found.'

Jaghatai Khan did not soften. The Lord Khagan would clearly not be mollified with gentle good humour.

'What now, brother?' asked the Great Khan.

'I have been examining the latest variables,' Dorn said, joining them on the platform. 'Each move our opponent makes reveals more of his intention. I'm beginning to see the Lord of Iron's strategy in some depth, which means I can predict where–'

'We do not need to predict,' said the Khan simply.

'This is a complex, multi-aspect battle sphere, brother,' Dorn began, then cursed himself inwardly. Jaghatai Khan's martial doctrines were very different from his own, but the Great Khan was a peerless, precise and subtle warrior. He did not deserve condescension. He did not need to have complexity explained to him the way humans did.

Jaghatai Khan shook his head. He looked weary, and that in itself was concerning. For a primarch to look tired…

'He wants our father,' said the Khan quietly. 'He wants unhindered access to the Palace. He has one foothold, he wants another. It is not complex, Rogal, not any more. Eternity Wall Port must be defended and held. Lion's Gate Port must be retaken. It is an offence they have claimed it at all.'

'It was unavoidable,' said Dorn.

'I'm not blaming you, Rogal,' said the Khan. He sighed. 'We must hold the ports. Deny them access. What forces they have already landed can be contained and butchered.'

'Jaghatai,' said Rogal Dorn. He cleared his throat, as if considering what to say next. 'I assure you, I have weighed every option. I applaud your determination, but it's not quite as simple as you–'

He cut short. Jaghatai Khan was gazing at him. There was a hardness in his look that made Icaro take a nervous step back.

'I think you misunderstand me, Rogal,' the Great Khan said. 'I am going to take Lion's Gate Port back. I'm not asking you. I came here to tell you what I'm about to do.'

She asked, 'Why are you kneeling?'

He was renewing his oath of moment in a dingy cubicle a million light years from the place she'd first watched him perform the ceremony. His private arming chamber on the *Spirit*, that seemed like false memory, something he'd imagined but which had never been true. The metal walls lacquered pale

green, the smell of lapping powder, the noise from embark-
ation decks outside. Those images didn't belong to him any
more. The oaths of moment pinned to the wall under the
stencilled eagle, those too. They belonged to someone else.
They were deeds another man had done, and he was dead.

'To show respect,' he replied.

'Who are you kneeling to?' Always so insistent, so curious.

He shrugged. He had laid out two blades. Rubio's sword
looked dull in the candlelight. The force sword's blade was
inactive. It was an old Ultramarines weapon, gladius-pattern,
a form he was familiar with. It still had the Ultima mark on
the hilt.

The Mk IV long-pattern chainsword beside it had a dent
across the cowling and several teeth that needed to be re-set
or replaced. A repair unit stood ready, beside the frame
supporting his plate. The pale grey of the battered armour
segments was the colour of old bone in the gloom, like a
moon catching only back-scattered sunlight.

'Kneeling is an act of respect or fealty,' she remarked. 'Or it
is an act of reverence and devotion.'

'It's not devotion,' he replied, becoming annoyed at her
interruption and her questions. 'There are no gods. We burned
that lie.'

'Then fealty... but there is no one here to kneel to, so the
fealty is worthless.'

'The Emperor is everywhere.'

'Is He?' She looked amused. 'You kneel to the idea of Him,
as an act of faith? So which is it, fealty or devotion? Have you
destroyed false gods just to build another?'

'He is not false,' he snapped. The floor shook briefly. Dust
sifted down from the trembling ceiling. The closest batteries
and casemates had resumed firing, and their mass recoil was
flexing the fabric of the Palace.

'Is He a god, then?' she asked. She brushed away dust that had fallen onto the pauldrons of his racked armour.

'There are daemons now, so...' he began.

'So there must be gods too?'

'I didn't say that. What do you want, Mersadie?'

'To live. Too late for that now.'

The candles guttered.

What oath are you making? Loken imagined her asking. He wondered how he would explain. Oaths of moment were just that – specific, taken before battle. All those he had sworn, almost everything he had ever sworn apart from his devotion to the Emperor, had long been voided. He had decided to make his own, a crude and simple oath, enough to keep him going through whatever part of his life remained.

'I've seen slogans daubed on walls, in the lower parts of the Palace Precinct,' he said to the empty cubicle. 'A few to begin with, then more. I think the Imperial Army garrisons and conscripts scrawl them up. A mantra. I adopted it as my oath. Simple. Encompassing, and easy to remember. Just three words.'

He showed the scrap of parchment to the empty air, to the ghost memory of her presence.

To the death.

TWO

Theory versus execution
Angels among us
Only human

To see the Lord of Iron at work, that was a thing. A mighty thing. There was only one other mind in the known galaxy that could orchestrate mass war like him, and that mind was behind the monolithic walls they were trying to tear down.

Well, one or two minds, Ezekyle Abaddon thought. One or two, maybe three. And one of them might be standing here on the platform watching him work. But give the Lord of the IV his due. He had a true flair for it.

The others were about to push ahead and approach, but Abaddon raised his hand to stay them.

'What?' asked Horus Aximand. 'Afraid we might break the bastard's train of thought? Balls up his plans?'

Tormageddon chuckled. There was little love lost between the Mournival and the Lord of Iron. The war had spilled too much bad blood. But these things had to be set aside, for the time being at least. There was one, unifying goal to be accomplished, and the Lord of Iron was master of the battle sphere.

'Take more than the sight of you to derail his concentration,'

Falkus Kibre told Little Horus. The Widowmaker paused, and sneered at Aximand. 'I don't know, though...'

'Just shut up,' said Abaddon quietly. 'I wanted to watch him work. For a moment. It's a thing. A mighty thing.'

His Mournival brothers shrugged and indulged him. They stood and watched with him.

A formidable lifter throne had been brought onto the platform. The Iron Circle, six towering battle-automata that never left Perturabo's side, stood watch around it, impossibly still and alert. *Forgebreaker*, the Iron Lord's colossal warhammer, stood head down on a grav-pad beside the throne.

From the lifter-throne's broad arms and footrest, hololith plates were mounted on sooty servo-arms, surrounding him on three sides: left, right and ahead. Eighteen active screens, streaming with data, flashing with quick-cut pict-cap images from the fields below. The Lord of Iron was lit by their glow, immersed. He sat hunched, an ogre sheathed in massive, matt-anthracite metal plate that looked as though it could withstand a siege all on its own. The cold plate seemed to be perspiring a sheen of gun oil. Servo-cables and feeder-pipes laced his skull like roped plaits, covering his ears, sprouting from his neck, cheeks and chin. Precious little of his face remained visible. The mass of cables gave him the look of Medusa from old lore, writhing serpent-haired.

His head twitched, darting from screen to screen. His fingers scuttled across the throne's haptic surfaces, adjusting, deleting, moving, impelling.

Writing history, touch by touch.

Perturabo, Lord of Iron, twelfth-found son, stepchild of Olympia, primarch of the IV Legion, devisor of war, master of the art of attack, leveller of walls, demolisher of fortresses, unmaker of worlds. Siege-war was his craft, his genius. It had got them that far, through the bulwarks of the best-defended planetary system in realspace, through the orbital defences of the most secure world anywhere, and in through these walls, to his genefather's doorstep.

Perturabo could see the entire micro-detail of the theatre all at once, but only through the screens around him and the feeds in his head. He was oblivious to the actual world, to the view just a few metres away from where he sat.

It was quite a view, Abaddon reflected. My Lord Perturabo, the twelfth primarch, is so buried in his work, he's really missing something. A fine, fine view on a day like this. But that was probably why he was so good at what he did: acute focus, utter concentration, diligence, obsessive attention; processing data, distilling, making choices step by step to accomplish his goal.

Perhaps two goals, in truth. The commands of the Warmaster, waiting high above for the work to be accomplished, of course, that goal first and foremost. Take the Palace. But also Perturabo's own, private, iron-hard ambition. To best his estranged brother Dorn, to take the ultimate prize, to finally answer the question that had generated jealousy and rivalry from the very first days: immovable object, unstoppable force… Which ceases to be when they meet?

From the view at hand, it seemed to Abaddon that the smart wagers were an unstoppable force. He gazed out at what the Lord of Iron was so singularly failing to appreciate. They were on a landing platform midway up the artificial mountain of the Lion's Gate space port, an objective hard-won five days earlier. The port, wounded but able to function, rumbled with activity. The mass freight lifters and elevator assemblies were pouring manpower and machines down to the surface levels. The immense edifice was also possessed: Abaddon could hear and feel the cackle and slither of the Neverborn things that were coalescing around the space port's structure, taking form and flowing like oil, like rancid fat, into the open city below.

Every few moments there was a vibration, transmitted from kilometres above, as another bulk warship grazed the docking rings and locked into place. Smoke, in thick banks, clambered up from below, gusting from the base structure and skirts where fighting still raged. But Abaddon could see enough: the vast, vast heart of the Anterior Barbican laid out below, the towers and fortresses, the streets, the fires; the distant shape of the cyclopean Lion's Gate two hundred kilometres south-west, with its implacable rings of concentric walls and sub-gates; the shielded expanse of the Sanctum Imperialis beyond that, vague in the ash haze. A distant mountain range, but closer than it had ever been before.

Below, many hundreds of metres straight down, the fields of fire, the burning, blackened, mangled zones around the port, thoroughfares that had once been the majestic entrance to the most exalted citadel in the Imperium. A million fires like spilled coals, ropes of smoke, the fire-cracker flash of heavy artillery, the lightning pulse of engine main-weapons, aircraft and strike ships darting past like birds, flocking and mobbing. The last swirls of their long migration home.

Abaddon looked at the view. It was more than he had ever imagined, and he had imagined it a thousand times. He looked at the view, then at Perturabo in his cell of data, then back again. Theory and practice, side by side.

Practice. Execution. That was where Abaddon's heart lay. Naturally, he admired Perturabo's genius, his virtuoso art that had made this all possible. But he was so detached. When he finally triumphed, and he would, would it be by the touch of another haptic control? Would he make one last command stroke, and know it was done, and only then, at last, look up and see the reality he had wrought?

That was not Abaddon's way. A proper ending came with the blow of a sword, not the touch of a button. Blades and mettle had won the crusade, and they should win this. Not theory.

Not warp magic either. Not the shrieking, filthy warp-things manifesting in the port around him, or inhabiting the flesh of beloved brothers as though they were second-hand garments. This end-war was being too much determined by new methods. Abaddon trusted the old ones far more.

Freight-lifter doors squealed open behind him, footsteps thumped across the deck.

'Why do you wait?' Lord Eidolon asked.

Abaddon glanced at the III Legion champion. Eidolon's retinue trailed him, wretched and gaudy in their enhanced and augmented battleplate. Their faces, and in some cases their forms, had grown wildly misshapen. Their adopted colour schemes hurt the eyes. They were the cream of the Phoenician's men, the Emperor's Children, grotesquely and excessively ornate. Haughty bastards. Why did they preserve the name? Did Fulgrim fear offending his father somehow? Names could be changed. There was honour in that. When the time demanded, wolves became sons. Sons of a better father.

'Respect?' Abaddon suggested.

'Also, there's a wonderful view,' said Horus Aximand.

'Respect for what?' asked Eidolon. His voice was unnatural, sonically phased. He regarded the four warriors of the Mournival, and the row of black-burnished Justaerin Terminators standing honour guard behind them. Abaddon could almost smell his scorn, and the look in Eidolon's eyes spoke of the very special place he kept in his heart for the XVI Legion. A place swimming with contempt.

'There is work to be done,' he announced.

'I'm aware,' said Abaddon.

'My beloved lord,' said Eidolon, 'grows–'

'Many more supple breasts every day?' asked Aximand. Kibre snorted loudly.

'Don't goad him, little one,' said Abaddon, smiling despite himself. 'It really might put our good lord Perturabo off his stroke if we started brawling with our brothers while he worked.'

He looked at Eidolon.

'Besides,' he added, 'it might dent that lovely armour. Which would be a terrible shame.'

He stroked his fingers down the ludicrously decorated pauldron of Eidolon's plate. Eidolon caught his hand, stopped it, clenched it very tightly, and smiled back.

'It's good we can still have fun,' Eidolon said. 'A tonic for the toils ahead. I've always enjoyed indulging your juvenile horseplay.'

His smile did not diminish. His teeth were perfect, like fine ivory. His face was not. It was like a painted parody of human features, fixed like a carnival mask. Frilled sacs breathed either side of his throat.

'I was trying to say,' he continued, his voice oddly modulated, as if an ultrasonic shriek wandered and skirled behind the words, 'if I'd been allowed to finish, that my beloved lord grows fatigued by the delays. He is impatient. Almost listless. It's a tragedy to see. He is–'

'Not the man he was?' asked Little Horus.

Eidolon forced out a courtesy laugh.

'Oh, how you play, Little Horus. He *is* changed. Aren't we all? All of us, made glorious? Even those in your own clumsy ranks?'

He looked at Tormageddon. Tormageddon was still gazing blankly at the lifter-throne. Something was purring inside him, and fluid seeped from his cracked lips. Abaddon eyed him. Tormageddon was not what he had once been. Death and resurrection came at a price. The hulking fourth member of the Mournival wasn't Tarik Torgaddon, who had once been the best of men, nor was it Grael Noctua, whose flesh had been borrowed. There was, disturbingly, something of both of them in the warrior's features, but there was something else too, something underneath that stretched and twisted the face into a bloated pastiche. Abaddon disliked Tormageddon's proximity, disliked the fact he was any part of their quartet. They bore him with them like a scar, the cost of doing business. Whatever lived in Tormageddon's armour and meat, Abaddon had no desire to know it any better.

'Yes, we are,' he said. He pulled his hand from Eidolon's grip.

'My Lord Fulgrim grows impatient. I thought this was to be a planning session? He has sent me to propose an acceleration of attack. Now the engines are down, a full and frontal assault of the Lion's Gate. Let's split the Sanctum open and have done with this delay.'

Abaddon sighed. 'Eidolon, I am dismayed to find myself agreeing with you, and with the desires of your lord and master.'

'Really?' replied Eidolon.

'You know how very much that must pain me,' said Abaddon.

'I am gratified that good sense can be spoken between us,' said Eidolon, 'that we may put aside our trivial contentions and stand as one mind. The war is, after all, the most important thing.'

'I enjoy teasing the shit out of you,' said Little Horus, 'but there is a time and place. The Warmaster wants Terra taken, and we would not disappoint him with delays. We all serve the Warmaster.'

'We do,' said Eidolon, after too long a pause.

'All well and good,' said Falkus Kibre. 'But your Lord Fulgrim's suggestion won't be entertained.'

'How so, Kibre?' Eidolon asked. A fluting sob of noise echoed each syllable.

'Because there's a plan,' said Kibre. 'The Warmaster has issued his objectives, clearly stated, and the Lord of Iron is executing them. Seize the ports, land the host, raze the city, then take the Palace. A methodical undertaking, old school.'

Eidolon laughed. 'This is no undertaking,' he said.

'It really is,' said Aximand.

'What? Are we... bringing Terra to compliance?' Eidolon giggled.

'Yes,' said Abaddon. 'It may be the Throneworld, and it may be an uncommon undertaking, but it's what we have always done. The suppression and conquest of worlds that counter the interests of the Imperium.'

'You're serious,' said Eidolon.

'Someone's got to be,' said Abaddon.

'Lord Fulgrim's proposal of a full and focused assault is attractive,' said Kibre. 'But it will be dismissed. It is contrary to the Warmaster's instructions, and to Lord Perturabo's plans.'

'Besides, the aegis of the Sanctum Imperialis remains intact,' said Abaddon. 'The voids and the telaethesic ward. This process is an attrition to wear them down. Until they fall, we can't mount a full and focused assault because our Neverborn assets cannot be brought to bear.' I can't believe I'm defending that aspect, Abaddon thought. We can't unleash our daemons. When did a war hinge on that?

Eidolon looked in Perturabo's direction.

'I say we bring this meeting to order and put it to the mighty Lord of Iron. See what he thinks.'

'After you,' said Abaddon.

As Abaddon had anticipated, the Lord of Iron was not receptive to Eidolon's proposal. He did not, however, rage at them, as Abaddon might have expected, no matter how much hatred brewed in him for the Sons of Horus and the Emperor's Children. Petty feuds no longer had any place in his mind. It seemed Perturabo was in his element, relishing every moment of a game he had played out in his head over and over again for years. He dismounted the lifter-throne to converse with them, looming over them, and addressing Eidolon's remarks in a blunt but cordial manner. He praised Eidolon, and so by extension Primarch Fulgrim, for his enthusiasm. He was fierce-eyed, vital, eager to show them the complex beauty and ingenuity of his grand stratagem. He tilted some of the throne's screens so that he could describe certain patterns and tactical nuances.

'I've never seen him so… happy,' whispered Horus Aximand. 'That is what it is, isn't it? That's the Lord of Iron *happy*?'

Abaddon nodded. 'Like a grox in shit. This is what he was born for.'

And it *was* beautiful. The summary Perturabo gave, the casual yet absolute knowledge of the data, the subtle expression of field strategy – adjusting for this, predicting for that, reading the battle sphere fifty moves ahead, like a regicide grand master. Abaddon's regard for Lord Perturabo's gifts reached new levels of awed respect. He was the right man for this greatest of undertakings. No one could come close to doing it better. Abaddon found himself taking careful mental notes, fascinated by the game plan that Perturabo laid out.

'Great lord,' he said, pointing. 'There, to the south. You just mentioned it in passing. It seems a valuable opportunity. Will you not implement it?'

The Lord of Iron looked at him, and almost smiled. His eyes were black pits, but points of light blazed in them like distant suns.

'You have a sharp mind, Son of Horus. Few have the acuity

to notice the elegance of that. Sadly, it does not comply with the approach your genefather has ordained. I am obliged to hold it in reserve, for now. I would not risk the Warmaster's ill will by deviating from his wishes. But in the unlikely event that Dorn shows some final spark of wit, and manages some last rally, then it's a gambit I can employ.'

'A shame, lord,' said Abaddon.

'I don't see it,' said Eidolon. 'What are you referring to?'

'Never mind,' said Abaddon. 'Trust me when I say it's a shame.'

A glare of rancid light bathed them all. Tall figures solidified in teleport fields, on the platform nearby: Ahriman of the Thousand Sons, regal and impassive, accompanied by initiated warriors; Typhus of the Death Guard; three archmagi of the Dark Mechanicum; Krostovok, acting Legion commander of the small Night Lords contingent active on Terra; and four lords militant of the Traitor Army host.

'I see we are all gathered at last,' said Perturabo. 'I'll brief now, so you may all communicate my directives to your respective forces.'

At Gorgon Bar, nine hours of uninterrupted shelling suddenly came to an end, as though a switch had been thrown.

Halen threw a switch of his own, a neural signal that deactivated the noise suppression systems of his helmet. He still felt deaf, as though his ears had blown, but he realised he could hear himself moving, hear the scrape of ceramite as he clambered out of the blast box.

'Look alive,' he said. The dust-caked visors of his brother Imperial Fists watched him. He hand signed: *restore audio*. They began to stir.

'Look alive,' he repeated, now they could hear him. 'We know what's coming next.'

Halen pushed through the blast curtains, and moved down the narrow defile to the front of the casemate. His mind was still adjusting. After almost nine hours of generated white noise to withstand the constant, jarring onslaught, the stillness and quiet seemed unnatural.

It had been impossible to maintain vigil on the outworks. The saturated shelling had been too intense. Traitor armour and artillery had focused their wrath on a three-kilometre stretch of the outworks: squadrons of Stormhammers, Fellblades and other super-heavies, hulls-down; Basilisks, Medusas, thousands of bombards; Krios Venator units of the Dark Mechanicum. None were visible; all were firing from rubble fields and dead plazas eight kilometres out, files after files of them, discharging in concert.

The Space Marines had been obliged to pull the Imperial Army, Solar Auxilia and conscript strengths off the outworks and the first circuit wall. No humans could withstand the ceaseless noise and concussion, not even those in heavier field armour. Their human cohorts had been sent back to the hardened bunkers and subsurface shelters to the rear of the second circuit wall, leaving their emplacements and wall batteries unmanned. Even there, shuttered in dark, shaking pits, there had been casualties, as overshots sailed across the outer lines, striking the second circuit or dropping behind it to split open bunkers.

The Imperial Fists had stayed on alone, and even they had been unable to hold guard at the wall. Suppression dampers active, they had sheltered in the blast boxes built into the back of the first circuit – compartments of rockcrete, ceramite supports and ballistic sacking that they had further reinforced by wedging their siege shields against the exterior wall and sitting with their backs to them.

Still, they had died too. Four boxes had been hit and

gutted by high explosives, and in others, including the blast box where Halen had been sheltering, superheated shrapnel fragments had punched through the shuddering wall, perforating rockcrete, lagging, siege shields and the brothers huddled behind them.

Fisk Halen, captain of 19th Tactical Company, recognised that this was merely the prelude.

He stepped up onto the silence of the first circuit wall. Brown dust hung in the air all around, making it seem as if his wall position were the only patch of the world left. He'd expected the worst, but it was worse still. The front edge and parapet of the bulwark looked as though it had been gnawed away by a ravenous giant: ashlar blocks split and bitten through, the parapet entirely blown out in many places, buttressing reduced to shingle, the thick armour facings of the wall crumpled and shredded like metal foil. Most of the wall guns, the macro cannons, rotary nests, las-platforms, were gone.

'Assemble,' he told his brothers as they clambered out around him. 'Make good. Begin vigil. Tarchos? Call the Army strengths back into position. Quickly.'

'Captain,' said Sergeant Tarchos.

'And get me a link to the second circuit batteries. We're going to need them.'

'How do we hold this?' asked Brother Uswalt.

'I doubt we do,' replied Halen.

'Agreed,' said Rann, moving along the shattered line to join them. Halen threw the lord seneschal a quick salute. His men began to do the same.

'No ceremony, brothers,' said Fafnir Rann. There was no time to waste on decorum.

He stood beside Halen, gazing out into the eerie haze of dust. Their optic units clicked and whirred as they tried to adjust for distance and definition. Halen was aware how stiffly the lord seneschal, captain of the First Assault Cadre, had been moving. He'd taken wounds at the Lion's Gate action. He wasn't close to being healed.

'Sudden cessation,' remarked Halen. 'Does he think we're broken?'

'He works on percentages,' replied Rann. 'Nine hours shelling, whatever percentage saturation, however many thousand tonnes of munitions. Enough to break our teeth and whip us to our knees. Then round two.'

They called him 'he'. They meant Perturabo. He was the personification of their foe, the demigod they faced. Not the Warmaster. Horus was the toxic spirit of malice that inspired the traitor host. Perturabo, Lord of Iron, was the instrument of execution, the facilitator of Horus' will. Though Perturabo was probably hundreds of kilometres away, it was his decisions and doctrines they were fighting. He was their true opponent, the architect of the traitors' scheme, though architect seemed the wrong word for a creature who brought walls down.

'He thinks he's softened us, does he?' asked Halen.

'Oh, I think he has, and he knows it, Fisk,' said Rann. 'First circuit and the outworks are hammered to non-vi. Let's see what he pushes up. Maybe run interference for a few hours, give them a slap while we drop back to second or even third and dig in there.'

Non-vi. *Non-viable*. Rann did not rate the first circuit wall as a viable defensive position. He clearly had doubts about the second circuit wall too.

'If we pull to third,' said Halen, 'we're reducing our opportunities.'

'I know, Fisk, I know.'

Gorgon Bar had formerly been known as Gorgon Gate when the Palace had still been a palace. 'Bar' denoted that it was a civilian structure converted into a fortification, as opposed to one built explicitly as a bastion. It was part of the outer ring, the initial circle of defences on the approach to the Lion's Gate and the Sanctum Imperialis. The Gorgon Gate had never been a fortress, just a magnificent triumphal arch on Anterior Way. The Praetorian had armoured it, just like he had armoured everything in the Imperial Palace, during the exhausting months of siege preparation. Decoration had been removed; walls reinforced and built out; utilitarian armour added to encase the once beautiful marble, ouslite and dressed ashlar. Four hemispheres of defences had been built before it, covering what had once been Trajanus Park and the Sonotine Gardens. Four hemispheres: four new, concentric circuit walls, bristling with casemates and defence batteries, and the outworks beyond them, all of them linked by redoubts and supportive trenchwork. In six months, the ceremonial gate, a site noted in monographs on palatial architecture for its tranquil beauty, had been retrofitted into an ugly, five-layer fortress.

Halen understood why. Every prep simulation had shown it would be attacked. Why drive at the actual bastions and fortresses protecting the Lion's Gate, like Colossi or Marmax, when you could break through a ceremonial landmark and drive all the way into the Sanctum itself?

Gorgon would fall. Halen knew that, Rann knew it, Dorn knew it. Perturabo knew it. The question was, how long could it stand? How long could it delay the traitor advance? How much materiel cost could its defenders wring from the traitor host in taking it? How much could it deplete enemy strengths before they reached the Lion's Gate?

'We've got partial aegis still,' said Halen, checking his auspex. 'Retaining void cover over eighty-eight per cent of the circuits.'

'So it'll come from the ground,' Rann nodded. 'Any armour?'

'What we held was drawn back to third,' said Halen. 'Except the stuff from the first sorties.'

At the start of the onslaught, fast Vindicator and Cerberus units had run from the ramparts to hunt and execute the bombarding forces, each hoping to get into their formation like a fox in a fowl-coop. But they'd failed. The tank destroyers had been obliterated by heavy flanking fire. As the dust began to clear slightly, Halen could see blackened hulks to the south, some still burning.

'Draw armour forward, lord?' Halen asked.

Rann shook his head. 'Just to have them roll back again? No, we'll need them at two and three. But get them to stand to and wake engines.'

Halen turned aside to issue vox instructions. Someone called out.

It'll come from the ground.

Assault lines were approaching through the dust and fyceline fumes. Infantry in their thousands, fanned out, moving fast. Some light armour too: Predators, assault tanks, troop carriers, winnowing the brown dust back around them like the wakes of jetboats.

The ground forces came first. Charging.

'Line up,' Rann commanded calmly. Siege shields clattered into place along what was left of the parapet. Bolters locked into firing loops. Crews cycled and turned what wall guns remained. Some refused to move or traverse, fused in place. Imperial Army support was still seven minutes away.

Halen upped his optic gain. The charging horde, in hard zoom: abhuman beastkin, like fairytale ogres, spittle flying from wide, braying mouths; assault units of the Dark Mechanicum, like nightmares conjured from the very darkest ages of Technology; Traitor Army formations, brandishing banner-obscenities. Among them, hulking Death Guard and Iron Warrior legionaries, moving more slowly, advancing inexorably. Halen didn't up his audio gain. He had no wish to hear the howling chant again.

'Hold or withdraw, captain?' he asked. There was still time to make the second circuit their line.

'I'm tired of hearing them shout that,' Rann replied. 'I think we'll stay and slit some throats.'

Halen could hear the chant by then anyway.

The Emperor must die! The Emperor must die!

'Target,' Rann commanded.

All along the wall, a series of whirrs and chimes sounded as boltguns ranged and auto-locked.

'What do you think, Fisk?' Rann asked. 'Thirty to one?'

'Thirty-five, maybe forty.'

'Praetorian odds,' Rann replied. He took aim. *Whirr-chime.*

'Another day on the wall,' Halen replied.

'Hah. For that, friend, you get the shout,' said Rann. 'Thirty metres out, please.'

'Yes, captain.'

Halen raised his Phobos R/017, felt its targeting systems slave to his helm's auto-senses. He had a perfect headshot on a striding Iron Warrior. He ignored his target lock, and watched the distance meter climbing down. Two hundred metres, one-seventy, one-fifty…

'To your glory, brothers,' he called out.

'And the glory of Terra!' they all sang back, even Rann.

Seventy-five metres, sixty, fifty, forty… thirty-five… thirty…

'Commence,' said Halen.

The bolters began to fire. Sharp flashes stippled along the top of the circuit line and from defence boxes in the face of the wall. The first impacts were scored. Every hit a kill-shot. The front of the charging tide crumpled. Bodies broke mid-stride, exploded, toppled backwards, tripped others. Warriors fell, tumbling on the fallen ahead of them, or torn down by the next rain of bolt shells. The charging line hinged in on itself at its midsection, flank elements outstripping the punished centre. Halen barked instruction, and his own flank units cast wide, broadening the fields of fire to demolish the outrunners. Wall guns began to thump and chatter to his left and right. Traitor rows buckled. Mud and rubble blasted into the air.

Fire was coming back at them. Loose and wild, fired on the run, but heavy, hammering at wall faces, parapet lines and shields. Then a few more-accurate shots, the bolter fire of Traitor Space Marines, their weapons motion-compensating. Brother Imperial Fists snapped back from the wall, heads blown off, chests blown out. Halen changed clips, feeling his siege shield buck as it took fire. Though its front ranks were mangled, the traitor host was still streaming out of the dust. More than they had imagined, so many more.

They reached the outworks, pouring between shattered stone piers and cratered revetments. A dazzling storm of crossfire ripped between rampart and ground. At Halen's command, his brothers moved to defensive pairs, one firing down the wall face to clean off anything or anyone attempting to scale, his partner standing to cover him with the rim of his shield while maintaining fire into the mass. Bodies began to pile up at the foot of the wall, heaped like dead leaves, half-submerged in the mud and the slime-skinned pools of waste-water that had formed between the revetment piers.

The charge broke. The traitor host flowed backwards, staggering, disarrayed.

'We've persuaded them of their stupidity,' Halen said.

'No, brother,' said Rann. 'That was a feint.'

The traitor Warhounds strutted into view, emerging from the dust clouds, retreating infantry flooding around their ankles: three engines, Legio Vulpa, accelerating to fast advance. Behind them, more ponderous, lumbered a towering Warlord, a behemoth silhouette against the sickly, backlit dust. The wall began to tremble.

Yes, a feint. Throw infantry at the first circuit to keep the Imperial Fists in position, prevent them from falling back, then run the Titans in to burn them where they stood. That's how you wore down defences: bait and switch.

'A bad call from me,' Rann said to Halen.

'No, lord–'

'Yes, it was,' Rann snapped. He looked at Halen. 'Prepare to draw us back fast.'

Halen started to bark commands. The advancing engines were a daunting sight. Halen didn't know the Warlord giant. It looked Mars Alpha-pattern, but it had changed, like so many of the brothers that they had once stood shoulder to shoulder with. Its crusade insignia was gone. Feral crests and crudely daubed sigils covered its flanks, and its hull was blackened, as though it had walked a thousand leagues through roasting flame to face them. Chains swayed from its limbs and groin, and tattered banners proclaimed filthy concepts in runes that made Halen's gorge rise. What he first took for beads he realised were naked human corpses swinging from the chains. The engine looked sick, skeletal, its stride uneven as if limping, though from chronic disease rather than injury. Its armoured head, hunched between the massive yoke of its gun-platform shoulders, had been refashioned into the form of a massive human skull. Cockpit lights glowed in the eye sockets, and rotary cannons protruded through the open, screaming jaws like tongues. War-horns boomed. The hound-Titans escorting it, similarly malformed, stalked like flightless birds, first rushing ahead of their giant dam, then edging back skittishly to stay at the Warlord's heels and retain formation.

'*Solemnis Bellus*,' muttered Rann.

'You know it?' asked Halen.

'Barely,' Rann replied. 'Just a few traces left of the engine it once was. Throne, I weep to see such a glorious weapon so debased.'

The weapons of the advancing engines began to fire. Megabolter. Turbo laser. Torrents of blast-shot from the rotator mounts of the three hounds. Devastation ripped across the circuit line. Ferrocrete shattered. Wall sections erupted, collapsing in avalanches of masonry, dust, flame and plate debris. Yellow-armoured bodies were tossed into the air. Casemate 16 subsided, the throat of its turret torn out, its entire gun platform sliding off its mount and dropping down the wall face, munitions cooking off in a frenzied stream of overlapping detonations.

'Fall back!' Halen yelled into the vox. 'Fall back to second now!'

A blast took him off his feet. Grit and flame swirled around him.

A strong arm pulled him to his feet.

'No, brother,' the Angel said, looking down into Halen's cracked visor. 'No need. Not yet.'

Sanguinius let him go, and turned to the mangled lip of the wall. He leapt off, into the wallowing curtains of fire, wings unfurled.

'Did I see that?' asked Rann, hauling Halen into cover.

'He's with us,' Halen replied.

The Great Angel wasn't alone. Legionaries were rushing onto the wall line from the defiles and back access wells. Warriors in blood-red plate gripped brothers of the VII by the hands in greeting as they pushed forward, pulling them back, giving them a moment to reload and reset while they took over the positions. The bolters of the Blood Angels began to roar.

Fresh blood, but still just blood. Even concentrating their fire, the guns of the Space Marines couldn't bring down a war engine.

The Great Angel of Baal was another thing altogether. He soared across the slopes of rubble at the foot of the crippled wall, across the tumbled and twisted enemy corpses brought down by the Imperial Fists, into the miasmal fog of dust and smoke and fire, surging on powerful wingbeats that spiral-eddied the smoke in his wake.

He swept low, like a hunting eagle, banked magnificently between the streams of turbo laser fire trying to track him, and ploughed into the snout of the nearest Warhound. He drove his spear straight through the top of its command compartment, through inhuman symbols, through ancient armour, through sub-system skins, through power trains. It dug deep. Sanguinius twisted the haft, feet braced on the hull canopy, wings beating hard to maintain balance. The Warhound squealed and faltered, a misstep, cumbersome weapon limbs flailing in a vain attempt to brush its attacker off its face, like a child flailing against a hornet's persistent attention.

The Great Angel wrenched the spear free, and fell backwards. He dropped, then his wings grabbed the air, his fall turned into flight, and he raced like a missile across the churned earth that had been expecting his impact. The Warhound stumbled backwards, sparks spraying from the gaping puncture in its head. The Warlord, annoyed and protective of its fledglings, declined both principal limb guns and opened fire, swinging at the waist as it tracked Sanguinius' low and rapid line of flight. The catastrophic firepower ripped earth, mud and rockcrete slabs apart, chewing an enormous burning crescent in the ground.

Sanguinius swept clear of the chasing hail of fire. His wings carried him faster than the Warlord could traverse. He banked again, turning in, climbing, his wings beating at the limit of their strength, and came at the right flank of the engine that had once been proud to call itself *Solemnis Bellus*.

He powered up its side, a vertical climb. The Great Angel

dragged his spear as he ascended, raking the blade tip through flank armour, ripping a long, ugly gash from hip to breastwork that spewed cinders and black fluid.

He crested the Warlord, forty metres off the ground, hung for a moment, and dropped onto its shoulders, straight onto the armoured nape behind the skull-head.

The *Spear of Telesto* slid into the back of its head.

Ugly, choking snorts echoed from the engine's war-horns. The huge Warlord shook and swayed. Both eyes blew out, flames and fragments of cockpit glass bursting from the skull sockets.

Sanguinius tightened his grip. The spear, harpooned deep into the base of the engine's skull, glowed briefly, and pulsed energy into *Solemnis Bellus*. Sub-detonations went off in its waist assemblies, its hips, and out through the back of its drive compartment. Sanguinius plucked the spear, raced forward, and took off, lofting clear of the machine's prow as the death blast claimed it.

Bright fire, an internal blast of devastating force, burst through its torso and sheared off one of its weapon limbs. It fell sideways, legs locked, and hit the ground so hard it slapped up waves of mud and soil. The earth shook. The wall shook. Halen reached out to steady himself. As it came down, the giant's head connected with the outspur of a stone revetment, and was twisted backwards so it ended neck-broken, gaping at the dead sky.

Secondary blasts rippled through the immense metal carcass. A magazine blew up, showering flames and molten steel. The mud, polluted water and debris hurled up by its gargantuan impact began to rain down in a half-kilometre radius, a torrential downpour of slime, fluid and metal fragments.

Sanguinius landed on the butchered earth, facing his kill. Backlit by the god-machine's huge pyre, he rose, wings furled, spear sizzling in his hand, and gazed at the three Warhounds. The one he had wounded was still vomiting sparks, and smoke trailed from its holed head. It whinnied and brayed. All three had come to a halt. They cycled their weapons and washed the Blood Angels primarch with target-seeking systems.

'Try, if you like,' Sanguinius yelled up at them. 'Shall we continue?'

There was a long pause. Then the Warhounds moved in unison. They took a step backwards, swung around, and ploughed back into the dust the way they had come.

Later, when the incident was recounted, someone insisted that even a primarch, even the glorious Great Angel, could not stare down three Titan engines. Their auspex must have painted Titan-killing armour – Shadowswords or Slayer-blades – that had been closing in, two minutes out.

But Halen knew what he'd seen.

Sanguinius flew back to the outworks rampart. The Blood Angels rose from their freshly taken positions along the parapet line as he swept overhead. The Imperial Fists drummed the butts of their bolters against their shields in a crude chorus of martial applause.

He landed. He leaned on his upright spear for a moment, as a man would rest after hard toil. The Warlord's black grease and oil-blood spattered his ornate gold armour, his beautiful face, the sunburst labarum behind his head. It dripped from his long, golden hair.

'Fafnir,' he said, greeting Rann with a nod. He clasped the lord seneschal's hand, dwarfing it.

'My lord,' said Rann. 'They will tell stories of this deed.'

'No, Rann,' Sanguinius replied.

'I am sure of it, lord,' Rann said. 'I'm lucky to have seen a myth being made.'

They knew the Great Angel of old. A heartfelt comment

like Rann's would have once provoked a smile and a modest laugh. But no smile appeared.

'No story will come of this,' he said. 'It was a tiny thing. There are too many stories, Fafnir, my dear brother, and most will be forgotten in a moment as the next takes its place. This is… This is everywhere.'

'My lord,' said Rann. There was silence all around them.

'I've seen it, Fafnir,' said Sanguinius. 'From here, to the gate, to the port, across Anterior, across Magnifican. This is everywhere and everything. Far too many stories, a million of them, all destined to be lost, for only the last line of the book matters.'

'Then we had better make sure we're the ones who write it,' said Rann.

Sanguinius did not reply at first. The smallest hint of a smile lit his eyes. It felt to Halen as though the sun had come out, dispelling the infernal gloom.

'Indeed,' said Sanguinius. He took a deep breath, and straightened up. 'Indeed, brother. So let's attempt to hold this line a little longer.'

Dorn left the bastion via the Petitioners Gate, and headed across the yard towards the walkway, two Huscarls in tow. The gate yard was half-empty. By the light of fat tapers enclosed in frosted glass hoods, groups of petitioners waited while liveried wardens dealt with their supplications. Most of the petitioners were high-ranking citizens, or civic leaders, and Dorn knew their requests were probably reasonable: increased ration allowances, medicae provision, permits for evacuation into the Sanctum. He also knew most would be denied. It was wartime, *the* wartime. Privations were a necessary burden to be shouldered by any who stood with the Throne.

His appearance caused a stir, a murmuring. Most averted their gaze, respectful, but he saw a few consider the notion of approaching him. Timidity got the better of them.

One small group, a mismatched band of men and women of various ages and stations, had taken seats on the stone benches by the arch. As the Praetorian passed, one rose and came to him. It was Sindermann.

'My lord–'

A Huscarl blocked his approach.

'I crave just a minute, my lord,' Sindermann called.

'Not now,' Dorn replied, and kept walking.

He paused, then turned back.

'This concerns remembrancers, Sindermann?'

'Yes, my lord.'

'I don't have time now,' said Dorn. *I may never have time*, he thought. 'But the project has my support. Diamantis will take your proposal and issue your permits, with my authority.'

Diamantis, one of the Huscarls, glanced at Dorn.

'My lord?'

'Take their proposal, get it sealed with my bond. Get them all attachment warrants in my name. Just make sure their proposal contains nothing too unreasonable.'

'On what criteria, my lord?' Diamantis asked.

'Use your discretion,' said Dorn. He turned and moved on without another word.

Diamantis looked at Sindermann. 'What is this about?' he asked.

'Remembrancers, lord,' Sindermann replied. 'A new order. A small one, I assure you.'

'I thought we were long past that,' said Diamantis.

'My Lord Dorn–' Sindermann began.

'I heard him,' said Diamantis. 'You have this proposal?'

'Here,' said Sindermann, pulling a folded parchment from under his coat.

* * *

Dorn passed under the old arch and onto the walkway. It was a broad, high bridge that spanned the deep gulf between Bhab Bastion and an annex of smaller drum towers to the west. The bridge was lit by more of the glass-hooded tapers. High above, the sky swirled with a darkness that looked like low thunderhead cloud. He could hear the creak and moan of the void shields, the uneven thump and rumble of distant, constant bombardment. The southern horizon was lit with a dull and throbbing orange light that made a silhouette out of the immense Lion's Gate and the neighbouring towers.

Far below the bridge span, the access streets and thoroughfares were choked with people, rivers of displaced citizens flowing into the Sanctum Imperialis. Officials and Adeptus Arbites with light poles were routing each long, migrating convoy towards temporary shelters: halls, libraries, gymnasia, theatres; any decent spaces that could be requisitioned and spared. The displaced were welling in through the Lion's Gate and the other gatehouses of the Ultimate Wall, driven from their homes in Magnifican and Anterior, desperate for shelter in the one zone of the Imperial super-palace that was still deemed safe and unviolated. Dorn could see people with small sacks of possessions, with handcarts, with children. How many millions had been driven out of the port zone and the northern reach of Anterior? How many millions more would follow?

Where would they go if the enemy breached the Ultimate Wall?

Midway across the bridge, Dorn realised he could hear an odd, incessant chime that his genhanced senses could detect above the moan of the aegis, the muffled bombardment and the low drone of unnumbered voices from far below.

He stopped.

'My lord?' asked Cadwalder, his remaining Huscarl.

Dorn raised his hand. That sound… Where was it coming from?

The lamps. The glass hoods of the bridge lights were all trembling in their holders, very slightly, invisibly, but he could hear their shiver. He realised the bridge was also vibrating very, very slightly, so little, a standard human could not have sensed it.

But it was there, the… What had Sindermann called it? The tremble.

The whole Palace was shaking. Not from fear. From the constant exterior impacts.

He started walking again, reached the horseshoe arch of the annex, and went inside.

The drum tower was as old as Bhab, but a tiny sibling of its vast and ugly neighbour. A Custodian Prefect Warden stood in the upper access, waiting for him; a regal golden statue with a draped crimson cloak, ornate castellan axe upright.

'My lord,' he said.

'Prefect Tsutomu,' Dorn replied. 'He awaits?'

'At your pleasure.'

The Custodian led them in. Dorn had requested a private meeting, away from bastion activity. None of the usual conference chambers or audience halls. Just a little gallery room in the thick, stone peak of the drum tower.

Constantin Valdor waited within. The captain-general of the Legio Custodes sat at the long table, his gleaming helm resting on the tabletop at his elbow. Scores of cylinder candles stood on the table, their flames the only light in the old room.

'Irregular,' Valdor remarked as Dorn entered.

'You'll excuse that, I'm sure,' Dorn replied.

'What's the business, my lord?' Valdor asked.

Dorn glanced at Tsutomu and Cadwalder, who had taken station inside the door.

'You may step out,' he said to them.

'Tsutomu can be trusted,' said Valdor, raising an eyebrow.

'So can my Huscarl,' Dorn replied quickly. He hesitated. 'Stay,' he told the two warriors, 'but appreciate the utter confidence of what is about to take place.'

He sat down, facing the master of the Legio Custodes. They were old friends, but there was tension.

'So… what *is* about to take place?' Valdor asked.

Dorn raised his index finger. 'Not yet,' he said. 'For now, small talk.'

'I don't believe I need to point out to you that we have precious little time for such luxuries these days,' said Valdor.

'Indulge me.'

Valdor shrugged. 'How did you settle things with your brother?' he asked, as if the subject were trivial.

'Jaghatai? Well enough. He wants to go for the port.'

'Of course he does.'

'Defensive doctrines are not his preference,' Dorn agreed.

'Not fair,' Valdor replied. 'The Khagan simply defends by attack. His Legion has always been energetically mobile. They are chafing. And the port is a logical and viable objective. Essential, some might argue.'

'And he did argue,' replied Dorn. 'It's safe to say I've never seen him that angry with me. Or perhaps angry with the world. Or me and the world. And I've never seen him so tired.'

'It's a sorry day for us all when the likes of you and your brother are fatigued,' said the First of the Ten Thousand.

'Everyone's tired, Constantin,' said Dorn. He sat back and watched the candle flames dance. 'The attrition rate in the bastion is savage. Officers falling sick, breaking down, suffering nervous exhaustion. Every few days, there are fresh faces to learn – new officers, new aides, new generals, stepping in, filling shifts.'

'The shift rollover is punishing. How long do they get to sleep? Three hours? Then there's the sheer volume of data-flow. We don't all have minds like yours, Rogal.'

'It doesn't help when Jaghatai storms in and dismisses two good seniors out of hand.'

'For what crime?'

'Being tired. Speaking too frankly. Being human.'

'Who?' asked Valdor.

'Niborran.'

'No!'

'And another. Ah…'

'Brohn, my lord,' said Cadwalder from the door.

'Brohn, yes. I'll find roles for them elsewhere. It's not as if we don't need good officers across the board.'

'Still, Saul Niborran's been there since day one,' said Valdor. He scowled.

'And he's probably burned out. It happens.'

'Isn't he too old for active line?' asked Valdor. 'I mean, the fellow's only human.'

'I don't think age limits factor in this any more,' said Dorn.

They both stopped talking. The candle flames trembled. Neither of them was good at casual conversation.

Only human. Valdor's words hung in the candle smoke. Neither of them was human. They had both been gifted with extended spans that were supposed to outlive war so they could aspire to things beyond it. But war was all they had known, and already they had seen through too many mortal generations. Humans had been born, lived, and died of old age several times within their lifespans, and still war persisted. Dorn and Valdor had never spoken of it, but they both privately feared they had, through necessity, become too moulded by the one role that they could never leave it. They could not talk easily or lightly, like men, or pause to consider the nuances of culture. They could not relax or reflect. Martial responsibility had pushed all other concerns out of them. Even the simplest conversation turned to logistics and strategies. Humans lived and died like gadflies, Dorn thought. Where did they find the time in their short spans to be anything other than warriors when I can't find it in mine? And I was supposed to find it. I was supposed to be so many things. Soldier was only one of them.

'We were born for more,' he muttered.

Valdor looked at him. The Praetorian realised he had spoken out loud, unguarded. He was about to brush the remark aside, but the captain-general of the Custodians held his gaze. Valdor simply nodded. His eyes betrayed a sad hint of empathy.

'We were,' he said. 'Born to fashion a future.'

'And enjoy it,' said Dorn.

'Enjoy it, yes. Be part of it, not just its midwives. When we were made, the future was full.'

'And now there is only war.'

Valdor exhaled, then laughed. He rubbed the stripe of cropped hair that ran across his otherwise shaven scalp.

'We will prevail, Rogal,' he said. 'One day, you'll break your sword and hang up your shield, and you will sit, and laugh, and from the window, see golden towers standing without fear or aegis or batteries, freed from all possibility of threat because of what we do now.'

'You believe that without hesitation, don't you, Constantin?'

'I have to. The alternative is unacceptable.'

'But, from the way you speak, you don't see that as your future, then?' Dorn asked.

'My duty will never end,' Valdor replied. 'The primarchs were wrought to build an Imperium. Your task, however hard, has an end. Mine does not. The Custodians were born simply to protect Him. It is what we will always do.'

'You always thought the primarchs were a mistake, didn't you?' said Dorn.

Valdor looked at him. 'I–'

'You had misgivings.'

'What I may have felt hardly matters,' Valdor replied. 'Especially now. We stand together. You and I, at His side, against this fall of night. We must be allies, without reservation or recrimination, and I trust that we are.'

He sighed. 'So…' he said, turning them away from contemplation quickly, 'you were saying. Your brother?'

'I let him simmer,' said Dorn. 'Then I took him aside. I told him he could have the port. Take it, with my blessing. It's not as if I'm going to go to war with him about it. I simply requested he took his force out to it via Colossi, and did a little work there first to bolster the line, so that strengths from the port could fall back if they had to.'

'He agreed?'

'Yes. It's mobile assault. The fight before Colossi is a running war for now. The White Scars get to slip loose. But he knew what I was doing.'

'Saving face for him?'

Dorn nodded. 'Jaghatai knows I can't spare one of my two loyal brothers in a gambit at the port, no matter the potential gain. But he'd said what he'd said. He knows Colossi is a shitstorm, and getting worse by the hour. He'll be locked there. He'll see it's where he's most needed.'

'And it's where you wanted to put him?'

'It's where I wanted to put him. The Khan at Colossi, the Angel at Gorgon. But it will feel, to him, that I'm acquiescing to his desire for aggressive tactics. Faces are saved and honour is retained.'

'So you handled him?'

'I did. And I don't like that.' Dorn sighed. 'He's the Khan, for Throne's sake. The great Warhawk. His doctrine of combat is superlative. As a warlord, I'd rank only Roboute above him.'

'And Roboute's not here.'

'He's not.'

Valdor nodded. 'I'd agree with your assessment. Roboute, the Khan… There's really only one other.'

'Don't flatter me, Constantin.'

Valdor smiled. 'I wasn't even including you, Rogal. You're Praetorian. The list starts with you. No, I meant, back in the day…'

'Ah. Yes. Him.'

'Him, indeed.'

'Well, He's the damned reason we're doing any of this,' said Dorn. He paused. 'No, I don't like having to handle Jaghatai. But it's necessary. He is wilfully independent. The Angel, well, I just ask, and he does. It's a different kind of loyalty. And you–'

'Me?' asked Valdor

'I want you at Colossi.'

Valdor frowned. 'My sole duty is His protection,' he said simply. 'The Custodians are withdrawn to the Sanctum. That–'

'I need your power in the field of war,' said Dorn. 'We must be allies, and I trust that we are.'

'I suppose,' Valdor said, with reluctance, 'I can release a Custodian force into the field, provided the main bulk remains in the Sanctum on watch. Colossi, you say?'

'Yes.'

'To keep an eye on your brother?'

'No, to fight the bastards.'

'*And* keep an eye on him?'

'Yes.'

Valdor smiled faintly.

'I'm glad of the clash, to be fair,' Dorn admitted. 'Letting the Khan have his way a little.'

'Why?'

'This entire battle sphere is me against the Lord of Iron. Strategy, counter-strategy. Doctrine against doctrine. And we both know it. We're both reading each other, predicting... And we're good at it.'

'You've been rehearsing for decades.'

'I never thought it would come to a practical test. I just worry that we're both too good at it. Ploy, block, ploy, block... Stalemate. But if I can introduce a more random factor, one I haven't specifically crafted...'

'Like the Great Khan, cut loose?' asked the lord of the Legio Custodes.

Dorn nodded. 'It might introduce a small, unscripted element,' he said. 'It's what Perturabo did to us at the port of the Lion. He let Kroeger have his run, and it cost us. Perhaps I can do likewise, on a grander scale, with Jaghatai. Perhaps, in time, that might be enough to break dear Perturabo's expectations and skew his decisions.'

'So,' said Valdor, 'your complex and utterly comprehensive plan of war now includes the unplannable?'

'It is a strange time, Constantin.'

All the candle flames suddenly flickered. A couple went out, hoisting dribbles of blue smoke. The outer door had opened and closed without the Custodian or the Huscarl reacting.

They did now, belatedly. An odd, stilling pressure had passed through the room. There was a half-shadow near the table at Dorn's side, as though a patch of air had been smeared with grease.

Tsutomu and Cadwalder both realised what it was, and lowered their weapons.

Dorn had to concentrate for a second. Even right in front of him, she shifted so easily, like a peripheral image.

Jenetia Krole, Mistress of the Silent Sisterhood, saluted him.

'I'm glad you could join me, mistress,' said Dorn.

She signed a response, her pale face impassive.

'Yes, anywhere,' Dorn replied, reading the thoughtmark of her hands.

Krole took a seat at the far end of the table. She nodded to Valdor. The deadening, flavourless nothingness of her psychic nullity permeated the room like an absence seizure. They felt the wrongness of it in the air.

'I asked Mistress Krole to attend for the same reason I requested this unremarked location,' said Dorn. 'To ensure the privacy of our conversation.'

'So now we can dispense with small talk and begin?' asked Valdor.

An inner door opened. Malcador the Sigillite, robed and cowled, emerged from an anteroom. He took his place at the other end of the table.

'Now we can,' said Dorn.

THREE

Krole
Whisper it
Muster point

I am aware I am present simply as a cloak. I am an instrument, placed at the end of the table, so that others may talk unguardedly. I am nothing, and my nothingness gives me great value.

They barely see me. They try. Even with their immortal senses, they struggle. I am a smudge. A smear. A piece of stained light in which the image of a woman occasionally appears, if you strain to look. They don't, unless they are addressing me. I am hard to look at. Harder still to bear. I am an ache in their joints, a clench in their jaws, the taste of bile in their throats.

I see everything.

I don't participate. I'm not here to talk. I'm just here to be. So I watch, for there is nothing else to do. I watch the flames of the candles flicker. Never the same shape twice, like snowflakes. The rising smoke-streaks of the wicks that simply died when I walked in. The whorls of the wood in the tabletop, tight lines marking years gone by. The stone walls of the old gallery. Uneven. Covered in bas-relief carving once, the emblems long scoured back to faint shapes by the process of passing touch and faster-passing time. This was a chapel once. I read so, in a book. A holy place, when things were still allowed to be holy. I wonder what was prayed for here? Health? Victory? Long life? Good crops? What were the images of? That shape there... Was that a god? A bear? A stag? An altar? It's hard to know. I make sense of some shapes, but then one may make sense of clouds, and read dragons and gods and demigods in the sky. The mind does that. It fills in blanks, and provides a semblance of meaning where meaning lacks. It is impossible to say what was really on these walls. The myths have been erased.

Gods, demigods and heroes still exist, though. I sit, looking at them as they converse. I wonder who will write their myths, and whether they will endure, or be erased by time and the unfaithful memory of man.

They would make good myths. I hope they get the chance. Rogal, I admire him. He is talking. He is the focus of all our trust. Everything hangs upon him, like the heaviest case of armour ever made, plate forged from the hyperdense matter of a neutron star. His armour is surprisingly plain. Grand, yes, as befits a primarch-son, more ornate than the suit worn by his man at the door. But utilitarian. Functional. It is there to protect him, not impress others. His bearing does that. The high line of his cheekbone, the stark white of his hair, the tone of his voice, like the hush-surge of an ocean.

He talks. I do not pay close attention. I am not here for my opinion. I wonder if he even expects me to listen, or assumes my blankness is as internal as it is external. He talks of defence lines and intersecting strategies. I'm not sure how he keeps the surfeit of detail so readily at the front of his mind. This is the most complex battle ever fought. He knows every line of it by rote, like a favourite poem. I review his plan daily, and understand perhaps a third of it. I could not do it, and I have noted ability in that discipline. He was born to do this, and no other could.

Constantin listens, makes comments. He follows as well as I do, which is very well, but not well enough. I have known him the longest. He was the one that first took me to kneel before the Throne, and brought me into this life. He was the one who found a purpose to fill the otherwise hollow girl. My life has been unpleasant, but it would have been more unpleasant if he had not taken me out of Albia. I will be sorry when he dies.

And he will. He is a Custodian. That is a very specific duty. A warrior of the Legiones Astartes may die in battle, as a negative consequence of battle, but a Custodian lives to give his life. Like Tsutomu Pearlfisher Adriat Malpath Pryope Uranus Prospero Calastar there, at the door. I know him well, too; I know all the Custodians, well enough to know the entirety of the title-names engraved inside their auramite armour, even Constantin's one thousand nine hundred and thirty-two. They are not warriors, they are protectors. They live to die, to place themselves in front of the Throne and suffer any mortal stroke. Space Marines pledge to fight to the death. So do I, and all my pariah sisters. But Custodians, they pledge to fight for the life. It's not semantics. It means their deaths are inevitable rather than merely possible.

Constantin's armour is magnificent. A gold finer than gold, more ornate than the Praetorian's, for it is ceremonial before it is anything else. Rogal took down all the splendour of the Palace when he fortified it. I think he would have had the Custodians cast off their raiment and wear brute ceramite, too. Ornamentation does not serve a purpose in Rogal's mind. But I think the ostentation may be forgiven. If a demigod offers his life to protect yours, then you should garb him in gold to honour that sacrifice.

The Sigillite listens silently. He is the second oldest person I've ever met. In this room, he looks every one of his some six and a half thousand years, a tiny thing beside the two demigods. I make him uncomfortable. My presence negates his demigod mind as easily as I might pinch out the candle flames in front of me. He is shorn of his glamour, the psykana mask of health, wisdom and purpose I am told he manifests to those few he meets in person. In this room, he is a fragile thing, bird bones gathered in a tight wrapper of thin skin, hunched inside a worn robe. His eagle-staff, his rod of office, leans against the table as if it is too heavy for him to hold.

For him to show himself like this, to allow himself to be seen as he really is, marks how significant this meeting is. The Regent of all Terra has come naked among us, allowing his public mask to drop.

But I don't know why. Rogal is talking, but still it consists of logistical detail. He says that the siege, at this hour, is composed of four thousand and seventeen interlocking battles. His definition of battle, he says, is any engagement with more than thirty thousand troops on each side. We've taken worlds with less. The scale is mythical. But we know that.

He says the battle sphere is fuelled by two considerations. First, his strategic contest with Perturabo. He describes it like a game, but one of infinite complexity, a game with so many rules they would need to be encoded in spirals of DNA. The winner, Rogal or Perturabo, will be the one who identifies some missing allele somewhere, some trace phenotypic mutation, some tiny loophole that the other hasn't seen. That will be how this is decided. Like a game, with Terra as the board.

The second consideration is logistics. That may be the more fatal decider. We have simply what we have: three primarchs, three Legions, the Army Excertus, the Custodians, my Sisters, the engines. Barring the arrival of others, like Roboute or

Leman or Lion, we are obliged to play this game out with what is already in the Palace. And that is a vast, but finite resource. We pray they will come, of course. The Lion, the Wolf, the Master of Ultramar. If the friezes on this chamber's walls were carved today, that is the prayer this chapel would display.

But they may come too late. They may not come at all. Their deaths may already be myths we have not read. And Perturabo, Perturabo and the heretic-dog who jerks his choke-chain, they have no limits. There is no cap on how they may be resupplied or reinforced. Six, seven, maybe eight primarchs and their hosts, the war-masses of Traitor-Mars, untold armies. And then, what else? What unstemmed tides of war might flow here from xenos worlds with whom the Great Lupercal has made pacts? What rivers of Neverborn filth might break the levees of the immaterium, and flood the Himalazia Zone?

Rogal's point, and he makes it firmly, is that attrition is the gravest menace. We contest this with whatever we have within the walls. They do not. We grow weaker every day. They grow stronger.

I wonder if this is it. The reason for our privacy. The thing too dreadful to admit in the bastion, too crucifying for the staff to hear. It cannot be. We all know it. You would have to be stupid not to. The general staff see the data-flow every day. They may not, like me, understand it fully, as Rogal does, but they grasp the gist. We are outnumbered, and the odds in our favour decrease by the hour.

No, this could not be the revelation that Rogal fears to make elsewhere. For this, he speaks in private, excluding even his seniors? For this, Malcador suffers the indignity of letting himself be seen unmasked? For this, I am summoned to block out the world?

I am oddly disappointed. I reason Rogal was simply too

concerned for general morale to articulate our plight so baldly in front of others.

My gaze goes back to the candles. I watch their light dance reflections across Constantin's gold plate. I smell the tallow, the dead smoke, the oil in the table's wood, the dust lodged in the clefts of the rafters. I smell the sweet perfume of the balms anointing Tsutomu's skin; the clean, unfragranced body odour of the Imperial Fist Cadwalder, sweat-less, like a warm, dry dog. I think of my duty, and wonder how it will end. I have been six hours on the walls today, ten yesterday, eight the day before. There are spots of blood on my gauntlets still. My fingers smell of resin. My sword has never been cleaned so often. Their blood is so black. The wind on the ramparts smells of cancer and decomposing rockcrete.

I have never felt so tired.

I am older than I care to admit, and older than I look, if anyone could see me. I have nothing to prove. My battle honours lack for nothing, even set alongside the records of these demigods. The Wars of Succession, Red Frost, the harnessing of Albia, the Pacific, Last Unity, Compliance 9-13, Pentacanaes, Mournful Gate, Skagan, Itria, the Witch Wars, Asmodox, Calastar in the webway. My formation of protectorate detachments allowed the Censure Host to torch Prospero.

Nothing to prove. I think of those times. My record is my identity, for I am lacking a visible one. Am I a myth too? Surely no one will write mine if I am. I have no one to tell who will listen. My proloquor is dead. I buried her myself. I have not taken another. My lamed hands will speak for me.

I wonder if, when my end comes, I will register any satisfaction. Any fulfilment. I will have done my duty, and I have never flinched from that. But duty is cold. It is functional, like Rogal's plate. It serves its purpose. It has never filled the hollowness in me. I was born hollow. I watch the candle flames. I think, perhaps for the first time in a lifetime spun out unnaturally long by alchemy, I think I might cherish some sense of fulfilment. Just something, in whatever are my last few seconds, that is more than mere duty. The thought that I have done something no one else could.

The candle flames flutter. Rogal has gestured for emphasis. He is speaking of the Eternity Wall. No, not the wall. The port named after it. I have drifted and lost track. I realise he is now saying, at last, what he could only say here.

I listen. He is re-emphasising our logistical deficiencies. He is reiterating our decreasing odds. He mentions again the four thousand and seventeen interlocking battles currently raging.

He says, of those, in the coming days, there will be four crisis points: Gorgon Bar, Colossi Gate, Eternity Wall Port, and a fourth.

What is the fourth? I ask. My hands ask. The demigods do not notice my thoughtmark. Constantin and the Sigillite are watching Rogal speak.

He says that we will only hold three. There it is. The unutterable truth that must be blanked. We cannot hold them all. We can only hold three. We are on the brink.

Constantin won't have it. He interrupts Rogal and starts to speculate about contingency. A redeployment effort to cover all four. A shift of doctrine. When Rogal counters every suggestion with cold data, Constantin asks if it is time. Time to bring *Phalanx* in. Time to take Him away. The last-ditch option. Get Him clear. Abandon Terra and rush the Emperor to safety.

Rogal looks at the Sigillite. He waits for the Sigillite to speak. It's a decision only the Regent can make.

I don't know if he is going to speak at all. He hasn't so far. Before he can, I rap my knuckles on the tabletop.

The candle flames shiver. A few more go out. All three of

them look down the table at me, their eyes straining as they make an effort to resolve me.

What is the fourth? my hands ask.

And Rogal says, 'Saturnine.'

'There is a weakness,' said Dorn, looking back at Valdor and Malcador. 'Infinitely small but very credible. In the wall line, near the Saturnine Gate. It hadn't been detected or factored in before.'

'They've struck at nothing that far south-west,' said Valdor.

'But they can, and they will,' replied Dorn. 'I would.'

'Why was this missed?' asked Valdor. 'How–'

'It looks like nothing,' said Dorn. 'I caught it by chance, entirely by chance, a few days ago. Something off-hand someone said to me. A tremble.'

'What does that mean?'

'It doesn't matter,' said Dorn. 'I've been analysing it since. It's proven. Certain.'

'But if you didn't notice it until now, why would he?' Valdor asked.

'Because he's Perturabo, and one of us was going to slip sooner or later. The deciding mistake. I cannot risk assuming he has not.'

'A strike at Saturnine, if it worked–' Tsutomu began.

'Station, Custodian!' Valdor snapped.

'Let him speak if he likes, Constantin,' said Dorn. 'He's here. He heard.' He looked at Tsutomu. 'Go on.'

'If it worked,' said the Prefect Custodian, 'it would cut to the heart. He would be into the Palace Sanctum. The Palatine core.'

'Decapitation strike,' said Malcador, speaking for the first time. His voice was like a dry wheeze, like a creak of weight-stretched rope.

'Decapitation strike,' said Dorn, nodding. 'Very quick and very sure.'

'Then we fortify–' Valdor began.

'Of course,' said Dorn. 'Of course. But this is my point. We are stretched too thin. The crisis points, Constantin. Perturabo drives at Gorgon Bar. If he breaks us there, he takes the central line of aegis generators and splits the Sanctum open. Best case, once that happens, two weeks.'

'You have Sanguinius at Gorgon.'

'And more besides,' said Dorn. 'So I trust we can hold it. The Lord of Iron also focuses effort at Colossi. A breakthrough there would take him right to the Lion's Gate. The very door of the Inner Palace. Best case there, a month. We anticipated they'd get there eventually if things continue as they are, but if Colossi falls, it cuts five months off our projected hold-out time.'

'But your other brother stands there,' replied Valdor firmly. 'Jaghatai, thanks to your handling, and I will be at his side.'

'So, again, I trust in our forces prevailing,' said Dorn. 'Then there's the port.'

'He can't take another port,' said Malcador. 'He has one. Eternity Wall Port would more than double his capacity to land ground forces. The result would be devastation.'

Dorn nodded. 'The loss of a second port would escalate this siege. I estimate the advantage a second port would give him… it would shave four months off our holding threshold.'

'And deprive us of an exit route,' said Valdor. 'Lose that, and we would no longer be able to choose the contingency of evacuation.'

The Sigillite sat with his head bent, one bony hand cupped in the other, as though in prayer. 'He will never leave,' he said. 'The question went unanswered. I can tell you, He will not agree to it.'

'He might have to,' said Valdor. 'His safety is my duty. It's the one area in which I have final say. I won't ask. I will just do it.'

'He's fighting a war of His own,' the Sigillite rasped. 'You know that, Constantin. If He leaves the Throne, we lose more than Terra.'

'Four crisis points,' said Dorn. 'We can't afford to lose any of them. But we must decide which is the most affordable.'

'Sacrifice one?' asked Valdor.

'Give up a piece to win the game,' said Dorn. 'Sacrifice a queen to secure checkmate. It's ruthless, but sometimes it's the only option. Which do we give up?'

Valdor stared at the Praetorian. He bared his teeth in a half-snarl. 'You've already decided,' he said.

'I have. But I'm asking.'

'A rhetorical question,' said Valdor.

'We give up the port,' said Dorn. 'It is a massive loss, but it is the least worst of our options.'

There was a moment of silence. The annulled air was stifling.

'The port,' whispered Malcador with a frail nod.

Valdor sat back. He cleared his throat. The rage in his eyes was a terrible thing to see.

'The port,' he conceded.

Dorn turned and looked down the table. 'Mistress?'

The shadow of her shivered, as if she was surprised to be consulted.

The port, she replied as a thoughtmark.

'So, we draw back forces,' said Valdor. 'I suppose it's one less front to fight. We can redeploy strengths to–'

'No,' said Dorn. 'That's the bitter part.'

'There's a bitter part?' asked Valdor sarcastically.

'I'm sorry, Constantin,' said Dorn. 'We need to defend the port. Make a decent and convincing show.'

'A show?' Valdor shook his head in disgust. He looked as though he wanted to get up and leave.

'He can't know we know,' said Dorn. 'If we let go of the port, Perturabo will know we know about Saturnine.'

'So what?' asked Valdor with raw scorn.

'To undertake Saturnine successfully,' said Dorn slowly, 'he will send an elite force. It's a decapitation strike. He will use the very best.'

He let that thought hang.

'And if you're waiting for them, you take a significant scalp?' said Valdor quietly.

'Several, perhaps.' Dorn watched Valdor's face for a reaction.

'I take it you intend to run that line?'

'I do,' said Dorn. 'If Perturabo goes at it blind, thinking we are ignorant of the weakness, we may have a chance to accomplish something significant. Not just protect the Palace. That's paramount. But we may achieve a victory of true consequence. Strike a blow that puts a… a Saturnine in *his* strategy.'

'Allowing us to win this?' asked the captain-general.

'It could take us much closer to a win,' Dorn said.

'Who would he send?' asked Malcador, his voice as small as a hedgerow rustle, 'in your estimation?'

'It's a spear-tip strike,' replied Dorn. 'Who would you send? Who was always the master of that kind of war?'

Valdor breathed out heavily. 'Oh, Terra!' he said. 'Is that why? Is that why we haven't seen him yet?'

'You know him,' said Dorn. 'He wants that glory. In person. He wants to be the one that spills blood across the Throne.'

'We would be condemning every soul who stands at the port to death,' said Malcador. 'Without doubt. We would send them out there knowing. And we couldn't tell them. They cannot know or this ruse of yours falls down.'

'You're right,' said Dorn. 'It's not how I ever thought I'd

run a war. It's a burden we would have to bear. An unforgivable guilt.'

He ran out of words, and wiped his palm across his mouth, as if trying to stuff back in words he wished he'd never uttered. He stared at nothing. Valdor's face was set expressionlessly, like a death mask. He glanced at the Sigillite.

Malcador leaned forward and splayed a knotted-twig hand on the table, the fingers extending towards Dorn.

'Every loyal warrior is oathed to give his life,' Malcador said to the Praetorian quietly. The weight of his words stretched the old rope of his voice tighter still. 'For Terra, for the Emperor. That's why they commit and die. Rogal, that's all they need to know. It's all they know already.'

'It still sits heavy,' said Dorn. 'I am going to have to order men, to their faces, knowing–'

A sharp thumping interrupted him. He looked down the table. Krole had rapped her armoured knuckles on the wood again to get his attention.

'Mistress, what?'

Her hands moved.

'Yes,' said Dorn. 'There will be daemons there.'

On the nineteenth day of the fifth month, the north-east hem of the Imperial Palace began to vanish.

Magnifican, the eastern and greater half of the Palace megastructure, an immense super-city in its own right, had previously been breached, by traitor forces storming east out of the Anterior bridgehead, and by rabble hosts swarming up from the south-east. No one, not even the seniors on station in Bhab, openly admitted it, but Magnifican was already regarded as lost. It was *non-vi*. It could no longer be protected from external attack, or held. The vast territory of its sprawling district, comprising almost two-thirds of the Palace area, was now acting as a soak. It had become a massive urban battlefield where the loyalist forces, falling back, fought delay and denial actions to hold off the invaders, slow their inexorable advance to join the main engagements in the Anterior Barbican and face the proud gates of the Sanctum Imperialis.

On the nineteenth, the nature of that collapse changed. Detonations came first, and firestorms followed.

The first projectile strike consumed a street section almost a kilometre square. Large buildings at the epicentre were simply atomised. Then, a blast wave of churning flame and concussion levelled more, block after block, shredding civic stone, granite and steel, disintegrating buildings like petals in a tempest. That missile was only the first. Its immense fire cloud, boiling with a billion sparks that seemed to hang and linger in the air, was still unfolding when the next projectile fell, and the next, each one overlapping, explosions propagating from the first ranged point. Fire cloud blossomed beside fire cloud, and proud streets vanished, reduced to dust or whizzing fragments of stone. Incendiary payloads of sticky napthek and aerosolised pyrosene spewed outwards, engulfing neighbouring blocks, where buildings had survived the initial impacts. Their windows punched in like gouged eyes, they lit and were enveloped, whole boroughs and districts swept up in seas of fire thirty storeys high. A canopy of black smoke covered forty square kilometres. Ash and petrochemical waste fell twenty more beyond that. Outrush wind carried soot further still.

Three of the Lord of Iron's siege-breaker chiefs, warlords of the Stor-Bezashk schooled in breach-craft by Perturabo himself, had broken the walls at Boenition earlier in the day, a calamity that passed almost unnoticed because of the intense fighting in the Central and Anterior reaches. Hundreds of thousands of invaders swarmed across the mangled rubble. Labour gangs and Martian engines began to clear pathways, and slave armies hauled in the first of the massive petraries and mass bombards. These were the monstrous siege engines that had been employed to crack the wall and collapse the voids, but their work was not done.

By mid-afternoon – an entirely arbitrary division of time, as the skies were as black as night at every hour – the vast engines were repositioned inside the wall line, and had begun firing. Gastraphetes, gravitic ballistas and manuballistas whipped like cyclopean crossbows, launching colossal ceramite arrows or wall-felling blocks; torsion engines and graviton onagers fired low trajectory payloads; counterweight trebuchets, accelerator mangonels and manjaniqs slung high-trajectory missiles. Some hurled inert, high-density loads of ouslite or tungsten that filthy abhuman teams had to wrestle onto the sling-mesh. These wrought catastrophic damage by sheer kinetic force. Many of the payloads were slabs of broken masonry from the fallen wall or the ruins of Boenition District. The traitors were recycling the city, hurling shattered pieces of the Palace back against it to break it further. Other engines flung chemical or high explosive projectiles like pyrosene mines or drums of gas/fyceline intermix that exploded, spreading greedy fires that could not be doused.

By nightfall, which passed invisibly for it was already perpetual night and had been for weeks, the petrary units ranged inside the shattered line of Boenition had reduced the north-eastern rim of Magnifican to pulverised rubble and firestorms as large as cities.

They were not conquering. They were razing.

Each impact, and they were unceasing, jarred the earth, even from many kilometres away. Shards of glass and plex rained from pressure-blown windows in untouched streets. Soot swam like fog. Roofs shivered, split free and fell in avalanches. Terminal cracks rent buildings from foundation to eaves.

'Keep moving,' Camba Diaz instructed.

The streets they trod were largely empty, an oddly tranquil hinterland, like the eye of a monster storm. To the west of them, the immense roar of the Anterior warzones. To the east, the volcanic pandemonium of the razing.

People had fled, combatants and citizens alike. Willem Kordy (33rd Pan-Pac Lift Mobile) presumed they had fled west, hoping to find some kind of sanctuary in the Sanctum Palatine. Buildings stood empty, vehicles abandoned. The sky was an acid yellow smog, and white ash fell like snow, coating every surface.

The hulking Space Marine led them onwards, saying little. His instructions were simply: 'Stay grouped. Fire only on my orders. Retain formations at all times, no matter what.' They were moving north, that was Willem's guess. From time to time, they crossed the path of recent battles: buildings punctured with shell holes, or entirely collapsed; bodies; litters of hard-round casings brass-bright on the ash-snow. A bridge destroyed, except for its central span, still miraculously suspended. The gorge of a deep underpass canyon choked with rubble like a collapsed mine. Messages on walls or doors, frantic efforts to inform families and neighbours where the occupants had gone. On Caesium Rise, four Imperial tanks, squashed flat as if something vast had crushed them underfoot, and a fifth, burned out and embedded in the wall of a manufactory, six floors up, its broken tracks hanging like intestines.

At Traxis Arch, they found another band of stragglers from the 14th Line, forty ash-caked troopers led by two more Imperial Fists. The Imperial Fists greeted Diaz with respect, and from that, Willem decided Camba Diaz was more than just a squad warrior. He heard them call him lord.

'Willem Kordy (Thirty-Third Pan-Pac Lift Mobile),' said Willem. 'Where are you from?'

'Lex Thornal (Seventy-Seventh Europa Max),' replied one of the men. 'We were on Line Fourteen at Manes Place, but the engines came.'

'Noise there!' Diaz called out. 'Keep moving.'

The hydrogalvanic plants at Marinus Spire had been crippled by something. Reservoir cisterns had ruptured, and trillions of tonnes of water were flowing through the streets and plazas, fast-flowing and a metre and a half deep. The water was turgid, frothy and grey. It carried debris and bodies with it, a flotsam of bloated corpses, some trailing tatters of armour. The soldiers waded and clambered across islands of rubble and scree. There was a large rockcrete embankment running to their right, but Diaz refused to let them use it as a pathway as it, in his words, 'brought them up against the sky as targets'. They waded on, freezing, poling bodies out of their path with the butts of their weapons. Slicks of oil gleamed iridescent on the scummed surface of the flow. Ash fell like soft snow. To the east, beyond the rockcrete embankment, the sky was flooded with twisting amber light from the firestorms. They could feel the heat, but the water was freezing, and the ash snow fell unmelted. Jen Koder (22nd Kantium Hort), who had still been unable to remove her buckled helmet, sat down on the top of one of the rubble islands, and refused to go on. Willem knew her injury wasn't survivable.

'We have to leave her,' Diaz said.

Willem didn't know what to say.

'I can prevent her suffering further,' said Diaz.

'No, lord,' said Joseph Baako Monday (18th Regiment, Nordafrik Resistance Army). 'I will do it.'

'No noise,' said Diaz after a moment's consideration. 'A blade.'

Willem watched Joseph slosh his way back to the mound

of rubble. The rest of the party was already moving on. The inferno in the east cast dancing, orange reflections across the floodwaters.

Joseph reached her. She was blind. She jerked her head at the sound of him.

'Who is there?'

'Joseph Baako Monday (Eighteenth Regiment, Nordafrik Resistance Army).'

'Leave me,' she said.

'I don't want you to suffer,' he said.

'Mercy shot?' she asked.

'It's not permitted. I'm sorry.'

'I don't want a knife,' she said. 'There's no mercy in that. Or were you going to throttle me, Joseph Baako Monday (Eighteenth Regiment, Nordafrik Resistance Army)?'

'I honestly do not know what I was going to do,' he replied.

The oddest smile crossed her blood-caked face. 'You're very kind,' she said. 'This can't get worse for me, but I won't have it be worse for you. Go on your way.'

She showed him what she was clutching in her hand.

'I want it to be quick,' she said. 'It hasn't been quick up till now. Go on your way. I'll count to a hundred.'

He could not say goodbye to her. It seemed worthless. He splashed and scrambled back to join the others. A few minutes later, as they clambered up a steep incline of debris, they heard the sharp thump of the grenade behind them. The sound of it slapped off nearby walls and rebounded along the wet pit of the street.

Diaz looked at Joseph.

'That was stupid,' he said.

'I'm only human, lord,' Joseph replied.

Diaz stared at him. It was impossible to tell what expression

lay behind his glaring visor, but Joseph guessed it was a look
that said 'that's the same thing.'

It *was* stupid. Less than two streets on, drawn by the sound, the
reavers found them. A Traitor Army unit in rags and furs, with
skulls war-painted on their faces. They opened fire from cover
along a raised colonnade. The waste-water began to splash and
spray as las-bolts and hard rounds chopped into it. Two troopers were cut down, falling in clumsy splashes, then a third as he
tried to run. Diaz gave the order to shoot. With no cover except
the floodwater and a few atolls of rubble, the stragglers began to
return fire, their lasguns blazing in support of the bolters wielded
by the three Imperial Fists. The facade of the colonnade became
ragged, chipped and scorched. Bodies twisted in the archways,
slumped, slid or toppled forward into the water. The enemy
fire eased. Joseph thought they had been discouraged, but they
were preparing to charge. Feral figures leapt out of the archways,
jumping into the water, yelling as they tried to run into the tide.

'Hold ground. Selective shots. Fire,' Diaz ordered.

Freezing and soaked, they picked the traitors off as they
lumbered through the water to get at them. Each kill-shot cut
short another war cry. Joseph couldn't bear to hear the phrase.
He shot at faces and mouths to shut them up.

The Emperor must d–

At his side, Willem was murmuring, 'It's not your fault. This
is not your fault.'

It was, and it wasn't. Hell had no rules. Whatever you did,
or didn't do, it came back to bite you.

Some of the traitor reavers were abhuman giants. It took two
or three shots to bring them down. Then a true giant emerged.

It came through the colonnade at a run, as though it had
been drawn to the gunfire and death. Its running leap took it
through an archway and six or seven metres clear before it hit
the water. It was still running, somehow unencumbered by the

flood that was slowing the other reavers down. It kicked up sheets of spray. It was a Space Marine: a Traitor Space Marine. One of the berserkers they had seen destroy Captain Tantane and his group in the first hours of retreat. Bone-white armour badged in terrible signs, human pelts tied around it, a ragged cloak of scorched chainmail. A chainaxe, screaming.

World Eater.

Their firing line, ragged to begin with, broke, and began to scatter, despite Camba Diaz's previous instructions. Just the sight of the thing had unmanned them, that and the hideous, wordless howls it was shrieking. It rushed them like a charging simian, faster than anything had any right to be in the world.

But Diaz was fast too. He stopped being the grim, taciturn sculpture that had been gliding along with them, measured and ponderous. He moved like a blur.

He got between them and the charging World Eater. He met it with shield raised, and longsword swinging from its scabbard. The impact was like runaway trains hitting head-on. Water sprayed. Waves crashed out in all directions. Sparks fizzled blue and electric as the chainaxe's teeth hit the rising shield. The collision knocked Diaz backwards. Joseph thought, surely they should be evenly matched? Legionary against legionary. Transhuman strength against transhuman strength.

But the beast in white seemed far stronger. Bigger, too. Its scything axe caught Diaz's shield, and spun him off his feet. The beast bellowed, and chopped down at the floundering Imperial Fist. That impact made a ghastly, snapping sound. Sparks and chips of yellow ceramite flew up.

The side of the monster's head blew out. One of the other Imperial Fists had closed in, and brought his bolter to bear. The World Eater swayed, its head partly removed, blood and bone and teeth visible through the cracked ceramite. It reeled, and lashed out. The back-spike of its axe caught the Imperial

Fist who had shot it across the faceplate, and wrenched him sideways into the water. The third Imperial Fist was aiming his boltgun, but the axe smashed it out of his hands. The third Imperial Fist tried to stagger back out of strike radius. The World Eater roared, blood squirting and drooling from its ravaged head, and swung hard.

Camba Diaz came up out of the water in a wave of spray, and ran his power sword through it from behind. The searing longsword blade impaled it through the torso. Still, it refused to die. Diaz kept the blade in place, and held the beast fast, preventing it moving closer to the third Imperial Fist.

The third Imperial Fist wrenched out a compact-pattern bolt pistol mag-locked to the back of his waistplate. A hold-out piece. He emptied the sidearm point-blank into the chest and face of the monster Diaz had pinned in front of him.

The rapid shots made a huge, echoing report. The impaled World Eater bucked and shook as the explosive rounds shredded its chest, shoulders and sternum, shattering plate armour and chewing it apart. Flecks of blood flew six or seven metres.

It went limp, cored out and mangled from the belly up. Diaz eased his grip, and let the hulking ruin slide down into the bubbling water. He pulled his blade out.

The third Imperial Fist reloaded his pistol, clamped it back on his plate, and recovered his primary weapon. The second Imperial Fist regained his feet, a huge, bare-metal gouge across the cheek and bridge of his visor.

Diaz turned to the Army stragglers.

'Stay in formation when I tell you to,' he said.

Crossing wide, open yards that were flecked with rubble, they got a proper view of the firestorms to the north-east. None of them had ever seen so much fire before, a wall of it thirty kilometres long and higher than a rampart. The heat, even at that distance, felt unbearable. Boenition District was gone. Through their scopes, they saw survivors fleeing the edge of the inferno into the cratered wasteland of Damascus Park. 'Survivors' was the wrong word. They were limping, blackened figures, trailing smoke, some still on fire, unable to claw the burning napthek from their flesh and clothing. They walked out of the torrent of flames as if to escape, and then fell. The edge of the park was littered with smouldering bodies.

White ash and oily rain fell, like a blizzard and a tropical storm at once. Ahead, through the miasmal drifts of brown and yellow smoke, they saw a huge structure with outer barbicans and defensive lines. Willem wondered if it was Angevin Bastion, though he had presumed that the constant roar of casemate weapons coming from the west was Angevin.

They couldn't see the true size or shape of the structure they were approaching. Smoke filled the air, the whole sky, and obscured everything except the lower ground works and fore-batteries of the enceinte. Whatever the place was, it was of stupendous size. It promised safety and cover at last.

They approached the outworks along a trackway, an old transit route, passing scarred or abandoned habitations. Missiles began to fall behind them, two or three kilometres east, huge lumps of stone hurled by petrary engines that fell soundlessly, and struck with shivering force, each impact a numbing boom of incredible volume, a fireless explosion, a column of dirt and debris. At Diaz's order, they began to double time.

The outer defenders were waiting for them: ragged loyalist Army, Solar Auxilia, citizen militia. Their emplacements looked sound, some well-made, some makeshift. Support weapons in dug-out firing pits, ditches, ceramite revetments; bundled loops of stake-pinned razor wire and scattered spike-blocks to maim approaching armour.

They crossed the iron boards of a temporary bridge thrown out across a deep heat-sink channel that had been fortified into a defence ditch. Armed troops came out to meet them. A few of the soldiers in the straggler group began to weep in relief.

Willem saw a Space Marine emerge from the paling line. His armour was white, but it glowed like pearl. His markings were red. His head was bare, scalp shaved, bearded. The White Scar came up to Diaz, saluted, and then embraced his brother. They spoke, but they were too far ahead for Willem to hear what they were saying.

'From here, we can fight,' Joseph said to Willem. Willem nodded.

'A stronghold,' said Pasha Cavaner (11th Heavy Janissar). He wiped tears from his cheeks, embarrassed. 'Safety, thank the Throne.'

Joseph smiled at one of the Solar Auxilia troopers escorting them in.

'Joseph Baako Monday (Eighteenth Regiment, Nordafrik Resistance Army),' he said.

The man eyed him, and shrugged.

'Al-Nid Nazira, Auxilia,' he replied.

'What is this place, my friend?' asked Joseph.

'Eternity Wall Port,' the man replied.

FOUR

Conviction
The thunder of hooves
Hate everything, win anyway (objective tactical clarity)

The warden of the watch, a Solar Auxilia veteran called Vaskale, checked their warrants carefully. He ran them through the optical reader twice, frowning. He hadn't seen documents like them before, but the seal of the Praetorian was authentic.

'Kyril Sindermann, Hari Harr,' he muttered, handing them back. 'What's this concerning?'

'We are commissioned to gather reports,' Hari replied. 'To document in the fashion of–'

Sindermann stopped him, a hand on the boy's sleeve, a cautioning smile.

'Warden,' he said to Vaskale, 'our warrants are intended to remove the necessity of repeated explanation. Our work is urgent, and time is finite.' The air shivered. Distant thunder rolled. A bombardment of macro-cannon shells was falling like sleet across the aegis twenty kilometres away. Sindermann tilted his head at the sound. 'Finite,' he repeated.

Vaskale nodded, huffed. He took up his crutches, and led them through the inner hatch, each step a twin thump of the sticks planting together and a sliding slap of one boot. The effort made him grunt and wince.

The Blackstone was a large and hulking annex in the skirts of the Hegemon complex, built as robustly as any of Dorn's fortifications, but inside out. It was designed to keep things in. Its sulking travertine walls, thirty metres thick, were laced with buttresses of Cadian-mined noctilith, and every portal was a series of blast hatches and portcullis grates. It served the Imperial Palace as its primary penitentiary. Other prisons existed, for civil crimes, out in Magnifican, though fate alone knew what had become of them and their inmates. Only the sub-level known as the Dungeon, beneath the Palatine Central, was a more secure place of imprisonment. According to Vaskale, much of that had been cleared. He didn't know why. Traitors, political subversives and other recidivists had been transported to the Blackstone for incarceration.

'Throne knows what that's about,' Vaskale mumbled as he limped along. He was short of breath from the effort. 'We should shoot them all. Have done.'

'Shoot them?' Hari asked.

Vaskale shrugged, turning to them as he waited for one of his men to unlock the next series of hatches. 'Liquidate them. What? Time's not the only finite quantity, gentlemen. Space is, too. Resources. We're keeping these devils warm and fed, safe from harm. You've seen what it's like outside. Good people starving, begging for shelter.'

Sindermann nodded. They had. As they'd hurried through the streets around the Hegemon, they'd passed through throngs of the displaced and injured, past petitioners, past soup kitchens and welfare centres. The Sanctum Imperialis was flooded with refugees seeking safety, and Sindermann knew it was but a fraction of the pitiful host trying to gain access from the Palace zones outside.

'So you'd see these prisoners executed?' Sindermann asked.

'They have more space and better provision than any bastard out there,' Vaskale replied. He glanced at the guard. 'Hurry up, Gelling! You know the codes!'

Vaskale looked back at Sindermann and his young companion, searching their faces for some sign of understanding.

'The Blackstone's a big place,' he said. 'We could take overspill. Accommodate thousands. Temporary of course, but better than–'

'Out there?' asked Sindermann.

Vaskale nodded. 'We have set food and water rations every day for the inmates. That's a waste, isn't it? They're not on our side, or they wouldn't be in here. Why feed and house them, when we can't feed and house our own?'

'I think the answer to that lies somewhere in the field of ethics,' ventured Sindermann. 'In trying to maintain some kind of decent, human society.'

'Really? Does it?' Vaskale replied. He chewed that over. 'You, you're making reports, are you? Enquiring? My name going to be mentioned?'

'No, sir,' said Sindermann.

'I'm not ashamed of my opinion,' said Vaskale.

'And you're entitled to it.'

'No, I see that look. Snooty, superior, liberal-intellectual… I'm not suggesting some eugenic cull, I'm–'

'I never said you were,' said Sindermann. 'You're desperate. We all are. We're caught in the greatest siege history has ever known, and everything we have is dwindling and running out. You are obligated to keep and feed criminals and threats to our sovereignty, while good people go without. So you voice a pragmatic idea.'

'Pragmatic,' Vaskale nodded.

'Brutal, but pragmatic,' said Sindermann. 'I fear you're right.

It may come to that. I also fear that, if it does, then we cross a line and become no better than the things trying to break these walls in.'

Vaskale scowled. The guard had opened the hatches. He waved them on, down a long, dank hallway that was utterly without decoration or hope.

'Where were you injured?' asked Hari as they walked.

'Me?' asked Vaskale, glancing back. 'Dawn Gate, about three weeks past. Got unlucky. Lost my leg, mashed my hip. Can't fight on the line, but I'm sound enough to be turnkey here.'

'Where's the previous warden?' asked Hari.

'On the line with a gun in his hand,' Vaskale answered, chuckling darkly. 'We all of us do what we can, don't we?'

'We do,' said Sindermann.

Another guard opened another hatch, and the warden brought them into a broad stone chamber, a congressional for communal dining. Guard posts overlooked the bench tables.

Vaskale had voxed ahead to have the prisoner brought up from the cells.

The warden looked at them.

'I apologise if my comment offended you,' he said.

Sindermann shook his head. 'This is what we are now, sir,' he replied. 'We serve the Emperor the best we can. Fight, if that's what we can do. If we can't fight, or if we're wounded, we serve however else we can, but still the best we can. Each wound is pain. Each wound shrinks the Palace a little more. But we serve. What you suggested... Sir, I hope it doesn't become a necessity. You're not the only one seeing the worst, and understanding what that may force us to do.'

Vaskale half-nodded. 'Inform the guards when you're ready to leave,' he said, and limped away, his metal crutches clacking.

'You've met the warden, I see,' said Euphrati Keeler. They

sat down facing her across one of the scabby old dining tres-
tles. Hari took out his scuffed dataslate and set it down in
front of him.

'The warden's just a little closer to despair than we are,'
said Sindermann.

Keeler shrugged. 'Speak for yourself.'

Her hair was loose, unwashed and lank. Her skin was
unhealthily pale. She'd been given army surplus breeches, a
baggy linen smock and woollen mittens.

'It's good to see you again, Euphrati,' said Sindermann.

'Who's this?' she asked.

'This is Hari,' said Sindermann. 'He's with me.'

Keeler looked at the young man. 'Run, Hari,' she said. 'Being
with Kyril never ends well. Not his fault, but true.'

'I'm fine, mam,' said Hari.

'What's this about?' Keeler asked Sindermann. 'Do you
bear a pardon with my name on it? No, I doubt that. I hold
views that are considered dangerous. They're beliefs I won't
renounce. But you, you walk free. Did you renounce yours?'

'No,' said Sindermann. 'However, the Sigillite's terms were
clear. Freedom of movement and no prosecution for any
theist, provided they do not practise or promulgate the cult.'

'Cult?' she echoed sadly.

'His term,' said Sindermann. 'In truth, I've set aside my faith
for now. It was growing shaky, anyway. You were always more
of a figurehead than me.'

'Kyril, you were the voice of–'

'I have set aside one truth for another. The original Truth.
The Imperial Truth. The light is growing dim, Euphrati. Even
in the short time since we last met. Hell rises up around us–'

'And the Emperor protects,' she said.

'He does,' said Sindermann. 'And He may purge the theist
movement at any time. I value my freedom… Which is ironic,

given we are all trapped here. But I've set aside sacred ministry for now, in pursuit of secular work.'

Sindermann showed her his warrant. She studied it carefully.

'I have another for you,' he said.

'Really? Kyril? Really? This? Remembrance?'

'I was close to giving up,' said Sindermann calmly. 'Giving up everything. My faith gone. My faith in everything, including the rationale of our Imperium. Someone reminded me that we're not just battling for our lives. We're battling for our way of living.'

'I don't want a bloody iteration, Sindermann–'

Sindermann held up his hand gently.

'I know, Euphrati. What we were building together, whether we believe it to be sacred or secular, has begun to fall. It's our duty to fight for it. Every part of it. We're not legionaries, we're not even soldiers. There are other things to fight for, and other ways of fighting.'

'There's only one thing to fight for,' she said.

'And that is?'

'The Emperor, Kyril.'

'And what is the Emperor?'

She smiled. 'People get uncomfortable when I answer that question, Kyril.'

'Why?' asked Hari. 'What do you tell them?'

Keeler beamed at the young man. 'Throne, Kyril! Did you not brief this poor child? Doesn't he know what kind of poison I spread?'

'I think he's teasing you,' said Sindermann. He glanced at Hari. 'Are you teasing?'

'Little bit, sir,' said Hari.

Keeler laughed. 'Oh, I like you! My apologies, Kyril. I should have known you'd choose bright, clever people. He looks so innocent. How old is he?'

'Old enough,' said Hari.

'Oh, now you've spoiled it, Hari,' Keeler said, tutting. 'Trying to sound like a big, tough man.' Sindermann's companion didn't respond. Keeler stared at him, and frowned. 'What are you writing? What is he writing, Kyril?'

'I suggested to Hari he could make notes...' Sindermann began.

Keeler snatched the dataslate from the young man. Hari glanced at Sindermann, stylus in hand.

'Notes,' said Keeler. She sat back, scrolling, reading. 'I'm surprised they let you bring this inside.'

'The warden vetted our possessions,' said Sindermann.

'Yes, Kyril,' she replied, still reading, flicking through panes with her index finger. 'But a writing instrument? When I am so full of words? Isn't a slate considered a weapon these days?'

She paused, studying the text.

'Euphrati Keeler. Imagist. Ex-remembrancer,' she read aloud. 'Promulgator of the so-called *Lectitio Divinitatus* bracket theist bracket. Removed to Blackstone facility, Thirteenth Quintus. Pale. Hair untied, appears unwashed...'

She looked at Hari.

'They won't give me a tie, Hari. Or much water.' She looked at the slate, reading again. 'Appears healthy. U/R.' She looked back at the young man, quizzical.

'Uh, abbreviation, mam. Unremarkable.'

She sniffed, considering this. 'Unremarkable. Why, what did you expect?'

'It's just an abbreviation,' Hari replied. 'I make a lot of notes. Report any distinctive features–'

'You're right,' said Keeler. 'I'm not remarkable. Just a person with ordinary features and dirty clothes.' She held the slate so she could look at it, fidgeting with her mitten as if it was in danger of sliding off her hand. 'The only remarkable thing about me, Hari, the reason I'm in here, is the idea in my head. Apart from a little offhand mention, there's nothing about that. The way I look doesn't matter. The way I think does. There should be page after page about it. Hasn't Kyril talked to you about it?'

'No, mam,' said Hari. 'He hasn't spoken to me about theist ideology. Not to me, or any of the group.'

Keeler looked at Sindermann. 'I'm disappointed, Kyril,' she said.

'Really?' Sindermann replied. 'You thought I'd carry on without you? Publicly renounce, and secretly continue?'

'You could have done that,' she said.

'So could you,' Sindermann replied. 'Defying the edict of the Sigillite is sedition, Euphrati. And an issue of sedition inside this city is a problem we don't need when we already have enough of them. Does that make me a coward? You could be outside, preaching in secret, but something, I don't know... Pride? Something made you stand by your beliefs. And here you are, making a point where no one can hear you. So let's not go there. We both made a decision. We have both stood by them.'

'They watch me,' Keeler said quietly. She put the slate down, and slid it back across the table to Hari. 'They watch me closer than anyone. There's nothing I could have done outside. All I could do was keep my faith.'

'And I could not,' said Sindermann. 'Not the way you needed me to.'

'But it wasn't faith, Kyril,' she said. 'You had proof. The evidence of your senses. You no longer had to rely on faith. You'd seen it, so many times, Kyril! But at the port especially, with me, you witnessed–'

'Witnessing it is what broke me, Euphrati,' said Sindermann. She looked astonished. 'Faith has a very special quality,' he said. 'When presented with proof, the mind does other things. I was elated, for a day, maybe two. But evidence erodes the patience that faith supplies. I began to think, "if He is divine, and I have seen proof of that, why does He not act? Why doesn't He end this? Because surely He can! Why does He let us suffer?"'

Sindermann hunched forward, eyes down, rubbing his finger around some knot-mark on the table's top. 'My faith could not survive the proof,' he said. 'I could not bear the idea He was allowing this.'

He looked up at her.

'I'm sorry,' he said. 'An existential threat is about to over-whelm us. I found something else I could do, something practical. Everyone needs to work together, contribute in what-ever way they can. We need a unity of intent–'

'The Emperor is unity,' said Keeler.

'Don't preach to me.'

'I'm not. It's just truth.'

'Your truth,' said Sindermann, 'and it's a beautiful one, I still believe that, but your truth won't win this war. So I came to ask you to consider–'

'It will,' said Keeler. 'It might be the only thing that can.'

'Are you going to listen?' asked Sindermann. 'I think I'll let Hari lay it out for you–'

'I don't need either of you to explain it,' said Keeler. 'It's the same argument as when we set out to join the fleets. War is a necessity, but our culture is more than that. It has to be.'

'Rule of law. Freedom. Ethical values…' Sindermann nodded.

'Responsibly documented history,' she went on. 'Progress, not stagnation. Advancement beyond simple obligations of conquest. A human society that does more than extermi-nate external threats. Because that, to answer your question, is what the Emperor is – the embodiment of a great scheme.

His scheme, dreamed in the first ages. Mankind as a great, sentient power. Civilisation. A purpose. Why destroy threats if those threats threaten nothing but our lives? Why are our lives of any value? Because we are more than destroyers. We are not an army. We are a culture.'

'That happens to have an army,' said Hari.

'I'm growing to like him again,' she said.

'I've been asked to re-form a small order of remembrancers,' said Sindermann. 'It seems like a luxury at this hour, perhaps, but it's not. It represents the things we are fighting for. The essence of us.'

'The ethical framework that justifies us,' said Keeler. 'Like the decent treatment of prisoners. Yes, I've had long chats with the warden. He makes a good point.'

'Sadly, he does,' said Sindermann, 'which makes it essential we fight to cling on to the things that separate us from animals – knowledge, ideas, a moral code–'

'Is history really high on that list?' she asked.

'If we survive this, do you want to repeat it?' Sindermann asked.

She sighed. 'Who charged you with this noble calling, then, Kyril?' she asked.

'Dorn,' he said.

Keeler nodded, grudgingly impressed.

'The mighty warlord is full of surprises,' she said. 'He really wants this?'

'He wants it done. It matters to him. But he has his hands full. He charged me to assemble a modest body of remembrancers. Whatever else you are, whatever else you may have become, you are a veteran of that service, so I thought of you at once.'

Keeler picked up the warrant again.

'Nowhere on this does it say "remembrancer",' she remarked.

'But you guessed my purpose straight away.'

'Because you never change.' She looked at the warrant. 'This symbol, the "I" icon…'

'For "interrogation". We have a warrant to interrogate and record. The word "remembrancer" has unfortunate connotations for many. We will interrogate any who have the time to speak.'

'And publish where? When?' she asked.

Sindermann shrugged. 'Maybe nowhere, maybe never.'

'Because we're all going to die?' she asked.

'That, or the things we record are too sensitive,' Sindermann replied. 'Too hazardous for civilian consumption. Dorn has the final say. For now, we compile. Collect and compile. The material we gather may be published when this is done, or sequestered for official record.'

'Or burn with us?'

'The other possibility,' said Sindermann.

Keeler sat back, toying with the warrant. She looked at her old friend.

'I would imagine the things I might wish to record are just the kind of things our Imperium would restrict.'

'I imagine so, Euphrati. But that's no reason not to record them. I'd like your help.'

'I'd like to do more than just sit here,' she admitted.

'Unfortunately…'

The three of them looked around. The Custodian had appeared from the shadows. His gold armour seemed to glow like dying embers in the prison gloom.

'Unfortunately?' asked Sindermann.

'The Praetorian's seal conveys great authority,' said Amon Tauromachian. 'But in matters of ideological conviction, the word of the Sigillite carries more. My orders are plain. Keeler is not permitted to go beyond the bounds of this vault, because she refuses to relinquish the observance of her faith. She cannot leave. So, she cannot be part of your work.'

Sindermann sat back sadly. 'I feared that might be the case.'

'I'm sorry, sir,' said Amon. 'Unlike you, the Lady Keeler will not set aside her ministry. She has been open about that.'

'I believe the Emperor is a god,' Keeler hissed across the table at Hari in mock conspiracy.

'I know,' said Hari.

'An actual god.'

'I know, mam.'

'And that's not a popular concept,' she hissed, 'especially with the Emperor.'

'Please stop that,' said Amon.

'It's as if He doesn't want people to know, or something,' Keeler said. She looked at the Custodian. 'So I can't leave, Amon?'

'No.'

'How many inmates are there, Custodian? In Blackstone?'

'Nine thousand, eight hundred and ninety-six.'

'They all have stories too,' she said. She picked up the warrant and looked at Sindermann. 'I'll do it, Kyril,' she said, 'but I'll have to work from my place of residence.'

'What did you make of her?' Sindermann asked.

'Not unremarkable,' Hari replied. The visitors' gate of the Blackstone had closed behind them. They walked across the access bridge, past dormant anti-air batteries swaddled under tarpaulins, to join the busy foot traffic of the main thoroughfare. The stone mountain of the Hegemon rose before them, cased in shield-plate and strung with weapon emplacements that clung like ivy to every platform and ledge. Above them, the sky was a pulsing violet, threaded with black. Sindermann could almost see the rippling distortion of the aegis. To the east and north-east, the sky shimmered with saffron light. Abrupt white flashes, brief flourishes of bright sparks, spoke of titanic struggles dwarfed by the distance.

'She was slightly terrifying,' Hari admitted.

'Terrifying?'

'Not the right word,' said the young man. 'A ferocity. Self-possession. As though she has seen things she can't adequately relate, or knows things she can't properly articulate.'

'You didn't find her articulate?'

'Yes. There's conviction there.' Hari paused. 'But the notion that the Emperor is divine… That's just a comfort, isn't it? A production of the eschatological mindset.'

'Because our world is ending, she clings to whatever seems to offer hope?'

'It's a common syndrome,' said Hari. 'Like a… a deathbed conversion. In a time of powerlessness, we look for meaning and a source of strength. The Emperor is that, above and beyond us, so much more than human. It becomes easy to believe He is an actual god, especially as we face what other ages would have deemed to be daemons. The entities of the warp are explained in supernatural terms, because we have no sufficient language to describe their nature. If a supernatural darkness exists, then a supernatural light must exist also, because humans respond to symmetry. The Emperor manifests in god-like ways, ergo He must be a god. It's a comfort. The resort of the desperate. We seek to believe that some higher power will save us. The Emperor fits that bill easily, despite any evidence or proof. Because we want to be saved.'

'So it's a mental issue?' asked Sindermann.

'Clinically, I suspect so,' Hari replied. 'And entirely understandable. Superstition is rife these days. Lucky boots, lucky guns, lucky caps. We seek signifiers to reassure us.'

'You don't think the Emperor will save us, Hari?'

'I hope He will,' said Hari. 'I think He will. But not because He's a god.'

They walked on, across Hegemon South Plaza, through the crowds. A cloister bell was ringing clear, slow, dull notes above the murmur of the throng. It had started to rain, the acidic back-fall of secondhand atmosphere.

'Have I offended you?' Hari asked.

'What? No. I was just thinking you sound like me.'

'You when?'

'Seven years ago, Hari,' said Sindermann.

'You don't speak of it much,' said Hari. 'At all, in fact. You shared her beliefs for a while. Promoted them. What made you believe?'

'The things I saw,' said Sindermann.

'And what made that belief fade?'

'It didn't.'

Sindermann stopped, and turned to look at the young man.

'But it isn't a fire, the way hers is. And I don't speak of it, because it is too easily dismissed as a mental issue. Do you want to know the truth?'

'Yes, sir.'

'Religion was a blight that shackled us for millennia. Faith almost ruined us, many times over. Willing ignorance. The eager embrace of that which cannot be demonstrated. It held us back. Do you want to know another truth?'

'Of course.'

'That's what I'm afraid of. That's what makes me reticent. That she's right.'

'Oh,' said Hari.

'How much would we suffer, Hari, if we are forced to accept that gods and daemons are real after all? Do you want to know a real truth?'

'Yes, sir.'

'Then go and find it. Interrogate the world. Find it for yourself.'

Most of the others were waiting for them under the portico of the Hegemon's civic entrance. Acid rain drummed on the stone peristyle that had admitted congregations for public ballot for over two centuries. Puddles were forming on the flagstones, and a faint mist hung where stone was being gnawed by chemical action. The bell continued to toll. Ceris was there, bundled up in a quilted military jacket with a fur-trimmed hood; Dinesh in weatherproof slickers; Mandeep, and eight more of Sindermann's initial recruits.

Ceris looked excited.

'We have been given disposition permits and travel waivers,' she said.

'This is from Diamantis?' asked Sindermann.

'Yes,' she replied. 'He was grudging. I think we're a bother he wants to be rid of. But he has to do as he's told.' She produced a plastek folder, fat with official documents and tags.

Sindermann took it from her, and began to look.

'Grants of authority, so we can be dispersed among line units,' she said as he looked. 'Some in the Sanctum. Some in Anterior.'

'Some of these postings will be hazardous,' said Sindermann.

Ceris scowled at him. 'Duh,' she said. 'Where isn't hazardous? We stand here much longer, the rain will kill us.'

Someone laughed.

Sindermann looked up at them.

'You're prepared for this?' he asked. 'There are no names assigned, so we can choose. I don't want you all grabbing the high-risk places. They're high-risk, nothing romantic about them. And there's a lot of good work to be done inside the Sanctum. It's not all about the glamour of the front line.'

'I've already begun interrogations in the refugee camps,' said

Mandeep. 'I'd very much like to continue with that project. There is a great wealth of material from eye-witnesses.'

'Good, exactly that,' said Sindermann.

'I thought, perhaps, the manufactories,' said Leeta Tang. 'The munition plants in particular.'

'Yes, to chronicle that this immense war effort isn't simply about fighting,' said Sindermann. 'I think that's a valuable approach, Leeta.'

'May I look?' asked Hari.

Sindermann passed him the folder. Hari began to leaf through the dockets.

'I'd like to take this one,' he said, showing Sindermann a tag. 'I had family in the north reach.'

Sindermann read it, and nodded. 'If that's what you want.'

'Go and find it, you said,' said Hari.

'It may not be there.'

'Then I'll start there.'

'You don't get to choose, though,' Ceris told Sindermann.

'What?'

'The mighty Huscarl Diamantis was very clear,' she said. 'I got the feeling it was an instruction from the Praetorian himself. He wants you, and a companion, if you like. He has something specific in mind for you. You're to report to Bhab tomorrow.'

Sindermann glanced at Hari. The young man was studying the docket he'd selected. Sindermann looked away, back at the group. 'You, then, Therajomas, you come with me.'

He looked at the rest of them.

'Well? Let's begin our histories,' he said.

The enemy ramparts were advancing. A kilometre-wide stretch of them: plasteel-threaded ceramite plates, mounted like dozer blades on the frames of giant tractor units, rolling forward with their edges almost overlapping. Hounding fire crackled and sparked from loops in the plates, or came over the plate-tops from heavier batteries mounted under mantlets on the backs of the tractors. Behind the advancing rampart, in the driving rain, walked the heavy infantry, diseased storm troops, chanting as they trudged, smacking pike-shafts against shields in a funereal rhythm.

The Imperial line, ranged below the Colossi Gate outworks, began deterrent fire. Field guns began to crump and sling, teams working furiously in shuddering gun-pits that quickly filled with dust and smoke, despite the rain. The first shells fell short, lifting geysers of filth from the chewed flats. Others struck the advancing wall, puncturing ceramite, washing up great waves of mud that plastered the machines. Missile batteries and box-launchers on the outer wall above joined in, spitting rockets that streaked into the shield wall.

Infantry units stayed low in the outwork trenches, fixing bayonets and readying pole-arms. Chainblades test-revved. Fire gullies were lit. Most of the troops were mixed Imperialis Auxilia brigades, section-led by veterans of the Antioch Miles Vesperi and the Kimmerine Corps Bellum, both regiments of the Old Hundred. Among them, flashes of yellow and red, a few scattered Space Marines, spread out to bulk fighting units.

Banners rose and unfurled behind the travelling wall line. Their profanities shivered in the rain. White smoke was fuming off the open ground, almost pure white, like cirrus cloud, where the outwash of military chemicals and gas mixed with the acid content of the rain and tortured soil. At the fringe, the white billow was trimmed with a fine embroidery of hard black smoke running off the fire trenches.

The traitor forces had spent nine days pushing down from the fallen port. They had razed almost everything in their path, leaving a tumbled desert of smoking debris where once had stood an entire city reach. Colossi was the holding point, the northernmost and first of the huge fortress lines that guarded the approach to the Lion's Gate. Colossi had not been converted to defence like some of its noble brethren. It was not a civic structure reworked for war like the massive build-outs at Gorgon Bar. The Colossi Gate was a principal fortress of the Anterior Barbican, a massive series of wall lines and concentric fortifications, its inner lines fitted with their own void shields. It was designed to stop and break any advance from the north.

The enemy had stopped at first. Shelling from Colossi had driven them back, pummelling a landscape already cleared, on Dorn's orders, into extinction. They'd made their line at the eight kilometre marker, and set out their investment: an arc of contravallation, twenty-eight kilometres wide, ditches, trench systems, earthwork ramparts and reinforced palings. They were dug in, defended and capable of resisting any sortie or counter-strike Colossi threw at them. Armour divisions had duelled for a day and half, an inconclusive sparring. Air assaults had been punished by the gate's comprehensive circuits of surface-to-air weapon systems.

Now they pushed a section of their own ramparts forward, a few metres at a time.

Behind the advance, artillery and dug-in tank sections began to fire, looping a steady bombardment over the heads of the heavy infantry and into the outworks and lower wall tali. Explosions lifted in vivid bouquets: bright fireworks of incendiary, spitting flashes of phosphor, fire-splashes of napthek. High explosive hurled earth and brick into the sky. Penetrators shattered stone, and sowed the air with showering grit. Trench 18 was hollowed out. Trench 41 was lost in a welter of sub-munitions. Four field emplacements were annihilated in as many seconds as high-arc howitzer shells dropped into them, shredding the guns and atomising the teams. Men fought to keep the raging fires from spreading to the back-line shell magazines.

Most shells fell deliberately short, dropping into the mangled waste between the lines. They were ranged to kick off any mines spread by the loyalist garrison, though few remained undetonated. At the blast of a war-horn, rotating flails extended beneath the lower lips of the trundling plates, their chain lashes whipping the torn earth to trigger micro anti-personnel seeds.

Marshal Aldana Agathe of the Antioch Miles Vesperi jumped down the steps into Trench 40, and hurried along the metal duckboards to the fire control station. She could feel the heat-flash, the prickle of grit in the air. This would be assault sixteen, the first significant land-push. She dodged stretcher parties, yelled at malingering Albian infantrymen, ignored the snap salute of Vesperi hussars. At fire control, she looked at the auspex status. She kept thinking about her husband and her two children, back in Hatay-Antakya Hive, a quarter of the world away, the sunlight on the patchwork arable estates beyond Orontes, the vivid green of the irrigation circles, the cool of the plunge pool below the villas on Iskenderun Spur. Why that? Why now? She couldn't eject the thoughts from her head, and there was no space for them. The images were like drag weights slowing her down.

She waved her hand, and the adjutant brought her the vox-link.

Clear, precise now. Hatay-Antakya may not exist any more. This was the business now.

'Forty, forty,' she said. 'This is forty, forty calling.' She took off her chrome helmet and ran dirty fingers through her tightly curled brown hair. Grease, sweat and the helmet had flattened the natural ringlets and made her scalp itch. 'Range now two kilometres,' she said. 'Requesting air cover and wall guns.'

Big ask. Air cover north of their line had been decimated after the fall of the port. Wall guns in the main upper bastions of Colossi had been told to conserve munition stocks for possible engine assaults. Standing orders direct from Bhab. But Bhab had not reckoned on mobile shield advance. And this was the Death Guard. She could smell them on the wind.

At Emplacement 12, Militant General Burr of the Kimmerine heard her voice on the link, chopped by the overlap traffic from a hundred stations.

'Forget it, Agathe,' he called, thumbing the send button of his vox-mic. 'Ready foot for repulse, go.'

'They're ready,' she replied, her voice a twisted crackle. *'Is armour deploying, go?'*

'Engines hot, six minutes,' he replied, 'but the last strikes took down the dispersal ramps at Twenty. We're laying boards. Lag time, ten minutes.'

He heard her curse.

'There'll be no top cover,' said Raldoron, watching him. 'Tell her that.'

Burr glanced at the massive Blood Angel standing nearby. First Captain Raldoron's helm was off, and he was hunched to fit in the low Army dugout. Technically, Burr had seniority in the line section, but he deferred to the veteran legionary.

'I told her, lord,' Burr said.

'Tell her again, and make sure she knows.'

Bombs fell close by, shaking the bunker. Dirt sieved from cracks in the ceiling. Debris rained across the angled roof, pattering like a cloudburst.

Someone shouted out.

Burr got on the scope. It had been knocked out of alignment, the lenses blinded by mud. He squeezed past the Blood

Angel, and got up on the scaling ladder instead. Bright shoals of las-fire and tracer were shredding past overhead.

The advancing wall had parted in several places. Through the gaps, plated gun carriages were running out ahead of the line: small, light, fast. They'd harried the outworks before. The men called them gun-wagons. They mounted heavy auto and las cannons on their payload pintles. Their wheels were big and spiked, and often rode over mines that blew harmlessly against the armoured axles and angled bellies of the wagons.

Behind them came the first of the foot heavies, echelons of a thousand at a time, streaming through the wall gaps, striding at their tails, sheltered by the wagons. Storm troops. Trench fighters. The insane raiders, unafraid of death, who would rush the line and assault the outworks first.

'Line up, line up!' Burr yelled. Men scrambled.

Raldoron was calling him. He dropped back down.

'What, my lord?' he asked.

The Blood Angel showed him the vox signal.

'Hold fire, two minute count,' Burr read out. 'What is this?'

'Nothing, unless it's authentic,' said Raldoron. He remained patient. The siege made them all brothers, and survival required strict adherence to the chain of command Dorn had set. But, in Baal's name, humans could be so *slow…*

'You can see it is, general. The tag marker…'

'I can. Call the hold.'

Burr grabbed the vox.

'Lines, lines, all lines!' he yelled. 'Cease on my mark and hold! Seventy seconds!'

A barrage of queries answered him.

'Do as you are bloody told!' Burr shouted. Raldoron calmly fitted his helm into place. Burr heard the throat seals click and lock. It seemed like the loudest sound in the world. The only sound.

Burr watched the clock. He could hear Aldana Agathe yelling at him over the vox for confirmation. He ignored it.

'We're dead bones if this is a mistake,' he said to the First Captain. Raldoron drew a sword, a tactical gladius. For a moment, Burr thought the Blood Angel was going to strike him down for cowardice, and realised he didn't care.

'We're all dead bones in the end, Konas,' said Raldoron.

'Throne, that's the truth, lord,' said Burr.

'Let's delay that inevitability by trusting the Praetorian has a coordinated plan.'

'Yeah,' said Burr. He nodded. His mouth was utterly dry. 'Yeah, let's do that.' He was gripping the vox-horn so tightly his knuckles had gone white. He looked at the clock, clicking down.

Mark.

'Lines, lines, all lines!' he yelled. 'Cease and hold!'

The Imperial bombardment died away. Burr could hear officers yelling at men who were still blasting from the gun-steps. It wasn't silence. The thunder of the enemy barrage remained. But it was stillness, eerie. The stillness of death.

Burr put down the vox, and heaved his way back up the ladder. Assaulting fire was still coming in. Smoke was washing north across the Colossi lines. He saw a flash. The glint of light catching something moving in from the south-east, something exceptionally fast.

'Oh, Throne,' he said. 'Oh Throne and stars.'

The cavalry action was a technique of warfare seldom practised any more, except on some feudal or xenos worlds. It was a throwback to an antique age of conflict, when military superiority was weighed on a different scale.

But the technique had not disappeared entirely. It had evolved, and disguised its true nature under a veneer of modern technology.

That was what this was, the raw truth of it. A cavalry action. A charge. The simple rules had been laid down long ago, before man reached out to the stars.

The first: maintain formation. Start steady, and do not race ahead of your fellow riders.

The White Scars ran out of the ground smoke in a wide, blade-edge fan. A perfect formation. They came from the south-eastern end of the Colossi outworks, sweeping around north in an arc like the swing of an axe. Three hundred and thirty jetbikes, gunning together. The roar of them was like a scream. Slow smoke tumbled in their backwash, accelerated, whipped, tortured into streamers and whirls and even halos, as the White Scars punched through thicker banks. Crimson pennants bent and cracked from the red-and-white vehicles: Bullock-pattern, Scimitar-pattern, Shamshir-pattern, Hornet-pattern, Taiga-pattern.

Burr stared.

The second: put your spur to your steed only when the enemy is in range.

The formation, already moving, as it seemed to Burr, with dazzling speed, somehow accelerated. The agony-howl of the massed engines intensified. The enemy line, shield wall and extended storm-force had broken step and slowed. They had seen what was coming. Weapons drew up. The jolting gun-wagons began to turn, or stopped to traverse their pintle-mounts. Maintaining the arc line, the formation bore down on them, unfaltering, unyielding, low-level, a racing blur, like a pack of target-locked missiles. The stained light glinted off the blades of the ordu: lances, drawn tulwars, glaives. At the heart of the line rode the Khagan, the Khorchin Khan of Khans, astride his monstrous voidbike. His sabre rose.

Time slowed down, as time always seems to do when

something terrible is about to happen. The enemy columns started shooting frantically. The Great Khan's sabre swung down.

The White Scars began to fire.

Bike-mounted bolters, heavy bolters, some in pairs; rotary guns housed in the nostrils or chins of their snarling steeds; plasma and lascannons; volkite culverins. A raking hurricane of destruction. Contrails and streamers of grey and black weapons-exhaust dragged out behind the bikes like banners. The discharge of it was heart-stopping, the continuation of it numbing. The roar, a frenzied drumming of heavy bolters, sounded, to Burr, like the thunder of hooves, the stables of a god unslipped at full gallop.

There was no ranging fire. The White Scars already had their targets. The first gun-wagons exploded. Others lurched, hammered, buckling. Fireballs lit off across the extended enemy mass from east to west. The storm troop lines began to fracture. Some broke. Some ran. Some tried to retreat towards the sally gaps in the shield line. Whole echelons were mown down where they stood, bodies twisting and lifting, and disintegrating in clouds of churned earth and stitching impacts. A few, unscathed, tried to fire back.

Rule three: shock is the action's best weapon.

The White Scars ripped in, never for a second breaking formation, despite the gunfire that clipped at them and tore at their armour. One jetbike cartwheeled, gushing flame, rider lost. No one looked back. The bikes crossed the line of the already-dead, the blackened bodies littering the ground, and their anti-gravitic down-force bent, tossed and flipped the slain as they rushed over, their kills jerking and dancing.

Impact. The first ordu riders reached the standing lines. Their guns were still reaping the enemy formations down. They punched through the breaking ranks, crushing through upright men, running over them, smashing them into the sky. Broken forms were thrown up and back, spinning slack and disjointed. Others burst against speeding armoured prows, washing the white ground-smoke red with puffs of aerosolised gore. Lances impaled, glaives scythed. Swords flashed, hooked, slashed. Burr saw one White Scar streak across an overturned gun-wagon. A traitor on its flank aimed a volkite pistol. The White Scar's back-extended tulwar met his fist before he could fire, splitting the pistol end to end, the hand at the thumb, and the entire extended arm lengthways to the shoulder, where the blade-tip dissected the man's head too. A kill from the saddle. All in one forward rush. The jetbike was past and on, even as the man spun and fell, sliced through, the cell of his pistol detonating like a flash grenade.

They reached the shield line, slaughter in their wakes. At close range, the bike guns fractured and crumpled the thick sheets of storm-plate, but they could not break them. They broke formation instead, rushing in through the wall gaps or over the shield line, entirely.

Then they fell upon the vast host sheltering behind.

The fourth rule: if you break the enemy line, you are in the heart of them, and war becomes the melee of hand to hand.

From Emplacement 12, Burr could no longer see the White Scars. The shield wall and the smoke screened off the havoc that followed. It was, perhaps, a blessing he was spared the sight. It becomes hard to trust as brothers, those you have seen capable of unbridled savagery.

For the White Scars, the rapacious V Legion, the far side of the wall was another world. Speed, shock and rate of fire had swept them to the shield line with devastating effect. But crossing the wall line had robbed them of speed and line discipline, and the odds were reversed. They were inside the choking enemy mass. Each rider, in a second, had passed from the bright smoke of the open field into a vast back-line of standing infantry. The rain seemed heavier, a curtain unfogged by the blanket of smoke. The assault host was immense: thousands of storm pikes, dripping with rain, ranked for assault; hundreds of thousands of traitor infantry; ready lines of armour, engines revving; monstrous formations of the Death Guard.

The Death Guard. Of all the Traitor Legions, the Death Guard was the one most despised by the White Scars ordu, and the feeling was mutual. The war between the XIV and the V had become a blood feud that would never be cooled. Hatred was too small a word. Even on this precipice of history, the White Scars were known as wild hunters, carefree killers, warriors who laughed in the heat of action, delighting in the fire of war.

There was no laughter now.

Nor were the Great Khan and his warriors fazed. They had done this before. Indeed, they had all known, from the moment they committed to the charge, that this was the goal. Unless enemy fire brought them down in the charging line, this was the highest purpose of a charge action: to reach the enemy, to meet his main strength, to engage, to be in his midst. They knew what to do. Physical momentum had been lost, but a momentum of mind took over.

They broke into individual actions, maintaining as much speed as they were able, preserving what collective forward movement they could. They thrust through the waiting ranks, or dropped into them. The bikes themselves were weapons: their armoured prows, their mass and motion, the crushing downward force of their repeller systems. The traitor host, far larger than even the Great Khan had been expecting to find, was war-ready, but it was not prepared. They were drawn up in deep, pre-battle cohorts. Their sight lines generally blocked by the shield wall, they had no idea what was coming at them. Only the roar of guns and the scream of engines had suggested that anything was.

The White Scars riders slammed down into them. Many came nose up, rearing, allowing their lift-systems to hammer the first rows off their feet. Their guns cycled, chewing into the bountiful, waiting lines of targets. Some shots passed through two or three lines of bodies. This was greedy killing. They were spoiled for targets, because they were vastly unnumbered, surrounded on all sides by armed, but as-yet undeployed enemy combatants. There was a kill to be made in every direction.

The enemy mass collectively flinched from the points of attack, the host rippling like a pool of oil as it recoiled. Men fell against, and into, other men as they scrambled away from the killers entering their positions.

But the White Scars were truly outnumbered. Traitors mobbed them from all sides, blasting weapons point-blank, heedless of their own kin, striking and battering with whatever blades and mauls were in their hands. Riders and bikes became mired in scrums of attackers, fighting from the saddle in the driving rain, lopping off every hand and head and pole-blade that came at them. Thickets of pikes speared two of them from their steeds, punctured in a dozen places. Gunfire destroyed the engine of a running jetbike, and its rider leapt clear, allowing the burning, tumbling machine to power into the enemy files, killing a score with its shredding mass, and then another score with its detonation. But the rider, Kherta Kal, was on foot, alone, encircled and rushed.

The Death Guard surged forwards, fighting through their own dazed foot troops to meet the White Scars. They were driven by transhuman reaction, sheer outrage at the audacity of the assault, and, more than anything, hatred. The desire to close with and punish their arch-foes, who had been fools enough to ride in among them. The brute horror of the Death Guard was plainly visible, a spasm of sadness to the heart of every rider. They beheld their once-brothers, pitifully transformed: massive armoured thugs, their grey-green plate greased with rain, streaked with rust and seeping fluid, rank and diseased, their armour swollen as though expanded by infected bloat within, jet and ebon-iron visors formed like howling beasts and wild-wood predators.

Legionary met legionary, dots of gleaming white engulfed by tides of mottled verdigris. Tulwars and sabres slashed down from saddle height, splitting dark plate like rotten squash and pumpkin, spraying ginger and yellow gouts of pestilential matter. Filthy spears, black as charcoal, plunged into burnished white ceramite, squirting scarlet into the rain, unseating riders, carrying them down under weight of numbers, some White Scars taking eight or ten fatal blows before they hit the mud.

The ground beneath was a deep mire, a liquid black morass, thrashed up by the shield tractors and the advancing host. It spattered and clung to the boots and legs of the churning Death Guard, and splashed the flanks of the wallowing jetbikes.

Wild chaos. The deepest and most intense melee. No rules, no order. A frenzy. An overwhelming din of blows and impacts, bolter blasts, shrieking engines. A tulwar splitting a houndskull helm and the skull inside. A dirt-crusted warhammer breaking chestplate, bone and muscle, pulverising heart and organs. A White Scar lifting clean from the saddle, impaled on a dark serrated lance. A Death Guard squad leader mangling against the snout of a surging bike, knocked down, shredding in the repulsor field. Flying flakes of armour. A spinning visor, torn off. Dismembered limbs, spinning aside, some still clutching weapons or parts of weapons. Gore splashing up to meet the hellish rain.

In the heart of it, the Great Khan. Almost unassailable in his might, but the greatest focus of the traitor wrath. He had dared to come among them, to enter their heart. He had wounded them savagely, broken the day's assault, but it would cost him. His was the trophy-head they most desired, the unthinkable kill they suddenly craved. A chance, an opportunity no traitor heart had dared imagine.

They swarmed.

But to take their prize, they had to kill him, and Jaghatai Khan was not in the mood to meet death. The vast and feral melee in the traitor back-lines was not a dismal misadventure to end a glorious cavalry action. It was just the far-point of the rush, the true price demanded of the enemy when the charge began.

Rule five: if you have driven through the enemy mass, turn and charge them again from the rear.

The Khan swung his dao, cutting through armour like fat. The war-calls of Chogoris bellowed from his lips, drowned out by the impossible deluge of the battle.

Yet they were heard.

Jetbikes gunned. Engines rose at the sound of other engines shrieking. Bikes turned, ramming through bodies, swinging sideways to fell others with deliberate and brutal sideswipes of the flanks and rear ends.

The White Scars broke back. One by one at first, following the Khan's lead, then en masse, breaking free, accelerating, retracing their rush back to the wall. They turned high to break out, but then swept low again, prow-rams, chattering gun mounts and raking blades slaughtering any who had survived their outward run, or any who had been foolish enough to try and surge in at their backs.

Almost as many traitors fell to the rear-charge as had died during the in-rush.

The White Scars raced towards the rear of the shield wall. Kharash riders split sideways as they approached the shields, running the length of it, tossing saddle charges into the unprotected backs of the massive field tractors.

None had been set with more than a cursory fuse. The mines began to detonate, some only seconds after the Kharash rider had sped past. Tractor mounts blew up, shearing apart in searing clouds of flame, bodywork splaying, stanchions fracturing, frames collapsing, engines bursting, splintered axles spinning clear from each inferno.

Shield sections fell. They remained, true to their construction, for the most part intact. But, torn from their supporting frames, they toppled forward flat into the mud, a wall no longer.

Eight tractors died. The advancing rampart was broken, like a broad smile with teeth missing, black smoke swilling from the gaps. The White Scars burned through the heavy smoke, taking full advantage of the clear passage provided by the annihilated sections. Some Kharash paused as they turned out of their breaking action, halting to haul fallen or wounded brothers up onto the bikes beside them. Yetto of the Kharash found Kherta Kal still alive, drenched in gore, standing alone with enemy dead heaped around him. He pulled him onto the flank of his steed, and bore him out of hell.

Burr saw the first riders punch out of the seething smoke. He started to cry out, a whoop of joy and shock, but it died in his throat. There could only be a few of them. The glory of the charge had gone into the darkest pit of the enemy. Precious little could return from that.

But more appeared. Then more still. Not all, but a startling number. Dozens. Hundreds. Their return ride, harried by parting shots from a wounded enemy mass, had little of the original discipline in its formation, but formal discipline no longer mattered. Some riders were wounded. Others, running more slowly, carried wounded men with them, clinging to the sides, or even held limp across the hulls in front of the saddles.

'I'm dreaming, surely,' Burr murmured. He looked at Raldoron. 'How could any of them have survived? Not just any, but so many?'

'Are you awake, Konas?' Raldoron asked. He had removed his helm, and was staring out at the ruined enemy line and the returning riders. There was no expression on his face.

'I am, lord,' said Burr. 'I'm sure I am.'

'Then know, you have seen the White Scars do what the White Scars do,' said Raldoron. 'It is rare for any to witness it. I confess, I have relished it every time I've been lucky enough to watch it happen.'

'It's not...' Burr began. 'This isn't a game! A... display!'

'No,' Raldoron agreed. 'It never is. And certainly not here, in this time of darkness. What you just saw, Konas, was fortune favouring us for the day. But you should still enjoy it for what it was. Great art must be appreciated, no matter the situation.'

The first riders were approaching the outworks.

The entire cavalry action had lasted six minutes.

'I'll go no further,' said Horus Aximand.

Abaddon glanced at him. 'Why? Are you afraid he'll refuse?' he asked.

'No.'

'Then have you changed your mind?'

'No, no,' said Aximand. 'He does not like me, nor I, him. Better you make the approach.'

Abaddon glowered. 'He is focused, these days,' he said. 'No interest in old scores, no time for it. You saw that yourself. We have unity, Aximand. Cohesion of thought and purpose. Old feuds are dead.'

'Even so, I shall stay here,' said Little Horus. 'I will not risk opening old wounds. Speak to him. You, I think, he still admires.'

Abaddon nodded. 'Tell me you still trust the sense in this?' he said.

'I do. The Mournival will back you. I'll see to that.'

Abaddon turned away. 'Stay here then, and wait for me.'

The great vaults of the Lion's Gate space port rose above them, almost devoid of light. The vast structure creaked and moaned, stressed by the sheer weight of the materiel flowing down through it every minute of every hour, every freight lifter and cargo platform running at capacity. This was their artery, through which the lifeblood of their war pumped from orbit to surface.

Down through which the first tides of the Neverborn were running in an immaterial river.

Aximand watched his brother walk away into the gloom, footsteps ringing from the plate deck. He didn't want to stay, but he would. He was uneasy. It wasn't the skin-prickle of the malaetheric vapour flooding the place, nor was it his proximity to the Lord of Iron. These last few nights, since the port broke, the dreams had started again: dreams in his sleep and in waking moments too, dreams he hadn't had in months.

Breathing, someone was close. Close but unseen. Someone was coming for him. The dreams, which had started around the time of the Dwell undertaking, had bothered him until he had engaged with them, and seen, at last, the face of the someone: Loken… Loken, Loken. He'd put the dreams to rest, exorcised.

Now, they were back, the soft sound of breathing just behind his head. What was his imagined menace now?

He stood alone, Abaddon now out of sight.

'Go away,' he whispered, 'or let me face you. Either way, I'll cut you down.' The breathing did not change its soft rhythm. Aximand wanted to leave, but he knew the breathing would be with him wherever he went.

'Tell me where,' he whispered.

Nothing replied.

The battle-automata blocked his path, silent and huge.

'I would speak with him,' said Abaddon.

They didn't move.

'You know me,' Abaddon said. 'I would speak with him.'

A subsonic murmur, a command. They stepped aside.

Abaddon entered the chamber, a command station for docking control, twenty kilometres up the spire of the port. Vast observation windows on three sides, clouded with soot. The pale sub-orbital twilight spilling in, illuminating a derelict control centre where a thousand port officers had once run the daily business of the port. A cold blue gloom revealed ruined console stations, the wreckage of fallen monitors and overturned desks on the deck. On the corner of one console, a ceramic caffeine cup, half-full, miraculously still stood where it had been put down weeks or months before. Put down between sips, waiting to be picked up again.

'The contents of my last briefing haven't altered,' said Perturabo. 'I would have informed you. Why are you here?'

'To speak to you,' said Abaddon.

The Lord of Iron had retired for the evening, and taken himself to the quiet of this dead area, alone. Abaddon thought that odd. When did Perturabo's work cease? His vigilance, his constant moderation of the battle sphere.

'I thought to find you below,' said Abaddon, 'at your station.'

Perturabo sat off to his left. He had stripped away his armour. The implacable panoply of the Logos plate waited nearby, arranged systematically by the battle-automata on a ready rack, like a specimen of some titanic beetle genus, pin-spread for display by an entomologist. Stripped to the waist, Perturabo was still massive. His flesh was almost white, pocked by the circular punctum of plug sockets and the shadows of old scars, slabbed with brute muscles. He sat on a cargo crate, elbows resting on an unpowered strategium table on which a large, paper chart of the Palace had been spread and weighted down with bolter shells. A few small lamps and candles burned.

'I have withdrawn,' said Perturabo.

'From what?'

'From the data, First Captain, not the engagement. It's a trick I learned. You're disturbing me.'

'I apologise,' said Abaddon. He didn't leave. He stepped from the upper range of extinct consoles onto the main floor, and approached the table. His feet crunched over shards of armourglass and chips of spalled metal.

'From whom?' he asked.

'What?'

'This trick. What is it?'

Perturabo turned his giant head to gaze at Abaddon. Pure disdain. Somehow, unarmoured, he looked more terrifying, more capable of rising up like a seismic convulsion and annihilating the First Captain.

'I learned it from my brother Rogal Dorn,' he said. 'I trust that suitably amuses you, Abaddon.'

'I'd like to know it,' said Abaddon.

'Data,' said Perturabo, as if that were an answer in itself. 'Vast amounts, in any battle, any war. In this… you can imagine the scale.'

'I can.'

'It must be reviewed, monitored, moderated, modified,' said Perturabo. 'Constantly. When I was younger, I bent myself to that task. Unstinting. I would not leave the strategium or the noospheric uploads for a moment until the action was complete. I never took my eyes off the game.'

'I've seen you do it,' said Abaddon. 'And few can begin to do it like you.'

'One can,' said Perturabo. 'Test exercises, nine times, he beat me. This was in the early days. I couldn't fathom how. Do you know what I did?'

'No, lord.'

'I asked him,' said Perturabo. He made a sound, a grating sound, that Abaddon realised was a rueful, perhaps melancholy chuckle. 'I asked him, Abaddon. We were brothers then. Such interactions were possible.'

'And?' asked Abaddon.

'He told me… and understand this, he was willing. He was glad to share a technique with me. He told me that data can blind. The weight of it. The burden of detail. Especially if one engages with it without a break or rest.'

Perturabo looked at the chart rolled out in front of him.

'He told me he had learned to step away,' he said. 'Step away, even at the height of conflict, if you can believe that? To clear his mind and focus, to shed the extraneous and the superficial. To contemplate. To reduce the immeasurable complexity of the arithmetic down to simple principles. Thus renewed, he would return. Do you know what he would do then?'

'No, lord.'

'He would win, Abaddon. The bastard would win.'

'He has a talent,' said Abaddon.

'He does,' replied Perturabo. 'I am the first to admit it. Only a fool ignores the advice of a brilliant man. Only an idiot denies the good practice of an enemy. I took up the habit. Intense moderation, as had been my way, but then short periods of withdrawal. Entirely unlinked. No augur-feed,

no noospherics. He was right. The objective tactical clarity is
astonishing.'

Abaddon approached the table, and looked down at the
old chart.

'This is clarity?' he asked.

'It is. Sixteen thousand, four hundred and eighty-six individual engagements, as of the last hour mark. Or ten thousand,
nine hundred and ninety, if we use his scale. His definition of
battle differs from mine. I measure by twenty thousand troops
per element, he by thirty thousand. It's merely a difference in
doctrinal tradition.'

Abaddon stared at the map. The thick bolter shells, red-
tipped and brass collared, did more than weigh the map down.
Four stood upright on the map, marking Lion's Gate Port, Eternity Wall Port, Gorgon Bar and Colossi Gate.

'Reduced to the most spare basics,' said Abaddon.

'Yes,' said Perturabo. 'A paper chart with objects for markers. The old way.'

'No, I mean...' Abaddon gestured. 'To the essential clashes.
Sixteen thousand plus reduced to four.'

Perturabo had a bolter shell in his hands. He was toying
with it.

'Yes, those four. They are the key to this phase. I keep
considering placing this on Marmax.' He pointed, with the
shell, to the area of the map between Gorgon and Colossi
in the Anterior Barbican. 'But we won't take Marmax yet. We
can't. It's too strong, and insulated from the north by Colossi.
Once my brothers are done with Colossi, we'll roll through
both, one after the other. We'll level them on our way to the
Sanctum wall.'

He glanced up at Abaddon. 'You see? You strip it all down
to the barest essentials, and even the greatest battle ever fought
is reduced to a simple series of steps. Why are you here,

Abaddon? I hope you have not come to impart some private instruction from your genefather. Eh? Some whisper in my ear to do better and work faster? I don't want to hear it. Tell him I am accomplishing what he has tasked me to accomplish.'

'Lupercal is not aware of this visit,' said Abaddon.

Perturabo sat back. His brows knotted, intrigued. He studied Abaddon's face for some clue.

'I'm curious,' he said. 'You have my attention.'

Abaddon didn't reply. He reached over, picked up one of the bolter shells in use as an edge-weight, and carefully placed it on the map, upright, just south of the Ultimate Wall. Then he stepped back, as though he had made a move in regicide, and was waiting for his opponent to respond.

'The other day, you were the only one to notice that,' said Perturabo. 'To even understand it. You like it, don't you?'

'So do you, lord.'

'Yes. But I told you. We are committed – four key, focus sites. Moreover, they satisfy the edicts of the Warmaster. They'll get the job done.'

'How quickly?' asked Abaddon. 'A month? Two? More? How soon before relief arrives and we begin a war on two fronts?'

'Faster. Faster than two months,' replied Perturabo, irritated. 'This scheme works. The other is appealing. I will hold it in reserve.'

'It's more than appealing,' said Abaddon. He looked around, spotted another broken cargo crate, drew it over and sat down without invitation. 'It's a flaw. A vulnerability.'

'He will have seen it.'

'What if he hasn't? Isn't it exactly the kind of error you're waiting for? The tiny oversight? It's the error you've been praying he'll make.'

'Watch your mouth, Son of Horus.'

Abaddon raised a hand. 'But if it is? That flaw is the basis of a spear-tip assault. Done right, that would end this affair in a week.'

Perturabo stared at him, and said nothing.

'You saw it, my lord,' said Abaddon. 'You. It would make this triumph yours. The Triumph of Terra. By your command, not merely executed by you at my lord's behest. That's immortal glory. That's a place above all of your brothers at the right hand of the new order–'

'I know what it is. Don't try your flattery on me. Tell me this, why do you bring it to me?'

'Because I saw it. Because I want it. It's a military win.'

Perturabo began to smirk. He could at last detect the hidden fire behind Abaddon's eyes.

'Oh ho, now I see it,' he said. 'You were always the warrior, a fine one, I'll confess. You want a piece of this glory too. You want to prove what you are. A soldier. Not a child of the warp. An Astartes.'

'It's what I've always been,' said Abaddon. 'I won't lie. I want the glory, and I want to win it with the skill of my blade and the superiority of my troops. As I did in the old days, as I have always done, as an Astartes. That is how the compliance of Terra should come. That's what carried me here. And carried you too.'

'Perhaps.'

'No perhaps about it,' said Abaddon. 'Tell me it wouldn't be sweet. For you, most of all. To settle the score. Brother against brother. You and him, decided warrior against warrior.'

'I am going to win this, Abaddon. The rivalry will be decided in my favour at the last.'

'I know you're going to win. Eventually. Entirely. You will best Dorn. But it's not the result. It's the means. Surely? To beat him on his own terms. Astartes against Astartes. Military rules. The true crafts of war, pitted according to the games you've played against him so many times, and too often lost.'

'I said watch your mouth–'

'I don't think I will, because you know it's a fact. Beat him this way, and no one can deny your supremacy. No one can say, "In the end, the Lord of Iron won, not because he was better, but because he had the warp at his side."'

'You little bastard.'

Perturabo stood up so violently the cargo crate crashed over on its side. Abaddon found himself a metre off the deck, his feet swinging, the Hammer of Olympia's right hand gripping his throat.

'No one by-blow manipulates me like this,' hissed Perturabo.

Abaddon clenched his teeth.

'I sincerely apologise,' he grunted, slowly choking, 'and take back any word I have uttered that was not true.'

Perturabo squeezed his grip more tightly. He was trembling with rage. With a sharp crack, one of Abaddon's collar seals began to buckle.

The Lord of Iron spat in Abaddon's face, then threw him across the chamber like a discarded doll. Abaddon fell into an abandoned monitor station, smashed it, bounced off, and sprawled on the deck.

He raised himself slightly, small fragments of plastek and glass tinkling off him. He pulled at the broken throat seal that was drawing blood from his neck. He looked at the primarch.

Perturabo had turned away. He stood, breathing hard, staring out of the observation port at the polluted darkness outside, staring as though he could see something, something bright but far away, that only he could make out. His monstrously broad back, lined with ancient cicatrix, raw neural plug-ports and the traceries of sub-dermal circuitry, heaved and flexed.

'You'd have your rabble do this, would you?' asked Perturabo in a low voice.

Abaddon got up. He wiped the spittle from his cheek.

'It would please the Lupercal if his own loyal sons were the instruments of this act.'

'I'm sure,' murmured Perturabo. 'A reason, but not a good enough one.'

'It's a spear-tip strike, my Lord of Iron. It is our proven speciality. You are the unrivalled master of military analysis, so tell me, loyalties and grudges ignored, who would you send? Think clearly now. Objective tactical clarity. Who would you send?'

Perturabo turned his head slowly to look at Abaddon.

'You know the answer to that,' he said.

'I do. I'd hear you say it.'

'The Sons of Horus. The Sixteenth. No, the Luna Wolves. That's who I'd send, if I had them. Hell, but you goad me, captain. As if you had come here to make me kill you.'

'Not that,' said Abaddon. 'I came here to make you take me seriously.'

Perturabo crossed to the table. The shell markers had fallen. He picked them up, set them back in position, then held up the one Abaddon had put down.

'The Luna Wolves are gone,' he said, 'and the Sons of Horus are assigned. Here, here and here. I cannot release their strengths. They are locked into the plan.'

'I don't need them all,' said Abaddon. 'First Company, maybe one other, the Justaerin. The Mournival.'

'A savage execution force, but scarcely a host,' said Perturabo. 'Not enough for this.'

'This offers another opportunity,' said Abaddon. 'A chance to deal with other problems that you contend with.'

'Such as?'

'We stand unified,' said Abaddon. 'Undivided. The greatest war-host in history. Differences and disputes set aside or ignored. But for how long? You know that's the invisible danger. Our own unravelling. You use every fighting asset at your disposal for maximum effect, but you are also obligated – against, I venture, your temperament – to act with a degree of diplomacy. To keep the multifarious factions content, and your brothers satisfied. It won't be long before they start to get their own ideas. Lord, to maintain our trajectory towards triumph, you need to keep them all in line.'

'The Phoenician.'

'The Phoenician, yes,' said Abaddon. 'He'll be first. Well, Angron has already snapped your leash, but at least his rampage serves your plan. Fulgrim is your immediate problem. He is wilful, he doesn't take to the bridle, and his attention span is woefully short. He is growing listless. I know this for a fact. Give him something to do that feels significant, and you can keep him in check.'

'His bastard children are deployed–'

'Who cares where you've placed them, or what you've charged them to do? Another few days, they won't be there anyway. They will have decided for themselves what action to take. But this bright objective would focus their attention, and allow you to channel them to genuine effect. And it would flatter him. He likes to be flattered.'

'I can't approach him,' said Perturabo, 'I can barely stand the sight of him.'

'I can,' said Abaddon. 'Through back-channels at company level. I can secure them for this, I'm sure of it.'

'And keep them in line?'

'Long enough to get this done. And once we start...' Abaddon shrugged. 'It doesn't matter then. The Third will give us the meat and muscle we need for grand scale assault. Cannon fodder for whatever greets us.'

Perturabo nodded slightly, thinking. That prospect clearly made sense and, more importantly, entertained him.

'They provide the necessary mass, I provide the scalpel, and you are the glorious architect,' said Abaddon. 'And this work is done inside a week.'

He walked over to the table, took the shell from Perturabo's hand, and put it back on the chart. The base squarely covered the middle of the words *Saturnine Gate*.

'If this is some ploy, if you renege...' Perturabo began, quietly.

'It's not, and I won't,' said Abaddon. 'This matters to both of us. It's the achievement we both long for. Forget Dorn's genius strategies, my lord, forget the prospect of loyalist relief. Time is our greatest enemy, fraying and eroding the patience of your brothers. We must find our friends where we can, and make those bonds count.'

Then Perturabo, Lord of Iron, did the most terrible thing Abaddon would ever see him do.

He smiled.

FIVE

Leave-takings and dialogues

Dorn was in the Grand Borealis when Vorst brought him the day's deployment summary. He took it, and skimmed it quickly. The date at the top, the twenty-first day of Quintus, then almost forty pages of logistic data. Each day, the document took him less than a minute to approve. Apart from any specific requests he made, it was assembled by the War Courts, usually through statistical analysis algorithms.

He was intensely busy at an augur station, reviewing North Anterior tactical schemes with Master of Huscarls Archamus, Mistress Tacticae Sandrine Icaro, Mistress Tacticae Katarin Elg, and twelve Excertus warchiefs, but there was one section of the document he wanted to review.

He saw the names: companies, regiments, divisions, officers, support cohorts and auxilia. They had been selected due to proximity, mobility, ease of transfer. They had been chosen by cool machine logic. His jaw clenched slightly. He had been waiting for this tight moment of necessary pain.

He handed the report back to Vorst, and returned to the augur display.

'You were saying, Mistress Icaro, that–' He stopped. 'Wait, I'm sorry.'

Dorn turned away from the station again, and called Vorst back.

'A problem, my lord?' the veteran Huscarl asked.

'Just give me a moment,' said Dorn, scrolling back down the list.

There it was. It had not been mistake of memory.

The vast bastion chamber seemed to close in around him, the babble of voices like a mocking, hectoring chorus. He looked around. The others were waiting for him. Old Vorst was attentive, dutiful, but frowning. There was no one Dorn could tell, no one among the thousands present who knew, no one who could know. And Dorn couldn't leave his post or the review. In the great, uncaring scheme of things it was nothing, a trifle, just a name on a list: a tiny, irrelevant detail compared to the defence of the Palace.

Dorn saw Cadwalder at station by the chamber door, far away across the sea of faces and urgent activity. Cadwalder knew. He'd been there, and he'd heard it. The Huscarl was the only other soul in Bhab Bastion who would understand.

Dorn caught his eye, and the Huscarl immediately made his way to his lord's side.

'My lord?' Cadwalder asked.

Dorn quietly, quickly, showed him the name on the list.

Cadwalder nodded.

'You understand the–'

'Sensitivity, yes, my lord.'

'This bothers me,' Dorn whispered to him. 'I would appreciate–'

'I'll go and see if I can stop it, my lord,' said Cadwalder.

'I'm grateful,' said Dorn. 'Be discreet.'

'I will, my lord.'

'Just… do something about it, if it's not too late. Safeguard him.'

The Huscarl put his fist to his chest, nodded, and strode away. Dorn turned back to the waiting chiefs.

'My apologies,' he told them, 'I noticed a minor transcription error. Let us continue.'

Leeta Tang had been waiting at the door of Munition Manufactory 226 for nearly an hour. There seemed to be some problem with her warrant. No one cared to explain what. Supervisors came and went in the cold, utilitarian atrium, and she could hear the noise of industry from beyond the inner hatches: the clank of conveyor assemblies, the drone of lathes, the periodic echo of safety sirens. She wanted to get in, perhaps to the canteen. Interviews with munition workers seemed like an ideal starting point. Sindermann had urged them to seek out the ordinary people, the workers, the menials, and hear their stories, stories that grander histories all too often ignored. Almost a hundred thousand people worked at MM226, one of the principal armament factories in the Southern Palatine.

An Imperial Fist strode into the atrium from the manufactory's yard. For a moment, she thought it was Diamantis, come to resolve her access problem, but it wasn't. The Space Marines all looked alike to her, but this one had the laurels of an officer, a company captain, not the ornate plate of the Huscarl detail.

'Sir,' she said, 'could you–'

'Not now,' the legionary snapped.

'But–'

'Really, not now.'

The Imperial Fist spoke to a supervisor, who let him through the inner gates immediately.

'Hey!' Leeta yelled after him.

'What was that about?' the captain asked the supervisor as they walked down blast-proofed tunnels, past the rhythmic thump of the automated casing press chamber. Smoke-wash from the annealing halls streamed past their ankles, drawn to the floor grates of the manufactory's humming extractor system.

'A remembrancer, lord,' the supervisor replied.

'I thought they were a dead breed?'

They stepped aside to let a steward pass, driving a train of cargo-carts laden with freshly stamped shell casings. Some of the rattling cylinders still glowed pink with residual heat.

'Apparently not,' said the supervisor, as they resumed step. 'She has the right warrant. All proper and correct. The mark of the Praetorian. But...'

'Go on.'

'I didn't think it was right to let her in, so I was delaying her. I was worried she might see...' He shrugged.

The legionary nodded. He knew what the man was trying to say. Munition plants like 226 were running low, their stockpile bunkers almost empty of explosive, propellant, intermix, charge-powder and alloy. Just a few – a very few – weeks of capacity remained, and then they would be spent, with no possibility of resupply. That was the kind of information that couldn't be allowed to get out, the kind of information that would damage public morale. No remembrancer could be allowed to wander in to ask questions, or see empty, echoing storage vaults.

They walked on, in silence, past bustling depots sheathed in rockcrete, the entrances to vast machining halls that rang with the squeal of air-buffers and the clatter of constantly running conveyor lines, and the curtained hatches of eerily quiet filling rooms.

'Anyway, he's in here, lord,' said the supervisor at last, as if they had been talking cheerfully for the past several minutes. He ushered the captain through a blast-curtained arch, into a dry room that stank of fyceline. The walls were clad with thick concussion padding and stacks of water-filled bowsers designed to absorb any accidental detonations. Sprinkler rigs and fire-suppression systems hung from the ceiling. Inside sterile and inert priming tents, tech thralls and arachnoid assemblies of servo-arms were precisely measuring charges, and delicately packing them into test canisters.

'Station six, lord,' said the supervisor, pointing.

Maximus Thane nodded.

'You!' he called out. At a nearby desk, a tech-magos looked up, puzzled.

'Yes, you,' said Thane. 'Arkhan Land, correct? Magos Arkhan Land? I need you to come with me.'

'What's this about, captain?' asked Arkhan Land as he followed Thane out into the manufactory yard. Acid rain was drizzling across the broad, high-walled gateyard, and heavy transporters were backed up to the factory's loading docks.

'You're needed for the war effort,' replied Thane.

'I was engaged in the war effort,' replied Land, jerking a thumb back over his shoulder. 'Very much engaged. Vital work. I was refining a new powder intermix, using tetraheldyl in granular form rather than volate-nineteen primer...'

He glanced at the Imperial Fist, who didn't appear to be paying any attention.

'Because resources are depleting,' he continued. 'We may run out of volate primer entirely in the next eight days. But a viably stable form of tetraheldyl could be used as a coactive accelerant, allowing us to extend the primer supply.'

The captain still did not respond. He was intently leading the way across the yard to a waiting armoured carrier.

'You don't know much about the composition of explosive charges, do you?' asked Land.

'I know what to do with them,' Thane replied. He gestured for Land to board the carrier via the rear hatch. Land clambered up, hauling his kitbag after him, balancing his chirruping artificimian on his shoulder. Thane swung in after him, closed the hatch, and banged his fist twice on the metal partition. The carrier spluttered into life, and began to move.

'So,' said Land, sitting back in the battered, bare-metal compartment. 'You were saying?'

'I was not,' replied Thane. He sat facing Land, his helm clutched on one thigh.

'Well, start,' said Land. 'I was engaged in essential work. Essential war effort work. And you're taking me away from it.'

'Your abilities are required elsewhere, magos,' said Thane.

'I'm not actually a magos,' said Land.

Thane frowned. 'You *are* Arkhan Land?' he said.

'Yes, relax. I prefer the term "technoarchaeologist". I'm not, in any precise or official capacity, an ordinate of the highmost Mechanicum though, of course, I am a true servant of the Divine One. "Magos" is a... what you would call a "brevet" rank, in your parlance. I adopted the title to facilitate my service, attached to the tech-priesthood, for the duration of the war. I am, I assure you, honoured to serve in whatever way I can. Successful prosecution of this hideous conflict is essential so that we can achieve the great goal.'

'The liberation of Mars,' said Thane.

'Ah,' said Land. He smiled, and adjusted the goggles on his brow. 'You're feigning ignorance, captain. You've read my file.'

'I have. You are a renegade technicist, and your paramount driver is the salvation of the Mechanicum world.'

'Terra first,' said Land. 'The Throneworld must be protected, or there is no hope for Mars. I am entirely committed to the cause at hand. And "renegade"? A little harsh, I feel.'

'There is no record of your assignment to Manufactory

Two-Two-Six,' said Thane. 'You just turned up there, and took it upon yourself to work in the development department.'

'One serves the Divine One where best one can, captain,' said Land. 'I had appreciated the impending crisis in munition supply, so I thought I should deploy my expertise there.'

'Without asking.'

'Well,' said Land, folding his arms. 'If you're going to get formal about it.'

'I don't care, Land,' said Thane. 'You're required elsewhere. Formally.'

'Is this Zephon? Did Zephon send you?'

'Zephon?' asked Thane.

'Captain Zephon, the Bringer of Sorrows,' said Land. 'Of the Ninth. A colleague of mine.'

'No,' said Thane.

'Oh. Where is he?'

'If I knew, I wouldn't tell you,' said Thane. 'This is wartime. Need-to-know basis only.'

'Exactly. I need to know some things,' said Land. 'Like where we're going.'

'I'm not at liberty to discuss anything,' said Thane wearily. 'I'm merely your escort.'

'Well,' said Land. He frowned. 'I will deduce, then. The Divine One has sent for me. He values my specialist expertise. I've met Him, you know? Oh yes. He knows my name. He's sent for me.'

'You deduce this how?'

'From you, captain... I don't know your name.'

'Thane.'

'From you, Captain Thane. You're not merely anything. My escort? No one sends a line captain of the Seventh on a personnel escort duty during time of war. Oh no. A man like you can't be spared for such a lowly function, unless the

Divine One requests it personally. I'm flattered, of course. But this wasn't necessary. He could have simply summoned me.'

'You talk a lot,' said Thane.

Land pursed his lips. The psyber-monkey on his shoulder chattered, and grimaced at Thane.

'And I don't know what that is,' Thane added, pointing at the artificimian with distaste. 'You'll have to get rid of it.'

'I very much won't,' said Land indignantly. 'This is my companion. My familiar, if you will. He helps me think.'

'I'm not remotely surprised to hear that,' said Thane. He sighed. 'Land,' he said, 'I'm here at the behest of the Praetorian. You have been summoned to assist my primarch.'

'Oh,' said Arkhan Land.

'This one?' asked Amon Tauromachian. Keeler nodded. Amon signalled to the sub-warden at the end of the block to open the cell door.

'We have to start somewhere,' said Keeler. 'I propose to work in simple alphabetical order.'

'This one is a murderer,' said the Custodian. 'Multiple homicides. Other, unsavoury crimes.'

'Everyone in this place is profoundly guilty of something, Custodian,' she said. 'I am obliged to work with what I have.'

The cell door began to grind open. The sound of sobbing echoed down the Blackstone's cold, damp gallery from another cell.

Keeler stepped into the opened cell. Amon hesitated, then followed her, bowing slightly to swing under the frame.

'Edic Aarac?' she said. 'My name is Euphrati Keeler. I've come to interview you.'

Bulk landers and troop ships were lined up across the wide, wind-blown space of the Field of Winged Victory, north of the Palatine. Their loading ramps were open, hatches ratcheted wide like hungry beaks. Thousands of troops and support personnel were lining up to board, huddled in greatcoats, lugging weapons and kitpacks, clutching deployment notices.

Cadwalder dismounted his jetbike, and pressed through the throng, his optics whirring as they hunted to make a facial recognition match, though he was looking for features he knew well enough. The faces all around him were pinched with cold, squinting into the gale that was sweeping the field, a gale generated by the aegis weather systems.

Cadwalder had always felt the Field of Winged Victory to be a significant place. From this massive parade ground, in the very shadow of the Palace, great musters and departures had been made, warriors assembling to set off into history, or to make it. The Great Crusade had begun here, so very long ago.

It was a glorious place to return to, too. The field beneath the Pharos Tower had seen great heroes come home from victory, seen the mass parades that had honoured them, seen the shining laurels and citations bestowed on them.

No one had returned to the field for a hundred days. With a sick heart, Cadwalder knew that none of the faces around him were destined to return here, ever.

Cadwalder had carried the private burden of that knowledge with him since the meeting in the drum tower five days before. He'd set it out of his thoughts, to contain it. He'd only known because he'd been present, by chance. He had been trusted.

But seeing the men and women marshalling for departure, he felt the weight of it return. He keenly understood his lord primarch's secret grief. To spare just one…

He spotted his quarry, on the ramp of a Stormbird painted in Excertus drab. He wasn't too late. He had been concerned he might miss the departure of the first flights.

'My lord,' he said, approaching. Waiting troopers parted to let him through.

Lord General Saul Niborran turned from the officers he had been chatting to. He wore a long storm coat and the cap of his old regiment.

'My worthy Lord Cadwalder?' he asked, frowning. 'How can I help you?'

'General, I...' Cadwalder hesitated. Now the moment was on him, he wasn't sure what to say. Since Dorn had given him his instructions, he'd been concerned with the simple act of getting to the field in time. He didn't know how to begin.

'My lord general,' said Cadwalder. 'I must inform you there has been a small mistake...'

Hari Harr's warrant got him a seat on one of the transports assembled at Aurum Gard. He'd been told the overland route would be gruelling. The convoy would have to go out of its way to avoid the battle zones in Anterior, and once it entered Magnifican via the Ballad Gate, there would be no guarantee of safety.

The transport was a battered old Brontosan-pattern, the bulk cargo version of the Dracosan. There were eighteen in the convoy, showing signs of rust and age, the emblem of the Solar Auxilia flaking on their side-plates. A line of Aurox units formed the munition train, and six Carnodon tanks waited, engines coughing, to act as armour support.

The air stank of exhaust fumes. The transports had been fitted with twin decks of cramped seating areas to max-imise personnel conveyance. Men were loading on, jostling, laughing, shoving: Solar Auxilia, mainline Excertus squads, militia, service staff. It was rowdy, almost convivial. Troopers were passing flasks around, telling jokes, boasting of martial feats they were yet to accomplish. Hari perched on a bench seat at the back of the lower deck, squeezed against the hull.

He wrote down a few observations on his slate. The mood. The camaraderie. The ebullience. Small details, like a man sewing his cap badge back on; another showing picts of his wife and children, explaining how safe they were in the Palatine shelters; the way they all, as a practised habit, stuffed their kitbags under the crude and uncomfortable bench seats, and then cradled their weapons in their arms like infants; the words of a song someone started to sing; the manner in which a pack of Solar Auxilia veterans ousted militia men, and claimed a block of benches for themselves; the smell of sweat, and of clothes that had been only superficially washed.

A man sat down beside him, taking up too much space.

'Piers,' he announced, offering a dirty hand. 'You're not a soldier, boy.'

'No, I'm not.'

'What you doing here, then?' the man asked. He was in his late fifties, overweight and solid, an Imperialis Auxilia trooper with a hugely bushy horseshoe moustache. Hari didn't recognise the insignia on the man's patched red greatcoat. He was clutching a bearskin shako, and had an antique plas-caliver that he rested upright between his splayed thighs. The hefty weapon was made bulkier still by the fat grenade launcher unit clamped on as an under-barrel mount.

'I've been sent to make reports,' said Hari.

'Reports?' the man replied, brow crinkling in suspicion. 'What, like conduct reports?'

'No, uhm, for posterity,' said Hari.

'Oh,' the man said, frowning, thinking about it. 'Like a... what'sname... remembrancer.'

'Very much like that,' Hari agreed.

'You're young,' said the man. His tone had altered. It had become slightly more avuncular. 'You know what you're getting into, don't you, boy?'

'The main warzone. I understand that.'

'You've seen war, have you?'

'Not up close.'

'It's not nice, boy.'

'You've served have you? Seen action?'

'Served? Oh yes! Olly Piers, corporal, Hundred and Fifth Tercio Upland Grenadiers. I've served me share. Dawn Gate. Helios retreat. Pons Magna, that were a one. Then Marmax, 'course. That's where I lost the leg.'

Hari looked down at the man's heavy and all too real legs.

'Your leg?'

The man guffawed. His breath was sour, almost as unpleasant as the onion-sweat reek of his armpits. 'Oh, ball-bags, boy! Oh my life! If you want to see a war, and record stuff for posterity, there's things you should know, like, for one, soldiers lie. All the time. Everything's bravado. Lies and jokes. Jests and boasts. It's all bluff, boy, to keep the spirits lifted. Reckon as I'll die with a lie on me lips. Reckon you could take every man-jack in this fine and luxurious carrier, and not find a strand of truth in the lot of us.'

'Duly noted,' said Hari.

'Aha ha ha!' the man burst out. 'Unless I'm lying.'

'I have noted that too,' said Hari.

Hatches clanged shut. The men aboard cheered as one, uttering war-whoops and praise to the Emperor. The troops packed into the upper deck space stamped their feet, making the thin metal sub-floor shake and flex over Hari's head. Now its engines were running, the entire carrier vibrated.

'We're off, boy!' Piers yelled. He joined in with a rowdy song that was being sung by most of the personnel on board. By the time the lumbering carrier had cleared the cavernous transport bunkers under Aurum Gard, and passed through the fortress' chain of gates, he was asleep, his head dropped on Hari's shoulder.

The carrier trundled on its way. The vibration and the rumble of the engines didn't ease. Re-circ systems were evidently broken, and the air quickly became close and foul. Excertus adjutants moved down the aisles between the tightly packed men, swaying for balance against the vehicle's motion, hooking open the covers of the gun loops in the hull to improve ventilation. Despite the weight of the slumbering Piers pressing him against the hull, Hari found that, if he craned his head, he could peer out of the nearest slot, and glimpse fragments of the city rolling by: the redoubts and guntowers of Aurum, like tombs in the rain; the grey streets of Anterior, buildings empty or armoured, or both; the passing shadows of bridges and skyways; the deep nocturnal chasm of Nilgiri Himal Way, where it rose through a canyon of towers and manufactories like a river through a gorge. Hari could smell rain and tar, fyceline and exhaust. Every now and then, to the north, he saw sheet flashes in the sky, like summer lightning, though he knew that they weren't. Twice in the first hour, the convoy halted, for no apparent reason, and they waited, engines idling, hearing men shout and argue outside.

Piers slept through it all, compressing Hari into an involuntary body pillow. Hari had one arm free. Tentatively, without waking the corporal, he took out his slate and started to read back through old note files.

Three hours into the journey, Hari found a file he had not put on the slate himself.

'I don't understand, lord,' said Niborran.

'An error,' said Cadwalder. 'In assignment. My lord the Praetorian expresses his apologies.'

Niborran smiled. They had boarded the Stormbird while
it was being loaded, and sat alone in the seats at the back of
the cabin. The brown leather upholstery of the flight seats was
worn and cracked. The 'bird was as old as Cadwalder.

'With respect, the error's yours, I think,' the general said. He
had an easy, fluid manner to him that Cadwalder had always
liked. 'I was dismissed, lord Huscarl. Removed from my post
by the Great Khan himself.'

'As I understand it,' said Cadwalder, 'that was a heated
incident. You are a senior officer militant, with great tactical
insight, and a valued member of the bastion's command cadre.'

'Well, that's kind of you, lord,' said Niborran, 'but I won't
be going back.'

'The dismissal was a lapse, general,' said Cadwalder. 'The
Praetorian has instructed me to tell you that he'd like you to
return to your position. He thinks highly of you.'

'You can tell him I'm grateful, Cadwalder, and flattered. But
I have my posting.'

'A clerical error–'

Niborran raised his hand, and smiled again. 'I was done,
Cadwalder. Honestly. Sixty years of service, the last dozen
without a weapon in my hand. The Grand Borealis is a gruelling tour, I don't need to tell you that. It burns the best
of us out, and I was burned out. Harder than any front-line
post. The Great Khan was right. I don't want any special
treatment. I put my name back in the system. Brohn did
too. We requested line posts. I think it's time I remembered
I was a soldier.'

'No one's forgotten that, general.'

'I think I have,' said Niborran. 'My deployment was selected
by the War Courts. They've given me zone command. I'm
delighted by that, and I won't back out of it. It's where I want
to be. At the front again, fighting the fight, not orchestrating

it. I want a last taste of active service, Lord Cadwalder. I've got nothing useful left to give to the cadre.'

'Well, then, I will organise an assignment to the Anterior Wall, or to Marmax–'

Niborran stared at him. The general was frowning.

'My lord… there's something you're not saying, isn't there?' he observed gently.

'I can't explain, general. I'm sorry. You will come with me now, and we'll cover the necessary reassignments.'

'Cadwalder, the port needs to be defended,' said Niborran. 'It's a priority.'

'It is, yes.'

'And when I was selected for zone command there, I was overjoyed. There, of all places, command of what's likely to be the most crucial fight of the next ten days. Maybe this whole show.'

'Understood, general, but–'

Niborran sat back. His smile had faded. He took off his cap and his leather gloves.

'I think I see what this is,' he said sadly. 'The Great Khan saw my shortcomings at the Grand Borealis. He could see I was done there. I accepted that. I did. But the Praetorian doesn't think I'm fit for this either, does he? He thinks I'm burned out full stop. That's the clerical error you're talking about.'

'It's not–'

'Don't dance around, Cadwalder. Please,' said Niborran. 'It's not dignified for you, and it shows me no respect. Just say it. Dorn thinks I'm old and washed out, and not fit to command a zone as vital as the port. Just out with it. I'm a grown-up.'

Cadwalder hesitated. Then, in a low voice that only Niborran could hear, he explained. The port would and could not be held. It was going to be sacrificed if necessary. The defence operation was for show only, necessary cover and distraction for another operation that Cadwalder wouldn't name.

Niborran listened impassively. The silver irises of his augmetic eyes dilated slightly.

'A show?' he whispered. Cadwalder nodded.

'I've come here as a personal favour to my Lord Dorn,' said the Huscarl. 'He is stricken with… with regret over this matter, as it is. There is no choice, but he is bitter that he has been forced into such a deplorable tactical calculus. Then he learned of your posting. He doesn't want to lose you.'

Niborran sat quietly. He gazed down the cabin, watching the junior officers as they began to board.

'Well,' he said softly. 'Not what I was imagining at all. I am flattered, truly, that he thinks so highly of me. That he'd jeopardise the confidence of what must be a critical operation to pull me out. Tell him I'm honoured and immensely grateful.'

'You can tell him yourself when–'

Niborran reached out and clasped Cadwalder's armoured hand.

'I *have* to go now, Cadwalder,' he said. 'Do you think I can just disembark and watch these good men go on without me, now I know what I know? Could you do that?'

'General, I–'

'I won't be spared by sentiment. War doesn't work that way. I have to go. The port needs the best defence, no matter what its strategic fate.'

'I shouldn't have told you,' said Cadwalder.

'Maybe not, but I'm strangely glad you did. I know my worth now, and I know the odds. Few commanders ever get that luxury. Thank you, Lord Cadwalder. Now, you get off before the ramp shuts. And tell Lord Dorn I am thankful for his faith and his consideration. Maybe…' Niborran chuckled slightly. 'Maybe, if I'm as valuable as he thinks I am, I can win the unwinnable anyway.'

Cadwalder breathed heavily. He wanted to argue. He considered picking Niborran up and physically removing him from the craft. He didn't have to respect Niborran's rank. Legion and Excertus were different branches, and Legion always took precedent. But his primarch had insisted, from day one, that loyalist victory had to be based on mutual regard and cooperation between command structures. It was an imperative. Niborran was about as senior as a human could be. No option seemed appropriate. Everything he might do seemed an unforgivable insult to Niborran's uncomplicated heroism.

Just… do something about it, if it's not too late. Safeguard him.

The Praetorian's instructions echoed in the Huscarl's mind.

'I know that look, Cadwalder,' said Niborran. 'Don't keep trying, my lord. You've had your answer.'

Cadwalder nodded. He got up.

'Have a good war, lord Huscarl,' said Niborran. 'To your glory, and to the glory of Him on Terra.'

'And to yours, general,' Cadwalder replied. He turned to the acceleration seats, built into the rear bulkhead of the cabin to accommodate Space Marines, and began to strap himself in.

'What are you doing?' asked Niborran.

Do something about it. Safeguard him.

'Coming with you,' said Cadwalder.

The guns had begun to speak. All along the lines at Gorgon Bar, guntowers and watch bastions started to unleash into the towering, murky dust banks beyond the distant outworks. Wash-smoke pooled back from redoubts, and wreathed from casemate turrets. The noise and concussion was physically painful.

Ceris Gonn had made her way up to the parapet line of the

Bar's central fortification. From the fighting step, she could see across kilometres of tiered defences: three further walls and the hazard-line of the outworks beyond, vanishing into the haze. The wall lines below her were packed with troops. She could make out the glint of red and yellow plate, a huge number of Legiones Astartes, along with the grey, drab and beige units of the Imperial Army. She wasn't sure how anything could ever get through a defended fortification this massive.

She was also disappointed. She'd wanted to get to the front, to see the front, but the true edge of Gorgon was kilometres away at the fighting line of the outworks and first wall. Her requests to move down from the principal fortress had been denied, despite her warrant.

Then again, the scale of it numbed her: to stand at the lip of the bastion, to see the millions below her, to feel the deluge of the guns. She pulled up the hood of her quilted jacket. The noise and blast shock was unremitting. It hurt her teeth and her diaphragm. The air stank of something that smelled like burned plastic, a dry chemical odour that caught in her throat, and made her eyes run.

Someone spoke to her. She turned. A subaltern of the Imperial Militia was staring at her, annoyed. She frowned, a hand to her ear. She couldn't hear him over the constant, air-splitting thunder of the guns.

'I said you can't be up here!' the man yelled.

This again. She showed him her papers.

'I don't care,' he replied, shoving the warrant back into her hands. 'The Bar's no place for civilians or observers.'

'I am very far away from anything,' she shouted back. 'I can't see a thing. What are they even firing at?'

He frowned at her. 'The attack,' he yelled. 'Are you an idiot? The attack.'

She couldn't see any attack. She could see smoke, banks of

it, streaming off the outworks, huge clouds of roiling black. A few sparks, little dots of light.

Wait–

She pulled out the scope Mandeep had lent her, and zoomed it into the distant line. The view was only slightly better. It was too fuzzy and she couldn't stop her hands from jumping at every salvo. But in the confusion of the smoke, she could see the little sparks more clearly. She realised what she was looking at. Blizzards of las-fire, swarming around the outworks and the first wall, thousands of shots flickering out, and being returned.

Ceris laughed. She'd been on the wall for fifteen minutes and hadn't realised she was looking directly at a massive engagement. A battle, right there. Not a skirmish, a full-scale war front.

'How do I get closer?' she yelled at the man.

He yelled back.

'What?' she shouted.

'You don't!' he barked. 'Throne's sake, what are you? A fool? You're not even safe here! You're not supposed to be–'

'I'm allowed,' she shouted back. 'Approved! And I need to get closer!'

Maybe the third wall, she thought. At least the third wall. Still a long way from the leading edge, but good enough. Get in among the troops, to watch them operate. See some Space Marines closer up. Witness something worthwhile she could document. Maybe even speak to them when the action lulled. Hear their experiences first hand. Perhaps… perhaps even glimpse the Great Angel. She'd heard he was here, commanding the repulse in person. Just to see him, even from a distance.

But not this distance. She couldn't see much of anything from this distance. She might as well have stayed in the Sanctum and used her imagination.

'I need to get down to the third wall,' she shouted at the subaltern. 'Please show me the way.'

He took her by the arm.

'Hey! You need to leave!' the subaltern yelled. 'This is not a safe area!'

'Get off!' she snapped.

He started to drag her along. 'You can't just stand there!' he shouted. 'Poking your head up for a look! The Bar's rated mortalis from front to back! I'm having you escorted down to the back-bunkers.'

She started to tell him what he could do with his back-bunkers. But something odd happened.

The noise stopped. The crushing thunder surrounding them simply ceased. There was a perfect moment of quiet.

Then she could hear ringing in her ears. Dull at first, then louder, like sounds from another room. Her face was wet.

She was lying on her back.

Sounds rushed back, muffled and soft. She sat up.

Twenty metres away, an entire section of the wall was missing. It had simply vanished. All that remained was the rough, bitten edges of rockcrete, and the twisted ends of sheared rebar, still glowing. The wall top was shrouded in smoke. Everywhere there was grit, dust, lumps of rubble and shards of stone. As she sat up, pebbles and debris trickled off her jacket.

She flinched, and cried out as another shell struck the wall, a hundred metres away. A vast cloud of flame, rising from a flash-burst into a slow toadstool. She felt the air bulge with pressure. More debris rained down. A guntower, six thousand tonnes of masonry, plate and cannon cradle, tilted slowly, and then fell like an avalanche.

Ceris got up. Her legs were rubbery. Her ears were so hurt, everything sounded like it was under water. She looked for the subaltern. He had been clutching her arm.

Half of him was lying on the parapet to her left. Something, perhaps a sheet of fractured ceramite plate, thrown out by the impact at the speed of a bullet, had cut him in two. His head and most of one arm lay to her right. There was blood everywhere, the settling dust sticking to it like a film. It was all over her, the whole front of her, from head to toe, painted in it.

Troops and medicae were rushing onto the wall top, yelling unintelligible muffled sounds, running to the fallen. They were all around. Men and women crumpled in the dust, blood pooling from crush and debris wounds. There had been three or four dozen people on the wall top when the shell hit. She was the only one who had got back on her feet.

'Move,' a voice said.

She turned, swaying. The Blood Angel towered over her. He placed a huge, gauntleted hand around her shoulder to steer her away.

'What?' she said. Her own voice sounded dull and muted.

'They have ranged the main line. You cannot stay here.'

She nodded. She looked back at the subaltern.

'He–'

'Move.'

He led her off the wall top towards the rear defiles and blast-boxes. The injured were being brought in. Some were being carried. Some were walking unaided, but as though in trances. Some wept. Several were screaming. She saw facial wounds, burn injuries, medicae teams fighting to cinch off mangled limbs that were hissing arterial blood. Everyone was coated in dust, rescued and rescuers alike.

'They have ranged the main line,' she said.

'What?' asked the Blood Angel.

'You said–'

'The foe is close to the outwork line,' he said, his voice an expressionless crackle from his visor. 'Artillery.'

'But it's so far away,' she said.

'If our wall-guns are firing, so are theirs. We both possess weapons of great range. Why are you here? You are not militia.'

'I have no idea any more,' Ceris replied. She looked up at him. 'What's your name, please?'

'Zephon,' he replied. He cocked his head, hearing something that all of the humans around him, including her, could not. Instinctively, he took her in his arms, pulled her to his chest, and turned to put his back towards the wall.

The next shell hit a second later, and fire took everything away.

I am leaving now. I haven't asked permission. I am my own permission. His grace fills me, as it always has done, and I know where I must go. I tell almost no one. No one will miss me or wonder where I am. It is hard to miss those who are never noticed. No one will come to the sanctuary asking for Krole with their hands or their mouths.

I tell Aphone. My hands tell her. In my stead, she will lead the Raptor Guard. If my duty is failing, or His grace does not sustain me, she will almost certainly be Vigil Commander after me. I think she is perplexed by my departure. I say, my hands say, it is the right thing. Not just to serve, but to serve where one is most needed.

I do not tell her the rest. My fingers are too clumsy to express the idea. Satisfaction. A fulfilment. Something more complicated than cold duty. The hollowness in me has always yearned for that. It is not vainglory, nor is it weary eagerness to meet certain death. Nothing is certain. Can I even explain it to myself? Not easily. I can justify it. The infamous Lupercal will suspect a ruse if the port is not adequately defended, and my kind is part of that defence. There will be daemons there. I also think, some proud part of me thinks, that it is not decided, no matter what Rogal has declared. We have won greater victories against worst odds.

I have won greater victories.

It is not vainglory. I am certain of that. If I fall, no one will remember me to heap plaudits on my name. No myths will form. My name won't vanish, for it has scarcely ever been.

I watch Aphone's hands. *Should she pick a unit and come with me?*

My hands say no. *We cannot spare any main force. Later, He will need us here.*

A squad, then?

My thoughtmark is insistent. *No. I must arm now.*

She helps me secure my hair, and clothes me in my artificer armour, piece by piece, the old, slow ritual. She hangs the voidsheen cloak around my shoulders, and pins it. We choose my instruments: *Veracity*, of course, she will be with me to the end; *Mortale*, the aeldari sabre, as a second blade at my back; *No Man's Hand*, the long dagger, for my hip; my archeotech pistol, long-snouted and ornate, older than the Imperium, which has never had a name, for it speaks for itself.

Aphone looks at me, and nods. I realise she is actually looking at me. Seeing me. That is so rare. One null to another. I have not really noticed the shape of her face before. This seeing is distressing. I fear, in that moment, she sees me so well she can see the truth. The secret Rogal struggles to keep. The coming danger. The impossibility. My selfish urge to do something that no one else can.

If she does, she does not speak of it. She shakes out the folds of my cloak, smooths the fit across the shoulder.

Then she embraces me. I don't know what to do. Neither of us are used to this. Contact with another. Connection. We are all so used to being utterly alone. I hold her. Our embrace is tight, like frightened children. It lasts, perhaps, ten seconds. It is the most intimate moment of my life.

She steps back.

Her hands say, *Come back*.

Mine reply, *I will*.

I walk the dark halls. My feet make no sound. In the gloom, the ancient statues pay me as much heed as any living thing has ever done. The soaring ouslite walls, monolithic, seem so permanent. I reach out and touch one, cold stone, my hand flat. This place will not fall. My fingers make the vow.

The landing docks are quiet. I have sent a transmission, in orskode, to order the servitors to prepare a Talion for me. The gunship waits on a platform, underlit in the darkness, its flanks slate grey, the leaves of its prow retracted to expose the iris valve entry. The servitors are detaching the feed cables, and locking the munition hoppers, sliding them back into the hull recesses. They do not notice me.

Then I see Tsutomu. He is sitting at the edge of the platform.

I walk up to him. Only when I am very close does he react, belatedly seeing the grease-shadow in the air that he has been watching for.

Why are you here, prefect? my hands enquire.

'I am compelled,' he says. 'Like you, I think. We are both party to the same sad secret.' I find it amusing that, even though he is looking at me, he, even he, can barely keep me in focus.

We were both present, my hands agree.

'Then, you understand,' he says.

You were just a sentinel at the door, I mark.

'And you were just a veil, but we were both there anyway.'

I do understand. The Legio Custodes, they are not manufactured blood-warriors like those of the fine Legiones Astartes. They are intricate and individual expressions of His will, they are extensions of His grace. That is why they so often operate alone, autonomously, going precisely where they are needed.

Where He wills them to be.

Just as my lamed hands are the instruments I use to speak, they are the digits He uses to communicate. Tsutomu was not the prefect at the door that day by random assignment. Fate placed him, so he could overhear, just as I overheard.

'My mind has dwelt on the matter since then,' he says. 'A certainty has formed. A–'

Compulsion? my hands finish.

'Yes.'

He has, of course, been monitoring the dock stations. He has seen my orskode command. We will go together, it seems.

I turn to board. He is not following. He has lost track of me. I look back, and snap my fingers loudly.

Come on then, my hands say.

He nods, picks up his helm and his castellan axe, and walks up the ramp behind me.

'Damn the bastard,' said Gaines Burtok. 'Screw Him, screw His eyes. His plan? His dream? A dream of shit.'

He sat back.

'You did ask,' he said, with a sneer.

The cell was damp. The oppressive black stone glistened with moisture. The reek of the rusted slop bucket in the corner was wrenching.

'I don't think this is the kind of sentiment you wish to record,' said Amon quietly.

Keeler shrugged. 'I don't know,' she said. 'Should history be selective? Shouldn't it be written by everyone in order to be true? Not just the victors?'

'Or the High Elite?' put in Burtok. He grinned. His teeth were tobacco brown.

174 DAN ABNETT

'Or them,' Keeler nodded. She glanced at Amon. 'I think the purpose is to record everything, without exercise of censor or mediation. As a starting point, at least. Plus, this is the fifth interview, Custodian, and Mister Burtok is the first subject to provide us with anything like a vehement opinion on anything, even if it does make your hackles rise.'

She looked back at the prisoner. Burtok was sitting on the cell's soiled cot. She was sitting on the small chair that she had insisted Amon fetch from the guard post after the third interview and the third hour.

'Your passionate distaste for the world,' she said, 'for society? Is that why you butchered those women?'

Burtok nodded. 'Indeed so, miss. An expression of my inner rage. My contempt for the conventions of this shit-hearted civilisation. A scream of anarchy. It was my life's work, really. I conducted it for many years, until I was caught. My so-called crimes were a protest, an articulation of the rage so many people feel. I'm a political prisoner.'

'Not really,' said Amon.

'You carried out these killings over thirty-five years,' said Keeler.

'One hundred and sixty-three, I did. They only found eight of them. Shall I talk about my methods?'

Keeler raised her hand.

'Not yet,' she said. 'Talk more about your protest. If it was a protest, how was it being made? You concealed the bodies of your victims. Only a few were discovered, by happenstance. Your statement, if it was a statement, was invisible.'

Burtok tutted.

'I thought you were smart, miss,' he said. 'They know. They shitting-well heard. The High Elite, they see everything.'

'You keep using this phrase, "the High Elite"–'

'The secret rulers of the world,' said Burtok. 'The ones of

wealth and influence. High-born, inherited power, handed down through generations. A tiny minority, making decisions for the rest of us. He's one of them. The most powerful of all. And now, not so secret. All their work down the ages has been to get Him to the top. Unassailable supremacy. Absolute power. Surrounded and guarded by His witches and His mind-priests. They treat us like cattle. Ninety-nine point nine per cent of the species, treated like livestock, to feed them and sustain them and get them where they want to be. And it'll get worse. If you think we lack rights now, lack a voice, just wait.'

'You seem very sure of these facts,' said Keeler.

'I've lived in this world,' said Burtok. 'Where have you been? You can see it everywhere. If this cell had a window, I'd invite you to look through it. This Palace? It's obscene. The paraded wealth, the flaunting of grandeur. And yet, there are famines. Pestilence. Hives where the poor eat dirt. Nomad cities of beggars in the Asiat. Whole sectors of Europa without clean water. Infant mortality. How is that a great Imperium? A great dream? Shit on Him. Screw Him and His dream of shit. This serves only Him. Everyone else is an expendable slave.'

'You don't believe He's a god, then?' she asked.

'I think He wants to be,' said Burtok. 'I've heard there are some who treat Him as such. That won't last long. Another few generations, no one will remember what He used to be. Everyone will accept it. Do as you're told, because He's god. Do your duty, because He's god. Die, because He's god. Worship Him–'

'What was it that He used to be?' asked Amon. It was the first question he'd asked any of the subjects.

'You should know,' said Burtok. 'Weren't you there? A warlord. A king. A conqueror. Chasing power, bringing rivals into line by force. Unification? That's a euphemism. Power grab. He's strong, I grant you. Him and the High Elite. Unnatural strong.'

'You acknowledge He has abilities that are beyond human,' said Keeler. 'But you do not accept Him as a divine being.'

'He has wealth,' said Burtok. 'Wealth like His, you can create those abilities. Build technologies that run like magic. Make scourging demigods like him.'

He gestured to the Custodian.

'These days,' Burtok said mournfully, 'there's few that can see it for what it is. See that truth. See beyond the global lie. Few who are as courageous as me to rage against it.'

Keeler nodded.

'Amon is a fearsome being,' she said. 'I am wary of him, his size, his splendour. You say these things without fear that, if what you say is true, he might strike you down for saying the unsayable.'

'I'm not afraid of a little passing pain,' said Burtok. 'Let him strike me. I've been in here twenty years, isolation. How much worse could it be for me?'

'I would invite you to look out of the window,' said Keeler, 'but as you point out, there isn't one. And if you saw what was happening outside, around the walls of the city, I fear it would only convince you further that you were right.'

She rose, and picked up her chair.

'But I assure you, Mister Burtok, it can be very much worse, and it may soon be very much worse. The future you fear is not the future that is bearing down on us. Thank you for your candour.'

'Won't you stay?' Burtok called. 'I haven't yet told you of my methods. The details of how I went about my protest–'

Amon looked back at him.

'How was skinning your victims part of your statement?' he asked.

'That?' Burtok shrugged. 'Oh, that bit was just for fun.'

* * *

After five hours, the convoy came to a halt. A ten-minute rest, they were told. The troopers scrambled off the carriers to flex stiff joints, to urinate, or to empty the bottles they had urinated into along the way.

It wasn't clear where they were. A haze lay over them, a low and overcast sky that grew darker to the north. The area was rubble, as far as the eye could see. The ghost marks of streets. Burned-out wrecks of machines, military and civilian.

'South of Palatine Tower,' said Piers. He had got off the carrier without a word to Hari. He stood, buttoning up his fly. He nodded his head. 'That there, boy. Palatine Tower. Ten kilometres, maybe.'

Hari looked, but he couldn't see anything except atmospheric murk.

Every part of him ached. Five hours of discomfort, sweltering airless heat, and being used as a bolster by a man twice his size.

'How much longer?' he asked.

Piers shrugged. He had put on his shako at an accidentally jaunty angle, and was carving slices off a foul-smelling cured sausage with his bayonet. Around them, troopers milled, stretched, pissed. One of the escort tanks grumbled past, kicking up dust.

'Interesting that,' remarked Piers, through a mouthful of sausage. 'That thing what you were reading.'

Hari glared at him. The grenadier had been asleep for over four hours, the weight of his head never shifting from Hari's shoulder.

'Just resting my eyes, boy,' Piers grinned. 'You should be careful with that, though. A theist tract, eh? Get yourself into trouble. That stuff is banned, as contrary to the Imperial Truth. Could get yourself shot.'

'I didn't put it there,' Hari said.

'Will not stand up in court,' Piers replied. A fleck of sausage had got caught in the bristles of his moustache. He hacked off another slice, offered it to Hari on the tip of his blade.

Hari shook his head.

'Actually,' Hari said, 'it's not banned. The preaching of it is banned, but the belief itself is tolerated.'

'You a believer, then, boy?' asked Piers, his cheeks stuffed with sausage.

'No,' said Hari. He'd read the file through twice since he'd found it. It appeared to be a copy of the so-called *Lectitio Divinitatus*. He had no way of telling if it was complete, or what complete even meant. He wondered how it had found its way onto his slate. His first thought had been Sindermann, but that seemed unlikely. Sindermann would have just given it to him, and asked for opinions. Hari wondered about the woman in the Blackstone. Keeler. She'd taken his slate from him. Had she secretly loaded a copy? Perhaps from a data-storage ring hidden under those mittens? Prisoners smuggled things into their isolation, especially items dear to them. If it had been her, why had she done it?

'Are you?' Hari asked.

Piers stopped chewing, and swallowed. He wiped his mouth. 'A believer?' he asked. 'That's a question and a half. Do I believe He's a god? *The* god? I don't know what any of that means. Is He high above us all, a Master of Mankind, divine in His grace? Well, I have to believe so. Otherwise, what's the point of any of this?'

'Is He not just–' Hari began.

'What? What is He?' Piers asked. He sat down on a block of rubble, eased off one boot, and tipped grit out of it. His thick, dirty toes stuck out through holes in what once had been socks.

'I'm from the Uplands, I am,' he said. 'Born and raised. Upland Tercio, hooo! There's faith up there still. In a lot of places. Don't give me that eye, boy. You know it. People have to believe, it's wired into them. They need it, that's my slant on the matter.'

'They need it?'

The grenadier nodded, and began to make a clumsy effort to get his boot back on.

'We've always needed something,' he said. 'Deep down. You do, I do. Everyone. The faiths, the old religions of the back-then days, well, they're all gone. Erased. They was a crutch, so it's been said, we didn't need. They was holding us back from our potential as a species.'

Hari raised the slate and wrote that down.

'You like that, eh?' asked Piers. 'You like that, do you? I read that in a book once. Don't look surprised, boy, you know I can read. I was doing it over your shoulder.'

'So, faith persists?' asked Hari.

Piers nodded. 'It's a part of us we don't let go. We need it, I think, like air. Like food. Look at us here. Would we be doing this, any of us, if we didn't have faith in something bigger than us? Something bigger, with a plan for us?'

'We had orders,' said Hari.

'You didn't.'

Hari sighed.

'In the Grenadiers, when I joined up,' Piers said, 'we had a confraternity. Just private, unofficial.'

'Like a warrior lodge?'

'No!' Piers snapped. 'Not like that Astartes bullshit. Just an association. We offered thanks, for surviving battles and such, to Mythrus. Some say she was a god. From a long, long time ago. A god who watched over warriors.'

'She?'

'I called her she. I call my weapon she.' Piers patted the heavy caliver leaning against the rubble beside him. 'I believe in *Old Bess* before anything else. Gender's not the point here–'

'Gender is fluid?'

'Shit,' Piers groaned, and shook his head wearily. 'Let's stick to one matter at a time. Your mind's everywhere. Mythrus looked after us. I don't know if she was a god, or used to be a god, or what. I don't know if any of us even really thought she was a god. But it made us feel better. A little faith, see? To keep us warm through a cold night in the trench, to keep us safe in a firefight.'

'Two minutes!' an officer yelled out from behind them. Piers got his boot back on.

'Gods come and go,' said Piers. 'Religions, creeds, they come and go. Sometimes they die out. Sometimes they fade, or get suppressed. Sometimes they lose their identity, or we forget about them. But they linger, that's what I think. They remain, under the surface. They are there, for when we need them again. So sometimes, they come back. They might have old names, like my girl Mythrus. They might take new ones. The creeds don't matter, see? That's just dressing, ritual palaver. The need in us, that's what counts. The Emperor, is He a god? I don't know. Maybe we're making Him into one. Maybe He's become one along the way. Or maybe we're mistaking Him for one. Does that matter? Or perhaps, just saying, He was a god all along, and we're only just realising it.'

'You think that?' asked Hari.

Piers raised his hands.

'I'm not coming down on any side of it,' he said. 'I'm just suggesting that it's us. We need something. Need something to believe in. He's either truly that thing, or–'

'Or?'

'Or He'll do, boy. We look around, and He's the obvious choice. The only choice. He fills our need, see? He's the new name we've latched onto to keep us strong. He's god, by default. We need Him to be, or all of this is mass insanity.'

The officers were calling again. Troops were trudging back to the carriers, complaining.

'Are you lying again?' asked Hari.

'Yes,' Piers grinned. 'Or was that a lie too?' He got up, stretched robustly, and gleefully ripped the loudest, longest fart Hari had ever heard.

'Better out than in,' he declared.

'Better out here than in there,' said Hari.

The hatches slammed. The vibrations resumed. They began to roll. Piers filled the seat next to him, lolled, and was soon resting the dead weight of his head on Hari's shoulder. Hari held the slate, hunched up, and began to read through the file again.

He could see Piers' reflection in the glow of the small screen.

His eyes open.

Corbenic Gard had fallen on the eighteenth of Secundus. Fallen easily, brutally. The first of the bastions that protected the approaches to the Lion's Gate, proud and haughty, it was gone, its defenders put to the sword. Now it formed a vantage from which to oversee the mass assault on the Colossi Gate, a far greater prize.

Corbenic's fabric had been shattered. Its walls were split, and barely any of its roofs remained. Dust was everywhere, dust like chalk powder. It coated every surface, and drifted in the air. The light was sallow. From the broken ramparts, Ahriman watched the advances below: tides of infantry, of war machines, rolling past the ruins of Corbenic like the delta of a vast, black river, flowing from its source to the north, at the Lion's Gate space port, then down the floodplain of the broken Palace to encircle Colossi.

Ground-attack craft flew past, heavy and fat, droning and

glinting like blowflies. Eighty, then another eighty, growling south at low level.

'I understand the Great Khan has already presented his credentials,' Ahriman remarked.

Mortarion slowly turned his immense frame from the rampart's splintered edge, and glowered at Ahriman. The white dust caked Mortarion's armour and his face like the dry clay of a tomb. He had rested his scythe against the cracked wall nearby, but Ahriman knew the huge weapon could be in the Pale King's hands, and striking in a nanosecond.

'*Goading me is not advisable,*' Mortarion said.

'Not a goad,' Ahzek Ahriman replied, though it had been. The scythe, named *Silence*, was preposterously huge, even by the theatrical standards of the Legiones Astartes warrior-kind. Ahriman wondered if Mortarion would ever understand what true strength was, the strength they had come to be blessed with. Under the drape of his cloak, Ahriman's hands were empty, but just as ready as the Pale King's blade. The idea of pushing the spectral prince was tempting, but this was not the moment. 'Not a goad at all,' Ahriman repeated. 'An observation.'

'*Hmm.*' The primarch-lord of the XIV Legion grunted, then sneered. '*Yes, he's there. Jaghatai. He has tested my line, the usual show. A mere sortie. This will see an end of it, though. These next few days.*'

'Of the war, my lord?'

'*What? Yes, that too.*'

Ahriman knew where the Pale King's focus lay. Mortarion despised almost everything, but the war had bred in him a particular animus with the Khan and his Scar-brood, and that had festered into a complex obsession, a battle too long unfinished. It was useful to harness that, to keep the Pale King's eyes on a singular goal and prevent him from lashing out at those around him, most of whom he reviled.

Like the Thousand Sons. Their battlefield alliance, Death Guard and Thousand Sons, so ordained by the Lord of Iron, would inevitably be a difficult thing to manage.

'Ah,' said Ahriman. 'You mean, specifically–'

'Of course I do,' murmured Mortarion. *'Let them laugh, let them try to laugh, as my blades cleave their faces. They have lasted this long only by running from me. There is nowhere left to run.'*

'I'm sure your victory will be severe, lord,' said Ahriman. 'But I urge you, the Great Khan's warriors have more talents than mere speed of mobility. They don't have our numbers. Your numbers. But they have always displayed great merit in warfare...'

'Urge me not, Ahriman,' said Mortarion. *'I seek no advice from witches.'*

'Yet here we are,' said Ahriman.

'We are,' the primarch replied. *'Where is he?'*

'Approaching, lord. Be patient.'

'That's twice you've told me what to do,' said the Pale King. *'There won't be a third time.'*

'Understood,' said Ahriman. Mortarion turned back to the wall. Ahriman saw him wince. He could taste the suffering in him. He could smell it. A pestilential stench leaked from the Death Lord's armour. Flies buzzed around the seams and joints of his panoply. He was decaying inside, and would decay forever. The torment was unimaginable. It was extraordinary that anyone, even a being as insanely strong as Mortarion, could endure it and remain standing.

We all get our gifts, Ahriman thought, each one tailored to our needs by the Great Ocean, all ruinous, in their way, but some more callous than others. I am whole, at least. Blessed with exquisite wonder. Gifted beyond measure.

Ahriman raised his left hand, his iridescent robe parting like mist. He let the motes of dust that thickened the air around them fall on his open palm. The dust of Terra. The home world. From which we came, and to which we now return. And all will be dust in our triumph.

The Crimson King had sent Ahriman ahead of him to Corbenic Gard, to gauge Mortarion's present demeanour. Though now riddled with it himself, the Pale King still deplored warp-craft and witchery, a blight he considered personified by the Thousand Sons. It was utter hypocrisy, of course. Mortarion had swum deep in the same intoxicating Ocean. He was like an addict... no, an inebriate. A rabid advocate of strict temperance who had then fallen to drink, and who then raged for weeks at a time in drunken excess, only to hate himself when the bout was done, and swear never to touch another drop again, until the next relapse came.

Pitiful. To obtain such gifts and not appreciate them. Mortarion's tragedy was that he had become what he had spent his life opposing. He hated himself. He could not reconcile his own drastic transmutation in his mind. The pestilential stench seeping from his plate was, as much as anything, shame.

For our part, thought Ahriman, you are the enemy, Pale King. How ironic you are content to be known by that title now, the name of the very monsters you used to hunt with such glee. Mortarion, witch-burner, purger of wisdom. Louder than any other voice, yours was raised against our being from the very start. There were other accusers too: Dorn, Russ, Corax, Manus, but none as loud or as self-righteous as you. Because of you, Prospero burned and Tizca fell. Russ was the implement, and dread Horus the architect, but you were the instigator who fomented the prejudice to begin with. We have longed to see you punished for that, and this is sweet indeed. Look what has become of you: Manus is long dead; Corax and Russ are broken, and lost from the field of war; Dorn is cornered and sweating out his last hours in a prison of his own making as oblivion descends.

But you. You couldn't even cling on to your principles, unlike them. You, the loudest critic of all, have become one with us. Your strength counted for nothing. You have submitted to the warp, and you loathe yourself for doing so. And we can now watch with relish as you rot and hate yourself for ever.

Behind his gold-and-azure mask, Ahzek Ahriman smiled. Placing the main strengths of the Thousand Sons and Death Guard Legions side by side in the same formation had seemed an insensitive decision, typical of the Lord of Iron's blunt and tone-deaf paradigms. This great siege was Perturabo's to orchestrate. He expected his ally lords to set aside their differences and work together without complaint. Of course, the Lord of Iron had not made that decision, though he thought he had. With a deft twitch of his fingers and a touch of his mind, Ahriman had adjusted Perturabo's precious and detailed mental scheme at their last meeting without the Lord of Iron even knowing it.

Despite the presence of the Death Guard, the Thousand Sons had chosen to fight here.

'*Do you hear voices?*' Mortarion asked, without looking around.

'No,' Ahriman lied.

'*I keep hearing voices,*' said Mortarion.

'Just the wind,' said Ahriman.

'*In my sleep?*'

'Do you sleep, lord?' Ahriman asked gently.

'*No,*' Mortarion admitted.

The voices were there. Ahriman could hear them all. The Neverborn were gathering to the north, building like a storm at his back, seeping under the telaethesic ward where it had fractured at the port, and manifesting to advance.

He could hear their voices. It was not his turn to answer them yet. He longed to shackle them and wrench their secrets from them. There would be time for that, when the war was done. For now, they were malformed, new-fleshed, learning to live and move in realspace. Some, like old Samus, chattered incessantly, repeating his dirge over and again: *'That's the only name you'll hear. Samus. It means the end and the death. Samus is all around you. Samus is the man beside you. Samus will gnaw on your bones. Look out! Samus is here.'* Others, like Balphagora and Ka'Bandha, Sahrakoor Elekh and Amnaich, spoke in tongues Ahriman had yet to master. Some sang. Some mewled like abandoned infants. Some, like Ku'Gath and Rotigus and Scabeiathrax, made the whirring drone of insect plagues or the infrasonic croak of frogs. N'Kari and Orbonzal and a thousand others gibbered, issuing noises of inhuman pain, of despair, of glee, of anger, of hunger. Inarticulate sounds. They had yet to find their languages.

A million immortal voices. A million million. One rose from the cacophony, quiet and clear.

Is he prepared?

+He is, my king,+ willed Ahriman. +As much as he ever will be.+

I approach.

The air writhed open. The motes of dust swirled, flurried, and swam together, forming a great, pointed archway that looked as though it had been fused from calcified bone. Cold light burned through the arch.

Mortarion turned, raising his hand to shield his eyes against the glare. Ahriman bowed.

The light shafting through the skeletal arch dimmed, sucking back like a tide to be absorbed into the figure that stepped out. The arch cooled, blistered, turned to vitreous stone, then flaked and blew away into the air like ash.

The Crimson King had arrived. Ahriman could not look upon him. His glory was too raw and bright.

'*You are late,*' said Mortarion.

'*My brother,*' said Magnus. His radiance dulled. Just as he had chosen the magnificence of his arrival to establish unequivocal power, now he selected his form carefully: a human face, one eye socket simply empty; a helm of wide, downturned ivory tusks to subliminally suggest deference; a modest scale, gigantic still, but deftly measured to be slightly shorter and slighter than the towering shape of the Death Lord; plain plate. Even the billowing silk over-robes were demure and unpatterned, to indicate submission.

'*I am glad to see you, and to stand with you,*' said Magnus.

Mortarion glared. Ahriman rose again, watching, delighting in the Pale King's discomposure.

'*I…*' Mortarion began.

'*Be at ease,*' said Magnus. '*Please. We are both yoked under instruction from our brother Perturabo. We are to abide by his plan. I would not have chosen to discomfort either of us by standing shoulder to shoulder with you. The Zone Imperialis is big, with many, varied theatres. But still, who am I to question the Lord of Iron's intricate scheme of war?*'

'*The Warmaster has faith in his abilities,*' said Mortarion cautiously.

'*So do I, brother, so do I,*' said Magnus. '*No finer exponent of siege-craft. So, we are obliged.*'

'*It seems so,*' said Mortarion.

Magnus nodded. '*So, Colossi?*'

'*Colossi.*'

'*Your mighty strengths and my… qualities,*' said Magnus.

'*I have no need of your qualities,*' said the Pale King. '*I can crush this by myself.*'

'*No doubt at all,*' said the Crimson King with a smile. '*But I go where I am sent. You seem so wary, brother. Surely our old disagreements are behind us?*'

'You bring that up?'

'I read it in your face.'

'And I have always read yours, Crimson King,' said Mortarion. 'Of your qualities… deceit has always been the uppermost.'

'There is no deceit today, brother,' said Magnus. 'That is why I came in person, to assure you. We are as one. We stand together. The Lord of Iron has charged us with a task. We must be undivided. So let us take this moment to unburden ourselves of tiresome histories, and reconcile. Things have changed. You. Me. I say this, all of this, so that you may know I forgive you.'

'You… forgive me?' Mortarion snarled.

'We are both now what you hated. It's unbearable, I know. The pain–'

'The pain is nothing.' The Pale King's voice was an empty husk. Magnus stepped closer to face him.

'The idea is not,' he said. He looked Mortarion in the eyes. 'Your suffering gives you power. The sort I promised from the start. Your submission was not weakness. There is no shame. I bear you no ill will. I understand.'

It took the Pale King a moment to find a reply.

'I hate this,' he whispered.

'I know,' replied Magnus softly. 'It should ease your torment to know I harbour no resentment towards you. Not now.'

Magnus placed his hand gently on Mortarion's shoulder. The Pale King flinched slightly, wary.

'What are you doing?' he growled.

'I have had my gifts for a lot longer than you have,' said Magnus calmly. 'Let me show you how they may be harnessed.'

A golden light seeped from Magnus' fingers, and suffused Mortarion's ragged plate. Mortarion blinked, straightened slightly, and took a breath. He seemed taller, less bowed by pain and wrack. His eyes had become fierce and unclouded.

'You are kind to me…' he murmured, puzzled.

'There is only one enemy now,' said Magnus. *'The Lie-Father. We face Him side by side.'*

The Pale King nodded. He clutched his fellow king's hand for a second, then turned away, took up his scythe and stepped over the ragged battlement. They watched his giant figure bounding effortlessly from block to block, descending the slope of rubble and calling for his captains.

'Compassion?' asked Ahriman.

'A temporary respite,' Magnus replied. *'He is made to endure, more than any of us, but pain dulls his abilities. He must learn to love what he is, or he will be of no use. And he and his Legion are fine blunt instruments.'*

'To crack the walls?'

'To crack the walls. To open the way. To let me reach the place I need to be.'

'If he realises you are using him,' Ahriman began, 'if any of them do–'

Magnus looked at the Corvidae captain sharply. *Not out loud*, he willed.

+Very well. If, for a moment, they appreciate that your true concern is not the united effort to topple your father's throne, but something more personal…+

'They won't,' said the Crimson King.

SIX

Dialogues and arrivals

+Garviel.+

'I am occupied, lord.' *Evade. Sidestep. Swing, left blade. Decapitation.*

+So I witness, warrior. What is your tally today?+

'Eighteen.' *Turn. Adjust. Block. Block again. Right blade, under the guard. Impale.* 'Nineteen.' *Adjust again. Back step. Re-address.*

Four more, coming from the right. Heavy storm troops, battle-armoured, intending to mob and overwhelm.

+A slow day for you, then?+

'It's barely begun.' *Adjust grips. Low address.*

+Does spinning your blades like that, one in each hand… Does it help? Or is it merely a flourish?+

'It cleans off the blood, so they bite better.' *Block two. Kick the third back. Snap that blade. Thrust. Kill.* 'It also shows them my intent.'

+I wouldn't know. I need to speak to you, Garviel.+

'You're speaking.' *Block to the face. Down-cut. Kill. Step out. Evade. Side-cut. Kill. Slash to block. Lock and hold. Cross-guard thrust. Kill.*

+Face to face.+

Loken stepped back, and lowered his blades. The chainsword continued to purr. In his hands, Rubio's sword was just an inert metal blade, but a fine one. He looked around. The balustrade section, now littered with dead, was clear. Below him, on the sub-wall line, Excertus repel-squads had torn down the last of the siege ladders. The fighting now raged ten metres below him.

'I won't leave my post, Lord Sigillite,' said Loken. 'They've been assaulting this section since dawn.'

+A mere harrying action, Garviel. Marmax West is not a priority objective for them.+

'Tell that to the men with me. Tell that to the dead.'

+Loken, your efforts on the wall have been tireless. I commend you. Especially your efforts to rally and coordinate the common army units.+

'I have no Legion to stand with, Sigillite. What you call the common army are my brothers now.'

+Loken, I have a particular service I need you to perform.+

'I'm not your hand any more, lord.'

+I know. Though a place was set aside for you.+

'And I refused it. You know why.'

+I don't.+

'To be one of your chosen, to walk in the grey, I would need to have my mind woken. Those were the terms, the requirements of membership. You said so. I've never had a trace of that talent in me, but you say it's there. Latent. Well, perhaps it is. It can stay that way. I have no wish to become that. I have seen too much of what it costs.'

Loken walked to the parapet, Rubio's blade rested across his shoulder, the chainsword growling low at his side. He looked over. The fight was thickening. Traitor squads had broken in across the lower redoubts, and the repel-squads were being slowly forced back into a choke point along the edge of the earthworks.

+It is nothing to fear, Garviel.+

'You're speaking to me, in my head, in the middle of a battle, from hundreds of leagues away. Only a fool wouldn't fear that. I've given you my answer. I serve the Emperor. I have one cause.'

+Vengeance.+

'Don't say it as if it's a weakness. It's all I have left.'

+And it's why I've turned to you. The service I require is specific. It speaks directly to your cause, and it comes directly from the Praetorian. This is, you must understand, a great confidence. He needs men like you, but you especially. One who knows and understands a very particular foe.+

'Explain.'

+I don't need to. I feel your heart rate elevate. I sense you already understand my meaning. Dorn's needs match yours entirely. Garviel, this is what you want.+

Step up on the parapet. Judge distance and depth. Multiple targets below, unaware.

Blades out. Leap.

'I'm listening.'

The Mournival entered the war camp down a long avenue of cowled and kneeling adepts. Binharic chants formed versions of the warrior's names, and crooned them to whatever dark aspect of the Omnissiah Mechanicum they adored. Behind them, the sheer and gargantuan cliffs of the Katabatic Slopes dropped away to dark plains far below, and violet lightning storms boiled and fractured through the roof of the world. Before them, visible beyond the structures and siege-machines of the Mechanicum's war camp, rose the southern aspects of the Imperial Palace, Adamant, the Ultimate Wall, far away but still staggering in their magnitude.

The place was known as Epta. It was one of the circumvallation

strongholds, a war-steading raised by the menial hosts and
Martian levies in preparation for the siege, part of the traitor
host's great, encircling investment. Abaddon liked the Mechanicum as little as he liked the Neverborn, but they were a useful
tool. They had the engines and devices he needed, and the surplus manpower. This visit was a necessary compact, a sufficient
display of respect to secure the efforts of the traitor host's most
capricious and inscrutable allies.

'My lord captain,' said a senior adept, moving forward to meet
him. She was entirely blind, her organic eyes removed. Sensory
acquisition nodes bulged out of her augmeticised forehead, an
ugly enhancement that she kept mercifully hidden, until she
swept back the cowl of her black robes and stood, long-necked
and proud, before him, as if seeking his admiration. Her mouth
and larynx were still human, unmodified. Abaddon suspected
this was why she had been chosen as interlocutor.

'Epta welcomes you,' she said.

'The ceremony is unnecessary,' he replied. 'This is a simple
formality. The Lord of Iron has supplied you with a list of
requirements.'

'It is received,' she said. 'A long list. Specialised. Our
resources are great, but not unlimited. The reserves of this
steading and the others are drawn upon every hour to fur-
nish the siege effort.'

'I'm sure my Lord of Iron made it clear this was a special
favour to him.'

'He did so, through subtle use of hard cipher and nuanced
encryption. He speaks our languages well.'

'And the confidence of this matter?' asked Kibre.

'Assured, Lord Kibre,' she replied. 'We do not fall to the
whims of human weakness. We do not gossip or whisper. But
to fulfil these needs, to deploy the assets, we require details of
the undertaking specifics.'

'And I'm here to give them to you,' said Abaddon. 'Do you
have a name?'

'In flesh? Eyet-One-Tag. It is short for–'

The adepts around her chorused a long sequence of binary
code-forms.

Abaddon nodded. 'Can we converse in private?'

She spread her hands. 'We are all a linked unity, Lord
Abaddon. All that is Epta is private.'

Aximand touched Abaddon's arm, and inclined his head.
Abaddon saw what he was looking at.

'Eyet-One-Tag, perhaps you could review the specifications
of our request with… *Lord* Kibre and *Lord* Tormageddon in
your control station? Out in the open seems so vulnerable to
un-linked beings like us. I have to step away for a moment.'

The adepts led Kibre and Tormageddon towards the nearby
modular out-build. Little Horus followed Abaddon past the
ring of crackling watchfires to the perimeter beside the steading's landing pads.

'What does he want?' Aximand asked.

'I suggest we ask him,' said Abaddon.

Argonis, equerry to the Warmaster, was uncoupling the
over-segments of his flight armour. His Xiphon-pattern Inter-
ceptor, its sleek lines dressed in the colours and insignia of
the XVI, stood on the dock behind him, vapour fuming from
its cooling hull.

'I'm surprised he's let you out on your own,' said Abaddon.

'I've duties to perform, First Captain,' replied Argonis.

He removed his helm and stared at them.

'What are you doing, Ezekyle?' he asked.

'What do you think I'm doing, Kinor?' Abaddon replied.

Argonis sighed. 'I think,' he said, 'that you're organising an
unsanctioned operation that is contrary to the Warmaster's
wishes.'

'Untrue, on both counts,' said Abaddon. 'It's sanctioned. A formal component of the Lord of Iron's strategy. Check, if you like. You know how Perturabo likes to help people out with trivial questions. And it is in exact accordance with the Warmaster's wishes.'

'Then why is it confidential?' asked Argonis.

'To ensure maximum effect,' said Abaddon.

'Why, what do you know?' asked Aximand.

'Nothing, except that First Company, including both the Justaerin and the Catulan, along with Goshen's Twenty-Fifth and Marr's Eighteenth, have been rotated out of the active line, without explanation.'

'What does he know?' asked Aximand.

Argonis glowered at Little Horus. 'He knows you can't be trusted,' he replied. 'Other than that, he knows nothing. Yet. Serving as the Great Lupercal's equerry is an honour. But it is thankless. I won't suffer his rage until I know who to blame.'

'That's fair,' said Abaddon. He didn't envy the equerry's testing role, but he admired Argonis Unscarred: a true, Cthonian Son of Horus, brutally effective and maliciously loyal. He also knew that, as Chieftain of the Isidis Flight, Argonis had been oath-bound to First Company for many years. He was the finest pilot Abaddon knew of, and the fact that Argonis still wore a burnished crest of feathers across his sea-green chestplate showed he remained proud of his former post and his former loyalties. 'How long can you keep it that way, Kinor?'

Argonis mouthed a soft, Cthonic curse. 'What *is* this, Ezekyle?'

'I asked how long?'

'As long as I have to. But it's better I know what I'm protecting. For your sake, at least.'

'An opportunity has arisen,' said Abaddon. 'Swift and complete compliance. Perturabo likes it very much, and so do I.

But it will stall and fail if word gets around. If… *people* get involved.'

'People?' said Argonis. 'You mean him?'

'He has a way of dominating situations,' said Abaddon. 'Of making them his own. This will please him, but if he learns about it too early, he will get involved. Stamp his mark. Make… improvements. Potentially kill it before it can fly.'

'Oh, quite probably,' said Argonis. 'I'm surprised he's leaving the Lord of Iron alone to run his schemes. Perhaps he understands that Perturabo will not perform optimally if he's interfered with. In all honesty, I'm amazed he hasn't dropped yet to join the brawl and lead the way. It's not like him.'

'He's still on the *Spirit*?'

'He is,' Argonis nodded. 'Almost in seclusion. Withdrawn. Ah, I don't know what to make of it.'

'Perhaps he wants to use his brothers, and all of us, as cannon fodder to topple the walls,' said Little Horus. 'Then just, you know, stroll in across our corpses and take the prize.'

'These days,' said Argonis, 'I wouldn't put anything past him. He's not himself. I… I don't know what he's becoming or where his mind is. He…'

The equerry trailed off.

'What?' asked Abaddon. 'Kinor, if there's a problem, I need to know it more than anyone.'

Argonis sat down on a wheel-arch of a munition trolley. He took off his right gauntlet and flexed his fingers. His flesh showed the old, white flecks of knife-fight cuts. His nickname was an ironic reference to the fact that only his face had remained unscarred through his long career.

'He sits alone,' he said quietly. 'He studies plans, and Perturabo's reports. He reads. Books and manuscripts. I don't know where they come from, or who gives them to him.'

'The Crimson King?' Abaddon suggested.

'I doubt it. That fiend hasn't been near him. I'd venture that little shit Erebus, or even Lorgar, except neither of them have dared to show their faces here. The books, papers, they're just *there*. I don't know what language they are written in. I don't even know if they're made of paper.'

He swallowed. Abaddon crouched down in front of him, and peered into his face. He knew that Kinor Argonis, like him, took little pleasure in the manifestations of the warp. Aximand remained standing, looking on with creeping concern.

Argonis glanced at Abaddon. His face was drawn, tired, tight with anxiety.

'I love him, Ezekyle,' he said.

'We all love him.'

'He's Lupercal. The Lupercal. Our genefather, the greatest man, the finest warrior that…'

He shook his head.

'I cannot bear to see him this way,' said Argonis. 'Withdrawing, alone. He… he calls for things, just little things, like a cup of wine, or a stylus, or some object from his chambers, and then, when I bring them, he doesn't remember asking me for them. Or he… holds them. The objects, usually trophies of old victories I've had to fetch from his shelves, he holds them, and stares at them for hours at a time. He talks to himself. At least, I hope it's to himself. And sometimes, he–'

'He what?'

'He calls me Maloghurst. At first, I laughed and gently corrected him. But he still does it. I don't think it's a mistake. I think he thinks I'm Maloghurst, or at least… that's who he sees when he looks at me.'

Argonis got up sharply, cleared his throat, and began to lock his gauntlet back into place.

'When I heard these rumours,' he said, 'These... deployment discrepancies, I came to find you. Only the Mournival could have authorised them. I didn't want anything to come out that would unsettle him. Not now.'

'Kinor,' said Abaddon, slowly straightening up. 'I need you to keep this confidential. Keep it away from his eyes until we're done. What he doesn't know can't trouble him.'

'But if he finds out I've been screening things from him,' said Argonis, 'or worse, if he finds out you have... I fear the consequences of that.'

'What we're doing will save him,' said Little Horus.

'What?'

'Aximand is right,' said Abaddon. 'Once executed, this operation will win the war, outright. And early, long in advance of even the most optimistic estimates. He will rejoice. It will lift his spirits and restore him. It will bring back to us the Lupercal we adore.'

'How certain are you?' asked Argonis.

'Certain,' said Abaddon. 'I'm doing this for him.'

'Not for your own glory?'

'Oh, that too,' said Little Horus. 'Always, that too.'

Argonis laughed involuntarily. Abaddon laughed too, to demonstrate that everything was safe and secure between them.

'I need you to keep this close, for now,' Abaddon said.

'Then show me what *this* is,' replied the equerry.

Falkus Kibre looked around, and narrowed his eyes as the three of them entered the command station.

'What's he doing here?' he hissed to Abaddon.

'Go with me,' whispered Abaddon. 'We need him.'

Argonis had crossed to the hololith display that Eyet-One-Tag and her adepts had set up to review the assets. The adepts, twenty of them, stood to one side, as silent as the deadpan figure of Tormageddon, who had said nothing for hours.

The equerry looked at the three-dimensional display. He raised his hand, and folded the light to enlarge one image.

'Three Donjon-class siege engines,' said Eyet-One-Tag.

'Good grief,' Argonis breathed. 'Abaddon, this is no minor operation.'

He flicked up another image.

'Twenty Terrax-pattern–' Eyet-One-Tag began.

'Damn it!' Argonis spat. 'These are major assets!'

'Considerable,' said the adept. 'Especially when one factors in the support squadrons, menials and surveyor drones. A total of perhaps six thousand personnel. Though the secondary assets are rather more substantial.'

She changed the images with a twitch of her head.

'Eighteen hundred batteries, mixed artillery, heavy ordnance and petraries,' she said, 'plus munitions and teams. The sustained bombardments of the Europa Wall section and Western Projection Wall section represent an extensive materiel debt.'

'Europa and Western Projection are two of the strongest wall-runs in the line,' Argonis exclaimed. 'You're throwing us against them? Abaddon, you're out of your mind! Three companies, even of our best, won't be enough to break them!'

'I agree,' said Abaddon. 'But I'm not going against Europa or Western Projection.'

'But–'

'They're distractions, Kinor. Loud and very big distractions.'

Abaddon leaned past him, and rotated the chart display. He pointed to a spot on the wall.

'This is my target,' he said.

'But that… that's impenetrable too,' said Argonis.

'Not as much as you would think,' said Abaddon. 'Or as

much as anyone would think. Especially the Praetorian. Our Lord of Iron has found a chink in his armour.'

'Now do you appreciate why secrecy is paramount?' asked Little Horus.

The equerry nodded.

'Good,' said Aximand. He turned and wandered to the exit, stepping out into the cold air. His hands were shaking. What Argonis had described, the state of Lupercal's mind... it had been hard to hear. That talk of listening to voices, speaking to things that weren't there, or to people who were long dead...

Beside him, in the darkness, something breathed gently. When the lightning flashed its fitful glare, Aximand could plainly see he was alone.

'Go away,' he hissed. 'Go away or tell me where. Name a place.'

From behind him, in the station, he heard Argonis ask, 'When exactly does this operation commence?'

And Abaddon reply, 'Any moment now.'

A minute later, at the adept's binharic cue, the sky lit up. To the north of Epta, cascades of fire as large as cities burst against the flanks of Europa and Western Projection. Once begun, the bombardment did not pause or cease.

The insane roar of it, the thunder, sounded like the howls of a tormented god.

Amber 'prepare' runes lit on the forward bulkhead and along the ridges of the cabin's armoured ceiling, but Niborran already knew, from the shift in engine note and the gentle dipping away to starboard, that they were commencing their final approach.

He opened his despatch case, and put away the slates and papers he'd been reviewing during the journey. He'd been trying to assess an overview of the port's current defensive capabilities and strengths, but the data reports were wildly contradictory and incomplete. Vox and noospheric connection in the Northern Magnifican had been patchy at best since the void collapse, and very little hard intel had come through to Bhab. Niborran didn't even know who he'd be accepting zone command from. He didn't know what he was dropping into.

Except, of course, he did.

He put that out of his mind. In the seats around him, officers and staff were stirring, and prepping, if necessary, for a hostile disembark when they reached the ground.

His stomach and ears told him the 'bird had begun dropping steeply. Combat approach. He opened his seat-window's blast cover. Daylight, a creamish haze. They were still high up. As the 'bird banked in a wide turn, the surface swung into view. The palace-city of Magnifican, an endless vista of towers, blocks, fabricatory complexes, plazas and highways. It rolled slowly below him. A few plumes of smoke, and occasional patches of damage in the street plan. Not as bad as he'd heard, or feared.

The command Stormbird dropped lower, arcing west in what felt like a leisurely curve. He saw a distant blackness that looked like a mountain range, then realised it was an immense wall of smoke, a band some thirty or even forty kilometres wide. He gazed at it in shock for as long as it remained in view. North-east... That had to be, what? Boenition District? Tortestrian? In the name of Terra, a whole swathe of the city gone, on fire...

Now they were passing over debris fields and the outlines of ruined streets. What was that? Could it be the remains of the Celestial City that adjoined the port, and served its needs? Surely not.

The 'bird banked north. The huge, rising curve of the Eternity Wall space port swung into view. Niborran had always loved the place. It was still impressive, even with its upper ridges and vast, ascending pylons hidden behind thick banks of atmospherics and smog. One of the great structures of the Imperial Palace, a monument of grand scale architectural engineering to rival the Lion's Gate or the Palatine Tower or the soaring superstructures of the Sanctum.

It had been the site of his first footsteps on Terra, all those years ago. He'd been born in the rings of Saturn, and raised in the strict disciplines of the Saturnine Ordos. Then he'd come to Terra as a trained but green young officer, ready to take up his inaugural active command, and he'd stepped off the boat here at Eternity Wall Port, his first glimpse of Terra and the Palace. The port had seen him off, too, on his first combat lift as a young officer, Setuway 55th, heading out to join the crusader fleets. He'd come and gone many times since then, arriving and departing via the Lion's Gate space port or Damocles, and once or twice through Eternity, but Eternity remained his favourite. It was the place where he felt he'd properly begun as a warrior. The place from which he'd first marched out to active war.

The view distorted. The 'bird had activated its voids. Low approach. Was it just a precaution? He saw puffs of brown smoke, and felt a slight judder. No, airbursts. They were taking fire from ground positions. Enemy anti-air batteries, off to the west, by his estimate, harrying anything that came across them.

The overhead runes went red.

In the seat in front of him, Brohn turned and looked back, grinning.

'And I thought we'd get there in one piece,' he said.

'We will, Clem,' Niborran replied.

'Well, that's half the battle,' Brohn replied with a chuckle.

Not even the half of it.

The run had been surprisingly clean. Once they'd paced

out through the Lion's Gate, the air convoy had been obliged
to skirt heavy fields of flak and anti-air over Marmax, and it
had grown worse as they lengthened their stride and crossed
the heart of Anterior. The ride had been a boneshaker. They
hadn't been able to climb, because the aegis limited their operation ceiling. They'd been obliged to run the storm. Twice.
And Niborran had recognised the distinctive thump and jolt
as the pilot had been forced to dispense anti-missile canisters. Niborran had heard, though it hadn't been confirmed,
that the convoy had lost two troop lifters crossing Anterior.

Once they'd gone through the Ascensor Gate into Magnifican
airspace, things had steadied. 'Unless you'd been told,' Clem
Brohn had joked, 'you wouldn't even know there was a war on.'

You would now. Niborran sat back, and checked his harness. They were picking up speed. Combat approach indeed:
low and fast, and then a short, dead drop onto the landing
zone at the very last second.

He'd always loved this part. It scared the living shit out of
him every time.

'I've lost them,' said Camba Diaz. Shiban nodded towards
the south.

'Low,' he said. 'One minute out.'

Combat approach. The train of air transports, just black
specks in the southern sky, had dropped, tracking in so low
they were out of sight below the edge of Monsalvant's landing
platform. Diaz could see the anti-air well enough: stippling
clusters of russet smoke-pops that were turning the entire sky-
line into a leopard's pelt.

Shiban Khan looked to his second, Al-Nid Nazira of the
Auxilia, and nodded. Nazira hurried away. They'd cleared the
platform for landing safety, but the honour guard was waiting
on the dock ramps ready to hurry into position.

'How many is Niborran bringing?' asked Diaz.

'My guess, not enough,' Shiban replied, 'and probably fewer than he set out with.'

They could suddenly hear the scream of burners. They took a step backwards into one of the blast alcoves used by ground crew.

The huge, bat-delta of the Stormbird burst up into view over the lip of the platform, blotting out the sky. Its gear was already down, like the grasping talons of a stooping falcon. Its engines howled as the pilot slammed main power from forward thrust and lift to reverse and brake. Too much gun, and the huge craft would simply overshoot the platform and have nowhere to go, and no space to climb.

It set down hard, spread wings bowing slightly on impact, the weight of it shivering the entire platform. Its engines shrieked to a new fury as they reached maximum reverse to suck in forward momentum. All the brake vanes on its wing-line were vertical. The airframe shuddered, and it rolled to a halt and stood there as though it were panting. Vapour spewed from its aft vents. The piercing shriek of the over-stressed engines began to die back.

Shiban Khan clapped his hands. Captain Nazira ran the honour guard out of cover. They began to assemble on the foredeck. Sixty troopers, mixed units. Four of them struggled to raise the huge banner. It showed, in a sunburst, the Emperor Ascendant, rays of light streaming from His golden face to form a halo. The banner had become tangled by the jetwash.

'Get it straight, damn it,' Diaz muttered as he and Shiban strode forward, side by side. The boarding ramp of the Stormbird began to lower. The 'bird was painted in an Excertus drab, a tawny brown that made Shiban think it was in its winter plumage. Lord General Niborran emerged, a tall, noble figure in a long storm coat. He put on his cap, and walked down the ramp to meet them, followed by six of his senior officers, and, Diaz noted with surprise, a Huscarl of the Imperial Fists Praetorian cadre.

Diaz and Shiban halted, their fists to their chestplates. Shiban set his guan dao pole-arm upright at his side. He was an imposing figure, heavily augmeticised for a warrior of the V. On the flesh of his face and neck were the hard, pink lines of old scars, from both injuries and surgeries, that spoke of his exploits and the immense efforts that had been made to place him back in the field. Shiban had grown a beard, which Diaz presumed was an effort to disguise some of the repair-work scars, as though he was ashamed of augmetics, but the beard had odd seams in it, like tribal markings, where it had been unable to grow back across the worst scarring.

'High Primary General, we are honoured,' said Diaz. 'Welcome to Eternity.'

'Well, isn't that a phrase to be reckoned with?' Niborran replied, with a wry smile. He took the salute, then offered Diaz his hand. 'Lord Diaz,' he said, 'I have to say, I am astonished to see you here.'

'Fate takes us where it will, general,' Diaz replied. He gestured to the White Scar at his side. 'This is Shiban, khan of the ordu Fifth, known as Tachseer.'

Niborran nodded to the White Scar, and then started to say something to Diaz. His voice was instantly drowned out.

The rest of the transport convoy was coming in, passing low overhead: heavy lift transports, bulk cargos, Thunderhawks, support gunships. Their shadows washed across the platform, each passing craft shaking the air with noise as it went over. They were heading low towards the combat hangars in the south face of the port, just half a kilometre beyond the platform. Two of the transports were trailing smoke. Over the thunder of thrust, Diaz could hear sirens starting to wail in the hangars as emergency crews scrambled to receive some less than perfect touchdowns.

'You arrive in force,' remarked Diaz.

'Some force,' replied Niborran. 'All that could be gathered. Additional reinforcement will be arriving overground in the next day, Emperor willing. You had better bring me up to speed rapidly, lord. And begin with… how does the lord castellan of the Fourth Sphere come to be in command here at Eternity?'

'You have misunderstood, general,' said Diaz, 'I am not in command. Shiban Khan is zone commander.'

Niborran looked at the White Scar. 'Really?' he said. 'My apologies.'

'I have effective seniority through rank,' said Diaz, 'but Shiban has precedence. He was running the port zone defence when I got here, and I saw no reason to disrupt the effective command structure he had established.'

'We built what we could with what we had to hand,' said Shiban. 'Some troop elements that were stationed here at the beginning, but mostly companies, squads and even individuals that fled here after the lines collapsed in Magnifican. You will not find much uniformity.'

'How many do you have, khan?' Niborran asked.

'Last count, eight thousand,' said Shiban. 'Mostly field infantry, Auxilia and militia. About four hundred main division Excertus, a little armour. And the port defence systems, of course.'

'Wait,' said Colonel Brohn, standing at Niborran's side. 'The lines collapsed in Magnifican?'

'Yes,' said Shiban, 'on and after the eleventh. Everything in the Northern Reaches broke when Lion's Gate Port fell. Mass enemy incursion followed systemic shield collapse. Most comm coverage was disrupted at that point too.'

'No, go back–' said Brohn.

'I'm sorry,' said Niborran, 'this is my chief of staff, Clement Brohn.'

'Which lines?' Brohn asked Shiban. His look was intense. 'Which lines collapsed? Fourteenth? Fifteenth?'

'All of them,' replied Shiban.

Brohn blinked.

'As far as we can tell,' said Diaz, 'and I was out there, there is no longer any coordinated Imperial defence in the northern reaches of Magnifican. Perhaps nothing north of the Processional. Gold Fane's gone, Angevin too, we think. There are some Army brigades active in the field, but they are principally fighting for survival.'

'Shit,' murmured Brohn.

'We had no idea,' said Niborran. 'Bhab Bastion has no idea. Nothing's coming through. They're into Anterior, you see. Burning up to Gorgon, Colossi, Vitrix, Callabar. I think Corbenic's gone already. We didn't realise it was this bad east of the Anterior Wall.'

There was a long silence, stirred only by the port-side wind.

'Do you stand ready to receive zone command, general?' asked Diaz.

Niborran cleared his throat.

'There'll be time for that, Diaz,' he said. He looked at the ragged honour guard, who were trying to look as presentable as possible in their motley array of dirty uniforms. They had finally got the grand banner unfurled. 'Those men have been waiting patiently for a long time,' he said. 'Let me greet them and we can turn to business.'

'As you wish,' said Shiban.

Niborran walked the proud line. He shook hands and exchanged a few words with each trooper in turn.

'Your duty and vigil here will be remembered,' he told them.

'Getty Orheg (Sixteenth Arctic Hort),' the next man said. Niborran glanced quizzically at Diaz.

'It's become a habit, general,' Diaz said. 'Since their units were fractured. I can't seem to make them break it.'

'I don't think you should, lord,' Niborran said.

He turned to the next man.

'Willem Kordy (Thirty-Third Pan-Pac Lift Mobile).'

'That's quite a banner, Willem Kordy (Thirty-Third Pan-Pac Lift Mobile),' said Niborran.

'We support Him, and He watches over us, sir,' said Kordy, staring rigidly straight ahead.

'As it should be, soldier,' said Niborran. 'Can you free one hand long enough to shake mine?'

'It's a little heavy, sir,' said Kordy.

Niborran reached out and gripped the banner pole with his left hand, supplying enough support for Kordy to let go with his right and accept the handshake.

'We'll support Him together, what do you say, Kordy?'

'Yes, sir.'

'Is he in charge now?' asked Pasha Cavaner (11th Heavy Janissar). The command party had left the platform, and the honour guard was standing down and rolling in the banner.

'That is how I understand it,' said Joseph Baako Monday (18th Regiment, Nordafrik Resistance Army). 'I liked him. He asked me if I came from Setuway Hive, and I said no, Endayu, but I know Setuway, and he told me he had done early service there, at Setuway, and he knows Endayu well. I wanted to ask where he had lost his eyes, but I didn't dare.'

'He's the High Primary General,' said Oxana Pell (Hort Borograd K). 'The High Primary. They have sent us the supreme commander, no less.'

'He's an old man,' said Cavaner. 'An old human man. We've had the bright Astartes here to lead us, Lord Diaz, and Khan Shiban. I thought more Astartes were coming. That's what we need. Space Marines. Not some old man. What does he know?'

'He wouldn't have been sent if he wasn't good enough,' said Willem Kordy (33rd Pan-Pac Lift Mobile). 'Now, grab the other end of this, will you?'

The general's retinue followed the dank transit tunnels from the platform down into Monsalvant Gard, principal bastion of the port's southern line, a fortress built out of the skirts of the space port's superstructure.

Diaz fell in step with Cadwalder.

'Glad to have you here,' Diaz said. 'Were you sent to ward the general?'

'Safeguard him, yes,' Cadwalder replied.

'On the Praetorian's orders?'

'In a manner of speaking,' Cadwalder replied.

'I don't know what that means,' said Diaz, tersely.

'Likewise,' said Cadwalder, 'it's beyond me why a White Scar was running this zone and not a lord castellan.'

'Shiban had already pulled it together,' said Diaz. 'We're on a knife-edge, and he had it balanced. He's a fine warrior, Cad. A real leader.'

'I'm sure.'

'I'm telling you,' said Diaz, 'he's one of the Khagan's senior men. Ordu commander. Would have made Master of the Hunt–'

'*Would* have made?'

'Injury, I think. He has a good doctrine. "No backward step".'

'Very ordu. And simplistic.'

'It's Terran, in fact, as I understand,' said Diaz. 'And not a million leagues from our own philosophy.'

Cadwalder glanced at him.

'If this khan is a friend of yours,' he said, 'keep an eye on the command staff mood, particularly if Niborran's got to work with him. You see that man? Brohn? Colonel Brohn?'

'I know him.'

'See that look on his face, like someone's put a turd under his nose? Every time he looks at Shiban. He can't hide it. Niborran's doing a better job.'

'What are you saying?' asked Diaz.

'Niborran and Brohn were command staff, Grand Borealis.'

'Yes, of course. Niborran is High Primary, and Brohn is one of the best. That's why the Praetorian sent–'

'They were dismissed,' said Cadwalder. 'Summary expulsion.'

'Why?'

'Said the wrong thing to the Khan of Khans, and the Khan of Khans was not in the right mood. Vorst said he nearly took their heads off.'

'For what?' asked Diaz.

'It doesn't matter. Something or nothing. They were tired, he was tired. My point is, I don't think White Scars are their best friends.'

'Wait, if they were dismissed–' Diaz began.

Cadwalder stopped, and brought Diaz to a halt. The rest of the party moved on down the tunnel.

'They were done, strung out,' said Cadwalder. 'Bhab is chewing through senior commanders like… The burn-out rate is atrocious. The Khagan lost his temper, and they were out. They chose not to go back, though Dorn wanted them. They volunteered to return to the line, and this is what they got. They want to be soldiers again, and see active service. They want to hold a gun, not look at an augur screen.'

'Because *that's* so demanding,' said Diaz.

'It's different,' said Cadwalder. 'You haven't been in the

bastion for a good while. It's punishing. Overwhelming. Things… things are not going well for us, lord. I think… Killing the enemy face to face might actually be easier. More meaningful, certainly.'

'Are you telling me they're non-vi? Incompetent?'

'No, they're very competent,' said Cadwalder. 'Niborran especially. Not just by dint of his supreme rank. There's a fire in him, like he's gained twenty years. He's exactly the zone lead we want. But we're going to need to support him, our full support. Clear any extraneous problems out of his path, like–'

'Like Shiban Khan?'

Cadwalder nodded. 'Yes. It's not the White Scar's fault. But I doubt they'll take to him. We need Niborran at the top of his game, because this is going to be hell.'

'I thought it might be,' said Diaz.

'I'm telling you,' said Cadwalder, 'it definitely will be. To the glory of Him on Earth, trust me on this.'

'You know what they say about hell, Cad,' replied Diaz. He turned and set off after the others.

'What, lord?' asked Cadwalder.

'It's just a chainsword deep.'

Euphrati Keeler leaned back against the wall, exhaled a long sigh, and rubbed the bridge of her nose. Her brow furrowed.

Amon Tauromachian handed her a cup of water. 'We should finish for the day,' he said.

'No,' she sighed. 'One more.'

'You are tired,' he said.

'I won't sleep. One more.' She took a few sips from the cup, and handed it back. She straightened up, and turned to face the next cell door.

Amon hesitated. The air was cold. Nearby, rainwater pattered from the ceiling onto the friendless stone floor.

'Not this one,' he said.

'Alphabetical order,' she said. 'Systematic. He's next.'

'Not this one,' said Amon. 'Skip this one.'

Keeler looked at him.

'Well, now I'm just intrigued,' she said. 'Today I have spoken, in turn, to some of the most unpleasant individuals ever sired by the human race–'.

'I told you Sindermann's entire effort was misjudged,' he said.

'And I told you,' she snapped, 'if you let me out, I could do it better. But this is the hand you've dealt me. So, how much worse could the next one be? Amon? Custodian?'

She frowned, and took the dataslate from his hand. She read the next entry.

'Open it,' she said.

Amon gestured. The cell door rumbled open.

She stepped inside.

The prisoner was nothing to look at. A very small old man, his undernourished child-frame swamped by the dirty inmate overalls he'd been given. His forehead was broad, his eyes sharp. He reminded her of a small owl, or certainly some form of bird: perched on his cot, head tilted, eyes unblinking, everything about him small, fragile and entirely breakable.

'Hello,' he said.

'Basilio Fo,' she said, checking the slate. 'Secured captive fifteen years ago by the Sixty-Third Expeditionary Fleet, following the compliance of Velich Tarn. Interesting. And it says he was held in the Imperial Dungeon.'

'One of the transferees,' said Amon.

'The Dungeon was getting too full,' said Fo, 'or too empty. They didn't tell me which. I would imagine the former.'

'It says you were a biomechanical engineer,' said Keeler, checking the slate. 'A self-professed "worker of obscenity".'

'I wanted to put "artist",' said Fo, 'but apparently that wasn't an option on the form. Your culture has never really appreciated my work. Hardly surprising. Yours is a very conservative civilisation.'

'My culture?' asked Keeler.

'The Imperium of Man. That's what you call it, isn't it?'

Keeler looked back at the slate. 'There isn't much detail here. It looks redacted. It says he's a genius. By some abnormal measure, neurotypically. And it… Wait, that can't be right.'

'Can't it?' asked Fo sweetly.

'According to this, you're in excess of five thousand years old,' said Keeler. 'That must be a mistake, surely? Active on Terra before the fall of Old Night?'

Fo shrugged.

'What can I say?' he asked. 'I look after myself and exercise regularly.'

'That's nonsense,' said Keeler.

'Biomechanism and organic engineering were my areas of speciality,' said Fo. 'I learned very early on how to prolong my mortal fabric. Of course, for the past fifteen years, without access to my studio, I have been ageing naturally. It's miserable. I avoided it for so long.'

Keeler stared at him.

'Were you really born before Old Night?'

'Oh, that's not the question you've come to ask me, is it?' said Fo. He moistened his lips with the tip of his tiny bird-tongue and smiled. 'Is he here? Has he come now? These last few weeks, I've been hearing terrible sounds outside.'

'Who?' asked Keeler.

'When I met him,' said Fo, 'he called himself Lupercal.'

'You mean Horus?'

'That's the one.'

'You've met him?' she asked.

'He was the one who captured me,' said Fo. 'Have you met him? You have. Isn't he quite the most awful thing?'

He looked at Amon. His smile was gone.

'But then, they all are, aren't they?' he remarked.

'What question did you think I was going to ask you, Fo?' Keeler asked.

'Well, I presumed you had all finally come to your senses and decided to ask me for my expert advice.'

'About?'

Fo frowned. 'About how you might kill him,' he said.

'Kill Horus?'

'Well, you clearly want him dead, don't you?' asked Fo. 'It's plainly becoming quite an imperative. Survival, as I found out a long time ago, triggers the most basic, fundamental responses in an organic form. An individual, a species… It will do almost anything, evolve in almost any way it can, in order to stay alive. I called it the Existential Maturation Trigger.'

Fo sat back on his cot, and rested his head against the wet stone wall. He gazed up at the ceiling.

'I have a few suggestions,' he said. 'No guarantees, but they have a reasonable chance of working. I've had time to consider the problem, and formulate some recommendations.'

'Based on?' asked Keeler.

'Based on the fact,' Fo replied, 'that fifteen years ago I came very close to killing him myself.'

The six missiles had been travelling for two kilometres at one and a half times the speed of sound when they hit the convoy. All came from the west, and the impacts were virtually simultaneous.

They struck the hulls of the target vehicles broadside and to port. The tip of each projectile was a high-explosive shaped charge of volate-19 and compressed imotex, designed to create a narrow and ultra high-velocity particle stream. The super-plasticity created by these precursor charges bored through any hull armour and anti-rocket plating. The molybdenum liners around the precursors vaporised during contact detonation, allowing the much larger main charge of each weapon to penetrate each target vehicle nanoseconds later, via the puncture the precursor had created.

Two carriers and one of the escort Carnodons were wiped out instantly. A second Carnodon survived the initial strike, but caught fire. Unable to move or return fire, the vehicle was destroyed fourteen seconds later when the flames reached the main magazine.

A third Brontosan was hit at the wheel line. The blast lifted the entire bulk of the transporter, and flipped it on its side.

The sixth missile struck the upper deck of the carrier Hari Harr was riding in.

The impact was so sudden, so complete, it felt like something he was remembering from weeks before: a noise that was too loud to be heard; a pulse of monstrous concussion trapped and channelled by the vehicle's hull; a flash like the sun.

A vast ring of dirt slapped up around the carrier. The vehicle swayed, the side of it deforming inwards at first, then bursting out like a hatching egg. Seventy-nine per cent of the personnel on the upper deck were killed outright immediately.

Power failed. The carrier filled with dense smoke. The upper flooring bulged and collapsed, crushing men below. Many of them were already dead or dying in their seats, ruined by compression, burning gas or blast debris that had torn down through the decking into the lower compartment. Fire instantly engulfed the upper compartment. Those troopers still alive and conscious shrieked as they were consumed. The fire, a rolling wave, rushed down into the lower deck through the collapsed floor, and washed backwards. More men died before they could even rise. Others scrambled up, choking the aisles, and were engulfed or crushed by their own comrades.

Only those at the rear stood any kind of chance. Hull deformation had actually burst the access hatches open. Troopers in the last six or seven rows scrambled and fell out into the open. Several had clothes ablaze.

Olly Piers came out with his plas-caliver in one hand and Hari in the other. He dropped Hari within metres of the hatch, and fell to his knees. His moustache was singed. Hari found himself on the ground, his ears ringing. He was still clutching his dataslate as though he was reading it. There was a diagonal crack across the screen.

It was bright outside. The sky was a stained haze. The landscape was a wasteland of tan dirt, the dry ruins of some industrial zone. Dust as fine as sand rolled in across the wide road.

'Up, up, up!' Piers yelled.

Hari rose. Behind them, several vehicles were alight, spewing fat cones of smoke into the pale sky. He could hear the chatter of small-arms, the crump of the surviving Carnodons as they fired their main guns into the wasteland to the west. He could hear the moans of the injured, the screams of men trapped and incinerating.

The entire convoy had halted. They could see figures milling aimlessly around stopped or ruined vehicles, people too stunned to know what to do.

'Get rolling, get rolling!' Piers was yelling down the road. 'We're sitting bloody ducks, you shitting simpletons!'

Nothing seemed to happen. A tank fired again. Hari heard the thump, and saw the dust-kick. Then the Aurox munition train started to move, trying to draw up past the line of stricken transporters. They hadn't heard Piers, of course not, they were too far away. But someone had the same basic instinct for self-preservation.

The second volley of missiles found the munition train as
it was trying to pass. The flashes made Hari stumble back and
flinch. He saw huge fireballs lift from the road, an Aurox turning
over in midair. Then even bigger blasts came, as the munition
wagons cooked off, blasts that engulfed some of the stationary
carriers, and devoured the men out on the highway.

Piers turned, and ran up the highway, heading towards the
scrub waste to the right of the road in front of the convoy
position. He lugged his huge rifle. His gait was heavy and
ungainly.

'Where are you… Where are you going?' Hari yelled after
him. Piers kept running. Hari followed him. So did two dozen
or more of the troopers who had made it out of their carrier.

Hari suddenly realised he could see what the grenadier had
seen. It was so big, it was almost invisible: a vast, white cliff
some five kilometres north, veiled by the thick atmospheric
dust.

It was the port. It was the vast, beautiful superstructure
of the Eternity Wall space port, silent and massive like an
alpine range. They had come so close. They had come so close
without loss or incident and now, in sight of it, this.

They were running, piecemeal and with no order, out into
the scrub. Some soldiers had their weapons, some didn't. One
ran off in the wrong direction for no apparent reason. Piers
lumbered along at the head of the pack. He was fumbling
to load something into his trusty firearm as he ran, cursing
and spitting. Hari could hear the caliver whine as it charged
to power.

The port was further away than it looked. It didn't seem to
be getting any closer. They started to slow, out of breath, some
troopers stopping, heads down, hands braced on their knees,
panting. Hari looked behind him. The convoy was a quarter
of a kilometre back. A long, black curtain of smoke was lifting

from it, as though it were trying to mirror the white sweep of the port in negative.

It was so quiet. Scrub. Dust. The stir of wind. A few men gasping.

'Shit,' said Piers. He steadied his shako, and started to stride back the way they had come. 'Shit-cakes,' he added.

'What?' asked Hari.

Piers reached inside his heavy red coat and, with some effort, wrenched out an old service autopistol. He held it out to Hari without looking.

'What?' Hari repeated.

'Do you know how to shoot one, boy?' Piers asked.

'You know I don't!'

'Bloody take it anyway,' the grenadier snapped. 'You're about to learn.'

Hari found the gun in his hands. It was heavy, and it stank of oil. He stuffed the slate in his coat pocket, and tried to hold the weapon in some way that it wouldn't be pointing at him.

Piers turned to the others. He was settling the long mass of *Old Bess* against his shoulder.

'Get yourselves in a line!' he yelled out. 'A flaming line, right now!' His voice was a foghorn, though it had a ragged edge of fear. Some troopers stopped, bewildered. Most stepped forward, prepping whatever weapons they had.

'Who's got rank?' Piers hollered. 'Who's got a stripe?'

No one answered.

'Bloody me, then,' he growled. 'Come on, show some order then!'

'What's going on?' Hari asked.

Piers gave Hari the dirtiest look of contempt.

'We thought we'd stop for a picnic,' he said.

'No, I mean–'

The grenadier pointed. Hari saw.

Back on the highway, figures were moving around the burning vehicles. He could hear pings and cracks on the wind, like sticks being broken. Infantry. Ground troops, swarming the convoy from the west. There were hundreds of them. Black dots. Some were turning their way.

We've got a moment, Hari thought. It took us forever to run this far. They–

Some of the dots weren't dots any more. They were shapes, bounding across the scrub towards them, moving so fast Hari couldn't quite make sense of it.

They weren't human.

At first, at first he thought dogs. Big dogs. Attack dogs. Then he thought apes. Then grox, galloping. The creatures rushing them weren't any of those things.

They might, once, have been men. Some appalling process had swollen them, enlarged their torsos, put humps of muscle bulk across the tops of their spines, and dropped them back down the evolutionary ladder onto all fours. Olly Piers was the biggest man present, and each of these things was twice his size. Their faces… their open mouths… the smell of them…

'What are they?' Hari asked, very quietly. 'What are they? What are they? What–'

'I dunno,' muttered Piers. 'I don't care. But I'm thinking daemons.'

Hari made a sound that almost had a question mark on the end.

'Daemons, boy,' Piers repeated. 'Shit-arse, for-real daemons.' He spat, and put the caliver up to his cheek, sighting. He started to mutter, 'Mythrus, war-lady, you useless bitch, wherever you are, send your old soldier some grace now, for shit's sake, I'm begging you…'

The things were closing.

'There's no…' said Hari, trying to sound as clear and certain as he could, as if that would clear everything up. 'There's no such thing as daemons.'

'Oh, we're all right then,' said the grenadier.

He snuggled into his aim.

'Ten metres!' he yelled.

'We're bloody dead, Olly!' someone shouted.

'You bloody will be if I hear you say that again!' the grenadier roared. 'Ten metres! Final offer! Going once, going twice...'

The things came up to them, bounding, leaping, eager, their jaws open to bite and snap. The ragged line of troopers began to shoot. The rippling barrage made Hari jump.

The grenadier's first shot was a raking beam of blue-hot light.

It burst the frontrunner, splitting it apart from front to back and dropping it in the dust, steaming, bloody bones open to the sunlight. To the big grenadier's left, an Excertus squadder with an old autocannon slew a second, ripping it into chunks of meat with a burst of fire. Lasrifles and hard-round guns cracked and popped.

Old Bess whined back to power, and Piers fired again, knocking another beast off its feet. The beam left a smoking hole the size of a dinner plate clean through its body. The squadder's autocannon kept blurting, cones of flash dancing around her muzzle, spent casings flying out in a jingling spray. A militia man with a lasrifle scored a kill. It had taken him four hits to do enough damage to stop his target in its tracks.

The grenadier's caliver whined back up to power. Slower this time, straining.

'Come on, Bessie me girl, come on,' Piers crooned, taking sight. 'Upland Tercio, hooo!' he yelled above the volleying gunfire.

He fired a third time. The caliver let off a less emphatic beam. It clipped a beast, and knocked it flat, but it writhed in the dust and got up again, blood bubbling from a gouge in its shoulder.

'P-piers…' Hari mumbled.

The caliver whined, struggling to cycle.

'Piers!'

The wounded beast lunged. Piers fired again. Just a bolt, a clumsy spit of light, but the thing was almost on them, and it was enough. It collapsed within metres of his feet.

There were two more right behind it.

The grenadier changed grip. He tucked the caliver's butt under his right armpit, and reached forward for the under-barrel grip. The weapon was whining again, but it sounded feeble and exhausted, trying the best it could to reheat.

'Come on, then!' Piers roared at the things bearing down on them.

He squeezed the forward grip. The under-barrel tube coughed out a grenade with a hollow thump. The small, heavy projectile flew like a piece of well-aimed fruit, struck one of the incoming beasts head-on, and disintegrated it in a cloud of flame.

Piers pumped the under-barrel slide, and thumped off another grenade shell. It blew the second dog off its feet, and sent it cartwheeling.

He pumped again.

But the dogs, the beasts, were now in among them. The squadder with the autocannon was carried over. She shrieked, trying to fight her killer off, but it savaged her relentlessly, until she stopped making any sounds. Two beasts caught the militia man, and fought over his corpse, pulling it apart. Four more troopers were slammed off their feet: crunching impacts, soldiers brought down in tangles of limbs and snapping bones. Other men broke the line, and tried to run. Most didn't get far.

One beast came for Hari. He saw its eyes, wild and inhuman, its mouth swinging open, its belly as it launched into its leap.

A beam of blue light snatched sideways, and sent it tumbling. *Old Bess* had finally recharged.

'Piers!' Hari yelled.

The grenadier turned. The dog that had killed the squadder was coming at him from the left, its face plastered with gore. He had no charge developed. Piers thumped a grenade into its chest point-blank. The blast killed it, but the air-smack knocked the grenadier off his feet too. He got back up on his knees, dazed, ungainly, coat twisted, shako off. Another dog was running at him. A frantic pump of the mechanism. A hollow pop. The grenade demolished it. Yet another came in, from the left again. Piers swivelled, still on his knees.

'Suck it, you ugly ball-bag!' he said, and destroyed it with his last grenade.

Piers looked up at Hari.

'Sorry, boy,' he said.

A shadow slid across them both.

Something thunderous mowed the ground around them. It felt as though multiple lightning strikes were earthing all at once. Hari and Piers sprawled together, arms tight around each other. It wasn't entirely clear who had grabbed whom, or who had pulled whom flat.

The thunder continued. Huge sprays of topsoil and dust flew up, like giant stalks of corn, stippling the ground around them. The earth under them quivered, vibrating like the skin of a drum. Beasts jerked and shredded, caught in the ferocious kinetic downpour. The air choked with yellow dust and sheets of drifting red mist.

Hugging Piers tight, Hari looked up, almost rigid with shock. He wiped a slick of blood and dust off his face with one splayed hand.

There was an aircraft hanging almost directly over them, hovering no more than thirty metres up. It was just a dark shape against the sky. He could feel the pummel of its down-wash. Weapon pods on its underside were howling out a hail of suppression fire. The dogs, the beasts, were being slaughtered and driven back from the small knot of cowering soldiers who still remained. The ground was being systemat-ically cleared around them.

But a second and larger wave of beasts was already bounding in, a surging tide of what the grenadier had called 'daemons'. A hundred or more, drawn by the scent of blood, flooding in from the ravaged convoy to feed.

The aircraft swung away, and dropped lower to face them. Its pods chewed at the approaching tide, the rotary canons buzzing like rapid metal hammers, one long blurt of sound rather than individual shots. The gun-pods' snouts were spin-ning crowns of flame.

The entire front-end of the slate-grey machine opened. It sort of hinged and unfurled at the same time, plates of metal spreading, overlapping and sliding over each other.

Hari saw something golden catch the light.

Prefect Tsutomu exits the Talion. He is more use on the ground. I don't know if there's anyone left to save. We have arrived too late. This relief convoy is miserably annihilated. But these things must die. They are the first Neverborn I have seen inside the Palace zone.

They are not full-blown creatures of the warp. They are human shells, soldiers of the traitor host, I believe, now a different kind of host. Mindless vessels for Neverborn spirits that have infested their flesh and remade their form. I have seen such things before in the depths of the webway, but not here, in the realspace of the Throneworld's heart. The Custo-dians named them 'witch-dogs', but I always felt that was insulting to witches.

I maintain suppressive fire from the helm. The prefect clears ten metres from the front hatch, and hits the ground running. He accelerates into a blur. He fires bolts from his poleaxe as he sprints, crippling and killing, cracking their line to make an opening. Then he is among them, and his castellan axe starts swinging.

The form is superb. He has been at this duty for a long age, and has mastered the very specific skills a castellan axe requires. Elegant but brutal, a fine balance of transhuman strength, constant momentum and subtle balance. It is like a dance, a whirling ballet that, once begun, cannot be halted. Unlike a sword, with which one might strike, break, re-address and strike again, axe-work must flow, stroke into stroke, or momentum will be lost and the axe become unwieldy, even for Tsutomu. In combat, a castellan axe must be kept in motion. It is a narrative of violence, not a dialogue.

Tsutomu knows this. Blade-stroke becomes blade-stroke becomes blade-stroke. The butt of the haft is a weapon too, breaking skulls on the through-swings and returns.

But there are many of them. From my seat, I see him: a lone figure of gold, reaping amid a broad field of dark forms. I will intercede. This work is why I came here. I set the lift systems to autonomous-hold, the gun-cogitators to auto-selective. I leave the gunship to hover and kill on its own.

I move to the open hatch. I draw *Veracity*, though I won't need her.

It is not far to jump.

'What is that?' Hari whispered.

'A Custodian, boy,' Piers said. He started to laugh. 'A Talon of the Emperor Himself! Balls of glory, look at him kill!'

The grenadier let Hari go, and got to his knees. He began to clap and cheer, as though it was a performance just for him.

The Custodian was a smudge of moving gold, fogged in a billowing cloud of blood. The bodies of beasts, none of them intact, littered the dust around him. He was leaving a trail of them.

But Hari hadn't meant the Custodian. He had meant the chill, the sudden cold. A shadow that had just passed over them, darker than the shade the aircraft had cast when it hovered over their heads.

Something else was here, something else–

'Oh shit,' murmured the grenadier. He got to his feet, pulling on his dusty shako. He was staring, but at what, Hari couldn't see.

The dogs, the beasts… stopped. They froze. A few yelped and yapped. They pawed backwards, heads low, whimpering, then turned and fled, every one of them that was still alive, or what might be termed alive. They raced away in, as it seemed to Hari, sudden and abject terror. They ran back the way they had come, in their hundreds, leaving their abominable dead behind.

The Custodian stopped swinging. He came to rest, a golden blur becoming a gilded giant. He lowered the immense axe, and stood, watching the enemy retreat.

'She saved us,' Piers murmured.

'*Old Bess?*' asked Hari.

'What, boy?'

Piers walked forward. Hari stumbled after him. Everything tasted of dust and blood. The Custodian turned.

'Are you alive?' asked the Custodian. His voice was like a lead weight wrapped in silk. 'How many of you are alive? Trooper, make an account.'

'In His name, I thank you!' Piers stammered. He had taken off his shako, and was clutching it to his chest. 'All these years, I have left little offerings, all I could spare, so forgive me, but just what I had, little offerings to ask for your intercession…'

Hari came up behind the grenadier. Piers wasn't speaking to the giant in gold. He wasn't even looking at him. He was grinning inanely at the empty air to the Custodian's left, rambling, tears in his eyes.

The Custodian turned his gleaming visor towards Hari.

'Was this man injured?' he asked, clipped. 'Has he taken a blow to the head?'

'I have no idea of his life story, lord,' said Hari, 'but there's every chance.'

'Your intercession, all I asked,' Piers went on. 'I'll admit, I have cursed you, from time to time, when it never came, so I hope you'll excuse that, but you were saving it for now, saving it for this moment, weren't you? Saving it all up for the day I needed to be delivered from daemons!'

'Piers,' said Hari. He put a hand on the grenadier's arm. 'Piers. The lord Custodian is trying to talk to you.'

'Well, he can see I'm busy,' Piers snapped. 'I must abase myself before anything else.' He looked at the space beside the Custodian. 'Should I? Is that required? Should I abase myself?'

'To whom?' asked Hari.

'I wasn't talking to you, boy!' Piers snapped. 'I was talking to her!'

'To—?'

'To Mythrus, you flaming idiot! Show some manners, boy!'

The Custodian looked to his left. 'Agreed, it is unusual,' he said, as if in answer to something.

The air around them was so cold. Hari felt sick. He squinted, and realised there was something there after all, like a broken sliver of dirty glass standing upright in the settling dust, almost invisible.

A greasy smear of light. The impression, for a brief second, of hands moving, forming quick shapes.

Piers had dropped to his knees.

'Yes,' said the Custodian. 'It would appear he can see you.'

At that moment, a very long way away, half a world, a man arrived at his destination. It was his last stop along the way before journey's end.

It was the right time, and the right place, within a reasonable margin of error: the deep and stubborn heart of the PanAfrik north-west, baking in the heat, a great erg, a sandsea. Just a few miles out; he still measured things in miles. Perhaps a few days shy. A few miles, a few days. That was an impressive degree of accuracy, given the scale with which he was obliged to work. All of times, and all of spaces, the entire cosmic map, and he had nailed it to within a few days and a few miles.

At least, he hoped he had this time.

He had an appointment to keep. A meeting. He wasn't looking forward to it at all. It was going to be awkward. Too many big favours to ask from people who didn't like him. Too many big debts to call in, and apologies to make. A lot of apologies, probably. He had pissed people off over the years. A lot of people. A lot of years.

He was going to have to work hard, appeal to natures much better than his own.

He stood for a moment. Soft, red sand lay all around him, quartz dusted with ferric oxide. The rolling dunes of the erg lay in the *uruq* manner, the long ridges flowing with the sculpting wind, like frozen breakers. Between these great banks of sand lay avenues, the *shuquq*, hollows between the dunes bedded with soft gypsum and *seeq*. There was a rocky rim of flat, black hills to the west. The sun beat down from a sky so cloudless, its blue had gone dark and hard with heat. He was sweating already. He wasn't dressed for this.

He sighed.

'Right, okay,' said John Grammaticus to himself, and started to walk along the nearest shuquq into the west.

PART TWO

I AM THE FORTRESS NOW

ONE

The twenty-second of Quintus
Lateral cunning
Pons Solar

Yzar Chroniates of the Third Grand Battalion of the Iron Warriors, lord captain of the Second Armoured Century, came over the splintered rampart, assured his name and deeds had just become immortal, and that he would be remembered upon the honour lists as the first of Great Lupercal's host to breach the fourth circuit wall of Gorgon Bar. Massing over a tonne of augmented, artificed Cataphractii plate, he was the first legionary to crack the inner ring of the gate defences that had held them at bay, a bellow of rage and triumph on his lips, servo-steered flamer systems mounted on the colossal shelf of his shoulders, framed by spikes – huge scaling hooks that had brought him up the sheer stone cliff of the wall – curving like an eagle's talons from his forearms and shins, power claw spreading to strike, bolter already firing, first among conquerors.

And the blade came the other way to meet him.

Encarmine bit through etched plasteel. Through ceramite. Through refolded harness padding. Overlaid power systems severed and shorted in clouds of flying sparks. Coolant ducts ruptured. The blade's course continued, its edge slicing reinforced undersuit, segmented liner, yielding flesh, and then the solid skeletal shell of the carapace, the nested transhuman organs, the spinal cord.

Chroniates teetered on the lip of the wall, his bolter firing blindly, wildly. His thorax seemed to slump slightly into his abdomen, as though his immense panoply of plate was a rock face succumbing to a landslip.

The Brightest One wrenched *Encarmine* free.

Chroniates toppled backwards. As he fell, his torso hinged open, like yawning jaws, like some toymaker's novelty, power systems exploding as cabling tore. He plunged down the sheer drop, his dismantled bulk smashing others of his kind off the stone facing, their scaling hooks torn free: Tyranthikos and Stor-Bezashk specialists cast down from the height into the smoke below. His moment of immortality had been less than a second long.

Sanguinius did not watch his kill's long plunge. He was turning to meet the next enemy, *Encarmine* a whistling band of silver, the flicker of a sunlight ray from which armoured heads tumbled and limbs parted.

Everything was noise and motion. Blurred noise, fogged motion. The drench of blood, the shearing of metal, smoke in every seam and every pore. Feral war engulfed the Bar, accelerated to transhuman proportions, a battle of the ancient days magnified in scale, amplified in force and performed at inhuman speed. Industrial death, with no pause, no scant second of remission, no time for reflection on glory, no room for myth or even the merest kindling of myth. An eight-kilometre line of angled high wall, sheer as a mountain, covered in a carpet of bodies like a plague of gleaming beetles, like a mat of moss and trailing vine folded across a great stream-thwart rock, ranks of defenders above, writhing against the press of the scaling creeper-tides of traitor host ascending against them, like termites massing to overtop a rival mound.

Smogged air, bruised black, underlit and jarred by explosive flashes of crippling brilliance, the fire-spears of detonations lancing out in sunbursts, eating the wall, shredding all in their radii with hypersonic shrapnel, and the jagged fragments of those already obliterated and instantaneously perished. Chains of fire from defending flamers. Jetting infernos hosing from attacking units. Stitching interference patterns of tracer and bolt-rounds. Enemy forces, some advancing under shield or covered by plated sows. Falling bodies, alive and dead. Out-flung body parts, still armour-clad. The howl of focused and accelerated plasma. The shriek of chainblades. The eerie local distortion and fume of melta fields, auras of sub-atomic agitation. Red mist. Dirt. Ouslite chips flying from the teeth of scaling hooks as they dug for purchase.

Armoured belfries disgorging men onto walls. Escalade ladders slamming into parapet lines, or being poled back past the apogee, every figure clinging on and falling as the ladder toppled. Tower guns and wall batteries firing at the lowest declination, barrels glowing with waste-heat, shells jamming in swollen breeches. The drizzling chime of autoloaders emptying hoppers, raining casings in jingling blizzards that fell in metal drifts, and covered parapet steps like spills of mining slag, obscuring all definition of structure.

Lives leaking out. Slow bleeds. Massive and sudden blood losses. Grim mutilations of extraordinary scope that would surprise the most inventive anatomists. Guns too hot to hold or use. Blades broken and still swinging, jagged edges acting surrogate for the lost fine teeth of hallmark weapons. Screams of death, of pain, of hatred, of loss, of hope, of disappointment, of duty. Last breaths expended in long, slow, shuddering exhalations or brief and violent bursts. Final moments spluttering in bubbles of blood between gasped lips, final words whispered to no one, final hopes dashed into darkness. Noise too loud to hear, noise that could only be felt, with no meaning in it.

Bloodstained Blood Angels, vanguard of the line, their beauty revealed as it had always truly been: as cruel and merciless horror, their noble legend put aside so they could kill unashamed, the way their genefather had made them to kill. No false myth of noble angels, that guise gone so that they, though unchanged in aspect, had become the truest, oldest meaning of terrible. A coin reversed. A truth that had been obvious all along, but was now unmasked, unslipped. Their true selves, beings of awe, when awe is a weapon of itself.

Bloodied Imperial Fists, backbone of the defence, yellow panoplies so badged and washed with gore they could be mistaken for their Blood Angels brethren, taking not one step backwards, nor one forward, for there was nothing before them but the brink of hell. Shields tattered, lances shattered, swords cracked to jagged stubs clenched in Imperial fists. Fafnir Rann, plate dappled with blood, red spots on yellow, like some illuminator's garish notion of a heraldic beast, rampant upon a wall of bodies atop a wall of stone, paired axes hacking like pistons into faces, chests and pauldrons, hooking torn visors into the haze on the backswing. Rann's breaker-shield had been destroyed in the first fury of the assault, and he had cast it aside, unclasping his war-axe's twin to wield a cleaver in each hand.

Blow answering blow. The hammer of war, a million individual impacts falling so fast they became one noise that shivered and buckled the air. Unbreakable materials breaking. Unstoppable strengths being stopped. A devolution of war: blades when ammunition was spent, empty guns when blades were broken, mailed fists when blade stubs were lost, bare fists when gauntlets were shredded.

And up from the darkness, the Iron Warriors, the grey-black flood of a dam that had burst in hell, a deluge of siege-breaker armour and fury that would not stop or ebb until the wall and the bastion was washed away and reduced to fused and smoking pegs of rock, and the path to the Sanctum was opened.

Open all the way to the Lion's Gate, and the Palatine under-belly, and the last, unassaulted wall of Eternity.

It was the morning of the twenty-second of Quintus. In the last three hours, the Bar's outermost lines had fallen. After a day of long-range shelling, which had wounded even the central bastion, the mass had come, and the outworks and first two circuit walls had been lost, and then the third wall too, in catastrophically quick succession. The traitor tide had rushed in, higher than any forecast, sundering stone, drown-ing that which had been safe and close-held. Imperial Fists had died, overwhelmed as they grimly kept their place. Blood Angels had died, overtaken as they rushed to regroup and stem the flow. The hosts of the Army, unbearably mortal, had died in between the two, crushed to paste and bonemeal and blood-ooze by the iron avalanche.

The fourth circuit wall had to be the flood break. The fourth circuit wall, so impossibly quickly, had become the last line that Sanguinius was prepared to draw. 'No further'. It had not been an order, it had been a law: an Angelic commandment that allowed for no failure.

An hour of inarticulate horror followed that collision of might. The fourth circuit wall, Gorgon Bar, the twenty-second of Quintus. In other histories of other wars, it would have been a defining moment, a legendary clash. But in this War of Wars, it was just a sortie, a footnote fast forgotten in a cata-logue of equal furies.

There was no grace to it, no order, despite the stoic discipline of the Imperial Fists, the drilled resolution of the Iron Warriors, the elegant execution of the Blood Angels. All that dissolved in moments into blind murder. It was the most intense, most concentrated, most disordered battle of the Terran Siege thus far, and would remain so until the ghastly, inchoate slaughter of the final days.

Fisk Halen turned it in the forty-eighth minute of the assault. With Terminator squads at his side, and a deluge of support fire from Auxilia units along the bastion ledge, he drove into Katillon guntower and its adjacent wall top, and compressed the southern hem of the enemy influx with such severity that Iron Warriors tumbled from the wall like spilled beads, both down the scarred face they had scaled and off the inner range into the yards below, where Army halberdiers and skitarii hoplites mobbed and butchered any that the fall had not killed.

Sanguinius, Lord of Baal, his golden hair stained red and dripping, saw the break. He could not reach it, locked as he was in cataphract onslaught, but Rann could, and Furio could, and Bel Sepatus of the Keruvim, and those he directed with a voice that pierced the storm. Rann's tattered wallguard was the first to reach the crux, and they bore into the tide as if they had no other desire than to meet Halen face to face and clasp his hand.

And there it teetered, on the brink of loss and collapse, for seconds as dense and heavy as centuries. Then Sepatus and his Paladins, their tri-faced emblems obscured by gore, joined Rann's desperate extension, and bolstered it with their Cataphractii might. In the shadow of Katillon guntower, a burning stump of stone into which shells kept smashing, Imperial Fists and Blood Angels pincered and broke the enemy's back.

The traitor tide snapped. So many bodies, most of them still living, cascaded from the wall where there was no longer any space for them to exist. They became involuntary weapons, their plummeting armoured forms striking those behind and below, taking them with them, disintegrating ladder frames and scaling chutes, tearing down the rising breach-scaffolds and the belfries of the warsmith engineers. Legionaries rained, a black hail of bodies. Rann, his faceplate torn in half, threw three of them personally, grabbing them as they tried to counter and turn, and casting them bodily off the parapet.

The rest broke, their formation damaged beyond recovery. Like a sea going out, they rolled backwards in retreat, and the mangled third circuit wall of Gorgon Bar became the Iron Warriors' new fortification and investment of attack.

Quiet fell, smoke-muffled, somehow more oppressive than the noise that had preceded it. Gorgon Bar, its lines of resistance cut back to one last circuit, was disfigured, weeping smoke, sheeting flames, walls deformed by onslaught pressure, towers bent and gnawed away, as though the entire bastion line had contorted in a rictus of pain and death. A cinder pall, eight kilometres long, hung across the Bar, a smoke ridge visible from the turrets of Marmax, a funeral banner of annihilation barely averted.

Sanguinius bowed his head. His vision, unbidden, fled from the stilled carnage. It became elsewhere, else-*one*. It touched an anger still to come.

'Not now,' he whispered, but his prescience took no orders, not even from him. It was wilful and disturbing, and came when it chose. For a moment, his mind conjoined with that of one of his brothers, and showed him…

A future. An unbridled wrath. A battle-slaughter that would make the last hour he had endured seem tame. He did not want to look at it. He did not want to see with a traitor's eyes, feel a lost brother's infernal torment, taste a killing hatred so intoxicating.

But he wept in pity, for slayers and slain to come, and could not look away.

The visions had stalked him his whole life, sporadic and infrequent, but they had started to come more often in these last days. He never really spoke of them to others, not out of shame or fear of suspicion, but more because there was never an exactitude to them. It wasn't a talent, nor could he harness it to make it an art. He had never tried. He didn't divulge it, because it wasn't something that could be turned into a reliable tool of prognostication.

It was just a thing that happened to him.

He walked from the broken lip of the wall, too tired to fly, though he knew the sight of him soaring would lift the concussed spirits of the defenders. Too tired, too unsteady: the fleeting vision was already going, but the aftertaste of anger made him tremble, enflaming the autonomic responses kindled by the battle.

He knew what it was. At least, he had always believed he knew. They had always said he was like his father, more like his father than any other. He shared the numinous qualities of his genesire. He was no high psyker, no magician, no warlock of the warp, but the vestige was there, an inherited trait like eye colour or handedness. It was his talent, or perhaps a slow curse. From time to time, the future would glance his way, and he would lock eyes with it briefly. Since the start of the siege, since the grim vision he had seen during the turmoil of the Ruinstorm, in fact, Sanguinius' escalating visions had become very particular, very *specific*. Each vision showed him the future through the eyes of one of his brothers.

The specific intimacy his visions brought to him chilled him. He would glimpse something the way one of his brothers was going to see it: a prescience linked to kinship, to blood.

And there was blood at Gorgon Bar. Too much of it. It pooled on the parapet walks and anointed the broken crenellations. Blood of the Legiones Astartes gene-line, which traced its direct heredity through him and his brothers to the Father of All. Perhaps that, Sanguinius thought, was the raw truth of it. Perhaps that explained why his unwelcome visions had come more often since the start of the siege. The blood of his familial line, spilled in unprecedented quantities, in such a small space on one world, the birth-world no less, spilled in such concentration as to be an offering, a sacrificial libation that enflamed and amplified his latent gift. The shamans of old had spilled blood to coax secrets from the future. They had sacrificed their own kind.

'My lord?'

Bel Sepatus approached, with Khoradal Furio and Emhon Lux. There was blood on them too, coating their angelic plate. The currency of future exchange. Sanguinius' visions were fading, mere aftershocks, but this blood seemed to stir them again. In quick succession, Sanguinius blinked away flash-visions: an elemental end-storm beheld by Jaghatai's eyes, cyclonic force dumping rain and unimaginable lightning on the earth; a tower or wall collapsing, witnessed by Rogal, carrying him with it; a great chart of the Imperial Palace, laid out with its edges weighed down by bolter shells.

That last, the clearest, the longest-lasting, was a glimpse through Perturabo's gaze. Sanguinius felt the unpleasant prickle of sharing that place, of inhabiting the Lord of Iron's best-protected fortress, a recondite bastion of the mind where none wanted to be, not even, so it seemed, Perturabo himself.

It made sense that this should be the vision that lingered.

It was the blood of Perturabo's family branch that dripped from the warriors who faced him.

'My lord?' Bel Sepatus said again.

'Secure the Bar,' Sanguinius said. They hesitated, expecting more. He noticed their faces, their quizzical beauty. His words had been feeble. It was hard to summon words up past the pulses of sight. *Shell cases on a chart...*

He remembered himself, and reached out, clasping the side of Sepatus' head.

'You did me great service, Bel,' he said. 'A feat of arms. No one lacked. Not our crimson host, nor our brothers of the Seventh.'

'What troubles you, lord?' asked Khoradal. Sanguinius realised he had stumbled on the word 'brothers'.

'I fear, Khoradal,' he said, 'that before this is over, too many will witness the true terror of us.'

A half-lie, but sufficient. Khoradal Furio nodded.

Shell cases on a chart. A hand moves one...

'Secure the Bar,' Sanguinius said. 'Engineers, sappers, the magi of the Forge. Fourth circuit is our line now. We hold what we have.'

'There may not be time enough for full securement,' said Emhon Lux. 'They will come again–'

'They will.'

'Too soon for–'

Shell cases. Moved across the chart to the spot marked Gorgon Bar. This is the future.

'We have until tomorrow,' said Sanguinius.

'Surely they will seek to–'

'They will not come again until tomorrow,' said Sanguinius.

'You say that as if you know,' said Sepatus.

'Then treat it as if I do, Bel,' said Sanguinius. 'They have wounded us sorely, broken us hard, but we have shattered their momentum. They are in recoil. They are stunned. They did not close the action. We have until tomorrow. We have time for modest securement at least.'

All three nodded.

'Get to your work,' Sanguinius said. 'Convey my instruction. And commend me to Fafnir and worthy Captain Halen.'

'Where will you be?' asked Sepatus.

Sanguinius was already walking away.

He needed to clear his mind. The visions were not just more frequent, they were closer. No longer fragments from months or years to come, they were glimpses that were mere days away, hours, minutes.

How long, he wondered, before they simply became glimpses of the now?

During the Ruinstorm, Sanguinius had seen a vision of his own death, at the hands of Horus. That was a future he intended to deny, but how many others could he prevent coming true? He needed to see them clearly, understand them so he could stop them from happening.

The flashes were fading, the chart and the shell cases dissolving. A sense of Perturabo's iron will lingered. What strength he possessed! What control! Willpower ground to a sharp edge, a mind that had emerged from the shadow of some black sun, no longer an organ of the flesh but a cold and aimed weapon.

From his vantage – it was impossible to tell where, for the vision had been very close in focus – but from his vantage, Perturabo had been directing his warsmiths closely. As the outworks and ring circuit of Gorgon Bar had fallen, and fast victory had become a fair promise, the Lord of Iron's heart rate had barely lifted. He had not succumbed to hope. He had maintained his cool, logistical oversight. And when Fisk Halen, and bold Fafnir, and the valiant Bel, had turned the tide on that instant, Perturabo had not despaired. Sanguinius felt that clearly. Perturabo had not despaired or exploded in thwarted rage. He had taken it in his stride, immediately adjusting, amending, preparing for the counter. That was his brilliance: the calculus of siege, the dogged, relentless warfare of attrition; allowing no highs, no lows, just constant, grinding pursuit of the goal. Today was no dismal loss for him. It was just a step, a small component of a grander mechanism.

That's why Perturabo, Lord of Iron, so alarmed Sanguinius, perhaps more than any other of his turned brothers. His relentless prosecution. In a siege... in this, *the* siege... It made him the most dangerous of all. Sanguinius felt he would rather face the Lupercal, close, hand to hand, than Perturabo at a distance. When the time came, facing Horus, in whatever situation, would be a monumental deed: to face down that once-beloved brother, first in majesty, and thwart him, him who they had all always thought un-thwartable.

To contradict and overturn the vision of his own doom.

But Perturabo...

The visions were all but gone, just flash-echoes. As he crossed to the main bastion, moving further from the spilled blood with each step, they receded. Perturabo was why Sanguinius was glad to have Rogal stand at his side. In this manner of warfare, only Rogal, dear Rogal, stood any chance of matching the Lord of Iron like-for-like.

Is that how it must play out? Rogal games Perturabo into check and mate, so that the task of fronting Horus falls to me? Perhaps it must. Like for like. If any must face the Lupercal with even a modest hope of prevailing, then it must likely be me, even though I have been shown that I must fail.

He stopped, two-thirds of the way across the bridge that joined the fourth circuit with the bastion proper. He looked up at the punctured towers above, draped in smoke. That other flash, of Rogal falling with a tower. How far off was that? How literal a vision? The glimpse of Jaghatai, lit by lightning, had been shockingly real, a moment of crystal definition. But the sight-blink of Rogal, like so many other visions he had suffered in his life, had been more abstract, as though symbolic, metaphoric – like the styled meaning of tarot cards turned up. Death, but not literal death. A man hanging, but not literally hanged. A tower struck, but not literal lightning.

Sanguinius dearly wanted counsel. If his visions had any real value, if they were anything more than a curious quirk of inheritance, he wanted to know. To understand. If he could learn to use them, even belatedly, now was the time. He wanted to confide in his father, or if his father was occupied, as his father so often was, then the Sigillite at least. The old man knew of numinous things too, and surely he had the advantage of familial detachment. Malcador could help him.

But Sanguinius knew he didn't have the luxury of leaving the line. Gorgon Bar was his place, and had to be held. It had to be, and tomorrow was too close, and it would not stand without him. Yet if they were to lose Rogal...

He closed his eyes. He breathed deeply. Sooty wind from the canyons of the circuit walls shivered the feathers of his pinions. He tried to focus on the scraps of the fading visions, attempting to pull them back. The one of Perturabo, the chart, the shell cases, a departing ghost, almost just a memory. Bring that back. See that again. See better. See more.

There.

The smoking iron of willpower. The texture of the old paper chart. The weight of the bolter shells. A smell of dust and smoke. Sanguinius was briefly invested in a body that was heavier and slower than his own, a body too dense to soar and fly, a body as heavy as a neutron star, but flimsy compared to the concentrated mass of the unswerving mind within it. Perturabo's mind was a weapon. It was all weapons at once. It was fast becoming *the* weapon, the apex of obliteration.

The touch of it made Sanguinius shiver. The cold of it, the absolute zero of a negative star. But he forced himself to keep looking. He needed to *see*–

Shell cases placed at Gorgon Bar, at Colossi Gate. At other points too, but he couldn't resolve them. The names on the chart were hard to read. His hand, my hand, taking up another shell case. It seems hot to the touch, as if just fired, but it is fresh. What is that heat? Ambition. Yes, ambition and desire. And it has another flavour, the touch of another upon it. The print of someone who is no longer present, but was there recently, someone who picked up that shell and handed it to the Lord of Iron and, in doing so, invested it with terrible meaning and significance.

The shell turns in iron fingers, thoughtful. At his side, in the smoke that drifted across the bridge span, Sanguinius' fingers turned and rippled, unconsciously miming the action.

That trace. The scent upon it. The imprint of someone…

Abaddon.

Lupercal's first and chosen, the finest and brightest of all the First Captains, once a credit to all Legions and a model of warriorship. *He* gave it to Perturabo. *He* gave it its meaning.

The iron hand starts to move, thoughtful, considering a placement, as a master gauges his next play in regicide. It reaches over to set it down, to set it down upon the chart. Where? Where? *What is the move? Where will you put it?*

Sanguinius shivered. The vision was already fleeting again, sliding into nothing. He couldn't hold it. His will could not match the iron ingot of Perturabo's will, or the whim of whatever numinous cloud of knowing steered the visions to him.

'Just let me see it,' he whispered.

The hand, the shell, move. Reaching out–

Gone.

Sanguinius opened his eyes. So close. He'd almost controlled it. But the battlements were behind him now, and the ritual potency of the blood drenching them was–

He reached up, hand shaking, and smeared drying blood from the breast of his plate. He squeezed the matted strands of his hair until drops ran across his palm. Gene blood. Kin blood. The blood of Perturabo's branch. If there was power in it...

He put his hand to his mouth and tasted it.

The chart, for a second, very clear. The hand, the shell, going down–

Then fire. Raging fire. Pain beyond any bearable threshold. The chart and the shell and the weight of Perturabo were swept away in an instant, eclipsed by agony. The *first* vision again, the one that had originally come, unbidden, as the day's battle ended. Rage beyond measure. The eyes of another.

Not this. I don't want to see this. I want to see–

The vision could not be reasoned with. It could not be commanded. Sanguinius tasted blood in his mouth. He saw flames, an inferno, spitting fat, burning human long bones like logs. Pitiful corpses stacked up like split firewood. Dead machines and fractured walls. Stacks of skulls, grinning at their own doom.

He knew that none of it was enough, nor would ever be enough.

A sky bridge, like the one he stood on, but greater, more massive, and broken. A gateway plinth, its proud stone lion gone except for the stumps of paws. Rubble. A plaque on the plinth, cracked. Inscribed there, etched into heat-brittled stone, the name of the place.

Pons Solar.

Then the agony increased, more than any pain should be allowed to be, more than any frame, mortal or immortal, could bear to contain. A pain that begot pain. A pain that wanted to be shared with all others.

Sanguinius knew whose eyes he saw through. It wasn't the vision he had chosen to see, but it was the brightest, and it dispelled all others.

He fell to his knees in the middle span of the bridge at Gorgon Bar, and screamed out a pain that was his own, and a rage that did not belong to him.

Angron. It was Angron's.

In the south of the Sanctum Imperialis, the transport rolled to a halt and they got out, pulling up their hoods against the heavy precipitation of sub-void atmospherics.

Around them lay empty streets, lined with proud mansions and noble halls, all untouched by the war except they were shuttered and boarded. The district had been cleared recently, whole streets in the lee of the massive wall vacated.

'Where are we?' asked Therajomas, his young face pinched and puzzled.

'The Saturnine Quarter,' Sindermann replied.

He had reported to Bhab, as per instructions, and a transport had been provided without explanation. Then followed a long drive through the cowering citadel, slowed at times by columns of blank-eyed refugees. Then quieter streets, then empty ones.

Sindermann glanced around, rain in his face. The transport had already turned and departed. To the east, beyond the high ridge of the Ultimate Wall, the sky was bright with ferocious, churning light. To the west, a similar confusion of flame-cast. Western Projection and Adamant. In the span of the last day, the traitor host had begun fresh assaults on those two wall lines, the first such effort to come from the south. Sindermann had been told the assaults were unremitting, artillery bombardments from dispositions of the turned Mechanicum ballisteria and, it was rumoured, the Iron Warriors' Stor-Bezashk siege-breakers. The magnitude was terrifying.

Yet Saturnine was quiet, an empty quarter, bracketed by these two great assaults. Sindermann fancied it had been emptied in case Adamant caved, though why? If Adamant caved, then the Ultimate Wall was breached, and nowhere in the Sanctum Imperialis Palatine would be safe any more.

Nowhere on Terra.

Therajomas tugged at Sindermann's sleeve. Two soldiers had emerged from the blank double-doors of a high-gabled mansion, and were approaching them. Long black rain-cloaks over poppy-red dress uniforms trimmed in gold and white. Officers of the Imperialis Auxilia, the Hort Palatine. One carried a torch-pole.

'Sindermann?' he asked.

Sindermann showed him his identification and warrant.

'Who's this?' the officer asked, glancing at Therajomas.

Sindermann introduced Therajomas Kanze, and told him to produce his papers.

'I was told one,' said the officer. 'Just you.'

'We're hardly going to leave him out here,' said Sindermann. 'The transport's already gone.'

'It wouldn't be the worst thing that has happened,' the officer replied. He paused. 'I'll vox for approval. He can come in and wait at least.'

'You are?' Sindermann asked.

'Conroi-Captain Ahlborn,' the man replied. His accent was strong. Where was that? Tuniz? Aleppo? The Hort Palatine drew the best from all over.

'You are of the Hort?' Sindermann asked. 'The Imperialis Auxilia?' He'd thought so at first, the red uniforms were right, but as the men had come closer Sindermann had noticed discrepancies. The long black coats were not the grey paletots issued to the Hort, and the badge on them, a silver palatine aquila, was unfamiliar.

'Yes,' said Ahlborn, 'but seconded to the Command Prefectus Unit for the duration, at the Praetorian's order.'

'The Command Prefectus Unit?'

'It's a new initiative,' said Ahlborn.

'Handling what?' asked Sindermann.

'Security. Secrecy. Disclosure. Matters of confidence.'

'Such as?' asked Sindermann gently.

'People asking unnecessary questions,' replied Ahlborn with a tight, cold smile.

Sindermann nodded, and made a polite gesture of acquiescence.

'Follow,' said Ahlborn.

Inside the heavy doors, which Ahlborn's comrade carefully barred behind them, lay an empty atrium. Gloom and dust presided over a few items of furniture, pulled aside and covered with sheets. A walkway had been laid across the old tiles of the noble townhouse, the linked mesh-and-plastek duckboards of trench systems. Paintings had gone from the high walls, leaving negative shadows. Sindermann wondered who had lived there.

They walked down long, echoing hallways, following the walkway, and Ahlborn didn't speak. They descended two levels and then, to Sindermann's curiosity, passed through a hole that had been cut cleanly through the building's heavy wall. A heavy melta cut, precision work. The edges were fused smooth. Sindermann could smell the acrid residue. It had only been done a day or two earlier.

They were in another building now, adjoining the first. Here, long galleries were lined with bulk hydroponic tanks. The light of the low-setting solar lamps filled the hallway with a dull glow. The air was ripe with the smell of mulch and recycled water. Sindermann had heard that whole districts and some prestigious buildings had been seized, and turned into crop production centres in a desperate effort to maintain food stocks. He'd never seen it. This place had once been, what? A museum? A court library? Whatever exhibits or books had been held here had been cleared out wholesale, and replaced with something more precious, the basic engines of nourishment.

There was no one else around. Ahlborn kept them on the walkway route.

'These are high-yield systems,' Sindermann remarked, gesturing to the banks of crop-tanks as they strode past them.

Ahlborn nodded.

'They require constant tending to maximise growth,' said Sindermann.

'They do,' Ahlborn agreed.

'Where are the farm staff?'

'Dismissed yesterday,' Ahlborn said.

'Without care, these crops will fail,' said Sindermann. He stopped and looked at a tank of tubers where the shoots sprouting from the suspended rhizomes looked colourless and wan.

'They'll be moved,' said Ahlborn. 'If there's time,' he added.

'Time before...?' Sindermann began.

'Please, follow me.'

They came at last to a great hall, a cellar vault or perhaps a water cistern that had been drained. It was warm and damp, like a cave.

Diamantis was waiting for them.

'The companion is approved,' the Huscarl told Ahlborn. The Hort-captain nodded.

'Why have you summoned us here?' Sindermann asked.

'I haven't,' Diamantis replied. From his expression, Sindermann could tell that Huscarl Diamantis still regarded the
interrogator order as an annoyance.

'I sent for you.'

The Praetorian stepped through an archway, and entered
the hall. Sindermann felt the boy at his side recoil, and drop
to his knees. Diamantis and the Hort Palatines had put their
fists to their chests. Sindermann wondered if he should do
either, or both.

This was no chance encounter on a rooftop terrace. This was
not Rogal Dorn in his father's old robe, caught off guard. Dorn
wore his full battleplate. He was dressed for war. Moving leisurely, he still seemed impossibly powerful.

'Bid him stand up,' Dorn said to Sindermann.

Sindermann yanked Therajomas to his feet.

'You have assembled your order, Kyril?' Dorn asked.

'As you willed it, lord,' Sindermann replied. 'Small as yet,
but the members of the coterie are fine and eager. They are
already out, despatched to various points, to witness and
record. But you brought me here.'

Dorn nodded. He glanced at Ahlborn and his companion.

'Refreshment,' he said. 'Recaff or tea or something.'

The men nodded and hurried out.

'I brought you here,' said Dorn, 'for the same reason I willed
your order back into existence. To observe. To set down for
posterity. To provide meaning to what we do. To represent the
hope that there will be a future.'

'I am glad to–'

Dorn raised his hand, an index finger firm to halt Sindermann's reply.

'And for you, here, a specific reason,' he said. 'You led me
here.'

'I did?' Sindermann responded, baffled.

'Unwittingly,' said Dorn. 'But I have been too long in the cosmos to ignore the significance of coincidence and the idle play of fate. So I brought you here to see what you had put into my mind, and observe the consequence. For it may be the saving of us.'

'Then I am honoured, my lord.'

'Understand, Kyril,' said Dorn, 'you are at risk. If I'm right, this place will fall in harm's way and I cannot guarantee your safety.'

Sindermann shrugged. 'Terra is besieged, lord,' he said. 'You cannot guarantee the safety of any of us.'

Dorn's lips tightened, then he nodded.

'This is particular, Sindermann,' he said. 'If fate is kind to us, the greatest threat of all is coming here. And will find, to his surprise, we are ready for him.'

Sindermann ignored the 'him'. He didn't want to think about the 'him'.

'Here?' he asked. 'This... place? This cellar?'

'Saturnine,' said Dorn.

He gestured for them to follow him, and they fell in behind him with Diamantis at their heels. Through the broad brick archway, another, still larger cellar cavern yawned. Sindermann and Therajomas both stopped short, dumb with dismay.

A sub-vox snarl snapped at them, quivering their diaphragms, the growl of a mature carnodon. The huge, Ironclad-pattern Dreadnought swung towards them, motivator pistons hissing, and brought its weapons to bear.

'Peace, Venerable Bohemond,' Dorn admonished.

The Dreadnought, dressed in the colours of the VII Legion, stepped back and replanted itself, limbs grinding. It depowered its weapon systems. Its growl reduced to a warning purr.

But it wasn't the Dreadnought that had halted them in their tracks, nor was it the odd chemical stench swimming in the air. Nor, indeed, was it the missing rear wall, gouged out and reinforced, revealing an underground chamber beyond of staggering size, the grain cellars and cisterns of three dozen mansions opened into one vast space and lit by portable lamp rigs, troops and war machines milling in the pools of light.

Not even that.

It was the figure standing beside the Dreadnought. The Sigillite, robed and cowled, leaning his frail weight upon his staff.

'Kyril, welcome,' said Malcador.

'Great lord,' Sindermann answered, a tremble in his voice. Therajomas had averted his gaze, head bowed. 'Show respect,' Sindermann hissed at him.

'He is too bright!' Therajomas whispered. 'He is too bright to look at!'

Sindermann frowned. The awe he felt for the Sigillite was based upon authority and command, on Malcador's role as a direct instrument of the Emperor's will. What was Therajomas seeing?

'Come forward,' said Malcador, beckoning with a bony hand. 'Learn. And find some way to frame it in your chronicle.' His voice was like dried thistles, brushed against velvet.

'What should I learn first, lord?' asked Sindermann.

'That this is a trap,' Malcador replied. 'One devised by Rogal. Laid fast, but laid well, or so we hope. History has preoccupied your life, Kyril. Here you will see it being made.'

'Or being lost,' remarked Dorn.

'Is your confidence failing, Praetorian?' Malcador asked.

Dorn shook his head. 'Just my realism showing. This is an extreme gambit. If we'd had longer to–'

The Sigillite sighed. 'Time is all we have. To be quicker than the quick. To surprise the surprising. To seize opportunity from the opportunists. Lateral cunning. You said so yourself. We take this chance or we suffer the penalty.'

'A trap for what?' asked Sindermann softly.

The Praetorian looked at him.

'I have reason to believe the traitor foe will strike here,' he said. 'Perhaps within hours. They seek to exploit a weakness they believe we have not noticed. We aim to block that attempt.'

'And more than that...' Malcador chided.

'And turn it back upon them,' Dorn conceded. 'Blocking is imperative, but there is a greater gain to be made. One that might end our calamity.'

'They will strike here at Saturnine?' Sindermann asked. He swallowed hard.

Dorn nodded. 'I am sure of it,' he said.

'Because it's what you would do?'

'Yes, exactly that. One flaw in a perfect defence. I would not ignore that. And neither would he.'

'So a... a blind attack?' asked Sindermann. 'A stealth strike?'

'To the head,' Dorn replied.

'For that... for that to work, you would send your best,' said Sindermann. 'Not just elite. Specialists. Spear-tip assault, to cut through–'

'Now he's getting it,' the Sigillite murmured. 'Now he understands.'

'Throne of all,' Sindermann whispered. 'You're laying a trap to kill the Lupercal.'

'I have a story for you,' the soldier said. 'I hear you are gathering stories, to make a history.'

Hari Harr looked up at him, squinting against the harsh sunlight, and nodded.

'I've been instructed to do so,' Hari said. 'To document events and–'

The soldier shook his head and smiled.

'I do not need convincing that your work is important,' he

said. 'Stories are all we have, in the end. Better than grave-stones. They last longer.' He smiled, a big, bright smile. 'I think,' he said, 'gravestones are all we will get otherwise.'

'This story then?' asked Hari. He was sitting on a retaining wall, overlooking the emplacement at the eastern end of the Pons Solar. Below, soldiers on work-drill moved in teams, filling and passing sacks of earth to pack the talus of the ram-part. He took out his dataslate. 'Start with your name.'

'My name is Joseph,' said the soldier. He leaned his rifle against the wall, and sat down in the sunlight beside Hari. 'Joseph Baako Monday (Eighteenth Regiment, Nordafrik Resist-ance Army). But it is not about me, no. It is a story I heard last night, about a mighty hero, and about the grace of the Emperor.'

Hari nodded. He liked the soldier. Joseph Monday had an honest manner, and, despite everything, a cheerful disposition. But Hari had a feeling he was about to hear a story he had been told three times already that morning.

'There was a convoy, coming here,' said Joseph. 'Reinforcements for the port defence. Like the one that brought you, I'm sure.'

'I'm sure,' Hari agreed.

'It was attacked, my friend,' said Joseph, his hands moving expressively in a dramatic flourish, his tone turning solemn. 'A terrible attack. Many dead. The enemy was upon them, you see? But one man, just an ordinary soldier like me, he stood his ground. He fought like a devil. And when he could fight no more, the Emperor Himself came, in the form of a winged angel, and saved him. The angel, it flew down, like fire, and it killed them all, killed them *all*, all of the enemy dead. Because the soldier, you see, he had shown faith, and had held the enemy at bay, and the Emperor had felt alive to the soldier's great faith, and sent His grace to deliver him.'

'Was this soldier's name Piers?' Hari asked. Joseph glanced at him in surprise.

'You have heard it?' he asked.

'Versions...' said Hari.

Joseph shrugged, disappointed.

'But I want to hear them all,' Hari added quickly. 'I'm sure the various versions contain the truth of the story, one way or–'

'You see, there is your mistake,' said Joseph. 'That is the thing about stories. The truth is in all of them. I grew up in Endayu, and all the children there, they would trade stories, and the grown-ups would tell them stories, because that is how we learn about the world. If you're going to be a storyteller, my friend, you should know this. The truth is in *all* of them.'

Hari was making quick notes.

'Tell me about that,' he said.

Joseph frowned. 'I don't know how to say it clearer,' he said.

'Well, this story you just told me, about the convoy, I've heard different versions...'

'You mean different details,' said Joseph. 'The facts don't matter.'

'Well–'

Joseph laughed. 'All right, they do. They *do* matter. But they are like the scales on a fish. The fish can't swim without them, but the fish is what matters. You talk about your versions, my friend... Did the hero man have a rifle or a sword? Was he tall or was he short–'

'Or was he fat, with a big beard?'

'Or yes, that, however you like,' said Joseph. 'But the truth, the fish–'

His dirty hands mimed the sinuous motion of a salmon racing downstream.

'–the fish. Well. That is what you need to hook. The man, he was an ordinary man. A soldier. Army man. Just a man. But what he did mattered. His courage and his fortitude. He did not give up. And the Emperor came to him, like an angel, and saved him. Just as He will save us all. He watches over us. That is the story.'

'Do you have other stories, sir?' Hari asked.

Joseph looked doubtful. 'I am just an ordinary man.'

'So was the man in your story. How did you get here?'

Joseph Monday looked aside. He seemed reluctant, suddenly.

'I was on the line,' he said quietly. 'Line Fourteen, in the north reach. Eleventh of Quintus, Lion's port fell, and there was a terrible time afterwards. Terrible confusion. We had to run and fight. I saw many bad things. In the end, I came here.'

'What kind of things did you see?'

'I do not want to speak of them,' said Joseph. 'The story about the convoy is much better.'

'Isn't it the same?' asked Hari.

Joseph looked at him. 'How can it be the same?'

'Well, you said the man was on his way here, and then bad things happened, but the Emperor was watching over him, and He saved him. That's what happened to you.'

'The Emperor did not come to me. I did not see an angel.'

'Those are just scales on the fish,' said Hari. 'I'd like to hear what happened to you. What you actually saw–'

Joseph got to his feet. 'I do not want to talk about it,' he said.

'Can I ask you a question, then?' asked Hari. 'The way you are talking about the Emperor. It… it makes Him sound like a divine presence. A spiritual power. You know that it's decreed wrong to think about Him that way? The Emperor Himself doesn't want people to think of Him as a god. The notion is suppressed by order of–'

'A god doesn't talk about Himself that way,' said Joseph. 'A real god is modest. In the old times, gods were boastful and arrogant. That is why they fell away and were seen as false. A true god is humble.'

He looked at Hari fiercely, then crouched down again, staring Hari in the eyes.

'I have heard there is a book,' he said. 'A secret book. A text explaining the divinity of the Emperor.' His voice dropped to a whisper. 'I have heard there is a copy of that book here. Someone here in the port has it.'

Hari cleared his throat, and looked down at his dataslate.

'I would like to read that book,' said Joseph. 'But I do not need to read it to know the truth. This war, all this fighting and killing, there would be no sense to it if the Emperor was just a man. That is how I know what He is. We fight for Him, my friend, because we believe He will save us. We have faith in Him. Total faith. Because if we didn't, we would just lay down and die. That is how I know.'

'So… He has to be a god because you have faith in Him?'

'Faith is all we have. I have not read this book. I have not seen angels, or the daemons that they say have come. I don't need to.'

Someone was calling. Troopers were getting up from their rest break.

'I have to go,' said Joseph, looping his rifle over his shoulder on its sling.

'Thank you,' said Hari. 'For the story. If you change your mind, I would like to hear your story.'

Joseph laughed, but Hari could hear the sadness in his tone.

'It is really not a good story,' he replied. 'But I'll bring you other stories if I hear them. Where will you be?'

'I'm not going anywhere,' said Hari.

There was no chance of leaving now. Word was, the enemy was advancing on the Eternity Wall space port from the south, through the pulverised ruins of what had been the Celestial

City, and contact was expected within hours. Niborran, a commanding presence, was orchestrating a mass defence of the port's reinforced garrison. Hari had hoped his warrant might get him a few minutes with the lord general, but he'd only glimpsed him from a distance. It seemed pitiful to try and arrange an audience. The clock was counting down. Niborran had far more important things to do with his time.

The rubble wastes adjacent to the port were swathed in a golden fog of sunlit dust. The air was dry. Someone had said that supplies were low, water especially. There was intense activity in the skirts of the port zone. Around the freight quadrants to the south and south-east, fortifications were being constructed and reinforced. The main defence was Monsalvant Gard, a bastion that looked indomitable. Artillery positions waited in the bleaching light. The port's defence systems maintained a bristling watch for movement, audio signals or noospherics.

The atmosphere was as taut as the steel cables anchoring the silent vox-masts.

'I think you're wrong,' said Clement Brohn. 'Frankly.'

'I don't think you've been here long enough to make that judgement,' Shiban Khan replied.

'I've been here long enough to know we don't have the force strength to cover every–'

'Stop it,' said Niborran. The High Primary looked at his second and the White Scar. 'No arguments, please.'

'I am not arguing, general,' said Shiban. 'The assault will be multi-point. We need to maintain coverage.'

'I have noted your recommendations, khan,' said Niborran.

'But not acted on them,' said Shiban.

'My lord Niborran has command here,' Brohn said. His tone was hard, even though he was staring up at an armoured giant. 'You no longer have zone command, khan.'

'I am well aware,' said Shiban. 'I am also well aware that none of us have a full intelligence picture on which to base our calculations. We know nothing–'

'So we make an educated guess!' Brohn snapped.

'No, we cover wide, and stay flexible,' replied Shiban.

'I said stop it,' said Niborran. 'I meant it.'

The wind blew dust into the observation bunker high on Monsalvant Gard's southern battlements. Niborran shielded his silver eyes.

'You know what civil war is?' Niborran asked. 'Comrades fighting each other. You'd think the last few years might have taught you both that. Clem, go and supervise the munition decks. See if those damn hoists are working yet.'

'But–'

'Now, please, Clem.'

Brohn saluted and left the bunker.

'He's a good man,' Niborran said to Shiban.

'I have no doubt, general.'

'This war, it brings out bad things in us.'

'I know he doesn't like me much,' said Shiban. He looked at Niborran. 'I'm told you were both on the wrong side of my Khagan. That you are, in effect, here because of that.'

'There's more to it,' said Niborran.

'For you, I think, yes. A desire for field service. Not so much for Brohn. And I know what people think of my Legion. We may be Astartes, but we are barbarians. The White Scars do not enjoy the respect shown to the Imperial Fists or the Blood Angels.'

'You seek respect, then?' Niborran asked.

'No, general, I seek victory. It is the simplicity of that notion that makes people think of us as uneducated tribesmen.'

'You've nothing to prove to me, khan.'

'Yet,' said Shiban, 'I saw the dismay on your faces when you arrived. When you found out I was zone command.'

'A role you handed over without blinking, Shiban. And the very fact that Camba Diaz had deferred to you, even though he's a lord castellan. That showed me enough. Besides, Diaz has spoken to me about you. He rates you highly.'

'My recommendations are ignored.'

'No, Shiban. But a full perimeter makes us weak everywhere. We have only nine thousand.'

'A full perimeter guards us everywhere, when we know nothing.'

We know plenty, Niborran thought. *I know plenty.* He glanced at Cadwalder, who was standing by the entry hatch on watch, and had remained silent throughout. *I know the true burden of this. I know what is expected of us.*

'I *have* listened to you,' said Niborran. 'The internal transit routes of the port remain open. I didn't block them and mine them, though that's textbook, and Brohn was all for it. We can move strengths rapidly behind our own lines in response to threat or assault. We can't cover everything, but we can focus swiftly when assault comes. Mobile warfare. That's the White Scars way, isn't it? Mobile war inside a fortified zone. I *am* listening to you, khan.'

'Mobile warfare is just one of our traits,' said Shiban. 'It is the tag we're given. Hit and run. We are more than that, but we are regarded as simply that.'

'For Throne's sake, Shiban, I am trying to work with you.'

Shiban Khan nodded. 'I understand. I apologise. This is not going to be an easy fight, however we run it. I answer to you. Know that. But my intent is the service of my Korchin Khan of Khans and, through him, the Emperor. Victory is the only thing that matters, and if I have to argue with you to achieve it, I am afraid I will.'

'Good,' said Niborran. He smiled. 'Good. I expect... and want... no less.'

His smile faded.

'What if victory isn't an option, Shiban?' he asked.

'General?'

'You must have considered that,' said Niborran. He took a pitcher from the map table, and filled a glass. 'Not every battle can be won. Victory is not always a possible outcome. We don't know what's coming, but you can bet it's going to be bad. We're barely nine thousand, we're boxed in, without support, and we can't run if they break us. So what happens then?'

'We die,' said Shiban.

'Yes?'

'And we make our deaths cost them as much as possible. We damage them so badly that even in victory, they are bled weak, and reduced as a threat.'

'Correct answer,' said Niborran.

'Do you think that is the likely outcome?'

Niborran sipped his water thoughtfully. 'A year ago? No. But a year ago I didn't think we'd be fighting to cling on to every last square centimetre of the Imperial Palace either. Are you ready, if it comes to it?'

'You do not need to ask that.'

'Then we stand together, Shiban Khan. Now, tell me, three things you would do that I'm not doing. Three priorities.'

Shiban raised his eyebrows.

'I would… deploy on a wide front, but we've had that conversation. I would give up the western approaches, and the Western Freight, now. Retreat and mine them out. The area's too big to hold, and simply overstretches us. If we tighten the circle now, we concentrate and make better use of what forces we have. Third, I would–'

A siren began to sound. Its hoarse howl rose from nothing until it was echoing across the port complex and joined by others.

'Assault,' said Cadwalder. 'My lord general, signals indicate they are coming from the west. Incoming main strength.'

Men were rushing, running, scrambling with weapons, pulling on body armour and helmets they'd removed in the heat. Hari wanted them to tell him what was happening, and where he should go, but he knew the answer to the first question, and the answer to the second was hardly a priority to anyone.

The first explosions lifted dirt from the outer line down by the bridge. They made distant *crump* sounds, like heavy wet sheets snapping in a gale. Hari couldn't see the enemy, but below him, army units were mobbing into the dugouts and emplacements, along the bridgehead and the banks of the wide, deep gulf that the bridge spanned. The enemy was coming at the port zone from the west, out of the Dhawalagiri Quarter of Magnifican.

More shelling hit the eastern bank. Return fire began to chop from the bartizan turrets along the port hem. Small-arms fire licked from the dugouts and trenchwork.

Hari knew he should probably quit the area. Make his way back to Monsalvant, and keep out of the way. He glanced at the huge sprawl of the port megastructure behind him, just for a moment. Then he started to run after the soldiers.

He was here for a reason. As a witness. Running off somewhere wouldn't let him witness anything.

Camba Diaz advanced. As he walked, he spoke clearly and simply into his link, coordinating the units around him. Close to a thousand men, most of them mixed Auxilia platoons, had been tasked to protect the Pons Solar approach. They seemed to be responding very slowly to both the assault and his orders. He wondered if it was the heat – exhaustion from the fortification labour they'd been doing when the attack began.

Then he realised they weren't being slow at all. They were

being human. He was used to commanding squads of trans-human battle-brothers, who reacted with intense purpose in the blink of an eye. These soldiers, even the best of them, the Excertus elite, were brave and steadfast and well drilled. But they weren't Space Marines.

He would have to lead from the front.

Diaz held area command of the port's western areas that day. Niborran, and every other senior commander of the zone, was a minimum of half an hour away at Monsalvant Gard. Diaz ordered vox signals to be sent immediately, expressing the situation and requesting support. Additional armoured elements, at least, from Western Freight. He had no sense of enemy numbers yet, but when the enemy had a technically limitless ability to reinforce, calculations were academic anyway.

They were focusing on the Pons Solar.

It was the only viable route for ground forces coming from the west. The immense heat-sink gully it crossed was as deep and broad as a major river. Shiban had advised giving it up, and demolishing the bridge. He'd urged it several times in Diaz's hearing. But Niborran had been swayed by Brohn's argument that holding the bridge provided a potentially critical arterial route for reinforcement and resupply from Anterior. At its eastern end, the Pons Solar was protected by entrenched infantry positions, multiple field batteries and an Excertus tank unit. It also fell inside the gun-shadow of the port's outer line, the western stretch of the barrier wall extending from Monsalvant. The heavier wall armaments, part of the port's defence system, had begun firing, ranging shells and pulsed energy fire across the gully into Dhawalagiri. Auxilia combat engineers had raised an immense barricade of rock-crete blocks, razor wire and anti-armour obstacles across the mouth of the bridge.

Diaz skirted the barricade. When he reached the east end

of the bridge, the scale of the assault became apparent. He
scanned, his visor absorbing data, processing it and trans-
mitting it to Monsalvant command. Shelling had already
pulverised both trenchwork and batteries north of the highway.
A thicket of gunfire was drizzling over the spans of the bridge.
The bankside terraces were scattered with dead, and wounded
men were being dragged to cover. There was a massive wash of
smoke from churned-up dust, and from incendiary bombs that
the enemy had launched into the gully. Overhead, the barrier
wall's guns thundered and spat at an invisible foe.

A vox chime.

'My lord.'

Diaz turned. Bleumel and Thijs Reus were approaching his
position on foot. He was glad of the sight of them, the two
battle-brothers who had joined his ragged party at Traxis Arch
during his trek to the port, and had fought at his side against
the feral World Eater. He struck his siege shield gently against
each of theirs in a terse greeting. Bleumel still had the raw
metal gouge across the cheek and bridge of his visor, where
the World Eater's chainaxe had kissed it.

'What do you bring me?' Diaz asked.

'Repellers,' Thijs Reus replied. A platoon of Excertus heavies,
Gehenned Brigade storm troopers in bulky carapace armour,
were trailing him up the bridge approach. Bleumel had twenty
hoplites of the Solar Auxilia. They were lined up behind the
barricade, hefty and anonymous in their void armour. Big
soldiers, by human standards.

'We'll need them,' said Diaz. 'This shelling won't sustain.
The enemy wants the bridge intact.'

'We can deny that desire quickly, lord,' said Bleumel.

Diaz knew what Bleumel meant. It was what he'd do.

'Standing instruction from the zone commander,' he replied.
'The Pons Solar remains intact.'

'That's a contingency pending relief forces,' said Thijs Reus. 'The situation's changed.'

'Agreed,' said Diaz. 'But the instructions have not. I've voxed for clarification. I have not received approval to take the bridge down.'

'It has to be done anyway,' said Bleumel.

'This isn't a strategy meeting,' Diaz said.

Bleumel nodded curtly.

'Prepare for ground repulse,' said Diaz. 'We'll hold the brunt of it, armour in support, and hold until instructions change, or reinforcement arrives.'

They clashed shields again.

'To your glory,' he told them.

'Always,' they replied.

Thijs Reus and Bleumel moved back to instruct their heavies. The Excertus tanks were beginning to move up the bridge approach behind the barricade.

Diaz drew his longsword, and moved through the ranks of men in the trenches and bulwarks of the southside bank. Most were firing: selective shots from individual lasmen, and decent cover fire from the heavier support weapons. Diaz passed among them, making himself visible, his presence known. He knew the rallying effect the sight of Space Marines could have on rattled Army elements, especially novice Auxilia conscripts, who had already been through the flame several times.

'You! That team! Arc your fire to the left. You four, we need faster resupply of munitions! Spread out, get into the communication trenches, and impress upon the load-captains how urgently we need the flow to be maintained! Be firm, my authority! Tell any shirkers I'll treat them as enemy sympathisers.'

Men nodded. Men saluted. Men ran. Within four minutes of taking his place in the Bankside emplacements, Diaz could

see a palpable improvement in the defensive line, the holding
pattern and the fire-rate.

Not Legiones Astartes. Not Imperial Fists. But brave, mortal
men, well trained, obedient, willing to listen.

And with everything to lose.

They would make a fight of this. He would make a fight of
it. With luck, and will, they could hold the bridge until the
backup armour came in.

No word had come from zone command. Diaz suspected
that ranged vox was being jammed or scrambled. Niborran
was no fool. Diaz admired him immensely. A true warrior, a
great martial mind. He would have instructed on the basis of
Diaz's assessment if he had been able to.

An enemy shell struck close, annihilating one of the proud
stone lions that guarded the bridge-ends. Nothing was left
on the plinth when the smoke billowed away, except for the
stumps of its paws.

Grit rained down on them. Diaz waited, hearing the whimpering moans of the injured. Six seconds, ten. Twenty.

The shelling had ceased. A ground assault was imminent,
and there was only one way it could come.

He leapt from the emplacement onto the ramp of the bridge.
Stray, loose enemy shots spat past him. He took his sword,
and carved a line in the rockcrete between the lion plinths,
thirty metres short of the rockcrete barricade.

'Mark this!' he yelled to his men. 'This far, and no further!
We stop them here!'

He was answered by a rousing cheer.

Diaz squared up, and looked along the empty length of the
bridge. The enhanced optics of his visor showed him things
his human forces could not yet see. Heat tracks and motion
traces in the smoke.

The enemy had appeared.

'The hell are you doing, boy?' Piers yelled.

'I could ask the same of you,' replied Hari.

'What?'

'I said, I could ask the same of you, spreading your fables around the–'

'Shitsakes, boy! Get your head down!'

The grenadier pulled him into cover. They were in a trench working fifty metres behind the bridge's barricade line. A train of Carnodon and Medusa tanks was grumbling past, belching exhaust, threading single file along the causeway towards the head of the bridge. The shelling seemed to have eased, but las-fire continued to chop and crack overhead.

'The front line's no place for you,' Piers growled. He was loading grenades into *Old Bess*. Around them, troops from about nine different regiments, every one of them filthy, were prepping weapons.

'It wasn't the front line until just now,' said Hari.

'Shut your smart mouth,' Piers snapped.

'It wasn't. I was interviewing men from the work crews up at the emplacement,' said Hari. 'Then this began.'

'Well, here's what's going to happen,' said Piers. He slammed home the last grenade, and turned to look at Hari. 'You're going to follow this trench back to the communication line, then get your arse out of here. Just run. East. Towards the Gard. Don't stop. Don't look back.' He held up his right hand, and his index and middle fingers made scurrying motions like little legs.

'Thanks, I'm fine,' said Hari. 'The port is a target, I'm in the port, I'm not safe anywhere.'

'Don't give me lip,' said Piers. 'We've got about ten minutes before this place turns to a full bucket of shit, so do as I tell you.'

'I hear you've been telling stories about yourself,' said Hari.

'What? Oh, piss off. Soldiers talk.'

'You can talk for a whole regiment. I've heard it all over the place already today. You, the mythical soldier, standing alone, but for the grace of the Emperor–'

'And how is that not what happened?'

Hari shrugged. 'I… I mean, it's… it's a glossy version. All noble and heroic. It didn't feel very noble when we were in it.'

'You're a daft little shit, Harr,' said Piers. He spat out some dust. 'I never said it was me. I never said, "I did this". I said it was some guardsman called Piers. It's called morale, you little git. It boosts the spirits. I told you all this.'

'You told me soldiers lie.'

Piers grimaced at him. 'That's the truth. And I tell you what, boy, she came for me, didn't she? She came and saved me, didn't she?'

'Mythrus?'

'Yes, you little turd.'

'I don't know what that was. I know it wasn't a miracle,' said Hari.

'Tell my arse that. And yours. And there were daemons too, remember? You saw them with your own damn eyes!'

'I don't know what they were either. Enemy bio-weapons. Certainly not proof of divine agency–'

'Oh, shut up!'

Olly Piers simmered for a moment, then straightened his shako, and glared at him.

'Look around. Look at the shit around you, boy. This is what the very edge looks like. The very brink. This is what it looks like when you're holding on so desperately there's no skin left on your fingerbones. This is when it matters most. This is when it makes the difference between living and dying. You take whatever you can to blaze up your spirits. Anything. A truth, a lie, it doesn't matter. You use whatever you can to keep you going, and you share it with whoever's with you. Whatever you've got, you understand? Whatever keeps you going one more step. That's how you live. That's how you win. That's how you survive, and how your friends and your comrades survive with you, so you can all tell glory tales afterwards, and make even more bullshit up to get you through shitstorms to come.'

'Piers, that's a really cynical way of–'

'Oh, piss yourself off a cliff, you precious little high-minded historian shit-streak, and take your pious little notion of what truth and history means with you! It's your pissing history books that prove my case! The power of myths and lies and frigging stories have got us through thirty frigging thousand years of shit, so I'm gonna go out on a limb and suggest it's a pretty effective bloody formula!

'Besides,' he added, slumping back against the trench wall, his voice dropping, 'it frigging well *was* Mythrus. And I tell you what's more. That file you've got, that *Lectitio* thing–'

'Which you've been telling everyone about–'

'Exactly. Because you should be. You should be going from squad to squad, spreading that frigging word. Sharing it. There's not a man or a woman here who wouldn't be a better soldier for hearing it.'

He slithered forward, keeping his head below the trench lip as a volley of shots went over. He grabbed Hari by the shoulder roughly, turned him around, and pointed along the trench.

'What's that, eh?'

Hari looked. Twenty metres away, a squad of Auxilia were manhandling a battle banner upright. The Emperor Ascendant, in a sunburst.

'A banner,' said Hari.

'And look, boy, how it takes four... no, five, look... men to get it upright and displayed. That's five soldiers who could be firing rifles at enemy targets. But the idea matters more. It rallies us. It reminds us why we're here. It could be anything.

It could be a picture of a giant rabbit. It could be a picture of my hairy frigging arse. Doesn't matter. It reminds us, plain and simple, that there's a point to what we're doing, and a reason to keep doing it. Without it, we're just a bunch of frigging idiots shitting ourselves in a ditch. Now think on that, and get your sodding arse out of here.'

He paused. Along the trench, men were shouting. Piers risked a peak over the trench top.

'Oh balls,' he whispered.

TWO

Eaters
Concerning the dead
Another thunder of hooves

There are World Eaters on the Pons Solar. World Eaters and witch-dogs.

I move towards the crisis as fast as I am able. I run along the barrier wall from Tower Six towards the Pons Solar stretch. I pass gun crews and infantry squads who do not notice me. They are standing at the ramparts, watching the expanding plume of smoke darkening the sky above the bridgehead a kilometre away. They shiver, despite themselves, as I pass by. They think it is from fear at the sight of approaching doom, but it is only partly that. The rest is the fleeting touch of my presence.

I transmit to Tsutomu in orskode as I run. He is in the area called Western Freight. I tell him to come. He does not reply. Communications are broken and intermittent. I am receiving only shreds of data, scabbed by heavy interference. Several streams, from Lord Castellan Camba Diaz and other commanders on station in the vicinity of the bridge. They are patchy and incomplete. But they tell me enough. They tell me I need to be running faster.

I focus on Lord Castellan Diaz's signal. There is virtually no audio, and the metadata is mangled, but I get flashes of pict-feed from his visor. White, hulking shapes emerging through smoke, bearing down, galloping like wild animals across the open bridge towards me.

Towards him.

Camba Diaz is a fine warrior. One of the finest. No mere legionary is made a lord castellan. To achieve that role, a warrior must possess more than gene-bred advantage. Lord Diaz has an exceptionally sharp mind, a genius for war that echoes that of his genesire, Rogal. His role in the defensive actions of the Solar War was significant and invaluable. He has a surprising ferocity, contained in solemnity, which I find appealing.

We are lucky he is present. Blessed or lucky. I don't know if there is a difference between those two things, or if they are just different words for the same effect. He can hold the line, even with the meagre and exhausted forces available to him. He can hold the line for five minutes at least.

Yet, I see what he is facing. I glimpse them via the tattered feed. I know their names. Most of them. I have made a study of the enemy. The data is available to us, for we knew them when they were friends. My cogitator processes the blurry scraps of his feed, freezing and highlighting partial captures of faces, visors, plate details, and comparing them to my combat files. Matches are framed, enhanced, and flashed onto my retina with appended identity markers.

Ekelot of the Devourers. Khadag Yde of VII Rampager. Herhak of the Caedere. Skalder. Centurion Bri Boret. Centurion Huk Manoux. Barbis Red Butcher. Menkelen Burning Gaze. Jurok of the Devourers. Uttara Khon of III Destroyers. Sahvakarus the Culler. Drukuun. Vorse. Malmanov of the Caedere. Muratus Attvus. Khat Khadda of II Triari. Resulka Red Tatter.

Khârn.

Broken images. Broken men. Most are barely recognisable.
The Neverborn touch has transmuted the XII into things so
wretched my heart breaks, things so terrible my blood freezes.
Many of the partial captures cannot be matched with identities
at all. Only snarling Sarum-pattern helms, and the intimi-
dating curved mantles of the Caedere Remissum, identify these
monsters as once-legionaries. Those, and the skeuomorphic
traces of tally marks, warrior-brands, and painted tears.

For some, not even that.

This is the measure of our foe. To take a Legion already
infamous for its berserk terror and its fury, and make those
qualities deeper. Beyond inhuman. Beyond savage. Beyond
the pale of any martial culture.

There are steps at Tower Nine. I take them four at a time.
I am outside, in the light. I pass field gun batteries where
sweating men are working to re-train their guns. I pass a picket
of troops who do not notice me. I run.

I draw my sword.

The plasma fire of Thijs Reus' hoplites did not seem to stop the
charge. The range was short, the line of fire clear and the rate
sustained. The Solar Auxilia were void veterans, equipped to
fight in any environment, famed for their stubborn endurance.
Their man-portable plasma guns and volkite rifles had been
engineered for boarding actions, designed to cut a kill-path
into warships. Each beam lanced out with a shriek, lurid pink
and as bright as neon. The air was already wretched with the
choking stink of superheated plasma and leaking coolant.

But the charge did not falter. Across the top of his raised
shield, Diaz watched in resignation. The combined firepower
around him – heavy plasma weapons, volkite guns, the rotary
cannons of the Gehenned, the Space Marines' bolters – should
have torn a regiment to shreds.

The charge did not falter.

The World Eaters were crossing the bridge en masse. They appeared through the backwashed smoke howling, augmented voices braying like wild cattle. Wild cattle in a slaughterhouse, Diaz thought, stampeding to die. There was the most exquisite streak of pain at the heart of every war cry, like a vein of pure agony running through the booming rage.

They were massive. They seemed, even to Diaz, bigger than legionaries. Like the feral traitor he and his brothers had killed in that water-choked thoroughfare, they were bounding and galloping, some propelling themselves on all fours like great apes. They were lumbering ogres in size and movement, but their speed was shocking. The wave of white armour spewed across the bridge like a horizontal avalanche.

Some still wore the high horn-crests and roaring Sarum-visors that distinguished the XII, but many had passed through the recognisable forms of legionaries, and had become hulking, hunchbacked monsters, bareheaded and insane. Eyes and brows had receded, jaws had extended and swelled, mouths had become the screaming maws of salt-water reptiles; of cave bears; of giant, carnivorous ocean fish. Blood ran from stretched lips. Foam and spittle flew from hook-teeth and exposed gums. Beaded strands of hair and cranial cables whipped and shivered behind their heads in writhing manes. They brandished chainblades, executioners' axes, spiked mauls, maces, falx, cleavers.

Among them came other horrors. Baying Neverborn spawn that ran like hyenas, or tottered like biped goats and rams. Loping hybrids of man and aether. Scurrying vermin that dripped blood, and oozed warp light. Flocks of winged things followed the mass, flapping overhead or swooping across the gully beside the bridge. Some were half-feathered, half-flayed, the size of vultures, cawing like crows. Others were small, fluttering in clouds, with frayed moth wings or iridescent pinions that beat rapidly, and buzzed.

The hoplites kept firing. The Gehenned kept firing. Diaz kept firing. Bright pink beams seared into the onrushing mass. Rotary blasts mowed into armour and flesh. Bolter shells detonated. World Eaters burst, burned through and fell, crushed beneath the following tide. Goat-kin were torched. Swooping, bat-winged monstrosities caught fire and plunged into the gully like meteors.

But for everything that fell, split or seared or ignited or hollowed out by loyalist gunfire, there were more behind, trampling the dead underfoot, filling gaps, bearing on, heedless. Diaz saw a World Eater lose an arm, sliced clean off by a plasma beam. The arm tumbled away like debris. The World Eater kept coming, oblivious. A volkite shot tore away one horn and half the face of another. It did not stop.

The charge did not falter. The charge *would not* falter.

The berserk mass engulfed the defensive line at the head of the bridge.

The vast spans of the Pons Solar shuddered. In the final few seconds, Diaz clamped his emptied bolter to his thigh plate, and wrenched his longsword out of the ground where he had staked it. He screamed the war cry of his Legion, but it was drowned out by the howling and the mass collision.

From the moment the charge began, time had seemed to speed up. Diaz noticed that, as he gripped his blade and hoisted his shield. The experience of mass combat usually had the opposite effect. Time usually slowed to a dreaming ballet where battle became a detached eternity. But on the Pons Solar, time had run berserk, infected by the World Eaters' mad urgency. It accelerated, almost comically, like a pict playback jammed on fast-wind, devouring seconds as greedily as the World Eaters devoured distance and pain. Time ate itself, gorging on moments with a maniacal appetite that matched the World Eaters' deranged hunger to reach and obliterate their prey.

Frenzy followed. Skill was banished. Lunatic, hyperactive time allowed no opportunity for technique. Camba Diaz was strong. As strong as any Imperial Fist. He judged that every single World Eater coming at him was stronger by far, enhanced by rage and the warp beyond even transhuman limits. His only real weapon of value was his mindset, the heritage of the VII, the unquestioning, indoctrinated will to stand and deny. That focus kept him planted like a rock. The discipline, that praetorian defiance, branded on his genetics and reinforced by decades of intense training and the voice of Rogal Dorn, stripped all fear from him, annihilated doubt and hesitation, erased any notion that what he faced was better or stronger or faster or bigger than him. The mindset fixed him. It anchored him like extreme gravity. It locked Bleumel and Thijs Reus too. It pinned them in place, though time around them had unhinged, and become a psychotic blur that permitted no skill.

Diaz stood, in the name of his Lord Dorn. He brought his siege shield up. It held firm, absorbing the first impact, demolishing a roaring face. His sword swung, carving a World Eater through the chest and throat. A chainaxe struck his shield in a welter of sparks. He cleaved the face and shoulder of its owner. He hooked a keening goat-thing off its hooves, and cast it tumbling through the air. Blood sprayed. Torn meat spattered. In the name of his Lord Dorn, he shield-smashed a World Eater aside so hard it broke neck bones. His longsword speared into a howling maw, punching through the back of the skull. It tore free through cheek and ear and mastoid and occipital bones. Metal fragments spalled, glittering. A falx tore a chunk off his vambrace. A blade cut his ribs. He took a head off its shoulders, and sent it spinning like a ball. A piece of severed horn bounced off his visor. He broke a World Eater's jaw with his shield rim, and gutted him as he staggered aside. He split a head down to the lower teeth. In the name of his Lord Dorn. A beam of pink plasma screamed past his ear. A Gehenned fell against him, his face bitten off, and slid down his hip and leg. Diaz kicked. He disembowelled. He broke a power lance with his shield, and scythed off the arms wielding it. Diaz hacked. He carried a charging World Eater over his head on his shield, and cast him off the bridge rail. He impaled. He chopped a darting witch-dog through the neck and spine. Blood and black ichor filmed his plate. He barely noticed the chainsword gash across his right thigh, or the broken spear-tip protruding from his hip. Focus. Maintain focus. Diaz swung. In the name of his Lord Dorn. Broken teeth flew up, a cracked tusk, a whole eyeball ejected by crush-force. Chainblades screeched. Cinders. Arterial jets. A hoplite thrashed, burning alive. A plasma gun overheated, detonating. A dozen figures in the blast zone vaporised, or staggered, ablaze. Diaz struck off an arm. A face, on a downswing. Another head. A grasping hand. In the name of his lord. His Lord Dorn. Focus. A mist from steaming innards. Corpses lolled, still upright, unable to fall in the density of the press. An Excertus trooper flew overhead, flailing, eviscerated. Diaz swung. Blood erupted. The concussion of a mace. Unremitting impacts. Bleumel, at his side, mashed faces with his power hammer, swinging like a smith. Feet caught on unseen corpses. A carpet of bodies and parts of bodies. Diaz ripped his sword through ceramite and meat. Split a skull. Sliced a throat. Thijs Reus, in the name of his lord, struck with a captured falx, another falx impaled clean through his torso. The reek of death. Broken chainblade teeth pinged out like bullets. The stench of blood. The cloud of rage. A frenzy

in him that matched the frenzy he fought.In the name of
Dorn. Blurring violence. Diaz struck, sword buried deep in
plate and black carapace. Thijs Reus on his knees, stabbing. A
Gehenned screamed. A rotary cannon fired blind, point-blank.
Blood on everything. Bleumel, one pauldron gone, drove his
hammer into a monster twice his size, hair braids whipping
and snapping at the impact. Diaz struck. He struck. Again.
In the name of his Lord Dorn. Again. More. His longsword
snapped. He drove the broken blade into a throat, to the hilt.
He punched, empty-handed, breaking face bones. He killed a
World Eater with his shredding shield, wrenching the purring
chainaxe from the traitor's hands, rotating it, making it his
own. He swung. He struck. Thijs Reus knelt, headless. Diaz
drove the squealing chainaxe through World Eaters plate. A
fountain of gore. Thunder. Carnage. Time rushing, headlong.
In the name of his lord. Blood flying. Bone snapping. Flesh
tearing. Impacts. Collapses. Swinging. Striking. Pinned. The
name of Dorn. Frenzy. Glory. Diaz. Smoke blind. Blood blind.
Striking. Again. Camba Diaz. Thrusting. Cutting. Gutting.
Striking. Slaying. In the name of his lord. Pinned. Unmoving.
    Unmovable.
    The line he had sliced in the rockcrete of the bridge between
the lion plinths still lay behind him.

Piers held Hari Harr by the wrist so tightly it felt as though
he was trying to twist his entire hand off.
    'Move your feet! Move your feet! Move your feet!' the old
grenadier kept saying, as if it was some charm or mantra that
would make them invulnerable.
    'We can't–' Hari yelled.
    'Exactly!' Piers replied. 'Exactly. Now you get it, boy. Now
you're grasping it.'
    Hari wasn't grasping anything. Nothing had prepared him

for this level of confusion, not even the horror of the fight
at the convoy. That had been branded on his brain since it
happened, a traumatic scar he thought he'd never lose or ever
really get over. Now, it seemed like nothing. A vague memory,
a trivial anecdote that might slip his mind... *Oh yes, I remember
that. Rockets. Fire. Witch-dogs. When was that again?*

What was happening to him now made everything distant
and incidental, every single scrap of his life, all the things he
had once regarded as important, all the things he had ever
valued and treasured. His grandfather cooking pok h'chal with
too much fish sauce and tamarind. The noteslate and stylus
his aunt had given him when she heard he wanted to be a
writer. Prize day at the scholam in Tunzho, and the certificate
for prose merit. The face of the first person he had kissed. Blue
kites flying off the jetty of the old shipyards. His first meeting
with Sindermann. Memories were calmly and silently snow-
drifting in his head, piling up at their own pace, but they
weren't his memories. They were things that had happened
to a young man called Hari Harr, and that didn't seem to be
him, because he seemed to have become a moaning, wide-eyed
animal in filthy, sweat-drenched clothes, trying to hide, trying
not to lose control of his bowels, trying to remember how to
move around without falling down.

Piers slapped him hard.

'Move your feet!' the grenadier yelled into his face.

Hari blinked. He had no idea why soldiers lied. If this was
war, the actual inside of war, then why did they make shit up?
No tall tale, not even one spun by a skilled, serial liar like Olly
Piers, could ever hope to match the astonishing truth of war.
Lies were smaller than war. No lie, no matter how cocky and
outrageous, was ever going to take war on and win.

War was a scream in capital letters. It was a noise. It wasn't
even words. It had no syntax, no adjectives, no subtext, no

context. It communicated itself as suddenly, simply and unequivocally as a punch in the face. It was a thing, not a story.

Then maybe that was why. That was why soldiers lied. It was the only way, the only meagre, insufficient way they could talk about what they had endured. It was the only way they could give voice to something that defied articulation. War was so big, soldiers needed to get it out of themselves, spew it out, purge themselves, and lies were the only things that worked. It was either that, or punch someone else in the face.

Unless…

Hari blinked again. Now he grasped it. The lies weren't exorcism. At least, not completely. They were protection. After the fact, after the brute scream of war, the lies weren't a means to talk about something that defied words. They weren't approximate expression. They were curative. They were comfort. The lies were lies of glory and heroism, achievement and success. They weren't born out of arrogance or boasting or self-aggrandisement. They were just ways to talk about something that was otherwise unbearable. They were coping strategies to insulate survivors against the madness and the punch in the face. They were ways to make war feel like it had some point, some value, some lasting worth. Lies made war better for those unlucky enough to survive it.

Lies gave soldiers something to think about, and talk about, and cherish, so they would never have to… never, ever have to think about the truth.

'It's a stupid bloody time to figure that out…' Hari murmured to himself. He laughed, for want of anything else to do.

'What?' Piers yelled. 'What did you say?'

Hari looked at him. Olly Piers, shako on crooked, meal-tin spills down the front of his coat, rancid of breath, half-covered in dirt and grease, too old by far to be having to do this all over again. What a horrible life you must have lived, Piers, to have become such a magnificent liar. What terrible things you must have seen to make you need to lie so much. That's what you were telling me all along, and I was too stupid to comprehend. I had no frame of reference.

I have it now, thought Hari. I wish I didn't. I would give anything not to have had this experience, and not to be here. There is no truth here, no story, no words. There's nothing to take from this of any worth, and all my high-minded ambitions to come along and brave the dangers in order to capture something valuable were bullshit.

There is nothing here to cherish. Nothing here to learn. War is noise, sensory overload, pain, terror, horror. That's it. It's an inarticulate obscenity. It can't be communicated, and even if it could be, it shouldn't be.

Hari looked around. The sky was on fire. The barricade was on fire. The invincible column of tanks had long since vanished into the smoke. Things that looked a bit like crows circled overhead. Mutilated and disfigured men wandered past them, with no idea where they were going. There was a constant background roar coming through the rippling clap and thunder of explosions and gunfire, and it wasn't a human roar. Hari was almost one hundred per cent certain he was hearing War itself, roaring the one, wordless word it knew.

'I have to get you out of here, boy,' Piers said. 'We can't stay here.'

'You're lying again,' said Hari. 'You want to get out of here, and helping the non-combatant idiot is a good excuse.'

Piers slapped him again. 'You little shit,' he said.

Then he reached out, and clamped Hari by the side of the head with one big hand. He was shaking. The remorse in his eyes was unbearable.

'Everyone's going to die,' he said. 'The World Eaters, boy, they–'

'I know,' said Hari. 'Let's just go. Run. No lies. Just go.'

He turned and started walking.

Crossfire had mown across the trench ahead of them. The banner had fallen. Three of the bearers were dead. The remaining two were trying to get the banner upright again, but the task was beyond them.

'Or we could do something,' Hari said.

'Like what?'

'Tell a lie.'

Hari grabbed one of the banner poles, and began to help the two men raise it. The pole was wet with blood. Piers joined him.

'This isn't a lie, boy,' he said.

Hari wasn't sure what it was, except that it seemed to have some purpose. A way to reclaim some sense from a senseless, insensible event. He could run, or he could die, or he could do this – and this, like all the best lies old soldiers told, offered a shred of meaning to something that was otherwise meaningless. It was so foolishly insignificant, but he'd take insignificant over no significance at all.

The four of them got the banner upright. It swayed in the smoke. Las-shots had cut several holes in it. It was ridiculously heavy and cumbersome. Two more soldiers ran up to them, and helped them steady it. One of them was Joseph Baako Monday. He seemed unscathed, but he was weeping so desperately he couldn't talk.

'Hoist it up! Up now!' Piers was shouting. 'For the Emperor! Upland Tercio, hooo!'

Others had joined them, closing on the flag because the flag was the only landmark that wasn't on fire.

'We're all dead!' someone wailed.

'Shut your noise, we're not!' Piers bellowed. 'He'll protect us! He will protect us! Show a little bloody faith, boys, and gather around Him! Terra! Throne of Terra!'

A few took up the chant. Hari was one of them. The more troopers gathered, the lighter the banner became. Hari was able to take one hand off the pole, and lock it around Joseph's shoulders, keeping the shuddering, grieving man upright.

There were forty or more of them now, survivors from different units. Others were approaching. Some helped with the banner, others formed defensive lines, weapons ready, anchored on the rally point of the flag. They would defend that, at least. The bridge was lost, the bankside emplacement overrun, but they would defend that at least, because it was the only thing left in the hellscape of Pons Solar that had any value. When they died, they would die knowing it had been for a reason, however trivial. If they lived, their lies would be the best lies ever spun.

Piers was full-throated, leading the chant.

'Throne of Terra! Throne of Terra!'

For a very short time, probably no more than five minutes, though it felt like the entire lifespan of the universe, two heavy, notched poles and an old piece of embroidered cloth defied the utter meaningless-ness of roaring war, and gave what was left of their lives the semblance of a purpose.

The chanting faltered.

The first true monster had emerged from the smoke, striding past the ruined barricade and the blazing hulls of once-invincible tanks. The World Eater, from its immense horned helm to its giant steel boots, seemed like a statement of fact, as though war had sent them an undeniable truth to negate their fragile, hopeless lie.

It saw the mass of them, sixty terrified troopers, huddled around a tatty banner. It roared, louder than the screaming chainaxes in its fists.

A megalodon grin snapped open. Megalodon teeth gleamed in the firelight. Head down, it charged them.

'He will protect us!' Piers yelled. 'He will, boys! If we protect Him!'

The soldiers started to shoot.

There is no hope. I am running headlong into what is now clearly a catastrophe. The bridge is lost. The east bank is lost. Archenemy strengths, worse than anything we predicted, and amplified by the toxic fire of the Primordial Annihilator, are swarming into the East Arterial and the edges of Western Freight. We will be lucky to hold them at the barrier wall, or at Monsalvant.

We will probably not be lucky. I am painfully aware of Rogal's strategic intention with regards to Eternity Wall Port. His tactical calculations are seldom marred by errors, and he has a low opinion of luck. I call luck fortune. Fortune is fickle and unreliable, but I believe it does exist, and when it is present, it can act like oil to unmesh gears that were thought to have jammed. Fortune sometimes alters the inevitable.

But loss here is more than inevitable. It has already occurred. We need to pull back, to redeploy along the barrier wall, and save as many assets as we can for the coming repulse. Hundreds of troops are already dead, but those that have survived must be re-instructed. They are fighting a futile battle that will end only in their slaughter. At the barrier wall, and at Monsalvant, they can fight more usefully and not be wasted.

There is no one to issue those orders. As I track through the smoke and the carnage, I see no leaders. No officers. No sign of the lord castellan or any of the legionaries posted on this flank. High Primary Niborran, may grace preserve him, is not yet arrived, and all comms are degraded and dead.

I have authority. But I am unseeable, unknowable. Tsutomu has not arrived. No one can communicate my will for me.

My presence has some effect, at least. As I run forward,

my cursed aura comes with me. I am null, and the Never-born cringe at my arrival. Flocks of crow-spawn turn and wheel away, like vultures driven from a kill by an approaching lioness, or pigeons chased off crops by a gamekeeper's scattershot. Witch-dogs, bounding ahead of the main assault, come up short, whining. They sense me, or the lack of me at least, and turn tail, craven, whimpering as they gallop back towards the Pons Solar where the air is more to their liking.

The beast things, goat-faced and cloven-hooved, are more resistant. They cower, unnerved, but do not flee.

I kill them. *Veracity* cuts matted fur and horns and fat throats. My blade runs with their poison blood. It is not worthy work, but any kill made in the name of the Emperor counts. Any dent we make in their numbers and their strength inches us closer to triumph.

I leave their carcasses in my wake.

Not far short of the bridge, beyond a mass of burning tanks, I see the banner. I see His face first, through the smoke, and for one foolish moment I think He has come. I believe, just for a fleeting second, that He has finally joined us on the field of war, and that everything is about to turn. It will be like the days of the Great Crusade again, when victory followed sweet victory, and He, shining like a star, led us from the front.

But it is just a banner. There are shot holes in His face.

There are some three score soldiers gathered around the banner, the largest gathering of survivors I have seen. Three score who could make a true difference somewhere else, if they survive.

But they will not.

As I close in, I see the World Eaters. They are bounding past the barricade. One has crossed the approach road, and is bearing down on the huddled survivors.

Khadag Yde of VII Rampager. A giant horror, a skull-taker,

trophies of human bone and skin strung about his plate like fetishes and leather aprons. He is berserk, his sentience whittled down to an inarticulate kill-urge. He is moving at close to sixty kilometres an hour. He will plough through them like a runaway speeder. He will kill them and eat them, and not necessarily in that order.

I accelerate. Khadag Yde is, I judge, fifty times stronger than me. Six times my size. Ten times as fast. He wields a brace of chainaxes, each of which could split a troop carrier wide open.

This will be interesting. For all that I have studied these poor friends-turned-archenemies, for all I have marvelled at what monsters they have become, that was all theory. This will be my first practical engagement with the things the XII have become.

I have one battlefield advantage. I can see Khadag Yde. He is a horned giant in white plate.

Khadag Yde cannot see me.

I intercept him, head-on, five metres short of the banner line.

He senses me at the very last moment. The Neverborn anima fizzling in his bloodstream is triggered by my null-state, and flinches.

I put my faith in the Emperor. I put my strength in *Veracity*.

I put *Veracity* through his face.

The upstroke impact almost breaks my elbow and shoulder. My feet slide, furrowing earth like the skids of a hard-landing Stormbird.

Khadag Yde rises up. He leaves the ground for a moment, like a breaching cetacean, white armour shearing across his face and chest, fetishes splintering and flying, ducts and feeds snapping, blood exploding in a fountain – *his* blood and litres of ingested blood from his burst stomach. He flails, convulsing, churning backwards, opened from groin to brainpan.

He lands on his back with a noise of falling scrap metal, smashing mire-wash into the air.

I judge my first practical experience to be a success.

The men around the banner do not understand what has just happened. I imagine it feels like a miracle to them, an impossibility, the act of some god. They cannot see me either. They can only see the result of me.

But they roar out a cheer nonetheless, their chanting renewed.

I turn to them, and see the blind hope in their faces, the triumph in their eyes. They cannot stay here. They have to move. Withdraw. More are coming.

But I can't tell them that.

Except–

I see him. The old grenadier. The reprobate veteran soldier. The one from the convoy, who acted so peculiarly.

He is staring right at me, one hand on the banner pole, his eyes wide, his mouth open. Spots of Khadag Yde's blood glitter on his face, and twinkle in his beard.

He sees me.

I look him right in the eyes. I will him to see me even better.

And I point. I point towards the barrier wall. I point as emphatically as I can.

Go. Understand me. Please. Go now. Take these men while you still can, and get to the wall.

For pity's sake, see me and understand what I am trying to tell you.

Hari could hear Piers shouting. 'He protects us! He guards us! I told you, I told you, boys! He's with us! The Emperor's with us!'

It didn't make much sense. Something had just happened, some state-change as simple and silent as the sun coming out from behind a cloud. But it wasn't sunlight, it was a stillness, a dense cold as though war's scream had been muted. All the daemonic things, some too grotesque to look at, suddenly broken and scattered, whining and barking as they scampered and flapped away. And the monster, the feral Astartes monster, had been split apart, just metres from them, by some invisible force.

Hari stared at its immense, ruptured corpse. Steam was pouring from its split innards. It had been so big, so fast, charging them with such fury, it had seemed less like a warrior in war and more like a force of nature.

And what, under all the stars, could stop a force of nature except an act of god?

'The spirit of Mythrus is among us, boys!' Piers shouted. 'Fickle mistress of war! We're her chosen ones today! Bless yourselves, and follow me! Lift up that banner, and follow me! To the wall, boys! We're falling back to the wall! You hear me? Do it!'

The dead had been taken to the longhalls and blockhouses that filled the yards behind Gorgon Bar. In the aftermath of the savage push-back, work crews had toiled to clear the ramparts of bodies. The wounded had been carried or led to the medicae bunkers and field stations. Processions of them, bloodied and dazed, were being guided down the ramps and walkways from the Bar's inner walls. The dead, Astartes and Army alike, were borne down on carts and loaders to the longhalls. Medicae personnel ran final checks to confirm extinction, then the corpses were divided, legionaries to one set of halls, human dead to others. All would be stripped of any functioning armour or equipment, for everything was precious. Apothecaries would extract vital gene-seed and any serviceable organs. Chirugeons would harvest the human bodies for blood, tissue and organs to feed the flesh-banks of the infirmaries.

What remained would lay in state until there was an opportunity for formal disposal. It was solemn work, with no time for proper ritual or ceremony.

'I want to see him,' Ceris Gonn told the medicae who had treated her.

'I explained this, mam–' he began.

'You know what I mean!' she spat. 'I want to thank him, for…'

He led her to the longhouses by the hand. She could hear the squeak and rattle of the body-carts, the clatter of armour being stripped, the low conversations of exhausted medicae. She could smell the blood, the choking odour of mass death.

She could not see. Her eyes were bandaged. The medicae had told her that her sight might return in time, if she rested and healed. A month, maybe two. Sound was her world, until then, sound and smell. As he led her by the hand, he told her gently that the Bar was now running a full evacuation. Only the holding garrison would remain. Even medicae were to be shipped out. Transports were waiting to ferry staff and civilian crews back to the Lion's Gate. He told her of the battle that day, of the Bar's near collapse under traitor onslaught. A crushing assault that had broken everything back to the fourth circuit wall in the space of a single morning. How close they'd come to ruin, but for the Lord of Baal and the Blood Angels and Imperial Fists who had stood with him.

She'd seen nothing of it. The shell that had taken her down, and felled an entire part of the tower, had been just one of the opening shots of an engagement that had been the most savage and precarious of the siege thus far. She'd been unconscious for most of it, and when she'd woken on a stretcher cart, her eyes had already been dressed and bound in gauze.

She'd heard the battle, the immense din of it, ringing

through the Bar's immense fortification. A world-ending war on the other side of a wall.

'I can give you five minutes,' the medicae said. 'Then I have to get you on a transport. No arguments. What was his name again?'

'Zephon,' she replied.

They entered a cool space, a stone building, away from the smoke-brushed open air. Different smoke here: incense. She heard quiet activity: the purr of drills, the clink of surgical instruments, soft incantations that she couldn't quite make out.

'Why is she here?' she heard someone ask. The medicae holding her hand seemed lost for words.

'My life was spared by a warrior called Zephon,' she said, tilting her head blindly, not knowing which direction to face. 'A shell fell. He... he shielded me with his body. I would have died.'

'And?'

'I think he died,' said Ceris. 'I wanted to...'

'What? What did you want?'

'To pay my respects.'

She heard voices murmur. She twisted her head, trying to locate them.

'This way,' the voice said. It was a strong voice, but it was dulled, like a fine sculpture that had been left in a dark place, alone and unobserved.

The medicae didn't say anything, but she felt him tug her hand, and lead her forwards. His hand was trembling slightly.

'Zephon,' said the voice. 'A captain. Called the Bringer of Sorrows. His war was a long one, and painful. He was gravely wounded, and repaired with augmetics, all his limbs. The grafts were difficult. His body rejected them. He was not suited to line service after that. But on Terra, he received some treatment for his degrading bionics. The treatments were unorthodox, though they healed him. Made him whole again, enough to rejoin the honour guard and fight for these walls.'

'But he's dead?' she asked.

'Giving his life for you, it seems.'

She let go of the medicae's hand, and reached out. She felt the edge of a metal bier, then the hard surfaces of armour. A body laid out, silent and cold. Her fingertips felt the ash and soot coating the armour.

'I'm sorry,' she said. 'I'm so sorry. I cost him his life. One human saved. That's a poor return for a legionary.'

'The Legiones Astartes are the shield of mankind,' said the voice. 'Zephon was only doing what he was made to do.'

She traced the edge of the armour, the breastplate, the shoulder guard.

'I'm still very sorry he died,' she said.

'So am I,' said the voice. 'Why were you here?'

'My name is Ceris Gonn,' she replied. 'I am an official observer. I have… I have the warrant to prove it. The Lord Praetorian, in his grace, issued them so that I, and others like me, could bear witness, and record the events of this war for future generations.'

'A remembrancer?'

'Like that. The Lord Praetorian believes that history is a solace. An art that must be sustained, even in the darkest time. For the recording of history allows for the hope that there will be a future to read it.'

'That is unusually sentimental for him. Yet, quite like him, nonetheless.'

'Who am I speaking to?' Ceris asked.

'You will have to go now, Ceris Gonn,' the voice replied.

'I know. I understand. Gorgon Bar is at the brink. All non-essential personnel are to vacate, effective immediately. I've been told this. Besides, my work is futile. I had only just begun, and now I can't observe.'

'You can't,' said the voice. 'But I believe the Lord Praetorian is correct. A hope for the future is of value. Perhaps the only light we have. We must keep writing history, or our Imperium will become an unremembered empire. But you must leave this hall. The work of the Apothecaries is private. A solemn duty that humans should not witness.'

'Of course.'

She paused.

'What will happen to Captain Zephon?' she asked. 'Will the Apothe-caries–'

'His bionic augmentation makes the normal procedures more difficult. This is no place for such work. His body will be transported back to the Sanctum, and placed in stasis until time can be found for the proper retrieval to be done.'

'May I…?' she asked. 'May I travel back to the Sanctum with his body? May I… accompany him? Can I witness that, at least?'

'If you wish.'

'Whose authority honours me so?' she asked.

'Mine.'

The medicae led her back into the yard. She felt the day's heat on her skin.

'Which senior was that?' she asked. 'Which lord officer?'

'Throne above,' the medicae murmured, 'that was the Lord Sanguinius.'

'My lords,' said Militant General Burr, 'half a kilometre out, and closing.'

'Understood, Konas,' said Jaghatai Khan. The primarch glanced across at Raldoron and Valdor. 'The day's work is at hand,' he said.

Both nodded.

'Give the word, lord,' said Valdor.

The Khan smiled. 'The First Captain has zone command,' he replied.

'In fact,' said Raldoron, 'good Konas Burr has that honour. I am simply here to expedite fluid function between Army and Astartes.'

All three looked at Burr. He adjusted his collar, which seemed to sit rather too tightly all of a sudden.

'It is my honour, lords,' Burr said. 'With respect, I'd rather strip bare-naked, and charge those bastards alone than give any of you three an order.'

The Khan's eyebrows rose, then he bellowed out a laugh. Valdor smiled. Even Raldoron, the quietest of them, glanced aside to disguise his smirk.

'You're a good man, Burr,' said the Khan. 'We are all brothers in this, now and forever. This is labour for legionaries. Are your forces prepared?'

'Steady on the line, my lord,' replied Burr. 'Kimmerine, Vespari, Auxilia, Albian. Marshal Agathe reports tight hold and readiness. So too Colonel Bezzer and Militant Commander Karjes. Fire gullies lit. Artillery ranged.'

The Khan looked back at Valdor and Raldoron.

'Then let's take a walk,' he said.

'Sir! My lord…' Burr began. 'They are clearly trying to lure you out.'

'Oh, clearly,' replied the Khan.

'Tempt you into another charge–'

'Of course. They're not idiots. Diseased wretches, but not idiots.' The Khan looked at Burr. 'The brave Imperial Fists have a doctrine. Not one step backwards. Mine is rather different. It is easier to avoid taking a step backwards if you have already made several steps forward.'

'Should I prepare for line advance, lord?' asked Burr.

'No, you hold, Burr,' said Jaghatai Khan. 'Hold and wait.'

'For… what?'

'In case they come through us, Konas,' said Raldoron.

'In case we don't come back,' said the Khan.

They climbed the lip of the trench, and began to walk across the mud-wash, weapons gripped. Fire gullies blazed at their backs. Along the line of the Colossi Gate, Space Marines stepped out with them: the white-armoured ranks of the White Scars and, fewer, the flashes of red and yellow, the Blood Angels and the Imperial Fists.

And occasional glints of gold, the Custodians from Valdor's force.

Ahead of them, vapour. A smoke-mist. A dark mass.

'Never let them come to you,' the Khan remarked dryly as he strode forward. 'If they get to us, we've already given up our killing ground.'

Raldoron drew his greatsword. The moving blade flashed in the smoking light.

'The essence of your doctrine, my lord,' he said, walking at a steady pace to match the Khan's stride. 'The unexpected. Meet them coming in.'

'Meet them coming in, Raldoron. Meet them before they are ready. Meet them short of their target. Never do what's expected. Never allow the enemy to execute in full.'

He glanced at Valdor, on his other side.

'I imagine you dislike this, Constantin?'

'I get to war at your side, Great Khan. What objection could I have?'

'Heh. From you, Constantin, who are pledged to place and function?'

'You simplify my order's doctrine as casually as others simplify White Scars tactics, Jaghatai.'

'Then, my apologies,' said the Khan. He had drawn dao and

boltgun. Ash flakes fluttered down over the walking line like early snow. 'Though I know,' he added, 'you are only here to keep me in your sight.'

'I'm here to–' Valdor began.

'Tell me Rogal didn't send you, friend Constantin,' said the Khan. 'Tell me Rogal didn't despatch you to Colossi to keep an eye on his brother the unruly Khan and his capricious notions.'

'I have lived my life in secrets,' replied Valdor simply. 'But I have never liked lies. Of course he did.'

The Khan nodded, unperturbed.

'I will take back the port,' he said. 'I've pledged so. I'll do it. But this needs doing first. Colossi must stand. Once this fight is settled to our benefit, I will take the port. Oh yes, Constantin, dear Constantin, I am well aware of how Rogal thinks he's handling me. Keeping the barbarian on a short leash.'

'I don't believe that's entirely his thinking, Jaghatai,' said Valdor. 'But his strategy is central to–'

'It's peerless, Constantin,' said the Khan. 'Peerless. I weep at the beauty of his tactics. Rogal will orchestrate this, and win it, or we will die. I have faith in him. I will not disrupt his plans. But in the execution, they sometimes lack room for... improvisation.'

The three of them continued to stride into the closing fog. Their pace had increased slightly. The Legiones Astartes line moved with them, resolute.

'Like walking out to meet the enemy?' Raldoron remarked.

'Just like that,' chuckled the Khan. 'They expect us to hold the line and wait, or charge them like maniacs. Not meet them, with confidence, in the middle.'

The billowing smoke grew heavier. It carried glowing cinders in it, like fleeting stars. Their striding feet squelched in the ooze. Valdor held his huge guardian spear braced across one shoulder.

'I imagine it helps that he might be here,' said Raldoron gently.

'Helps?' the Khan asked.

'To focus your mind on Colossi, rather than the goal of the port?'

'He means Mortarion,' said Valdor flatly.

'I know what he damn well means,' snapped the Khan.

'To meet him, here?' asked Raldoron. 'That's incentive enough, surely?'

'I'm here, Raldoron,' said the Khan, 'because Colossi is vital. Vital. I don't need an incentive to plant my standard here.'

They took a few more steps.

'Though I'll be watching for him,' the Khan added slyly. 'Hell's blood, but I'll be watching for him. And if either of you see him once we're in this, stay out of my damn way.'

The clouds of smoke began to part.

They saw the enemy, unveiled. Dark shapes in the thinning smoke ahead of them; dark shapes, dark lines, a dark mass. A host of the Death Guard, spread wide, advancing on foot at a steady pace. They could smell the sickness in them, the rot, and feel the wallowing fever heat of infected bodies. They could hear the clotted gurgle of frothed throats and consumptive lungs. Flies swirled in the smoke, buzzing like migraines, fed fat.

The enemy mass gave no sign that it had sighted them. It just continued its steady, turgid advance. It had time and weight on its side. Even obscured by the drifting smoke, it was clear that the Prince of Decay had fielded a vast number of his warriors against the Colossi line, seven times or more than the Khan had walked forward from the trenches. The lack of reaction did not seem like brute stupidity, or even the preening confidence of a superior force. To Raldoron of the Blood Angels, it felt like a simple lack of response. The Death Guard did not react, in the same way that an encroaching disease does not react. It simply continues, at its own insidious pace, invading a body, multiplying, spreading. As a cancer advances through a body, through system and tissue and organ, as an infection spreads and overwhelms, it creeps at its own pace, heedless of the antigens and philtres dispersed against it, knowing that it will consume and envelop, that it will triumph, and it will be neither delayed nor rushed.

The Death Guard would not be provoked into urgency, not even by the sight of its enemy emerging from the smoke to meet it. It would approach at its own speed, slow and lingering and relentless.

For the lingering was part of its process. It was built to overwhelm eventually, but it wanted the lingering agony that preceded that end to last.

The torment was the point.

The Khan's rate of stride began to increase. No word or command was given or needed. The Astartes line accelerated with him, keeping pace. Fast strides, then a jogging measure, then a bounding run, heavy plated figures spattering wet mud and quaking the ground as they began to charge.

Shields up, blades lifting, heads down, weapons aimed.

Twenty metres from the advancing wave of grey-green diseased monsters, the Khan's force began to fire. Boltguns boomed and sparked, their muzzle flashes dull red in the twilight of smoke. Front-rank Death Guard crumpled and fell, spinning aside, toppled, blown open, punctured. Fractured armour burst from explosive impacts. Putrid meat and liquid discharge showered.

The guns of the XIV began to answer, blinking and roaring from the plodding ranks. The Death Guard had stirred from its brumation. Charging legionaries on either side of the Khan dropped, killed outright, or smacked off their feet as explosive bolts detonated against storm shields. With another ten metres clearance, the Death Guard mass would mow the loyalist strike force down entirely.

But it did not have ten metres. The Khan's war line was running, and it was already on them.

The impact was a rippling clatter of metal on metal, of plasteel and ceramite clashing, that ran along the battle line like the hammer blows from a thousand working anvils. It was so loud and fierce it could be heard by Burr and his men back in the trenches.

The assaulting Space Marines brought the force of momentum with them. They collapsed and splintered the leading files of the enemy, running them down and trampling them, finishing those that fell underfoot with stabbing blades and merciless execution shots, using their corpses as stepping stones to meet the rows behind.

Foremost were the Khan, Valdor and Raldoron. A triumvirate, they were the leading edge of the assault's blade. Constantin Valdor, a figure of gold, broke the enemy line like a siege ram. His Custodes spear had obliterated eight of the foe before he'd even made contact, the weapon held level like a spearing pike, the bolter mechanism spitting fire above the aimed blade-head. Once he was in among them, he scythed them apart, cutting through corrupted plate, cracking armour like porcelain, crushing helms like eggshells, flipping bodies into the dank air. Within seconds, his magnificent form was plastered with suppurating matter, back-spattered from his kills. Blades struck and broke against his auramite. A giant, he drove into the ranks, like a reaper hacking through dense vegetation, raking a pathway into the mass.

Raldoron was a crimson spectre. His greatsword glinted as it swung, refracting the infernal light. Nothing it met stayed whole. Bodies fell either side of him, cut through, severed, sliced segments falling and rolling in the mire. He howled the battle hymn of his Legion, the sacred songs of blood and wonder that fuelled every blow he struck. If Valdor was a demigod unleashed, then Raldoron was an angel, demonstrating the monstrous terror of an angelic being unbound. He was the face of revelation. Angels inspire awe: the grace and serenity they radiate in repose becomes astonishing fury when they are roused.

They fought at either hand of Jaghatai Khan, Valdor to his left, Raldoron to his right. The Khagan, Khan of Khans, was another thing altogether. His primarch frame towered over the enemies he raged upon. Death Guard broke hopelessly around him like storm waves dashing against a rock. There was a fire in his eyes that lit fear even in diseased minds. He was feral and elemental. It was not the wild ferocity of his gene-brother Russ, the shadow-savage killing lust of the wolf pack. It was pure, the clean, cleaving, unblinking razor of an eagle, focus-locked and emotionless, surgical. He was no snarling muzzle, tearing a carcass apart in a frenzy. He left that kind of manic killing to the Wolf King and his Fenrisian Rout. He was the cloudless wild, the splintering strike of lightning, the bone-snap impact of a striking hawk, the sharp cry of unheralded death in a wild and lonely place. He was the unmourned death of a far, forgotten cairn.

His bolter spoke. His dao gleamed. The enemy simply died around him. Every strike and every shot maximised its killing potential, an utter economy of destruction, as though death were a finite resource, and he was meting it out; unstintingly, but never more than was necessary, so as not to waste a single drop of it. Death Guard crumpled in his wake, many apparently still intact or whole, felled by an exact thrust, a single expert slice. Not overkill, just total kill. He had come among his foe to measure out death, blow by blow, each dose in a precisely lethal quantity.

His White Scars did the same. Along the line, they matched the superbly drilled and tireless precision of the Imperial Fists with shocking and relentless fidelity of their own. They fought

at the sides of Raldoron's ferocious Blood Angels and the staggering might of Valdor's invincible Custodians, and sowed
death with sure and rigorous lucidity, with the hardwired
focus of apex predators. None who witnessed it, Custodians,
Imperial Fists or Blood Angels, would ever demean them as
barbarians again. They would respect them as a man respects
the unnegotiable destruction of a storm.

The unwavering loyalist line buckled the front of the Death
Guard host, and compressed it, driving it into itself, in a tangled maelstrom of confusion and slaughter. The mud vanished
under a carpet of impacted and contorted armoured corpses.
The air hung heavy with a murk of blood vapour, smoke and
clouds of swarming flies. The brutal carnage was muffled by
the pall, as if everything was swaddled in thick blankets. The
blast of guns was dulled, the impact of blades hollow. For every
warrior, the world was wrapped tight, confined in a deadened
space where the loudest sounds were his own rasping breath
inside his helm, the noxious buzzing of insects and the ring
of weapons striking his plate.

Deep in the press of the slaughter, the Khan sensed the
enemy formation breaking around him, disintegrating into
retreat.

And he sensed flashing. There was flashing. Broad and
bright, banishing the smoke, strobe-lighting the entire killing
field. Sheet lightning, wide and amorphous, was shivering and
blinking overhead.

The Khan heard sharp pinging. Hailstones were raining
across them, chiming like bells as they bounced off his armour,
and off the plate of the bodies around him.

He put a warrior of the XIV to death with a wrench of his
sword, let the body flop backwards, and looked up. Pebbles
of dirty ice burst into powder and grit across his face. The low
sky was churning, pestilential clouds frothing and souring. The

sheet lightning became more intense, backlighting the heaving clouds with a blue, photoluminescent afterburn.

He knew that blight-taste. Knew it too well.

'Naranbaatar!' he yelled, trying to locate his senior Storm-seer in the sea of mayhem around him. Hail was bouncing off everything like spilled ball bearings.

'We must go as we have come,' said Qin Fai, reaching his Khagan's side. The loyal noyen-khan was smeared in blood that was running pink, the melting hail diluting it.

'Agreed,' rumbled the Khan. 'Sound it. Call it, Qin Fai. Let us draw back.'

'Not yet!' Valdor cried. He was close by, still at the Khan's left hand, demolishing Death Guard, who were tumbling before him. He looked back. 'Turn now? Jaghatai, we're breaking them!'

'They are breaking themselves, Constantin,' said the Khan.

He could hear a thunder of hooves. It was not the drum-roll thump of cannons that had made his charge, two days before, to resemble a cavalry action of old.

It was actual hooves.

The massed lines of the Death Guard before him were breaking, but not in overrun and retreat. They were parting to let something through. Giant hooves trampled the mud. Antlers and horns loomed through the smoke and hail, high above the heads of men.

The Neverborn descended. Brute monsters, warp horrors, cloven-footed, broad-horned, their legs jointed like goats, their hunched torsos like ogres, skins charred black and gleaming, their bristled lips drawn back from snouts and muzzles, from fangs and equine teeth that slobbered foam and spittle, and brayed and roared and squealed. Above those mouths, their faces were autumnal masks of moth-wing patterns, brown stripes and whorled dusty creams, dotted with asymmetrical clusters of spider-eyes.

From where he stood, the Khan could see eight of them bearing down, hideous to behold, like the devil-daemons in old and fanciful woodcuts. Not a single one of them was smaller than a Warhound Titan.

The sabre in his fist felt like nothing, as weak and useless as the ice flecks melting on his plate.

He felt the true ice of terror in his heart.

Ahriman lowered his hands. They trembled, as though a high voltage current was streaming through his fingers. Braying and howling rang up the vale to the broken battlements of Corbenic.

He looked across at Mortarion. The Pale King was watching the horror unfold below.

'*They ride out,*' said the Pale King.

'They ride out,' agreed Ahriman. 'They are summoned into flesh upon the face of Terra, and they walk. Your warriors have drawn the enemy into the open field. What mine have summoned will purge the field entire, and bring Colossi down.'

THREE

Guelb er Richât
Rules of hospitality
The Opener of the Ways

John descended into the eroded dome.

It was over forty miles across, formed of varying concentric rings of sedimentary rock and quartzite. From the air, it looked like a whirlpool with its circling bands of rhyolite, vegetation and sand. He knew that, because he'd flown above it, several times, years before.

Many years before. It had been her camp then, her retreat. Now, apparently, it had become her permanent home.

Some said it looked like an eye. An eye staring up at the heavens. It had been staring for a long time, since the primordial period known as the Cretaceous. The eye had opened long before the rise of man. It had gazed at the sky as man learned to walk. It had sheltered walking man, *Homo erectus*, in its wadis, and those walking men of the Acheulean epoch had left their bones and hand axes in its dust.

It had stared, unblinking, through time, through eras of humid vegetation and creeping glaciation. The land had come to be called Mauritania. That was the name John remembered,

at least. Names changed, eroded by time. The descendants of
the ancient Sheba and Thamud had named the eye *Guelb er
Richât.*

For so many aeons it had gazed up at nothing but sky and
stars. What gazed back at it now? John wondered.

The sky, dipping to evening, had turned reef-water blue.
White dust kicked up around his boots like bread flour. He
passed the first of the outer markers. Stone idols set on boulders. Pendulous Earth-mothers, full-bellied, and warding
fetishes made of bone and twig and straw. John was fairly
sure they were cautionary signs and had no power, no magic
in them. But there was a good chance they could be wired
with sensor-trip systems, or placed to conceal auspex pods.

He drew his pistol. Then he holstered it again. He wanted
to be noticed. He wanted to be found and greeted. A drawn
weapon would only invite violence.

Ahead, in the bowl of a wadi, he saw a cluster of dwellings.
Some rusted habitat pods, half-tented with draped tarpaulins, and large Berber tents were gathered around a central
structure. A few small enviro-tents, old and patched, dotted
the site. They, and the hab-pods, and the corroded vox-mast
poking up above the scraggy thorn and mastic trees, were the
only clues that this place was not exactly the way it had been
when man first came to the spring that rose here.

He could hear the spring gurgling in its old stone cistern,
the dull neck bells of goats grazing on the salt grass.

The central structure was a stone ruin, an earth lodge secured
and out-built with carved stone by the ancient Berber people.
No, they hadn't been called that in a long time. Berber was
a slur drawn from the Eleniki dead-tongue, *barbaros*, a word
for outsider just like barbarian. What were they called now?
Amizigh… 'free men'. No, that name was probably a long
time dead too. Numid? Whatever. The Berber were probably

long dead too. This wasn't their place any more. This was no one's place.

Except hers.

The earth lodge was half-buried in the soil. Its stone walls, above ground, had toppled and been rebuilt many times. Missing sections and lost roofs had been covered with stretched cloth, dyed indigo, as rich as the evening sky.

The place was so still. Was she even here any more?

Had everyone gone? Had he wasted his time?

'Hello?' John called out. His voice seemed an intrusion on the quiet.

'Hello,' replied a voice, right against his ear. The voice wasn't what concerned John Grammaticus, even though it had risen out of nowhere. What concerned him was the weight pressed against the back of his skull. The cold muzzle of a weapon. A large-calibre weapon.

John half-raised his hands, a casual gesture to display his submission.

'I'm armed, but not dangerous,' he said, trying to sound cheerful. 'You can take my gun.'

'I have.'

John glanced down. The pistol had been removed from his holster. Damn.

'Neatly done,' he said.

'Of course.'

'Well, now I'm not armed *or* dangerous,' he said.

'You're not armed,' said the voice. 'But you're definitely dangerous.'

'Oh, come on...'

'I typed you as you wandered in. Face match. Gene-print. I know exactly who you are, or who you're pretending to be.'

'Really?' asked John.

'John Grammaticus.'

'Ah.'

'John Grammaticus. Mercenary. Outcast. Rogue. Pariah. Agitator. Agent of xenos. Perpetual, to some degree. By any measure, dangerous. Would you like to take a moment to deny this? Or would you like to take this opportunity to lose the mask and admit a truer identity?'

'I have no mask,' said John. 'I am no shifted xenos, nor am I wearing a psykana disguise. I am what you see. John Grammaticus. Just that. I would quibble with your other descriptors. I haven't been any of those things for a long time, though I confess I have been most of them, a record that shames me.'

'It would shame the devil,' said the voice.

'Ah, well, he's hard at work on his own sources of shame. Can I lower my hands? Turn around?'

The weight withdrew from his head. John turned slowly.

He was looking down the barrel of a bolt pistol. It looked like a Phobos-pattern, the oldest pattern of all, and the weapon was a genuine antique. Cared for, it was, nevertheless worn and burnished by use. It had a patina of age that was impossible to fake. And no one mass-built them with a gold-wire grip and side-sights any more.

It was being aimed at him by a figure in plate armour. Legiones Astartes plate, and the figure wearing it was Astartes big and Astartes bred. But the armour was colourless and unmarked, not even the bare grey of the Knights Errant. It was pale, a sheened silver finish like a lead ingot.

The warrior wore no helmet and no smile. His face was clean-shaven, set hard, grizzled, as if he had a patina of age like the pistol he aimed. His hair was cropped straw. His eyes were indigo blue.

'What are you now, then?' the legionary asked.

'Just me,' replied John. 'A friend of the Emperor.'

'Well,' said the legionary, 'isn't that the most dangerous thing of all?'

'These days?' asked John. He chuckled. 'I should think so.'

'In any day,' replied the legionary, without a hint of humour.

'But you're one of His,' said John.

The warrior gently shook his head.

John felt his guts coil. Of course. He was too late. The Arch-enemy was already here. He was cornered by Traitor Astartes. Which faction? Which Legion? It hardly mattered, but he searched for a clue.

'I'm not His,' the legionary said.

'Then... the Warmaster?'

'Not his either.'

'I don't understand,' said John.

'It seems you never did. So she says.'

'You work for her?'

'Till the day I die.'

John had noticed something. A small stamp strip, like a hallmark, etched into the legionary's uncoloured plate just below the breast line. *LE 2*. What did that denote?

'I've come to see her. To talk with her,' said John.

'No,' said the Space Marine. 'She won't meet with you. She knows what you are. What you've done. You're lucky she didn't just send me out to sanction you. A gesture for old time's sake, I suppose.'

'I'm sorry, friend,' said John. 'I need to see her. I've come a long way to see her. A long time. I know I'm not popular here. I understand she despises me.'

'Just walk, John Grammaticus,' said the Space Marine. 'Walk now, back into the desert. Back to wherever you came from. I'll give you that one chance, because she wants me to. Walk now. This offer of mercy expires in a matter of seconds.'

'I need to see her,' said John, not moving.

'You're too dangerous,' said the legionary.

'For god's sake,' said John wearily. 'You must know what's happening. She must know. The hell descending on Earth. The hell overwhelming the Himalazia and tearing down everything that holds our civilisation up. Horus Lupercal is days away from destroying our species. And you think *I'm* dangerous?'

'So why have you come?'

'To stop it all,' said John.

'Horus? You can't.'

'Of course I can't,' John snapped. 'He's bloody Horus. No one can. I'm here to stop Him. Because He's the only one who can end this abomination.'

'That's the stupidest thing I've ever heard,' said the Space Marine. 'Even coming from a man who's spent his life making stupid decisions. How do you propose to stop Him?'

'That,' said John, 'is why I need her help.'

The legionary walked him into the earth lodge, keeping the old bolt pistol aimed at the small of John's back. They descended a flight of stone steps that had been bowed down by centuries of scuffing foot traffic. Above them, the last of the day's light shone through the sheets of indigo cloth that had been stretched across the gaps where sections of the old rock roof had fallen in.

The steps led down into a wide chamber of irregular plan. Canopies of silk and dyed cotton had been raised on wooden poles to screen off the low, damp stone vault of the ceiling. It felt like entering a tent, the sanctuary tents of the PanAfrik nomads. Woven carpets, their patterns bright and intricate, had been rolled out to cover the uneven brick floor. There was some low wooden furniture, heaped cushions bound in soft hides and silk; a few candles burned on copper dishes. More candles, a few ailing lumen globes, glowed within brass lanterns that hung from the tented roof on chains.

As much as it felt like the interior of a nomad home, it also felt like a shrine. It reminded John of the temples of Mythrus he'd visited a few times in his days as a soldier of the Caucasian Levies, a thousand years before. The Mythraic creed, the old, informal soldiers' religion, had still been a thing then, back when faiths still had a little life left in them. His comrades had tried to induct him, but he hadn't taken to it. This place was more comfortable than those dark and secretive underground chapels, but it had the same provocative quality of silence and mystery, an air of captured grace.

The effigies added to the shrine-like feel. They were everywhere, occupying alcoves in the old stone walls, or hung from pegs. More Earth-mothers, eyeless, sack-breasted and bigger bellied; a Catheric icon of the Theokotos; ancient figurines of Cybele, Persephone, Proserpina and Prithvi in chipped faience or battered bronze; clay votives of the Spider Grandmother; odd idols of tricksters, messengers and fertility gods; a terracotta vase showing Ninhursag; an ivory charm of Di Mu; a fid spearing a ball of red thread; Nwt, painted on a clay tile, surrounded by stars; the Hittite trinity of nursing midwives Hutellura, Isirra and Tawara. So many he recognised, so many more he did not. None were copies or replicas. The newest of them was twenty-five thousand years old.

He picked up a little wooden carving of a Hopi trickster, and studied it. 'I never took you for a person of faith,' he said out loud, knowing she was close.

'You never really knew me at all, John,' she replied.

'True,' he agreed, looked around. She had appeared from behind the silk screens at the back of the room, as silent as ever.

Erda was tall, by any human standards. He'd forgotten that about her. She wore a simple, floor-length thob of indigo cotton, waxed to iridescence, that veiled her figure, except for the pull at her hips. A purple tesimest was knotted over her shoulder, and then wrapped across her head in a cowl. There had to be psy-refractors woven into it, perhaps a null cap, because he had no read on her famous mind at all. Her eyes were vivid light blue, her skin like polished rosewood. Even modestly shrouded, her beauty was evident. John was sure it would be obvious even if she was fully veiled in a niqab. Like only one or two beings he had met in his life, her beauty was a radiance that came out of her, like an aura. He couldn't look at her for too long. What seemed in her beautiful reminded him too much of another numinous grace, and the memory of that made him queasy and nervous.

'So you have belief in these?' he asked, looking down at the carving in his hands. 'Any of them? All?'

'No,' said Erda. 'Those are just mementos, John. Gods have come and gone. None have any lasting power or influence, and most cause nothing but harm.'

'Ain't that the truth?' he replied, and put the carving back in its alcove carefully. 'I'm grateful for the chance to talk to you,' he said.

'That's not what this is,' she replied. 'I have admitted you because the al-kubra has rules of hospitality. The wastes are vast and harsh. Any traveller must be offered food and water, and a moment to rest, no matter the tribal or ideological differences between him and his host.'

'That's not what he said outside,' said John, jerking a thumb towards the Space Marine.

'Leetu was just doing his job,' she replied.

'Leetu – Leetu? Leetu can surely put his bolt pistol away now?' John said.

'No,' said the legionary.

'If it goes off, it could damage something very valuable,' said John, gesturing at the precious effigies and figurines. 'Like me.'

'You are a dangerous soul, John,' said Erda.

'Not as much as I used to be, really,' he said, shrugging.

'Long story, but one thing led to another, and I'm on my last life. No more perpetuity for me. It was fun while it lasted. No, that's a lie.' John sighed. 'My point is, the big guy there could tackle me easily, with that Astartes speed and strength of his, and he'd break me, and I would not get up again. Ever. He doesn't need the gun.'

Erda nodded very slightly. The Space Marine locked his weapon's safety, and clamped it to his hip. She nodded again. Three figures came out from behind the silks, an old woman in a niqab, a girl and a teenage boy. They carried lidded bowls, cups and a stoneware pitcher on brass mesomphalos dishes. They set them down on the low tables, and left.

'Food, water and a moment to rest,' said Erda.

John sat down on the cushions, and lifted the lids from the black earthenware bowls. Tahricht, stewed apricots, fine bouchiar wafers with butter and honey, a glossy tajine of squab. His mouth watered. He hadn't realised how hungry he was.

'This is great,' he said. 'Very welcome. I'm not sure the last time I ate. I mean, how long ago or when. I–'

Tears came to his eyes involuntarily. He'd been running on nothing but adrenaline and emptiness for too long. The relief was painful.

'Sorry,' he said, hurriedly wiping his eyes. 'Sorry. *That's* embarrassing.'

Erda squatted beside him, and poured water from the pitcher into one of the cups. She handed it to him. It was a small and delicate brown beaker, a kintsugi piece. Once broken, it had been repaired and healed with fine seams of lacquer and powdered gold.

'Eat and drink,' she said. He nodded, and did so.

Erda stood back up. The legionary was watching him. 'He is a strange man,' he said, speaking in a Hortsign battle cant from the Unification age.

'Yes, I am,' said John. Mouth full, he looked up, and grinned at the Space Marine.

'You can't disguise your words from him, Leetu,' said Erda. 'John is a logokinetic. He speaks and knows any language. He mindglosses. It is the only one of his gifts that he was born with.'

'Like I said,' said John, eating with his fingers, 'it's about the only one I have left. The others were given, and are now gone. I'm not a Perpetual any more.'

'You never were,' said Erda.

'Well, no. Technically, I was. A reincarnating immortal. Fun times. I was one of your lot by default.'

'By the manipulation of the xenos aeldari,' said Erda. 'Not one of us. You merely rhymed with us. And poorly.'

'Well, Erda,' said John, still chewing, a slight grin on his face, 'if your kind ever rhymed, as you put it, with each other, it would have been a miracle. I didn't rhyme with any of you, because there wasn't a tune to match. Show me the rhyme, Erda, and I'll sing along. But I don't think there is one.'

She sniffed.

'There is some truth to that statement,' she admitted.

John smiled, and took a sip of water from the beaker. 'Look at us, having that conversation after all.'

'Not at all,' she said.

'Come on,' he said. 'The food and water is welcome, the chance to just sit the hell down. I'm grateful. But that's not why you let me in. You're intrigued, and you want to talk.'

'I have not laughed in a long time, John,' she replied. 'I have not even heard the sound of laughter. I listened to what you said to Leetu. I have no wish to discuss it with you, but I let you in because I wanted to hear it from you. Directly. I wanted an excuse to laugh out loud.'

'Mmm. Tough crowd,' he said. He picked up another wafer,

then put it back, and wiped his hands. 'I don't think there's much to laugh about. Not these days. It's become a time quite devoid of laughter. You know what's going on. Of course you do. It's indescribably bad.'

'You helped stoke that inferno, John.'

'Yeah. I made things worse. I was used, in my defence. Had the shit manipulated out of me by the Cabal, by Alpharius' bastards… There's a long list, believe me. I was used. I could have resisted, I grant you. I didn't. I'll regret that to the end of my days, which isn't going to be that far off. Now, I'm my own man. No one's using me. I'm following my own path. Trying the best I can to salvage something. And my path's brought me here.'

'So this is redemption?' she asked.

He shrugged. 'If I gain some kind of absolution, great. That's not why I'm doing it. I'm doing it because someone needs to do something. It's probably too late, but someone needs to try. It should have been tried a long time ago. A long, *long* time ago. Back when there was still an iota of hope. Your kind. *Your* kind, Erda. That exclusive club. You should have done it. You should have got your heads out of your arses and started to rhyme. Worked together. The Perpetuals could have stopped this long before it ever started. But, oh no.'

He exhaled slowly, and took a sip of water. 'You don't accept I'm one of you,' he said, 'and maybe I'm not. I'm just a fake, an imitation, but don't you feel a glimmer of shame that an artificial perpetual, a johnny-come-lately wannabe, is the only one trying? Doing what you lot should have done long before I was even born?'

'I will kill him now,' said Leetu in Hortsign.

'Bloody have a go, big man,' John snapped back in the same battle cant. He looked at Erda.

'I tried,' she said.

'Yeah,' John said gently. 'Yeah, you did. Couldn't get the numbers on your side, though, could you? But yes, you did. That's why I came here. Tell me, lady, was it guilt that drove you to try? Like me?'

'What do you mean, John?'

'Well,' he replied, sitting back on the plump cushions, 'as you took great delight in pointing out, I've made things worse along the way. Collaborated with the Cabal, brought the Alpha Legion into play for the explicit goal of ending mankind. There were reasons for that. The Cabal's Acuity is *very* convincing. But anyway, I'm damned. Guilt fires me now. Guilt and anger at the part I played. So I'm guessing it drives you too. It's what made you try.'

'You think I'm driven by guilt?' she asked.

'You helped Him build it,' said John. 'You gave Him his damned children.'

'I love my sons,' she said. 'All of them. Even now. When I saw how things would go, I tried to stop it. The inexorable slide. I tried to make Him see. But there was no reasoning with Him. There never has been.'

'That's an evasion,' said John. 'You saw the truth of it long before you tried to act. Centuries before. More than *that*, probably. You knew what He was like, right at the start of it. You went along with it, and helped Him build the murderers. You acted far too late.'

She stared at him.

'Let us speak of evasions,' she said. 'You say you have freed yourself from the xenos Cabal, and that you walk your own path, but that's a lie. You work for Eldrad Ulthran, farseer of Ulthwé. You are still in the thrall of xenosform.'

John sniggered. 'You are well informed. But not accurately. I work *with* Eldrad, not for him. And I'm not the only one. Some of us are starting to rhyme, Erda. Maybe too little, too late, but we are.'

'Like who?' she asked.

'Oll,' he said.

'Ollanius?' She frowned. 'Is he really still out there? No, he would never... He was always so adamant. He refused to get involved. I think he knew it was hopeless from the very first day. You're lying again.'

'I'm not,' said John. 'It took some persuasion. But I'm good at that. And it took the burning of an entire world, and the destruction of the life he'd chosen. Not, before you ask, my doing.'

'Which world?' she asked.

'Calth,' he replied. He saw the look on her face. 'Lorgar razed it. Shattered the jewel of Ultramar. Oll escaped because Oll is Oll. I've been guiding him along. He's come around to the idea, at long last, that someone needs to make a stand.'

John reached into his jacket pocket. He saw Leetu flex for his bolt pistol, and made a show of doing it slowly. He took out a slim pair of ornate wraithbone scissors on a ribbon.

'Eldrad gave me these,' John said, showing the object to them both. 'He freed me from Cabal control. He rejects their strategy entirely. Sacrificing the human species as a firewall against Chaos? Despite what's at stake, that's savage even by aeldari standards. He believes mankind can be helped. We can survive – in fact, we have the right to survive – if we can be taught how to fight and resist the Primordial Annihilator. But we're young and we're new and we're woefully ignorant, and there's one big problem about us – the person we follow. He can't be reasoned with. You said it yourself. He thinks He knows everything, and He's wrong. His ambition is wonderful, but His arrogance is a mortal flaw of tragic proportions. Tell me you don't know that.'

'I know that,' she said.

'So,' said John. He put the scissors down on the low table.

'Someone has to make Him listen to reason, while there's still time. Mankind can survive. Mankind can save the galaxy rather than damn it forever. Hell, mankind might even ascend to a state of grace, and become greater than any species yet. We have potential, and Eldrad sees that. We have the potential the aeldari have lost. But there's very little time left to reverse things. And He, acting like the god He insists He isn't, is in the way. So… It's time to act.'

'Are those… scissors… intended to kill Him?' asked Leetu.

'Shit, no,' said John. 'I don't think they could. They're my passport. Eldrad gave them to me so I could get around. Move between moments. Snip and sidestep my way through the immaterium. It's not a great way of travelling, and it can be very hit and miss, but it got me here. Actually, I took a lot of wrong turns, and I missed the first time. Ended up about eight months ahead of now. By then, it was too late. Way too late. So trust me, I know of what I speak. We have a very small window left.'

He picked up the scissors again.

'These should show you the seriousness of the intent here,' he said. 'Even the aeldari seldom employ these. The causal risks are terrifying. They don't like to use them, let alone give one to a mon-keigh savage. Oll's travelling by similar means. His artefact isn't aeldari made. It's an athame of god knows *what* kind of provenance. But it does the trick. Anyway, you know that already.'

'What do you mean, John?'

John gestured to the lodge around him.

'I know this was all just testing,' he said. 'Sounding me out. You needed to be sure I was on the level, that I wasn't some Neverborn, wearing a human disguise. So you can bring Oll out now, and we can get started.'

'Ollanius isn't here, John.'

'We haven't got time for any more games,' said John.

'I am telling you, John, Ollanius is not here,' said Erda. 'I haven't seen him in a thousand years.'

John rose sharply, bumping the table so hard the pots rattled.

'No, no, no,' he muttered. 'He has to be. We agreed to meet here. We wanted to talk to you and get you on side, so this seemed like the best place to rendezvous. He should already *be* here.'

'He's not.'

'He has to be. He should have got here at least a week ahead of me. Probably more, because of the diversion I was forced to make.'

'Ollanius is not here, John,' said Erda. 'I'm sorry.'

'Oh shit,' he said. He sat down again hard. 'Oh shit. I thought he'd make it.'

'Might he have been intercepted?' asked the legionary.

'Yes, he might,' said John bitterly. 'As you can imagine, there are quite a few interested parties, keen to stop us executing this scheme. The Cabal, the damned traitor host, the warp itself… just for starters. Not really a bunch of adversaries you want to go up against. So, yes. There were forces trying to intercept us both.'

He looked at Erda.

'You should go,' he said.

'I'm not going anywhere, John.'

'Look, this is clearly unravelling fast. If they've got Oll, they're probably on me too. I might have led them here.'

'I'm not in hiding, John,' she said.

'That doesn't matter. They could be coming. And anyway, I'm surprised you're still here.'

'Where would I go?' Erda asked. 'The Earth is my home. Yes, I still like the old name for it. I live here, in a remote place, withdrawn, outside of the affairs of man. I have no power. Women and mothers seldom have. These days – for the longest time, in fact – humans generally have no power. Only He has. And He leaves me alone.'

'Maybe He does,' said John, 'but the end is coming. Nowhere, not even a place as remote as this, will be safe.'

'He won't harm me,' she said.

'Erda, He's not going to win. His children are going to destroy Him. The sons you made with Him are going to burn the world. And they will come for you once He is gone.'

'My sons…' she whispered.

'They are not…' he began. 'They are not as you remember them. The warp has taken most of them, even the best of them. They will show no mercy, no affection, no sentiment, no filial duty. They probably won't even know you, and if they do, it will be to hate you as they hate Him. You have to go.'

'What do you have to do, John?' she asked.

John shrugged.

'Now?' he asked. 'I don't have the first idea.'

'Perhaps Ollanius will yet come,' she said.

Full night had fallen, the great bowl of desert darkness, blue as ink and frothed with stars. John stood in the earth lodge, idly studying a figurine. It was so old, so worn, he couldn't tell if it was a trickster or a way-maker or both. Maybe Hermes Trisumagister, thrice great, opener of gates. And, as he recalled sadly, the emblem of the Jokers, Geno Five-Two Chiliad.

Erda had come in behind him without him hearing her.

'Interesting choice,' she said, nodding to the effigy he was holding. 'Azoth-Hermes. An opener of the way.'

'I was drawn to it.'

'I'm not surprised. It's very you, I think.'

He put the effigy back on a shelf.

'I was saying, perhaps Ollanius will yet arrive,' she said.

'Perhaps,' he said. He looked over at Erda. 'There's always hope. Well, there's always *been* hope. I think hope is a quality the galaxy is close to exhausting.'

'Will you wait for him? If he's coming here, you can wait.'

'Thank you. I'll wait a while. And if he doesn't come, I'll–'

'What? What will you do, John?' Erda asked.

'I don't know. Get on with it, I suppose. Alone. Try to reach Him. You could help.'

'How?' Erda asked.

'I need a way in. A way into the Palace.'

'I can't help you with that.'

'You're the most powerful of your kind,' he said. 'I mean, apart from Him.'

'None of us have ever been as powerful as Him,' she said. She sat on the heap of cushions, leaned back, and gazed at the silk canopy, which hung over her like a regal baldachin. 'That's always been the problem. He's not just more powerful, He is a different order of magnitude. A freak.'

'Really?' That made him smile.

'An aberration, even in terms of the Perpetual line, which is itself an aberration. You asked why we had never come together to stop Him or contain Him. There are many reasons, most of them trivial or personal, but the main one is that even together, en masse, the Perpetuals could not begin to match His power. We have many talents, many powers. We are what we are, transcendent mortals, who have often influenced the course of human life and achieved great things. We have been guides and steersmen, pilots and mentors, sometimes to whole nations and peoples. But He is something else, altogether. An engine of change, a font of power.'

'A god?' he asked.

'Not at all. At heart, He is a man. He has a personality, He has traits and flaws. All of those are magnified, of course. He is, truly, quite wonderful. Kind. Funny.'

'Honestly?'

'Yes. Funny. Witty. Articulate. Passionate. Incisive. Clever beyond genius. Charismatic. Devoted. Driven. Determined. From the earliest days of His life, He did what we all did. He saw His own power and tried to use it. He tried to steer mankind towards a better future. He tried to raise the human race up to achieve its potential. And, of course, because of His power, He was rather more effective than most of us.'

'Is that what Perpetuals do, then?' John asked. 'Is that what they are?'

Erda sat up, and looked at him. Her eyes were as blue as crystals.

'John, I tell you truly, I have lived a long life, and I have no idea what Perpetuals are. I *am* one, and I don't know. There are theories, and some seem convincing. The one I favour is that we are the next version of the human species.'

'How does that work?' he asked.

'Through history, the human species has reproduced along fairly neurotypical and physiotypical lines,' she said. 'The standard, mortal human, flawed and wonderful. But there are outliers. In every generation there are anomalies. Non-heterosic mutations. People born with unusual gifts or traits, unusual skills. The most obvious, I suppose, would be the psyker. Like you, John. As you were originally, before the xenosforms manipulated you. Born with a rare gift.'

'I'm a mutant?' John asked wryly.

'That's just a word. You're genetically atypical. That's all psykers are. Random variations from the baseline norm. That's how species evolve, John. That's how they progress. Rogue variations to the genetic norm, sometimes in response to environmental factors. Some of those mutations are failures and die out. Some are advantageous. A longer beak, a stronger jaw, an opposable thumb. Mutants born with those advantages tend to survive, *because* they are advantages. They pass their genes along, and their offspring share that advantage. Longer beaks and stronger jaws become the new norm. The variant gene survives and becomes part of the baseline.'

'And eventually, a species changes, and no longer resembles its earlier self?' said John.

'Yes,' she said. 'It takes a very long time. Longer even than a Perpetual might have patience for.'

'So you think Perpetuals are outliers too?'

Erda nodded.

'I believe the Perpetuals,' she said, 'which have been appearing for at least the last forty-five thousand years, are abnormally advantageous mutations. The theory suggests that we are what you might call *Homo superior*. The next step along for the triumphantly successful *Homo sapiens*. We are the next evolutionary form our species is intended to take.'

'Intended?' he echoed, and frowned.

She raised her hand apologetically. 'That was the wrong word. I do not subscribe to the idea of a divine plan, or the work of god. I meant the process of nature, advancing a species, enhancing it. I believe that the Perpetuals are the early appearances of the next generation of humans. Freak outliers appearing in very small numbers in advance of the evolutionary curve. And I believe, not because nature has any sort of plan, but because we are a fully sentient species, our purpose is to shape and guide the human race. Marshal its course and trim its sails. Use our gifts and longevity to drive it towards the future, to the point at which we are the new normal. To the point at which *Homo sapiens*, collectively, become *Homo superior*.'

'And that's what your kind does?' asked John.

'Generally. Mostly through individual efforts. There are very few of us, after all. Some have chosen to. Some have chosen not to. They have relished their gifts, and elected to indulge their lifetimes, succumbing to the whims of their personalities. For we are all still human. Some of us are selfish. Some insular, some petty, some lacking in altruism or empathy, with no care for the fate of the rest of humanity. In one instance I know of, one was psychopathic.'

'That's a story I want to hear,' said John.

'And I'll tell it sometime. It was long ago.' She looked down, thoughtful. 'And, of course, there are some who have not wanted to play the role. Ollanius is a great example of that. He is, I think, the oldest of us. He was always a man of faith, for he was born in an age when gods seemed real. He was never able to shake off the religiosity of his birth culture. Ollanius didn't believe that Perpetuals should meddle in the affairs of man. He thought the guidance of the human race was god's work alone. So he stepped aside, and lived his life, over and over again, never taking part. He wasn't the only one.'

'And the Emperor?'

Erda grimaced. 'You know, I loathe that term. It speaks to every part of His arrogance.'

'Does He have a name, otherwise?'

'Many. He has had many names over the millennia, none of them His own. I have no idea if He has ever had a true name. I knew Him as Neoth.'

'Neoth? His name is Neoth?' John shook his head in wonder. 'That's crap. And a huge disappointment.'

'No, that's just how I knew Him. It was what He called himself when I met Him. We were roughly coeval.'

'When was that?'

'In the time of the First Cities. He was a warlord even then. A king. And He was doing exactly what most of my kind do.

He had taken on the stewardship of the human race. He had a greater understanding of the universe than anyone, such was His power. He saw the dangers of the warp, the fragility of humanity, the recurring flaws of our species… credulity, anger, false-faith, yearning. Everything that was terrible and also wonderful about humanity. When I met Him, He had already begun on His path to shepherd mankind towards a brighter future.'

She looked at John. 'I believed in Him, John. I adored Him. Most of us did. It was hard not to love Him, hard not to be in awe of Him, harder still to perceive the dangers of His ambition. He wanted to achieve what most of us dreamed of, and He had the will and power to do it. Not just do it, but do it faster and more completely than any Perpetual could. He had the means to accelerate our efforts and accomplish, in just a few generations, what might otherwise take millions of years.'

John drew up a stool, and sat down facing her.

'Go on,' he urged.

'Over time He located, and tried to recruit, every single Perpetual on Earth,' said Erda softly. 'Some of us joined Him, others decided not to. Some of us fought Him. Several of the greatest conflicts in world history were caused by rival Perpetuals trying to thwart His programme. Did you know that?'

'I suspected so,' said John.

'He prevailed, John, though there were eras when He was badly set back. Over time, disaffection grew among our kind. Even the best of us could barely keep up, and I think He resented that. He is quite ruthless, and He is astoundingly arrogant. I suppose it would be hard not to be if you were Him. He was always right. He never looked for advice or counsel. He reshaped the world, and drove it forward, and He would not be questioned on the merit of His plan. To do so was… heresy.'

John raised his eyebrows. 'Hilarious. But you stayed at His side.'

'For far longer than I should have,' she replied. 'Most of us divorced ourselves from His efforts. He was taking risks. One by one, Perpetuals allied to Him slipped away. He was glad to see the back of them, I think. He was tired of their objections, and weary of their caution. He wanted results. He became angry with minds that could not match His speed of thought and His genius. So most of us left Him. They went away, into other lives, or went into hiding, or left the home world. A few stayed. The Sigillite, of course. He was always married to the cause. And, as I say, I stayed longer than I should have.'

'Erda, what risks was He taking?' John asked.

'The acceleration, John. He had no patience. He believed He knew everything He needed to know. He constantly pushed ahead. That's the irony. We are immortals, but He couldn't bear to waste time. Natural evolution takes millions of years. He refused to wait that long. He'd worked for twenty, thirty thousand years, and felt that was more than time enough. The natural stewardship of the Perpetuals, born through the evolutionary cycle, was not rapid enough for His needs. So once most of the natural Perpetuals had left His side, He built his own.'

'The primarchs,' John whispered.

'The primarchs,' she said, with a small nod. 'They're not actual Perpetuals, in any biological sense. They're the artificial equivalents of the Perpetuals, functionally immortal beings born from His blood and power and vigour, coded to accelerate His programme even faster. They were designed to live long enough to see His plan through to the end, and not die away so quickly, the way humans did, and they were indoctrinated from birth to follow His word, and not have opinions of their own, like naturally occurring Perpetuals. They were made to service His dream. He took what nature had wrought in the Perpetuals, and He built His own pathologised version. And through them, their genetic lines, the Legions.'

'He didn't do that alone.'

Erda was silent for a moment. Outside, the desert air sighed, and the neck bells of livestock clunked.

'He did not,' she said. 'I was still with Him then, one of the last few. Me, my colleague Astarte, a few others. I had misgivings, we all did, but He was very convincing. Compelling. And by then, He had become more powerful than ever. He needed a geneticist to work with Him, and that was my art. And He needed a biological source. A gene-stock rare enough to mix with His own. A Perpetual.'

'You.'

'Me. I was the other source. A genetic donor. He is the Father of Mankind. I am the surrogate mother. And the clinician. And the midwife. We made twenty fine sons. But He allowed me no influence. I was just a biological instrument. And once they were born, I began to properly understand the future He had prepared for them. The bitter destiny. The aggressively rapid and unnaturally savage evolutionary jump-start He was driving towards. No good ever comes of coercing nature, John. Through His sons, He would force the human race into the future, force it into submission, and defy the warp to do it. He had built artificial Perpetual-analogues and weaponised them, ready to resist the unbending cosmos. He was planning a crusade to retake the stars. To claim back in a bloody century or two what had taken millennia to lose in the first place. That was when I stepped away too. Astarte stayed, and finished the work on the Legion gene-build. But I left. I was heartbroken and bereft, but I stepped away.'

'No, not quite,' said John. 'This part I know. Eldrad told me. You didn't just step away, Erda. You tried to stop Him.'

'I tried to save my sons.'

'You scattered them.'

She sat forward, and stared at the ground, her hands across her mouth.

'I did. I took them from Him. I cast them onto the tides to spare them from His terrible ambition.'

'Shit,' John murmured. 'What did He do?'

'Raged, for a long while. I was gone by then. I hid for a long time. But He never tried to find me. I always thought that odd. I always expected His vengeance, for He could be vindictive, but it never came. Eventually, I came here, a place I'd always loved. I was born not far from here. I withdrew from the world, and He never came looking for me.'

She glanced at him, and smiled sadly. 'Because, I suppose, it was academic by then. He had moved on, fired and driven, as always. He sent the Astartes on their crusade anyway. A programme of reconquest, as He had always planned, but in truth it was just an excuse to find His sons. And His scattered sons were found again, of course, and returned to His side. I had failed. My efforts merely delayed His programme. I tried, John, but I did not stop Him.'

'Will you try again?'

'No, John. It's too late.'

'Please.'

'Everything is broken, John.'

John slumped. 'Oll's not coming. I can't do this alone.'

'Perhaps you shouldn't,' she said.

'Why not?'

'My fundamental objection to Neoth's Great Work,' she said firmly, 'is His haste and urgency. To supplant the natural flow of life with an artificial version that tramples ethics and morality and wise prudence. Artificial Perpetuals, John. That was His plan, and look, see how it has worked. And you, John, earlier you chided me and my kind for not taking action. You called us derelict that we had not made a concerted effort to block Neoth's progress, and that we should feel ashamed that you, a fake and neophyte immortal, should be doing what we should have long since done. You are an artificial Perpetual too, in a way, John, or at least, you were. I have no reason to trust your judgement, for you, like Him, and like my poor accursed children, are trying to hasten the movement of fate.'

'So, you'd leave it up to the cosmos and natural order, and see how everything turns out in the end? Erda, with the greatest respect, none of us are going to live to see what that end is.'

He moved across, and sat down beside her. The trays that had brought his repast were still on the low table. He picked up the beaker he had drunk from earlier.

'Kintsugi,' he said. 'I love kintsugi work. To take time and huge skill to rebuild a broken thing.' He ran his fingers along one of the beaker's crooked golden seams. 'Other cultures would discard it. Broken pottery. But no. The craftsman puts it back together, fusing each piece with gold. And he uses gold because he doesn't want to hide the fact that it was broken. It wears its scars and turns them into beauty. I think kintsugi pieces are more wonderful than the original, unbroken pots.'

'I agree,' she said. She smiled broadly. 'I am braced for your staggeringly crude analogy, John, so get it over with.'

He laughed. 'Fine. I was building to a big finish there.'

She took the cup from his hand, and turned it over.

'I understand,' she said. 'The cup is us. The Imperium. Humanity. Terra. Everything is broken, but it can be repaired.'

'If we just make the effort,' he said. 'Apply a little meticulous skill. And if we're not afraid to let the scars show afterwards.'

'It's still about force, not nature,' she said. 'The aggressive application of unnatural force.'

'Yes, it is,' he agreed. 'Because of where we are now. It's all about force. We are sitting in the eye of the greatest war that has ever been. We don't have the luxury of waiting. The pot won't fix itself. Here's the thing... You broke with the Emperor, because He forced the pace of fate in defiance of nature. And you're afraid that I'm doing the same. An artificial drive. An artificial Perpetual trying to push change. The embodiment of everything you tried to stop. Just another false demigod trying to alter fate. The difference is, He was driven by pure ambition. It was in response to nothing except the pace of evolution. My effort is simply in response to His. I am trying to apply force in *response* to force.'

She studied his face.

'Tell me, John,' she asked, 'who do you fear more, the Emperor or Horus Lupercal?'

'At this stage, it's hard to tell,' he replied. 'But only one can stop the other. Either way. Jury's out. However, Horus will only destroy. He cannot be reasoned with. But intervention might work with your beloved Neoth. I'm not talking about helping Him win the war. I'm talking about stopping it completely.'

'He has never listened, never learned,' said Erda. 'In the cycles of old lore, He is Saturn. Inflexible authority.'

'What?' asked John.

'He is Saturn. He is Cronus. He is Oanis. It depends on your pantheon.'

'You don't believe in gods.'

'I don't,' she said. 'But the symbols have always intrigued me, and through the ages He has styled himself on many of them, for effect. Mithras, the soldier-god, Tyr Hammerhand, the Wolf of the Romanii, Arawn, Enlil of Storms, Maahes the lion-headed, Seth. And Saturn, most of all. The father-god. The maker. In the acroamatic texts of alchemy, Saturn is glyphed as lead, the *prima matera*. It is heavy and it seals, and limits, and protects. It is cold authority. Saturn is a black, stone prison, caging all truth inside its chain of rings.'

'Great. You're telling me to forget it.'

Erda smiled at him. 'No. I am taken by your spirit, John Grammaticus. Your resolve. I believe you may be a trickster god, John, but tricksters have always had their vital place. They cannot be trusted, but they are needed.'

'You've lost me, Erda.'

'He is Saturn,' she whispered. 'The Saturnine aspect is lead. Lead is heavy. But lead, John. Lead can be moulded.'

'Lead can be moulded,' he repeated. He smiled. 'Yes, it can.'

'It can be shaped. It can be re-formed.'

He got to his feet.

'So you will help?' he asked.

'If I can.'

'Because He is the Saturnine father, and you are... what? Nwt? Ma?'

'I have no aspect as a mother any more, John. The effigies of fertility and vitality in this place are just memories of the past. But perhaps I could be an opener of the way. That's what you wanted, wasn't it?'

'Absolutely,' he said. 'I need to get into the Palace. You fled from there. I think you know a way in.'

'There are means, but John, you have Eldrad's shears. You are already an opener of ways. When I came in you were examining that figure of Azoth-Hermes. You said you were drawn to it. Your kindred aspect.'

'The Palace is warded, against even Eldrad's device. I'm no way-maker. Maybe you were right, and I'm simply the other aspect of Hermes. The trickster arsehole part.'

'I told you, tricksters play a vital role,' she said. 'Did you know that one of his names was *stropheos*? It means a hinge. It opens doors, but it also turns fate. Are you that, John? Are you the hinge of fate?'

'I can try.'

'In the early days,' said Erda, 'when gods were plentiful, every

culture had a version of the trickster. One who opens doors
that could not open, and changes things without warning, to
much delight or consternation. Among the Yoruba, the trickster was called Eshu.'

'Great story. Why are you telling me this?'

'Because,' she said, 'Eshu, like Hermes, and Azoth, and Mer-
cury, and all the swift couriers of fate, is the solution. The
solvent. It is the agent that transmutes lead and opens the
cage of Saturn's black prison. But it is also called the Enforcer
of Sacrifice. To get a god to answer your bidding, you must
make an offering. You must pay god his price. Are you ready
for that?'

He went outside. The night was clear, and had become very
cold. Some of Erda's companions, including the three who
had served him food, had gathered around a leaping bonfire,
inside the ring of huts and tents. One was singing, an old, old
song that seemed almost familiar. The others, especially the
younger ones, were dancing and clapping. Sparks flurried up
towards the unending stars.

When they saw him, they ran away, leaving the fire burning.
They became darting silhouettes that flickered in the firelight,
and vanished into tents.

Afraid of me, John supposed. Or afraid of the trickster god.

'Bullshit,' he whispered. Erda had a way about her, the storyteller's knack. For all she said she didn't believe in gods and
spirits, that they were tall stories from a more credulous age
of the world, she had a way of convincing you. Her words
carried weight, freighting meanings inside meanings. She had
an odd way of synchronising things, both real and symbolic,
aligning them so they made some new, bewildering sense.
John liked that. There was mystery left in her, and that was
precious in itself. For all the Emperor was secret, and moved,

across the ages, mysteriously, the way a god is supposed to, His ambitions were not. The direction of His Great Work was blatantly self-evident. He was unsubtle. He always had been. A blunt, brute monolith.

'There should be more mystery in the world,' said John. Mystery left room for all sorts of things, for doubt and ideas and exploration. The tales Erda wove blurred the line between myth and reality.

And that seemed right, because that was the cosmos now. A cosmos that denied gods, but accepted the existence of a vast otherness. Supernatural forms existed, Neverborn, reaching into the world. Some said if you acknowledged such spirits, you had to allow for the idea there might be gods too. John had heard that argument too many times in the last few years. It fell down on its basic premise. Just because one thing existed, it didn't mean the other had to. The universe was many things, but it wasn't symmetrical. The existence of daemons did not prove the existence of gods. There was just the warp, in its unfathomable immensity, and on the other scale, the tiny speck of mortal life.

John strolled down to the fire, and poked at it with a stick to make the flames rise up again. He could understand why men had begun to see the Emperor as a god. At least the Emperor had the decency to deny that. He was just a man, only a man, but on a unique and different scale to any other.

And yet… He was, to all intents and purposes, a god. A de facto god. And if He was that, then John was a trickster, and Erda was an Earth-mother. The real question wasn't whether the Emperor *was* a god or not, it was *should* He be.

John took the torquetum out of his vest pocket, and carefully unfolded its intricate mechanism. It was the compass that Eldrad had given him to negotiate his path through un-space, and guide the cuts he made with the wraithbone scissors. It, too, was made of wraithbone. It was as cold as the night air around him. No trace of warmth, or the tingle that hinted Oll might be getting close.

'There is no sign,' said a voice.

John started sharply. Leetu was standing right beside him.

'Shit, you could stop doing that,' John said.

'Sorry.' The legionary didn't seem sorry at all. 'I made a sweep, right out to the rim of the eye and back. I checked every sensor trap and data-snare. No sign of anyone. I thought this friend of yours might have been hurt or stranded somewhere, but–'

'Thanks for trying.'

'I did it for her,' said Leetu. 'This person–'

'Oll Persson.'

'Oll? Person? What did I say?'

'Just say Ollanius.'

'Whatever, he seems to matter to her. I think she cares about him.'

'I think they were old friends,' said John. 'I mean, a long time ago.'

John glanced at the warrior.

'Speaking of old, that's an antique piece.' He gestured at Leetu's thigh-clamped weapon. 'Mark Two Phobos?'

Leetu shook his head. 'M676 Union Model. Pre-Phobos. Mark Zero, you might say. Made before the accord with Mars.'

'How old *are* you?' asked John.

'Old enough to have been issued it new.'

Leetu unclamped it, and handed it to John. He struggled with the weight of it.

'This is a real antique,' John said. 'Sickle-form mag. Side-sights, chambered for seventy-cal. They use seventy-five now.'

'So I hear.'

'You don't hanker after one of the new patterns?'

Leetu took the weapon back and re-clamped it. 'Why would I?' he asked.

John shrugged. 'Something new to play with? Improved stopping power?'

'I stop all I need to stop,' said the Space Marine.

'I'm sure you do. So... what Legion were you?'

'No Legion.'

'Never assigned?'

'Never anything.'

'Right, sure, but which... bloodline?' John asked. 'Which primarch was your genesire?'

Leetu looked at him. 'My father was Neoth. My mother was Erda. I was one of the first. Before they spliced in the gene-stocks.'

'You were a prototype?'

'Template.'

'And your name? "Leetu"? That's just a contraction of your serial code, right?'

Leetu nodded.

'So what *is* your name?'

'I don't have one. I've always been Leetu.' Leetu looked at him, as if measuring him carefully. 'You've convinced her to help you, I gather?' he said.

'Yeah,' said John. 'I'm not asking for much, but yeah.'

Leetu frowned. 'I don't like it,' he said. 'I don't care for you. But if that's her will, I'll help you too.'

'Because you answer to her?'

'Always.'

John nodded. 'Well, friend,' he said, 'I'll take any help I can get.'

They were silent for a moment. The fire crackled and spat.

'So then,' said Leetu. 'I was thinking. You arrived too late.'

'What?'

'It's the twenty-second of Quintus. Earlier, you said you arrived too late. Eight months out.'

'That's right.'

'You had to go back. Find a new route. Retrace your steps, so you arrived today instead.'

'Yes,' said John.

'What if your friend did the same?' Leetu asked. 'Arrived too late? Or too early? I don't know how it works. But the shadow of the warp has fallen across this world, and pathways may have been distorted. Twisted and bent out of shape. Maybe this Ollanius wasn't intercepted. Maybe he got here. Just not at the right time. Like you.'

'Oh god,' said John, his eyes wide. 'Maybe he did.'

FOUR

Locked away
Let me back in
Unwanted gifts

'It is becoming quite disturbed out there,' remarked Basilio Fo.

The black stone walls and floor of his cell, deep in the Blackstone prison, had just vibrated.

'The whole Palace shivers,' he added. He was pacing, fidgeting. 'Should we be concerned?'

'We're safe here,' said Keeler. She glanced up at Amon. The Custodian disliked giving her any details about the conflict raging beyond the ambit of the Sanctum, but that morning he had mentioned, in passing, specific points of turmoil at the Colossi Gate and Gorgon Bar. The siege was a ring of iron and fire around their throats, constricting with each passing hour. It was becoming so tight that the Imperial Palace, a structure she had always felt was the biggest and most resolute thing anywhere, had begun to tremble in fear.

'I think you are naive if you think we're safe anywhere,' said Fo, with a pinched smile. 'Outside howls a daemonic horror, pounding to get in, and we are locked inside these walls with the Great Daemon who made it. I do not know which would be safer, inside or out. Nowhere on Terra. Nowhere full stop. We could be hidden on an end world at the farthest limits of galactic space, and I fear we would not be safe there either.'

'From Horus?' she asked.

'From him, or his father, dear girl,' said Fo.

'You were speaking, when we last met, of a weapon. A trigger.'

He pouted, and tapped the pad of his index finger against his lips.

'Well, Euphrati,' he said, 'to construct a weapon, one must assess the intended target.'

'Horus?'

'Yes. And to understand him, we must consider his lineage. His family background. His bloodline. His sire.'

'The Emperor?' she asked warily.

'Yes,' said Fo. 'I knew Him, you see. I knew of Him. Back in the Strife. No one could *not* know Him. Let me tell you about Him. I was there when He truly became a thing of terror...'

The noise was the worst part.

The giant Neverborn were appalling to behold, of course. They had ravaged Colossi's northern and eastern lines, scouring away the trenchwork and emplacements that had held off the XIV's assaults for days. They had pulped the land into a miasma, a churning lake of mud and flames. They had killed everything they could reach. Over seven thousand of the loyalist forces. Konas Burr was among the dead, lost in the first few minutes of their atrocity.

But the daemons were almost too awful to accept. To visually register. Vast daemon forms, like blockprints of the Apocalypse, animated as raging shadows in the smoke and haze. Marshal Agathe tried not to look at them more than she had to, but when she did, they seemed unreal. Preposterous.

A child's drawing of a nightmare. A child's unreliable account of the thing under the bed that had woken him.

The noise, however...

Under the Khan's command, Colossi's garrison had fallen back, an almost frantic effort to empty the outer lines. The Neverborn had lumbered in to shred those emptying emplacements, and while they were thus occupied, the Khan had directed the full force of Colossi's wall guns, and the artillery, and tank formations, to pound the zone.

The daemons survived the long and exhausting barrage. They survived, or they were blown to shreds multiple times, and simply re-formed from the ooze. It was hard to say. What had yesterday been the front lines was today a burning zone, a vast furnace of destruction, in which very little could be discerned, no matter how hard you trained your field glasses. Agathe did not look very often, because sometimes, startlingly magnified, things looked back out of the fire.

The desperate and sustained barrage, which had drained Colossi's munition depots back to a mere quarter capacity, had bought them time. It had slowed the daemons' advance, and allowed the Great Khan and his men to pull as many souls as possible back behind the curtain wall.

Not enough. So many lost. Poor Konas, her unlikely friend. He wasn't here, which is why the zone command pin had passed to her.

The Great Khan's efforts had also bought them enough time to realign the heavy defences. Army and Mechanicum gangs had toiled to exhaustion, during the hours of the bombardment, to reframe the aegis and the telaethesic wards. Many major voids had to be dropped, and pulled back, their projection discs re-erected along the curtain wall to face outwards rather than up. The defenders had lost leagues of outwork ground, and they had also lost a great section of the void

canopy that had protected them. The voids, crackling like
frying meat, now covered the wall, and a little overhead, and
the telaethesic wards had been revised to match.

The Colossi Gate had surrendered an immense portion of its
outer front and support territory. The bastion line protecting
the Sanctum approach had, accordingly, suffered a massive
reduction. Aegis cover, partial and damaged before, was now
almost gone on the northern run of the Anterior Bastion. The
Neverborn, previously active only at the Lion's Gate space port
and its environs, now had liberty to roam more freely into the
Palace zone, deeper and closer than ever before.

The voids and the wards had stopped them at the wall. For
the time being, anyway.

Then the noise had begun. Uncannily, it was far worse than
anything they could glimpse. Deep in the inferno before the
curtain wall, the half-seen fiends were clawing at the wards,
and pounding on the shields. It was a constant drumming
thunder, a scratching, a rasping, a squealing, like iron nails
on glass, like teeth on stone, like blades on metal. And behind
those excruciating sounds, sounds that made you flinch every
few seconds, there was the endless braying and booming of
daemon voices.

The noise was by far the worst part.

Agathe hurried to the blockroom. She kept bumping into
personnel in the narrow tunnels of the wall redoubts. An extraordinary plague of flies, perhaps the entourage of the daemons,
perhaps the work of the pestilential XIV, had got inside the
walled fortress. They were everywhere, seething mats of shiny
black bodies that covered faces and hands, and slipped into
sleeves and boots and gloves and cups and nostrils. Environmental officers suspected bacterial clouds too. Everyone had
suited in gas-gear, masks and respirators, partly to keep operat-
ing in the blanket of flies, and partly to keep breathing amidst

the ghostly billows of the pesticide that was being pumped and sprayed, around the clock, to try to rid the fortress of infestation.

There were reports of plague cases. Wearing gas hoods, it was hard to see, and hard to catch your breath. It was stifling. The eye-pieces of the hoods were tinted. Everyone bumped into each other, their boundaries lost, their periphery vanished. Agathe could see almost nothing. It was as if she were approaching death, and her vision was tunnelling into darkness.

But she could hear.

The constant drone and buzz of flies. The patter and fidget of them clustering on her ear guards and crawling on her flak coat. Her skin crawled in sympathy. And she could hear, no matter how hard she tried not to, the terrible noise. The braying and squealing and rasping of the daemons clawing at the shields.

The archway into the blockroom had been strung with gas curtains, for all the good they did. Colossi's massive regulation system had been adjusted to increase internal air pressure in order to prevent gas penetration from outside, but that did nothing about the swarms inside, and only seemed to add to the suffering of the personnel. Everyone's ears rang and thudded, everyone's sinuses throbbed, everyone's eyes ached. Agathe kept tasting blood in her mouth.

She flashed her command seal at the sentries, parted the gas curtain and entered. Flies blew in with her. There were flies inside the room already. They swirled in the warm air, and settled on people and the fascias of consoles. The Great Khan, now acting commander of the Colossi repulse, stood beneath the main display, remonstrating with three of his men. The sight of him ordinarily filled her with dread – transhuman dread, they called it. He was so very much bigger than every other figure in the chamber. Today, the bulk of him seemed almost reassuring to her. She was comforted by the notion that they had mythical beasts of storybook proportion on their side too.

She was also oddly calmed by the fact that there were flies settling on him as well. He was the only person present bare-headed and unmasked. Green and black dots crawled on his face, and in his beard, and trickled over the white curves of his armour. Not even demigods were spared the torment.

She couldn't hear his words, but the White Scars he was addressing were Stormseers. She knew the name of one: Naranbaatar, the leader of their kind. They were warriors, but they were shamans too, their armour strung with beads and fetish-charms. Agathe, her background pure military, had always felt uneasy about the use, by some Legiones Astartes, of psykana and aetheric craft. It smacked of a time humanity had left behind, of ignorance and superstition. But now, like the scale of the Great Khagan himself, the sight of them seemed reassuring. If Colossi was to hold, it needed sorcery. It needed magic to fight magic.

Agathe didn't know the right words. It seemed preposterous to think in such terms, but she had seen and heard what was at the door. The Stormseers worried her, though. They seemed devoted and serious, but everything they had conjured so far – again, such a term seemed wrong and stupid – had been inadequate. Whatever magic was clawing at the walls, it was far stronger than anything they could muster.

Nearby, the captain-general of the Legio Custodes was briefing a quintet of his men. Like the Khan, Valdor and his men alarmed her, more giants in their midst. But Valdor brought a stoic calm, speaking low and clearly. She noticed that fewer flies swarmed on him and his golden warriors. Little carpets of dead insects crunched beneath their feet. It was said that each member of the Custodian Guard was a personification of the Emperor, a sliver of His supreme will made flesh and extended out into the world. Perhaps that aura of grace was anathema to the infestation.

'Marshal.'

She turned, clumsy and half-blind, and found herself facing Raldoron of the Blood Angels. He was First Captain of the IX Legion, and equerry to the Great Angel of Baal, no less. He had been sent to their lines in the previous days to oversee unit coordination. The besieged forces of the Palace were a raucous patchwork of mismatched assets drawn from any and all sources. They dearly needed glorious and admired champions like the First Captain to inspire unity, and foster cohesion.

Glorious, she thought. Flies clustered on his beautiful armour like beads of oil.

'My lord captain,' she replied, speaking overloudly, because she knew how badly the hood muffled her voice.

'You've brought the updates?'

'Yes, lord,' she replied, fishing a dataslate from her coat. 'Disposition of all forces on the walls and emplacements as of twenty minutes ago. Also, munition levels.'

'Shield bearing?' Raldoron asked.

'We're waiting on that,' she said. 'The tech-magi speak of fluctuation. They are trying to calculate a reasonable estimate. Should I deliver these to the Khagan?'

'I'll do it,' said Raldoron. 'He's occupied at present, and you are doubtless due back at your station.'

'I am, lord,' she said. 'His seers look tired,' she added.

Raldoron followed her gaze. They stared at the Khan and his men, deep in discussion.

'Not tired,' said Raldoron. 'Our kind does not tire. To me, their bearing tells of helplessness.'

'Which is worse,' said Agathe.

'It is, marshal. The power of the Librarius varies from Legion to Legion. Some, indeed, eschew it entirely, like the Praetorian's brave sons. I had always thought of the White Scars as more than just dabblers in the esoteric. I've seen them harness the elemental power of wild places to a degree that would have horrified any hardliner at Nikaea. I think of them as serious proponents of the controversial art.'

'It speaks to their barbarian heritage,' she said.

Raldoron turned his visor to her, and stared with unyielding disdain.

'A word of caution, marshal,' he remarked. 'Don't let the Warhawk, or any of his men, hear you recite such truisms. The White Scars are painfully aware of the way those of oh-so-cultured Terra regard them. As savages. As uncouth heathens, feral in aspect, who barely deserve the honour of being of the Legions.'

'My pardon, lord, I meant no such thing–'

'The affect comes too easily, Agathe. The White Scars are not lauded as champions the way the Imperial Fists or Guilliman's Legion are.'

'Or yours, lord.'

'Or mine. The human public does not hero them, or worship them as saviours. They think them wild and uncivilised. I know better, and would urge you to remember that. It is a reductive attitude. The White Scars represent a greater third of the legionaries holding this siege. They have come to Terra willingly, to a warfare that is alien to their ancient axioms of combat. And without them, we would be lost already.'

'Again, my pardon, lord.'

Raldoron nodded.

'We'll say no more on it,' he murmured. 'Though, please watch for such attitudes among your soldiers. We must preserve a unity of respect. No, Agathe, my meaning was that, for

all their shamanic lore, the Khan's Stormseers are outclassed.
Environmental conditions are not conducive to their particular psykanic methods. And, of course, what intelligence we
have suggests they are facing the very worst of such adepts.'

'It's confirmed, then?' she asked.

'No, but more than reasonably likely. The Pale King's Fourteenth drives at us still, but the aetheric tribulation we are
enduring is not their work. The damned sons of Magnus work
some black art in support of them.'

'The Thousand Sons,' she whispered.

'Several of their sorcerous captains have been reported, perhaps orchestrating this atrocity from a distance. Ahriman, for
one, allegedly. Of all the Legions, lost or loyal, the Fifteenth
were the ones who took the concept of the Librarius to its
furthest degree, and made it the axle-beam of their doctrine.'

'We are damned, then,' she said.

'They are damned, Agathe,' said Raldoron. 'We are merely
doomed.'

Fo, in his fluttering little bird-voice, told them of ages long
dead, of things Keeler knew as only broken histories. The air
in the grim, squalid cell seemed to thicken, as though Old
Night had come to visit them and hear its story told.

'There were so many monsters in those days,' Fo said,
'towering monsters of pride and arrogance and ambition. Poor
Terra did not seem big enough to hold them all. Leaders,
kings, despots, tyrants. Your Emperor was only one of them.
But I understood His malevolence even then. It was singular.'

'I would caution your remarks,' said Amon tersely.

'Why?' asked Fo, amused. 'What are you going to do to me?
Lock me in a dungeon and deprive me of liberty for the rest
of my... Oh, wait.'

'Let him speak, Custodian,' said Keeler. 'Let him say whatever he likes. They are only words. The subjects we are speaking to here in the Blackstone need to be free to express themselves, or we will learn nothing of value. If they fear recrimination or prosecution, they will close their mouths.'

Fo was staring at them both, as though amused.

'I do not understand the relationship between the two of you,' he said. 'Prisoner and escort, which would make you, Euphrati, some kind of recidivist like me. Except you have been granted powers of interview, and the golden killer there shows you courtesy.'

'Who we are doesn't–' Keeler began.

'It matters to me,' said Fo. 'It's clear you're a prisoner too. Yet you have a modicum of power. And you are very much Him. I feel it in you. You are deeply loyal to the tyrant, yet you have committed some crime, which the pair of you skirt around.'

'Please, sir–'

'Between you,' Fo chortled, 'you seem to be a perfect symbol of this Imperium of Mankind. The terrifying warrior, inhuman, regal in his adornment and unswerving in his severity, paired with you, a kindly voice of reason, protesting liberty of speech and freedom of expression, striving to obtain some truth. There were so many like you, Euphrati, back in the old days, at the start. Reasonable-looking people saying reasonable-sounding things, strident in their belief in the righteousness of your master… Yet always with a transhuman terror at your shoulder, eager to strike.'

Keeler breathed deeply to retain her calm exterior.

'What was singular about Him?' she asked.

'That? Oh,' Fo said, making a diffident little shrug. 'I think, Euphrati, I think the others knew their flaws. Or cared little about them. Tang of Yndonesse was a zealot, and knew it. The artifice of faith was his uniting weapon. Belot… is his name still remembered? He was a warlord, and his interests were territorial gain by any means. Dame Venal sought to claim resources for her impoverished land, and spiralled into madness as she saw her own cruelty magnify, as she pursued her goals in the name of her people. Dume, aha, Dume. He was mad. Quite mad. But he fought for the security of his realm. He wanted to be left alone. Or so he told me.'

Fo ignored her expression.

'But the Emperor,' he went on. 'Your Emperor. Do you know, He took that name before He had an empire? That's weapons-grade hubris. I thought Him just another warlord at first, scrabbling for His share, but something stood out about Him. He was clever, of course. More than that. A genius. And that mind of His, which could not be contained. His rise was meteoric, and would have been under any circumstances. But the terrible thing about Him, the singular thing, was that He thought He was right. Never a shred of doubt. His confidence was unimaginable.'

Fo shuffled back on his cot.

'We were all monsters. I was, I know. But I just liked to play. I had an ability with genetics, with biomech systems. I would concoct things, just to see where they went. Sometimes that horrified people, and I gained an unfortunate reputation. But whatever I did, I never planned to conquer the planet. I never set out to unify. I had no great plan. I was just playing.'

He looked at Keeler.

'I fled Terra when I saw that He did. You would either be part of His plan, or you would be removed. I'm sorry... *illuminated*. I fancied neither.'

'You fled Terra, because you knew you would be punished for your crimes,' said Amon.

'Yes. Certainly, by His terms. For the only law was His. I saw what was coming. He would unify, for He had the power to do it, and such a lack of self-doubt to never question His intention or His means. I am named a monster, because of the things I made, but look what He has made.'

'An Imperium,' said Keeler.

'Built on the shoulders of genetic transhumans,' said Fo. 'Brought to compliance... ah, there's another telling word... by abominations far worse than anything I ever devised. Transhuman abominations capable of burning the galaxy down. Do you doubt me? Behold the world outside.'

'This is pointless,' said Amon.

'You would say that, warrior,' said Fo fiercely. 'For you are Him. A part of Him, of His mind, His will. I might as well be talking to Him, face to face, and He never – I mean *never* – took criticism. He would never be questioned. And you, dear girl, looking at me with those questioning eyes, so are you. A part of Him. You were not made that way, but you are filled with His power. You've allowed that to happen. You think of Him as a god.'

'I know He...' she began. Her voice dropped. 'I know what I know.'

'You know what He wants you to know, dear.'

'The Emperor has denied every attempt,' she said carefully, 'to apotheosise Him.'

'Let me share a secret with you, Euphrati,' said Fo, leaning forward, beckoning to her. 'There are no gods. That's the first thing. If there were, they would operate in silent and measureless mystery, their ways too sublime for us to perceive. But there are those who would have you *believe* they are gods. Who, I should say, *want* to be gods. And the first step they take to that end? They deny themselves. They assume a humble attitude and declare, "I am not a god... even though you might think I am." It is a psychological pathway to foster faith. I saw Him begin it all those years ago. I knew that, one day, He would be proclaimed a god. He is, after all, immensely powerful. He will become a god whether He likes it or not. Godhood is the ultimate tool of control. It is the pinnacle of tyranny. Faith drives your followers. Blind faith. You no longer have to make any sense at all, no longer have to justify your actions. You are followed blindly. If, like Him, you do not care to be criticised or doubted, it is a state to be wished for.'

'He has denied–' Keeler began.

'Yet you still believe! This is my point! The more He denies it, the more you believe! You do not judge the fact that He is, at heart, human, you embrace the lack of fact, because blind faith comforts you. Tell me, does He tell you, any of you, what His plan is? His scheme?'

'No.'

'There you go. Because then you would understand. Anything that is easy enough to understand is not powerful enough to be worshipped. A history of religion should show you this.'

'The Emperor is different,' she said.

'Only in that He is more, Euphrati,' said Fo. 'More powerful than any version of this lie that's come along before.'

He sighed wearily, and pulled the filthy blanket of his cot up around his legs.

'Mankind, in my experience,' he said, 'and I think we can at least accept I have more experience of it than most… Mankind has proven to be pathologically incapable of learning from its own mistakes. It blithely remembers the witness of history, but it does not apply the knowledge it gains. The Age of Strife was a terrible thing, inflicted by man upon man. Those few of us who lived through it, and survived it, no matter what part we played, no matter what crimes we committed, we all looked on it during the last years of its horror and said never again. Never again can we do this to ourselves. Yet, mere centuries later, Terra is about to fall, Terra and the galaxy with it, at the hands of engineered humans turning against their creator. This siege, your war, it is self-inflicted.'

His head dropped.

'We should be better than this,' he said quietly. 'We never learn.'

'Earlier, you said you knew how to end this,' said Keeler. 'A... weapon?'

'Yes,' said Fo. 'I have had a great deal of time to ruminate. I could build a weapon that would end this war and remove the threat. I would require access to extensive and advanced laboratory facilities.'

'What kind of weapon?' asked Amon.

'Biomechanical,' said Fo.

'What kind of weapon specifically?' the Custodian growled.

'Oh,' said Fo, 'one you really won't like.'

The Neverborn had fallen silent, all at once, and very suddenly. An uneasy quiet filled the halls and gunblocks of Colossi. The only sounds were the creak of the voids and the endless buzzing of the flies.

Agathe thought it would be a relief when the noise finally stopped, but it seemed worse somehow. The silence pressed in, and she felt claustrophobic. They had all been left alone with their thoughts, and the things they had seen, the daemons at the wall, were memories that began to stew and fester. As she walked her tour circuit, she became aware of the increasing distress among the men. They had been on station for hours, choking under their hoods, hearing horror, seeing nothing. Now, the silence was stretching out their wait, carving away what was left of their confidence, sweating out their courage, magnifying their dread.

'He needs to be more visible,' she said, very directly, to Raldoron, when she encountered him on the Seventeenth Platform.

'Meaning?' Raldoron asked.

'Meaning the Khan.'

'He is in vox conference with the Grand Borealis,' Raldoron replied. 'Negotiating the safe delivery of munition resupply.'

'Once he's done, then,' said Agathe. 'The sight of him inspires confidence. He should be walking the lines. I do not make the same visual impact.'

'I see.'

'Can you ask him that?'

'Yes, marshal. I can communicate your request.'

First Captain Raldoron had brought three of the White Scars Stormseers with him. They waited in a silent group behind him.

'We were coming to find you,' said Raldoron. 'The seers need access.'

'To? For?'

'As I understand it, they are formulating some new initiative to drive off the foe. But we need to see. To assess why the assault has fallen silent.'

'The observation ports–'

'No, commander,' said one of the seers. 'The open. The wall top.'

'With respect, lord, no,' she replied. 'We have sealed Colossi behind the voids. Closed the gas shutters. I can't allow–'

'The Khan has requested it,' said Raldoron.

Agathe shrugged, clumsy in her gas-gear. 'Then why even ask me?' she said.

'My Khagan wishes that the chain of command be respected,' said the seer. 'Your authority, commander. My Khagan would appreciate your consent. We must work together, not at odds.'

'I'm grateful for that,' said Agathe. 'Can we look first, make an assessment?'

The seer nodded.

'Your name is Naranbaatar?' Agathe asked.

'Yes.'

'How do I address you?'

'As Naranbaatar.'

Agathe bid them follow her with a gesture. They walked down the armoured hall, and crossed the retractable walk-bridge that spanned one of the massive munition shafts that spined the wall's midsection. She could hear the dull thump of the transhuman footsteps behind her, ringing on the metal, the firm clip of Naranbaatar's totem staff as it struck the deck, in pace with his stride.

'Rest assured, we will not engage,' Raldoron said to her as they walked.

'Rest assured, lord, I don't think we could engage,' she replied.

'Perhaps,' he agreed. 'But the Khan has ruled that only the Custodians seem fit to wage battle, in any hand-to-hand fashion, against the Neverborn. They seemed sanctified in a way the rest of us are not.'

'The flies die when they land on them,' she said.

'Quite so. The spirit of our master flows most purely in them, a light against the darkness. Perhaps our best weapon.'

'I'll tell my soldiers, if the walls are breached, to hold fire until a Custodian comes.'

Raldoron made some small sound behind his visor. A grunt perhaps, or a chuckle.

'He had a dry wit too,' the First Captain remarked. They had entered a garrison well beyond the bridge, past rows of blast-boxes that were filled with edgy, waiting men. The over-heads, glowing dull amber, were laced with flies.

'Who?' Agathe asked.

'Burr,' he remarked. 'Your predecessor.'

'My friend,' she said.

'Mine too, marshal. I liked him very much.'

'For a human?'

'I do not make such distinctions, Marshal Agathe. A good soul is a good soul.'

She stopped abruptly, and turned to look at him, square-on, so she could line up the blinkered gas hood and see him clearly.

'I think that's a luxury only the Legiones Astartes enjoy, lord,' she said. 'We see the distinction very clearly, every time one of you walks into the room. You remind us we are small. You remind us we are lesser things. And very mortal.'

'I am sorry to hear that.'

'I am... sorry to have said it,' she returned, and continued on.

'My presence here, and the presence of legionaries like me, was intended to rally and uplift, not diminish morale,' he called after her.

'I said I was sorry,' she replied.

'You understand, marshal, that we fight for you,' Raldoron said, resuming step to easily catch up with her. 'We were born to fight for you.'

'I hope so.'

'The soul of mankind–'

'Captain, my lord... it is very clear to me that you were born to fight for something. I hope it's us. I hope the life of mankind is the precious gift that gives purpose to your warring. But I am tired, and I am scared, and I am confused. I cannot see in this hood, I can barely breathe. I think of my family, far away, to give me hope and strength, and the thought of them destroys that hope, because I am afraid that they are already dead. I do not know what to think any more, or what to understand. I know you were born to fight for something. Right now, that's all.'

He caught her arm with one of his immense, plated hands, and stopped her.

'We fight for you,' he insisted.

Agathe stared at him. His warhelm, as always, conveyed no expression. He removed his hand.

'Through here,' she said.

She took them up a cargo ramp, past the oiled mechanisms of bulk autoloader systems that had become furry with adhered flies, and into one of the gun silos. The chamber was large, reinforced, and baffled with damping blocks. Six macro-guns, locked back in recoil position on their platforms, faced the gun slot. The blast shutters were down, as per her orders.

Gun crews and Kimmerine troops got up quickly as she entered with her Astartes escort. An officer approached her, and saluted.

'What's wrong with him?' she asked. Nearby, a Kimmerine subaltern was hunched by the foot of the guns, his hood off. He was shivering and weeping, oblivious to the flies crawling on his face.

'His brother keeps calling to him,' the officer said.

'Where is his brother?'

'Dead four weeks ago, mam.'

'Have him removed at once, please. Get him to the medicae. I want the obs shutter opened.'

Two troopers hauled the weeping man away. The officer stepped onto the observation platform, produced his chain of keys and unlocked the shutter bolts. He started to crank the handle to lift the blast cover that blocked the glass of the obs slit. Agathe swung down a heavy field scope on its brass armature.

The slit's glass was thick. Nothing but an orange glow showed beyond. She adjusted the field scope to look. Raldoron pulled down a second scope, and paired it with his visor systems.

Outside, a bleakness. A waste, shimmered by thermal radiation and the distorted signal-feed of the scope. They were a long way up. The Seventeenth Platform gun-boxes were over three hundred metres above talus, at the foot of the curtain wall.

The field outside Colossi was a mangled darkness. The outer lines, trench system and earthworks laid before the bastion had been ploughed up into a torn and tortured mire, where no trace of the original defensive structures or formations could be detected. A heavy smog lay across the view, slowly drifting banks of smoke and vaporised ejecta. Fires dotted the waste-ground, patches of flickering orange that danced between the few, scattered ruins of trees. Beside the leaping flames and the crackling distortion of the wall's void shields, there was no movement. No nothing.

Agathe was about to push the scope away. She froze. Trees. There were no trees on the approach to Colossi Gate. The things she had seen weren't trees.

They were the Neverborn beasts. She counted eleven of them. The huge, dark monsters had ceased their assault, and lowered their therianthropic forms to the ground. They were kneeling in the mud, some close, others further away, corded arms slack at their sides, heads bowed, antlers and horned crowns raised like the stark branches of winter trees. They were facing the fortress. It felt as if they were waiting.

Or praying.

Some simmering brimstone heat, a coal-red glow, pulsed slowly and softly in their shadowed faces.

'What are they doing?' she asked in a whisper.

Raldoron didn't reply. Agathe swallowed hard, and closed her eyes, trying to clear her head and block the ominous image. She heard a voice.

'What did you say?' she asked, glancing at Raldoron. But he

hadn't spoken. And it couldn't have been him. It was a human voice, light and far away.

'May I?' Naranbaatar asked her, gesturing to the scope. Agathe stepped aside, and let him look.

'Gathering power,' the Stormseer said. 'Perhaps they have expended their wrath for now, and are recharging their anima, or-'

'Or?' asked Agathe.

'Or they are performing some ritual,' he said. 'Focusing their spirits to reach out into the Neversea of the Immateria, to gain insight or strength.'

'Do you... do you know that?' Agathe asked him.

'I feel it. Sense it. Like a charge in the wind, a brewing thunderhead. An echo of their shadow-selves, calling to the darkness that spawned them.'

Let me back in.

'What?' Agathe asked sharply.

The White Scar turned from the scope.

'What do you ask me, marshal?'

'You said... Let me back in.'

'I did not.'

'I heard the words.' Agathe moved to the scope again. Naranbaatar stopped her.

'Do not look again,' he said. 'If you have heard the whisper, they are playing with you.'

'I will look,' she insisted.

'Please do not.'

Let me back in.

Agathe stared at him. 'I just heard it again,' she said.

'A trick.'

'I know the voice,' she said.

'Burr,' said Raldoron. He stepped back from the scope. 'I heard it too.'

'He's out there?' Agathe asked.

'No, marshal. Naranbaatar is right. They are trying to wear down our sanity. Konas is dead.'

Raldoron pushed both sets of scopes up into their cradles.

'Close the shutter,' he told the officer. 'Lock it. Marshal, if the Neverborn are quiet, we can venture up to the wall top. Take advantage of this lull, and let the seers make their preparations.'

Agathe nodded. 'You heard him too?' she asked. 'If there's a chance he's alive…'

'I saw Burr looking back at me through the scope,' he said without emotion. 'Staring, pleading. We are three hundred metres up, marshal. That's how I was sure he is dead.'

Amon Tauromachian checked the locks of Fo's cell door. The boom of its closing still echoed through the cold and draughty darkness of the prison around them. Amon picked up his lamp to lead them away.

'We should–' Keeler began.

'We should forget what we just heard,' said the Custodian.

'We can't!' she exclaimed. 'Custodian, we must take this to the Praetorian. To your master at least–'

'No,' he replied.

'Fo is loathsome,' she said. 'Beyond redemption, but his abilities as a biomechanic are in no doubt. His skills are listed in detail on his file.'

'I know.'

'Amon, if he says he can make a weapon, we must take him seriously. It doesn't matter who he is or what he's done, if he can provide a means of ending this, then we must–'

'That's not what he described,' said the Custodian.

'He can make a weapon to destroy the Lupercal,' said Keeler.

'That's not what he described,' Amon repeated slowly. 'He

proposed the manufacture of a biomechanical phage. Tailored and specific. I have no question that he is capable of it. The phage would kill Horus Lupercal, yes, because it would be coded to wipe out everything of that gene-altered pattern in the Imperium. Horus, yes. And every primarch. And every legionary. On both sides. It would exterminate the transhuman genetic lineage of mankind.'

She paused, then nodded.

'Yes, it would,' she said. 'And that's unthinkable. But we're standing at the edge of total extinction, and the triumph of the warp. This moment is the unthinkable. What price is too great to win that, and shut down the Primordial Annihilator, and let mankind live?'

'Not that,' he said.

'Yes,' she sighed. 'I agree. Nevertheless, Amon Tauromachian, the Praetorian must know about it. He is running this war, and every second takes us closer to doom. He must be aware of all his options.'

It took a long while for Amon to respond.

'Yes,' he said, 'he must.'

They rose into the gloomy air above the wall top, passing through gas shutters and blast shields, to exit onto the fighting platform of Artemis Tower, the central ravelin of Colossi. It was nocturnal. A warm, foetid wind blew in from the burning wastes. The air was drawn with smoke, and low with swollen brown clouds. Agathe kept her hazard gear on.

'Five minutes,' she said.

The Stormseers nodded. They wandered out into the open part of the wide platform, talking softly to each other. They were looking up at the curved edge of the void shields that shimmered overhead, like the ghost of a gigantic wave breaking across the wall. The void sections were secured vertically, and extended out across the fighting platform, and beyond, for sixty metres. Beyond that, they decayed to nothing. Colossi's energy shields covered the fortress like a shelf, a miserable relic of the mighty void system that had once screened the entire gate and outworks beyond, projecting for five kilometres.

'Go back below, marshal,' Raldoron told her. 'I will watch them until they are done. No need for you to be here too.'

'I'll stay,' she said, shifting uncomfortably in the hot, toxic wind.

'Please, Agathe, just go below,' he said.

'What?' she asked. 'What's the matter?'

'I am concerned for your wellbeing. You are not as robust as us legionaries.'

'Captain, that's not it at all. You're being disingenuous.' She tried to step past him. 'What are you hiding? You're trying to block something from me.'

'Please, Agathe.'

'I want to see, First Captain. I need to–'

She stopped in her tracks. She could see what Raldoron had been trying to mask from her with his bulk. An object placed on the crenellations at the edge of the fighting platform, twenty metres away.

It was small and pale.

'Oh shit,' she murmured.

'I'm sorry,' said Raldoron. 'You didn't need to see that. The Neverborn filth knew we were coming. They left us a gift.'

Agathe stared for a long time, and turned her back when she could no longer bear to look into the sightless eyes of Konas Burr's grey, severed head.

FIVE

Another angel
Hope is not an error
Olympos

As Sanguinius, the Lord of Baal, climbed the inner staircase to the fighting platform of the fourth circuit wall, he felt the pounding in his head resume.

The pulse came in time with the thump of the kettle drums the massing traitor hosts were beating, and skipped arrhythmically at every crump and pop of nearby combats. But neither the drumming nor the blast of munitions was causing it. Other minds were grazing against his again, other minds, *brother* minds.

One especially.

He walked, because his great wings ached, and his spirits were low, but he kept his face set with a stern yet kind aspect. He would not show weakness to his sons, or Rann's stalwart Imperial Fists, nor to any warrior of Terra or Mars who stood this line with him. He understood his chief purpose and role. Few beings in creation could match him in war, but in war of this scale he was but one small element. No matter his prowess, no matter his deeds, he would not turn the fight for Gorgon Bar alone. His role was as a figurehead, a living standard, to bind the defence, and nurse its strength.

And he knew his repeated absence from the line had already been noticed. Rumours were spreading that he was sick, or wounded. Sanguinius had tried to confine himself alone, in his chambers, while he staved off the plague of visions. He didn't want people to see him struggling. Too many soldiers had seen him fall to his knees on the walkway and cry out in agony. Word had got around. He could not let that happen again. When the visions came, and the fits took him, he stole away and endured them in private.

But he had been missed. His absence marked. Unease was brewing. The sight of him unmanned, in pain and distress, would break morale, but so too could the gap he left by not being visible. A figurehead only worked if it could be seen. Undone by the visions, he was failing as a warrior and as an inspiration.

It was a burden like no other, far worse than the uncalled-for responsibility of Imperium Secundus that Roboute had placed on him. The Great Angel was the protector. If he failed, then Terra would fail. Perhaps the visions afflicting his mind were the very weapons Horus would use to destroy him. It wasn't his literal death he had seen during the Ruinstorm: it was his symbolic failure, his disintegration as a viable force of good.

Soldiers on the steps saluted and bowed as Sanguinius passed. He paused to talk to some, to clasp hands and lift hearts. That was how it worked. A few words from the Great Angel reforged mettle.

Bel Sepatus and Halen awaited him on the landing stage below the parapet. The shiver of nearby fighting was louder. He could smell the smoke lapping across the wall.

'They mass?' he asked.

'To your schedule, so it seems,' replied Sepatus sardonically.

'Just sorties so far, lord,' said Halen, passing him a hardened dataslate. 'A dozen since dawn. Probing for weaknesses in our line.'

'Structural?' asked Sanguinius.

'And spiritual,' Halen replied. 'They aim to break us this morning. They are testing to see what sections are weak.'

'None are weak,' said Sepatus quickly.

'Indeed, captain,' replied Fisk Halen. 'I mean only that some are stronger than others.'

'Bel knew what you meant, my friend,' said Sanguinius. 'There's no shame in weakness.' He reviewed the data carefully.

'The Berengerian Fusiliers–' Halen said.

'Should be rotated out,' said Sanguinius, nodding as he read. 'They took the brunt on second circuit. They haven't been allowed a chance to stand down for nine days.'

'The company commander refuses to leave your side,' said Halen.

'And I embrace his courage,' said Sanguinius. 'But they are weak as they stand, dead on their feet. Pull them, Fisk, and give them six hours on the reserve line to rest and resupply.'

'I have two battalions of Prushik Kurassiers waiting in the yards for a place on the fighting step,' said Halen. 'Fresh from the Sanctum last night.'

'Make that change, captain,' said Sanguinius. 'Tell the Berengerian chief I have personally requested his brave men rest, for I have them in mind for a special action later. Use the word brave.'

'Special action, lord?' asked Sepatus.

'Holding Gorgon Bar,' said Sanguinius. 'He doesn't need to know specifics. He just needs a reason to stand down that will not bruise his pride.'

Halen nodded, and took back the slate.

The pounding in Sanguinius' temples had grown worse.

'Let's see the day,' he told them. He made himself smile.

Halen led the way up the combat ramp, shouting orders. Wall reserves raised lances and spontoons upright in attention as they passed, banners and company oriflammes billowing like sea snakes in the wind. Sanguinius held Sepatus back for a moment.

'On the subject of a special action, Bel,' he said softly, 'I need you to take your best squad, quit the line, and return to the Sanctum Imperialis.'

Bel Sepatus' face darkened. 'Why in the name of Terra would I do that?' he asked.

'I received a communication an hour ago, conveyed directly and in great confidence from the Sigillite. He requests my best squad, and my best man, without delay.'

'For what purpose?'

'It did not specify, and I did not ask.'

'I won't leave your side, lord. Not at this hour. And I am concerned for you. I have heard–'

'Will you obey my commands, Bel?' Sanguinius asked.

'Always.'

'Then this is my command. You, and your best squad, to the Sanctum.'

Sepatus ground his jaw for a moment, then nodded.

'The Praetorian has need of you,' said Sanguinius. 'It is some matter too delicate for transmission.'

'Dorn has his own men,' said Sepatus.

'If my brother has need of better angels,' said Sanguinius, 'I do not question him. The Praetorian commands over all. We follow his strategies, or the siege falls apart. His understanding of this war is far broader and more comprehensive than mine.'

Sepatus exhaled gently, steadying his silent wrath.

'I'll pass command of my formations to Satel Aimery,' he said. 'I'll take second squad. The Katechon. I will…'

'Bel?'

'I will miss the glory of this day,' said Sepatus sadly.

Sanguinius placed a hand on his shoulder.

'Glory, Bel,' he said, 'awaits you wherever you walk.'

The wall top was thick with troop lines, metal glinting in the bright haze. Sanguinius rejoined Halen. Below them, the vast circuit wall quivered as bulk auto-hoists brought load after load of munitions up to the macro-gun casemates. Above them, in the wan light, observation balloons drifted like low, stray planets caught in nets of golden braid, their pict systems whirring. Sanguinius could hear gunfire rippling from the line to his left. Pioneer parties were running an assault about half a kilometre down, and the wall guns were driving them back with desultory bursts.

To his right, about a kilometre and a half out, the traitor Warhounds had returned, making gun-charges out of the ruins of the third circuit wall to strafe and harass the wall below Parfane Tower. They had brought friends, six or seven Warhounds in total, and a supporting unit of corrupted Questor Knights. The tower's guns were clapping the air with their response. Blooms of white smoke from each salvo drifted along the wall. Sanguinius heard a cheer rise and build, rolling across the wall emplacements with the gliding smoke. A Warhound had been struck and brought down. He could see its twitching carcass, on fire, in the blasted gully short of the wall.

Sanguinius mounted the observation alure where Lord Seneschal Rann, Khoradal Furio and three lords militant of the Imperial Army were positioned.

'They are working themselves up,' was all Rann said.

'I'd need to work myself up a little, if I was coming against us,' said Sanguinius.

Fafnir Rann chuckled.

'I don't think it will be a mass wave,' said Sanguinius. 'They tried that yesterday, and it won them a lot, but it broke at the final step. And it cost them.' The ground, far below them, was still contoured with mounds of rotting dead. 'They're wary,' he said. 'Stung. They'll probe, then drive at a section or sections they perceive as weak.'

'None are weak,' said Rann.

Sanguinius smiled. From a Blood Angel, that remark would sound like stubborn pride. From an Imperial Fist, it sounded like an operational mantra.

'So I'm told, Fafnir,' he said. 'But pay attention, and watch for wavering. I expect two or perhaps three main drives, and they'll come at once.'

He stared out. The shattered, jagged shadows of the third circuit wall were a kilometre away. Beyond them, the overwhelmed ruins of outer circuits and the outworks. All of that, lost in one savage day. A great stain of smoke hung low over the enemy-possessed ruins. He could hear the constant batter of kettle-drumming, and see signs of bulk movement stirring in the gloom. A build-up. There was chanting, too. Enemy voices, chanting together, but boned out by the distance. The same words.

The Emperor must die! The Emperor must die!

Sanguinius closed his eyes, and saw different smoke, different ruins.

No. No, not now.

The other mind was there again, eclipsing his, a heat pulsing behind his eyes. He felt the fraternal bond that could never be broken, the raw hatred that could never be understood, the rage that could never be reasoned with.

Angron. Another angel. A redder angel. Where was he? Sanguinius tried to see. Just smoke. Just rubble.

He thought of the Sigillite's message that had taken Bel Sepatus from him. Malcador had simply asked, and Sanguinius had given, without question. How dearly he wanted to consult, to ask Malcador a question of his own. How do I still my mind? How do I keep these visions at bay? How do I stop the thoughts of my brothers invading my head?

What do the visions mean?

There was no *one* question. He wanted to know what use the visions were, or why they were now, as it seemed, continuous and contemporary. They had once been fleeting scraps of possible futures, little flashes he could ignore. Now they were the present, or the near future. Now they were constant, and as draining as a migraine.

That was no simple message to send, or simple answer to receive. To dissect his visions, and their cause and meaning, he would need to sit with the Sigillite, in person and in private, and spend hours unravelling it all.

He had neither the time nor opportunity for that. It would have to wait.

Maybe that was for the best. His greatest fear was that if he told Malcador, or Rogal, or anybody, they might deem him unfit. At best, perhaps, just troubled. At worst, they might believe it to be the first symptoms of creeping corruption, some deep flaw in him forced open by the sly ministries of the warp, like the tiniest crack in a bastion wall: prised at first, then widened by hammered wedges, then undermined and opened, until the wall collapsed under its own fissured weight, and the enemy tide flushed in to take the bastion entire.

They might order his removal from command. From the line. From the war. What was the term the Imperial Fists used? Non-vi. As good as *dead*.

The loyalist cause could not afford to lose a primarch. But Gorgon Bar could not afford an unfit one.

Fight it. *Fight it!*

Sanguinius opened his eyes, but the vision stubbornly remained, beating like a war drum. He saw it overlaid across the scene of mounded dead, smoke-drift and the shattered third circuit wall.

He saw another wall, whole as yet. Monsalvant Gard. A rain of bombarding fire. The rising towers, spines and peaks of Eternity Wall Port.

Angron was assaulting the port. The approach to Monsalvant had become Angron's next gladiatorial arena.

The Child of the Mountain, for all he had tried, had never left the slave pit.

The Pons Solar had fallen. The East Arterial was gone. The vast yards of Western Freight were all but overrun. The port's garrison had retreated behind the barrier wall, and only that, and the heavy fire of the defence systems, had brought the swarming World Eaters to a temporary halt.

The enemy had brought rams, huge column rams they wielded through brute manual force. They were pounding at the gate blocks and the sealed cargo entrances of Western Freight. On the loading ramps and cage-ways behind the barrier wall, troop strengths were lining up and loading, ready to hold the choke points of these precious causeways if the gates broke.

Niborran carried a lasrifle, slung across his shoulder. Every able body would count from now on. The chandeliers above him shivered and tinkled. They had claimed a reception hall in Tower Seven of the barrier wall to use as a meeting room.

'Batteries?' he asked.

'Another six hours,' replied Brohn, 'if we maintain the firing rate.'

'And we've requested–'

'Munition fulfilment from Bhab?' Brohn asked. 'Twice in the last hour alone. No response. No signal. I've had bulk landing pads cleared anyway.'

Maps and sheaves of documents had been spread out on the reception hall's long teak tables, a parody of the extravagant buffets laid on for worthy off-world dignitaries.

'Six hours…' said Niborran.

'For solid shells,' said Shiban. 'All energy and las-platforms will sustain longer, if we draw power from the port's reactors.'

'We'll need heavy cabling, secure networks,' Niborran said.

'In expectation of that need, I've had crews start work on the infrastructure,' said Shiban.

'I wasn't told,' said Brohn. 'We can't spare fighting men from the–'

'Civilian labour,' said Shiban, not even looking at him. 'Technicians and labourers from the port guilds, long-shoremen, cargo handlers. There are twenty-nine thousand non-combatants trapped in the port zone too. That seems to have been forgotten.'

Brohn scowled. 'All right, then,' he said.

'Can they be armed?' asked Niborran.

'When it comes to it, general,' said Shiban, 'I think they'll want to be.'

'Armour?' asked Niborran.

'We lost nearly a third of our complement with the Pons Solar,' said Shiban.

'The bridge was a mistake,' growled Brohn. 'The bridge was a bloody mistake. Intel said they were coming from the south. We should have mined the bridge down. There. Is that what you want to hear me say?'

He stared at Shiban Khan. A cocktail of terror and anger had done alarming things to his expression.

'I don't need to hear you say anything,' said Shiban.

'If the bridge is gone,' said Cadwalder, quietly from behind Niborran, 'then Lord Diaz...'

'Lost,' said Tsutomu.

'Lost or dead?' asked Cadwalder. 'Please specify.'

The Custodian glanced briefly to his left. He paused, then he looked back at Cadwalder.

'Dead,' he said. 'Dead along with almost all who stood with him.'

'Are we certain?' the Huscarl asked.

'She saw his body herself, during the retreat,' said Tsutomu expressionlessly. 'Still on the bridge, surrounded by the slain. He had not taken a step back.'

Niborran frowned. He had almost asked which 'she' the Custodian was referring to. Then he remembered, and glimpsed the smudge of light on Tsutomu's left. It was so bizarrely easy to forget about her, to miss her. And her presence explained the deathly air in the room.

No, he thought, it didn't. This wasn't the depressing malaise of her null effect. This was the moment, the plight they found themselves in.

'Again,' he said, 'I thank our sister for her efforts. Many lives were saved because of her. Lord Diaz is a hard loss. Terra, they all are. We will prevail here simply so we can mourn them later. I am reminded of a doctrine cherished by the Imperial Fists. Achievement through sacrifice.'

He clapped his hands briskly.

'Let's to our stations,' he said. 'I want the troops rallied and ready. Be visible. Stick to the plan. If the gates break, compartmentalise. Seal and close, one step at a time. The vox is clearly damned, so we'll use hardline links between operation points. Orskode, or Hortcode. Simple, basic.'

The garrison commanders nodded. Brohn saluted.

'Khan?' Niborran called as they turned to go. 'A word.'

Niborran stepped out onto a balcony that faced the port megastructure. Shiban followed him. Cadwalder followed too. He ghosted the High Primary General wherever he went. Outside, the noise of unwavering assault was much louder.

'Is this about Brohn?' Shiban Khan asked.

Niborran glanced at him, puzzled. 'What? No. I...'

He turned to face Shiban.

'Your instinct for defence has been excellent since day one. Since before I arrived. I've taken your counsel, but not enough of it.'

'We make our decisions in good faith, general,' said Shiban.

'You do, I think. I haven't had the honour of knowing you long, but I believe this is true of you.'

'I appreciate you saying that,' said Niborran. 'This situation, khan, this fight... I fear I've been taking too much of a text-book approach. Standard operational strategies, reliable ones–'

'Such as?' asked Shiban.

'Trying to keep arteries open in the expectation of further relief and reinforcement,' Niborran replied. 'That was foolish. An error forced by human hope, which is something you don't seem to suffer from.'

'Hope is not an error, general,' said Shiban.

'It is when one knows, for a fact, that there is nothing to hope for,' said Niborran. 'I knew, and yet I allowed myself to hope. I set out my lines according to standard operation...'

'Knew what?' asked Shiban.

'That no one is coming,' said Niborran. 'That we face this with what we have, and nothing more. I–'

He stopped. Shiban had raised a hand to halt him.

'How did you know that, general?' he asked.

Niborran glanced quickly at Cadwalder, then sighed. He unfastened his overcoat, took out a cigar, and lit it with slightly trembling fingers.

'It shouldn't matter, khan,' he said. 'It doesn't matter now. I should have assumed it from the first moment. Expect the worst, and anything else can only be better. I should have tossed out the rules of standard operation, and implemented ruthless...'

He exhaled blue smoke, and looked at Shiban. 'Too much of the old Saturnine Ordos schooled into me,' he said. 'The discipline, the rigidity, the devotion to codified rules of war. I see I must break out of the prison of those habits. The truth is, the port was understrength and underprepared from the very start. We must act on the principle that no one is coming to our aid. Treat that as a certainty. By implementing the strategies you suggested–'

'It's too late to implement any of them now,' said Shiban. 'The enemy is here, and it has already determined the path of battle.'

Niborran nodded.

'Yes,' he said. 'But forget the tactical specifics. The spirit of your intent still holds true. We only have what we have. We make best use of that. Best use of finite resources.' He gestured towards the soaring towers and pylons of the port. 'How finite does that look to you?' he asked.

Shiban did not reply.

'We are woefully short of dedicated military personnel and materiel,' Niborran said, 'but we have a whole port sitting there. How many non-coms did you say?'

'Twenty-nine thousand,' replied Shiban.

'Right. Many of them technical specialists, port crews and personnel.'

'Many are just civilians. Refugees from Magnifican–'

'Even so, we have specialists. Pilots, ferrymen, engineers, mechanics.' Niborran took out a dataslate. 'I ran checks on port cargo inventory. Nine billion tonnes of freight, still sitting here.

That includes munition loads destined for Anterior. There's at least a thousand lasrifles packed in shipment crates. Fourteen hundred autoguns. Two payloads of trench mortars.'

'So we can arm a few,' said Shiban.

'It's not just munitions,' said Niborran. 'Not just unshipped cargo. The space port is packed with specialised equipment. Systems and devices we can employ defensively.'

'Asset-strip the port?'

'To hold the port.'

'It's a question of manpower–'

'And we have unutilised manpower, hiding in shelters. And on the pylons and platforms, we have seven hundred and nine small craft. Lighters, ferries, tugs, shuttles, wherries–'

'Are you proposing an evacuation?' asked Shiban.

'No,' said Niborran. 'Our orders are to hold the port, not abandon it. And anyway, nothing is going to fly clear through this. But a Sysiphos-class tug, khan, it carries a massively over-muscled gravity array. It can drag a medium shiftship into low-anchor dock. If we get those arrays down here, to the surface, strip them out, mount them laterally...'

'Improvised gravity weapons.'

'Gravity walls, gravity screens,' Niborran nodded. 'Immensely powerful. Not even berserk World Eaters could claw their way through. At maximum output, a grav-array would turn them into paste.'

Shiban nodded. 'What do we need?'

'Lightermen to get them operational and move them down-pylon to the base platforms. Technicians to disassemble. Handlers and bulk servitors to move them and position them. Engineers to rig them.'

'We don't have much time,' said Shiban.

'The garrison is buying us all the time it can,' Niborran replied. 'The civilian and labour force will need motivation if they're going to act fast. They'll listen to a legionary. Jump to his word.'

'I was expecting to fight,' said Shiban.

'You will be fighting, Shiban Khan,' said Niborran, 'just not in a conventional fashion. Besides, once the enemy becomes aware of what we're doing, and it won't take them long, they will try to stop you. They want the port, but I don't think the World Eaters care how intact it is.'

Shiban nodded. 'I'll need a few men as supervisors.'

'Of course. Pick well, and be sparing.'

Niborran switched his half-smoked cigar to his left hand, and held out his right. Shiban hesitated, then shook it gently.

'No backward step,' said Niborran. 'Your doctrine, I believe? Lord Diaz told me that.'

'No backward step,' Shiban replied.

The White Scar left the balcony without looking back. Niborran glanced at Cadwalder.

'I want you on the line, Huscarl,' he said.

'According to my pledge to the Praetorian,' Cadwalder replied, 'I go where you go.'

Niborran tossed his cigar away, and swung the lasrifle off his shoulder.

'Then you'll be on the line,' he said.

Those who had survived the frantic retreat from the Pons Solar took shelter in the yards and cage-ways behind the barrier wall. Medics moved through the gaggles of sprawled troops, and sutlers brought food pails, water and tepid samovars. Someone was singing. Hari thought it was probably a hopeless effort to drown out the noise of the assault. The wall battalions and defence systems had taken over the desperate repulse.

He slept for a while, curled up in a gritty rockcrete corner. When he woke, the noise had not abated. He sat with his slate, trying to write down what he had witnessed. When, as he expected, he failed entirely to do that, he tried instead to write about the clarity he had found in the chaos. The importance of history, no matter how little truth lay in it. The clinical necessity of lies, from a soldier's point of view. He tried to explain, as simply as possible, the curative need for accounts of valour, even if they were inflated into fiction.

He was not pleased with the result.

He thought of Kyril Sindermann, and the pep talks the old man had delivered, with wry passion, to his early clutch of would-be remembrancers. The siege had already become an inescapable fact by then. Now here he was, caught up in a siege within a siege.

He remembered Sindermann saying, 'The historian's first duties are sacrilege and the mocking of false gods. They are his indispensable instruments for establishing the truth.' The old man had attributed that to some M2 mystic, but had clearly believed it. Hari had too. Now he found he believed it *inside out*. He had accepted it too literally, because it had been right and proper to do so. Reversing that was the sacrilege part. The false gods weren't the heathen deities the Imperium had erased. They were concepts, such as literal documentation and scholarly detachment. A history of war, and this Last War especially, needed to understand, and engage with, the spirit of those who fought.

He tried to write about that, but it sounded stupid, and lacking in any professional rigour. So he wrote down the story of the convoy ambush instead, just as Joseph had told it to him: the valiant soldier, Olly Piers, standing his ground, and then surviving through the grace of the Emperor, by merit of his unshakable faith. Hari used words like 'daemons', then thought better of it, deleted them, and replaced them with phrases such as 'the Great Traitor', or 'the power of Horus'. It came out reading like a child's fable. A parable.

Then he wrote, in a similar fashion, a plain account of the
stand at the Pons, while it was still fresh in his mind. Piers
rallying the men around the banner. How they had stood
before the face of the Emperor, and stared down the monstrous rage of the Great Traitor. How they had protected the
Emperor's image with their lives, mortal in the face of super-
mortal danger.

He wanted to add a gloss, a few paragraphs explaining the
mechanism of lies in these parables, how the symbolic values
were far more important than any literal, eye-witness account.

But a man had approached him.

'Do you need restock?' the man asked, standing over him.
Teams had entered the yards, lugging long boxes of ammu-
nition and energy cells for distribution. It was time to rearm.
Weary troopers were calling out calibres and slot-gauges.
The man, a trooper caked in dirt, had a clutch of las and
hard-round magazines in his hands.

'No,' said Hari. 'Thank you.'

'Are you…?' the man asked. 'Are you the historian? The
remembrancer?'

'Uh, interrogator. Yes,' said Hari.

'My friend told me about you,' the man said. He sat down on
the dirty rockcrete beside Hari without being invited. 'Joseph.'

'Joseph Monday?'

The man nodded. He put down his selection of magazines,
and held out a dirty hand.

'Willem Kordy (Thirty-Third Pan-Pac Lift Mobile),' he said.
Hari shook his hand.

'Is he all right?' asked Hari. 'I haven't seen him since we
made it back inside.'

Willem shrugged. 'Are any of us all right?' he asked.

'I found him during the battle,' said Hari. 'He was weeping.
Uncontrollable. I presumed it was the trauma of–'

'Nah, doubt it,' said Willem. 'We've been through a lot. Fourteenth line, that whole shit. Got here by walking through hell's arsehole. I expect it was just release.'

'Release?'

'That this was ending. That death was close, and it would all stop.'

'He wanted death?' asked Hari.

'He wanted it to stop,' the trooper replied. 'We all come to that place, sooner or later. I've seen it. I remember it happened to Jen.'

'Jen?'

Willem shook his head. 'We've seen a lot,' he said.

'I am trying to record accounts,' said Hari. 'Stories. It sounds like you have some.'

'I haven't got time to tell them,' said Willem. His team-mates were calling to him to hurry up. He got to his feet, and picked up the magazines. 'Anyway,' he added, 'why bother? Why bother with stories?'

'To create a history,' said Hari. 'To commit to the future by believing there can be one. And to help that future understand itself.'

'So the future can remember us?' Willem asked. 'Remember me?'

'Yes.'

'I like that,' Willem admitted. 'I like the idea that the future is watching me in its memories.'

Hari looked down to quickly note the soldier's phrase on his slate. When he looked up, Willem Kordy (33rd Pan-Pac Lift Mobile) had gone.

Hari found Joseph Baako Monday in a nearby yard. He was sitting silently, gazing at the far wall. His weapon, and a restock of fresh magazines, lay by his feet, waiting.

'You made it too?' Joseph asked, looking up at Hari.

'Why were you weeping?' Hari asked.

'Oh, because my angel had died,' said Joseph.

'Your what?'

'I said to you,' said Joseph, 'no angel delivered me. The Emperor did not come, or send His spirit, in my hour of need after Line Fourteen, not like He came to the soldier in the story. But that was a mistake. I was wrong. I see that now. Angels take different forms. The spirit of the Emperor, it takes many different forms.'

Hari sat down beside him, and took out his slate.

'Lord Diaz was my angel,' Joseph said. 'He found me and the others. He brought us through the fire. He was the spirit of the Emperor, sent to us.'

'Your angel?'

'I saw him die,' said Joseph. 'Only when I watched him die, did I understand that. He was on the bridge. The last living man on the bridge. He fought everything that came at him. He fought until they killed him to make him stop fighting. He fought as they butchered him. I saw what they did to him, before he died, and after.'

He looked at Hari.

'I wept, because the spirit did not come for him,' he said. 'It made me think that there was no spirit, that my faith in the Throne was a stupid waste. But then we were at the flag, all around the banner. And the spirit came again, like it came to the soldier in the convoy. It struck down the butcher that would have murdered us.'

'Who is Jen?' Hari asked.

Joseph looked surprised.

'Jen Koder (Twenty-Second Kantium Hort),' he said. 'My friend. She died because her faith had failed. She was too tired, too hurt. She did not see, like I did not see at the time, that Lord Diaz was the Emperor come to us. Maybe she did not have the strength left, even if she did see that. But she had some strength. Enough to make sure the enemy did not take her life.'

'Do you think what happened to us at the banner was a miracle?' asked Hari.

'What do you think, my friend?'

'I don't know what that was,' said Hari.

'I think there are miracles everywhere,' said Joseph. 'All around us, all the time. We just have to see them. Know to recognise them. And have the faith to believe in them. If we believe, we make them happen.'

He looked at Hari.

'You are writing all this down?' he asked, and laughed.

'It's my job,' said Hari. 'Do you have a slate?'

Joseph fumbled in the pockets of his litewka. He eventually brought out a battered, small-format dataslate, crusted in dirt.

'It does not work,' he said. 'No link, no noospherics.'

'But it can store, right?' Hari asked. He took the man's slate, and carefully transferred files across from his own device. 'These are the accounts I've taken down,' he said. 'Share them with anyone you like. Add to them. Add your own. I think it would help people here to read them. And you asked about a book. A secret book you would like to read.'

Joseph looked at him, curious.

'There's a copy of that there too,' said Hari. 'Share that as well, with as many people as you can. I think there's a strength in it, and I know we all need as much strength as we can get.'

Piers was in one of the cage-ways. He had the banner spread out on the ground, and was scrubbing it with a bristle-brush to remove some of the dirt and soot. Two other troopers, one male, one female, both as filthy as Piers, were sitting with him, using needles and threads from their uniform kits to sew up the shot holes.

'What's your name?' Hari asked.

Piers, on his hands and knees, looked up at Hari with a pained expression.

'You could help,' he said.

'What's Olly short for?' Hari asked.

'Why, boy?'

'I'm writing your story,' said Hari. 'I wanted to get your name right.'

'I don't have a story,' Piers rumbled, and went back to scrubbing. 'I have stories, plural. Many fine stories. But not *a* story. I am a complicated man. I will not be reduced or abbreviated.'

'Except to Olly.'

'Shut your hole, clever clogs.'

'Is it Oliver?'

'Pick up a brush, boy.'

'Is it Olias?'

'Give me strength…'

'Is it Olaf?'

'Is it?' asked the man working nearby, laughing. 'Is it Olaf?'

'Shut your bloody noise, Pash, and stop encouraging him,' Piers snapped over his shoulder. The two troopers grinned at him.

'What is this story?' the woman asked, rethreading her needle.

'The exploits of Grenadier Piers,' said Hari. 'There are many parts to it. He's been spreading them around. I'm surprised you haven't heard any of them.'

'I heard this one about a convoy,' the woman said. 'How the Emperor sent His spirit to save this brave soldier from daemons.' She looked at Hari. 'Are you his biographer, or something?' she asked.

'He's the historian,' said the other man. 'Piers said about him, remember?'

'Interrogator,' said Hari.

'I'm Bailee Grosser (Third Helvet),' she said. 'This is Pasha Cavaner (Eleventh Heavy Janissar).'

Hari made a note. 'Grosser... Cavaner...'

'Put the regiments,' she told him.

'Why?' asked Hari.

'It matters,' said Grosser.

'It's all we got,' said Cavaner. 'Put them in brackets.'

'I'm just writing down accounts from everyone,' said Hari. 'Like what happened with this.' He prodded the outstretched banner with his toe.

'Don't stand on His face, boy!' Piers snapped.

'I was there,' said Cavaner.

'You were?' asked Hari. He didn't recognise him, but then everybody had been caked in mud, and blood, and veiled in the abject terror of the moment.

The man shrugged. 'It was mad. We put the banner up. It was heavy. Blood all over it. But we stood before it. Stood in front of it, protecting Him with our lives.'

Cavaner reached down, and patted the banner.

'We stood in front of Him, and when evil came, we stood in its path, and the Emperor rewarded us for our faith, and struck evil down.'

'Getting the banner up was actually my idea,' said Hari.

Cavaner frowned at him. 'I don't remember you being there,' he said.

'I was,' said Hari.

'Putting yourself in my story, are you?' Piers growled.

'No,' said Hari. 'Is it Oleander?'

Piers sagged and sighed. He muttered something.

'What was that?' asked Hari.

'What did he say?' asked Grosser.

'I said, if you must know,' said Piers, 'it's Ollanius.'

Grosser and Cavaner burst out laughing.

'Oh my life!' giggled Grosser. 'That's an old fart's name! A grandad's name!'

'It *was* me grandaddy's, as it happens,' Piers protested. 'An old family name. A good Uplander name. Stop bloody laughing.' He looked up at Hari. 'Don't bloody write it down, boy!'

'Why not?' Hari asked.

'Make a better one up!' Piers said. He got to his feet. 'Something more heroic. I've never bloody liked it. No hero was ever called bloody Ollanius. Put something better!'

'Like?'

Piers hesitated. 'Olympos,' he suggested.

'I'm definitely not putting that,' said Hari.

'But it's proper heroic!' Piers objected.

'I'm putting Ollanius,' said Hari.

'You little ball-bag. Why does it matter so much?'

'Because there's got to be some truth in it,' said Hari. 'Something to balance out the bullshit and the lies. Of which, let's be fair, there's plenty.'

'Mythrus, Dame Death, she weren't no bullshit,' said Piers.

'No one saw her,' said Hari.

'I saw her!' Piers snapped.

'I saw what she did,' said Cavaner. He looked at Hari. 'If you were there, like you claim you were, you must have too.'

'I saw something I can't explain,' Hari admitted.

'There you go,' said Piers, as if that answered everything.

'And I grasp it now,' Hari said to him.

Piers simmered down a bit. He studied Hari's face.

'Do you?' he asked.

'I do,' said Hari.

Piers nodded. 'Good,' he said. 'Good, then.' With some

effort, he got back down on his knees, and began scrubbing the banner again. 'But tell it right, if you're telling it,' he added. 'What I'm saying is, do it justice. Make a proper tale out of it, eh? It wasn't no banner, it was the Emperor Himself. In person. I stood before the Emperor on the battlefields of Terra, to protect Him. Put myself in harm's way, for His sake. And it wasn't no raving World Eater, neither. Make it… say it was the Great Traitor himself. Big, bad Lupercal.'

'I'm not putting that,' said Hari.

'Why not?'

'No one would ever believe it,' said Hari.

Then the old grenadier says, 'They don't have to believe it, they just have to like it. It just has to be inspiring.' The young man thinks about this, and then types some more on his slate.

None of them can see me. Not even the old grenadier this time. Perhaps he is too preoccupied mending the banner, or perhaps he can only see me in the heat of things, when his adrenaline is pumping.

Or perhaps… Perhaps he can only see me when it matters. When it's necessary.

I don't know what force or power decides such things. If asked, I would say fortune, but I am no expert, and I have not made a study of these transmundane concepts.

And no one will ask me.

I believe the young man's efforts are worthwhile. I see now why the Lord Praetorian initiated the programme, and warranted the return of the remembrancer order. It has value, though I am not sure this is quite how Rogal imagined it. The act of recording history produces a sense of a future. It is, perhaps, the most optimistic thing anyone can do. We will always need to know where we have come from. We will always need to know that we are going somewhere.

I would have liked to talk to the young man. I have many stories to tell. So very many. But he is not even aware of me, and the Custodian is not present to translate my hands. I had considered making the grenadier my proloquor, but it is clear he does not see me all the time, and besides, he does not know my thoughtmarks.

I sit in the corner of the cage-way, and watch them for a few more minutes. Tsutomu has gone to the barrier wall, and I must join him. The enemy's rage grows worse. I have composed myself. I am centred and ready for what will follow. Of all the stories in my long life, I think it will be the very last.

I get up and walk away. They do not notice me depart. They did not notice me arrive.

SIX

All
Inevitable weapons
From the pit

Horus Aximand thought, for a second, that he could hear the slow breathing again.

But it was Lord Commander Eidolon, as he strode towards them, teeth glittering, his throat sacs heaving and puffing like the goitre frills of some foul marsh amphibian.

Aximand glanced at Abaddon. 'Is this where he reneges?' he asked softly.

'I'll gut him if he does,' said Abaddon, with a cold simplicity that told Little Horus he meant it.

'And I'll hold him for you,' said Kibre.

Tormageddon snickered.

'Brothers,' said Eidolon, infrasonic tones thrumming behind his words. 'Are you prepared?'

'Take a wild guess,' said Abaddon.

Eidolon sniffed sullenly, and gazed beyond the four warriors of the Mournival. The deep canyon lay sixty kilometres from Epta war-stead, a split in the lip of the Himalazian plateau. High above them, above the walls of the ravine, the sky twisted and raged, a now almost permanent storm driven across the entire region by gross atmospheric disruption.

Eyet-One-Tag's artificers and magi had already hollowed the base of the canyon out, drilled the cavity like rotten molars, and raised the immense ramp platforms for the machines they had supplied. The ugly Terrax- and Plutona-pattern Termite assault drills, and their far larger and uglier kin, the Mantolith-pattern, lay on the sloping ramps, nose-bores down, aimed at the earth. Engines were being test-fired, drill heads and melta-cutter systems checked.

Three complete companies of the Sons of Horus, the First, 18th and 25th, in full battleplate, stood ready to board. Officers waited, ready to take their oaths of moment. These were oaths the warriors were eager to make, perhaps the most significant of their lives.

The company captains, Lev Goshen of the 25th, and Tybalt Marr of the 18th, waited nearby, flanked by an honour guard formed of the Justaerin and the Catulan.

'I see you are,' Eidolon fluted.

'You've kept us waiting,' said Abaddon.

'Not polite,' said Kibre.

'My manners are impeccable,' Eidolon replied. He glanced at his escort guard, lavish warriors in full panoply, and smiled, as if at some private joke. They were gaudy warriors, parodies, but killers all. Aximand knew some of them. Von Kalda, with his wide-eyed child's face and ivory armour, equerry to Eidolon; Lecus Phodion, the vexillarius, who now insisted his rank was 'orchestrator' or something; Quine Mylossar, once a fine sword and a good tactician, now chromed like a trophy, with hideously long sabre blades extended from his vambraces, and peacock feathers behind his head; Nuno DeDonna, a noted master of assault doctrines, sheathed in plate that seemed both black and purple, yet neither.

'The question is, lord, are you prepared?' asked Aximand. 'Were you persuasive?'

'I am always persuasive,' said Eidolon.

'So the Third is with us in this undertaking?' asked Abaddon.

'It is, Ezekyle,' said Eidolon, 'it is. The concept is appealing. The speed of it, the finality. The Emperor's Children are with you.'

Abaddon nodded. He took a step closer to Eidolon. Aximand recognised the footwork. It looked casual, just a step forward with a half-step to the side, but it placed Abaddon slightly on Eidolon's off-guard side. The First Captain often used the same footwork to realign for a kill-stroke in a blade fight.

'Good,' said Abaddon. 'I am gratified, *brother*. You had sent no word, and I was beginning to fear we had over-committed in false expectation. My Legion, with the tacit approval of the Lord of Iron, has made significant investment in this endeavour. Without your promised participation, it dies before it even begins.'

'And I have kept my promise,' said Eidolon. He chuckled. 'I have been persuasive. I have been silver-tongued.'

'It looks blue,' said Aximand.

'You're funny, little one,' Eidolon giggled.

'What strength?' asked Abaddon. 'What strength do you commit? What has the Phoenician allowed you? I told you, I need five battle companies, minimum.'

'Yes, you were quite clear.'

'Then what strength?'

'All,' said Eidolon.

'All five?' Abaddon asked.

'No, Ezekyle. All.'

Abaddon narrowed his eyes.

'Is that a joke?' he asked.

'I do love jokes, as you know,' said Eidolon, fastidiously

flicking some invisible mote of dust off his coral-pink warplate, 'but no, it's not. You wanted our strength. You have it. You have the Emperor's Children. You have all the Emperor's Children.'

'The entire Third Legion?'

'The entire Third Legion,' echoed Eidolon. 'I hope that will be sufficient.'

Abaddon ran the tip of his tongue around his lips, thoughtfully.

'You've surprised me,' he said.

'I can tell that by the expression on your face,' said Eidolon. He clapped his hands in delight, and shrill little squeals burbled from his inflated throat. Behind him, his warriors laughed and hooted. 'It was worth it all, just to see that!' Eidolon added.

'It will be worth much more than that,' said Abaddon. 'It will be worth my gratitude, and the respect of the Lord of Iron, and the thanks of my genesire. What we are about to do will change everything, and the measure of your support will guarantee its success. I have underestimated you, brother. Underestimated the seriousness of your intent.'

He held out his hand.

'Forgive me for that, Eidolon, and receive my thanks.'

Eidolon's face split in a smile that even the features of a legionary should not have been able to accommodate. It stretched to his ears, revealing thousands of polished teeth. He took Abaddon's hand and clasped it.

'Think nothing of it,' he said. 'It's what brothers do.'

'How did your lord, the Phoenician, greet this idea?' Abaddon asked. 'You said you were persuasive, but he must have questioned the wisdom of deploying the whole of his Legion. He must trust you a great deal to lead it into this action.'

'Oh, he doesn't trust me at all,' replied Eidolon. 'Not even slightly. But I am so persuasive.'

'I… don't understand,' said Abaddon.

'He talked me into it,' said a voice.

One of the warriors behind Eidolon stepped forward, from between Phodion and Mylossar. With each step, his plate and gear, cloak and shield, peeled off him, disintegrating into embers that sizzled into the canyon wind. The legionary was naked for a moment, then, as he continued to walk, his unblemished skin became polished like opaline shell. He began to grow, becoming taller, leaner, a towering figure of athletic perfection. A soft, pearlescent radiance guttered beneath his nacreous skin, like candles fluttering inside a box of the thinnest ivory, and then his flesh was reclothed in ornate armour of the most extraordinary lustre and complexity. The beautiful, painful fury of Fulgrim's eyes bore down on Abaddon.

'It sounded like fun,' Fulgrim said, his voice made of silver and venom and sherbet syrup. He brushed a loose strand of long, snow-white hair away from his face.

Abaddon bowed his head, and sank to one knee. He knew he needed to show respect. He also didn't want to look. A single glimpse of Fulgrim's lethal beauty was enough.

Abaddon threw a curt gesture. The Mournival, and the companies behind them, knelt too.

'You honour us, lord,' said Abaddon.

'You honour us, Abaddon,' said Fulgrim. *'You offer us a chance to break deadlock and seize victory. You offer a swift end to this malingering. When Eidolon brought your modest proposal to me, I saw its finesse at once. I wanted to do more than lend you a few companies. I wanted to throw my entire support behind your effort. My children will execute the assault you have requested. I will lead them in person. Where my children go, I will go.*

'*Get up now,*' he added.

Abaddon rose.

'*Let's make our beginning,*' said Fulgrim.

The geo-imaging display turned slowly in the air.

'There,' said Malcador. 'And there. Do you see?'

'I am no geological expert, lord,' said Sindermann, squinting, 'but I see enough. The subcrust is compromised below the macrofortifications.'

'Both before and behind the Saturnine Wall,' said Malcador. His voice was dust dry, loose pebbles trickling down a dry stream course.

He cancelled the display with a twitch of his hand, and sat down on a gilded chair.

'We knew of the natural fault,' he said. 'Every potential flaw was assayed and plotted when Dorn began the fortification work. It was filled in. Rockcrete and ferroplast. But the bombardment of the Palace has been long and sustained. The cumulative effect has caused tectonic shifts. The old wound has split again. We weren't aware. We would not have seen it but for you.'

'It was an idle comment, made by chance,' said Sindermann. He noticed that Therajomas was still writing on his slate, furiously. 'Don't note that,' Sindermann hissed.

'The idle comment part?' asked the young man.

'No, the fact that I apparently noticed it,' said Sindermann.

'Why ever not, Kyril?' Malcador asked. 'Your role is part of the history now. A significant part.'

'A historian, lord, should show some modicum of detachment,' said Sindermann. 'I seek truth, not personal credit.'

'You seek odd things, Kyril,' said Malcador. 'You always have. The truth? What is that? The truth depends on who's looking. Who's telling. You found a hole in the ground, Kyril, and the only truth in that is, if Rogal's right, it will be filled with an enemy spearhead within days or hours. It is the way in they've been looking for. The one tiny chink in Rogal's defence. Perturabo will exploit it. There's no doubt about that. And the prize is very great, so the agency he sends to exploit it will be very great, also.'

'Can't you just fill it?' asked Therajomas suddenly, then remembered who he was addressing and swallowed hard.

'What did you say, child?' Malcador asked.

Therajomas mumbled something.

'My colleague was positing the idea that you could just "fill the hole", lord,' said Sindermann. 'Remove the flaw.'

'Oh, we can,' replied Malcador. 'And we are preparing to. The specialist, Land. That's his task.'

'Land?'

Malcador sighed. 'I am tired. Diamantis, point him out, will you?'

The Huscarl led Sindermann to the gantry rail. Below them, in one of the vast, excavated chambers, a man was supervising high-function servitors and diligent magi. They were in a lab space, working on an array of industrial machines that looked like pumping units and drill rigs. The rest of the chamber was filled with rows of immense storage tanks, the source of the chemical stink Sindermann had detected when he first arrived.

'Arkhan Land,' said Diamantis. 'Technoarchaeologist.'

'What's that?' asked Sindermann.

'I think only he knows,' the Huscarl replied. 'He's an annoying little bastard, but he's clever. In just a few hours, he has concocted a liquid filler. A sealant. He calls it lockcrete, I believe. Flows like water, but it sets fast. Massively adherent. It forms a solid harder than the ground rock. We've broken drills on it in tests.'

'Mars?'

'What?' asked Diamantis.

'He's from Mars? He's Mechanicum?'

'Something like that,' said Diamantis.

'I'd like to talk to him.'

'You really wouldn't,' said the Huscarl. 'He's obnoxious. Besides, he's busy.'

Sindermann looked back at the Sigillite. 'So, you can seal the flaw, this terrible vulnerability, at a moment's notice?' he asked.

'We expect to be able to do so,' Malcador replied. Perched on his golden chair, he looked very frail. He took a sip of something from a goblet.

'But you're waiting?' Sindermann asked.

Malcador nodded, and dabbed his lips.

'Because you want them to come in?'

'Whoever's coming will be a prize. A significant kill. Perhaps a decisive one. They don't know we know. We want to let them in.'

'And who's coming?'

'I don't know that,' said Malcador. 'But it will be someone worth destroying.'

'It could be him?'

Malcador wheezed out a chuckle. 'It is his kind of play. And we can be fairly certain he wants the glory. For himself. He's come a long way for this, Kyril. I can't picture him delegating the final step to others. Can you?'

Sindermann walked across the gantry, drew out another of the golden chairs, and sat down facing the Sigillite. 'It is the most extraordinary risk,' he said.

Malcador nodded. 'Without doubt,' he agreed.

'If it fails, lord–'

Malcador raised a bony hand to hush him.

'This is Dorn's game,' he said. 'Regicide. The grand master

play. I trust his schemes implicitly. We think of him… I dare say, we've always thought of him… as the master of defence. We are *not* masters of defence, Kyril. None of us even approach his level of insight and expertise. We presume, in our innocence, a great defence involves an absence of flaws. A perfect, impervious fortress, immune to any assault.'

He paused, and took another sip. His neck was as thin as a reed, and as knotted as a twig.

'Rogal understands better,' he said. 'A flaw can be an invitation. Especially to a mind like Perturabo's. It draws his attention. Of course, it helps that the Lord of Iron is clinically obsessed with besting Dorn. He won't resist. Dorn is forcing him into making a move, forcing him into an error.'

'It seems so counterintuitive,' said Sindermann. 'Exploiting one's own flaw–'

'I know, I know,' said Malcador, nodding. 'Rogal is full of surprises. That's why he's the Praetorian. We expect perfection of him. Faultless perfection. He is embracing imperfection. Seeing it and, rather than removing it, using it. I think he's learned that from Jaghatai.'

Sindermann frowned. 'This was the Khagan's idea?'

'Oh no, not at all!' the Sigillite replied, chuckling. 'The Khan is mercurial, almost capricious. Dorn is not. The Khan is fluid and adaptive. Dorn is not. The Khan adjusts his strategies on the move, as the environment changes. Dorn sets the environment in advance. Now they're working together, obliged to, caught in the same trap, back to back. A siege is Dorn's theatre. It is stifling to the Khan, so he's learning. Adapting. And Dorn, in turn, is watching him adapt. And learning from that.'

'They are learning from each other?'

'It can be fractious, but yes,' said Malcador. 'Rogal knows he needs Jaghatai. That's a given. But he's also come to understand that he can't box Jaghatai in, and force him to conform.

Dorn has perceived, quickly, that he needs to let Jaghatai be Jaghatai. Create a grey area in which the Khan is free to operate to his full potential. That grey area is still part of Dorn's structure, but is, of itself, not set.'

'A little, deliberate flaw,' said Sindermann.

'Quite right,' said Malcador. 'It means Rogal gets the best out of the Khan. But the real beauty of it, is it sets up variables that Perturabo can't read. Perturabo is anticipating Dorn's every move. He's studied his tactica for years. The Khan is an outlier. What he does, still, you understand, on Dorn's behalf, cannot be anticipated in the same way. The Khan's actions are not Dorn's. Through the Khan, Dorn seeks to generate unexpected moves that Perturabo cannot read.'

'And now he's adopted that idea himself?' asked Sindermann.

'Rogal has learned a flexibility. A sleight of hand.'

'Like letting our archenemy into the Sanctum Imperialis?'

'Yes. Letting him in, cutting his throat, and then sealing the flaw behind him. This Land fellow's lockcrete will close the flaw once the trap is sprung, and build a tomb for whoever comes.'

'We're meeting their decapitation strike with one of our own?'

'Exquisite, isn't it?' said Malcador, and laughed.

Sindermann sat back. 'Still, it is a risk,' he said. 'A gamble of terrifying magnitude...'

'Oh, absolutely,' replied Malcador.

He tilted his head, as if listening to something.

'We should attend,' he said. 'He's ready. Help me up, would you?'

They found Dorn in an adjoining chamber, one of the preparation halls carved out of the rock beneath the streets of the Saturnine Quarter. It was, Diamantis said, a deployment station adjacent to the line of the flaw.

Dorn, in full regal battleplate, was standing on a dais, with a baldachin canopy above him. The rich, draped material was embroidered with the Praetorian crest and the symbols of the Imperial Fists. Nearby stood the brooding Dreadnought Bohemond, several more Huscarls, a small group of tacticians from the War Courts, led by Mistress Tacticae Katarin Elg, and a phalanx of the Hort Palatine, fronted by Ahlborn.

Dorn nodded to Sindermann as he approached. The Praetorian helped Malcador onto the dais. Sindermann and Therajomas waited with Diamantis at the side of the stage.

Ahlborn listened to his earpiece, then looked at Dorn.

'My lord, the counter-assault officers are assembled.'

'Bid them enter,' said Dorn.

Four of the Hort troopers hurried across the chamber floor, and rolled open the heavy cargo shutters. A line of Space Marines walked in, side by side, and approached the dais.

Sindermann gazed, taken aback. He'd expected a command section of the Imperial Fists.

'Is that–' Therajomas whispered.

'Shhh!' Sindermann hissed.

He watched the warriors approach, side by side, a slow and steady pace. Each one was in full battleplate, unhelmed. Their faces were solemn and determined. Maximus Thane, Imperial Fist, captain of the 22nd Company Exemplar, a long-hafted warhammer resting across his right shoulder. Helig Gallor, once of the Death Guard, his plate now the sombre grey of the Knights Errant. Bel Sepatus, Blood Angel, a captain-Paladin of the Keruvim host, his tri-faced emblem gleaming on the chest of his crimson Cataphractii armour, his avenging longsword, *Parousia*, held across it in both hands, inverted. The massive Endryd Haar, the Riven Hound, World Eater turned Blackshield outcast, his power fist as soot-dark as the plate he wore. Nathaniel Garro, once battle-captain of the 7th

Great Company Death Guard, now a grey Knight Errant too, Paragon bolter clamped to his hip, the ancient broadblade *Libertas* braced across his pauldron. Sigismund, Imperial Fist, First Lord Captain of the Templar Brethren elite, his artificer plate the black of that order, badged in yellow, covered in an ebon surcoat that lacked any emblem, his powerblade bound to his right wrist by penitent chains, his shield to his left. Garviel Loken, Knight Errant, Rubio's dead sword strapped to his waist, a long-pattern chainblade suspended in his hand.

Loken's plate was not grey. It had been freshly refinished in the colours of a captain of the Luna Wolves.

The seven came to a halt, in line, in front of the dais. In unison, they saluted the Praetorian, each making the particular gesture of homage used by his Legion, or the lost Legion he had once served.

'Brother-sons,' said Dorn. 'Under a mask of absolute confidence, we have prepared this place of war, and drawn up our strengths. When the hour comes, and it closes on us fast, you seven will be the leaders of the combat. Every one of you is more than proven in battle. Every one of you is sworn to Terra. And every one of you, each in his own way, is fired by a personal longing to annihilate our enemy.'

There was silence. Haar nodded gently. Sigismund tilted his head back slightly, and clenched his jaw.

'And none of you more so than me,' said Dorn. 'You will follow me into this action.'

There was a murmur.

'You will lead us, lord?' asked Sigismund.

'In person,' Dorn replied. 'You have been briefed by Diamantis. Instructed, and assigned your complements. Mistress Elg will run tactical operations from the forward command established here. Its cipher is Trickster. Narrowband datacast only. Secrecy is paramount. General vox and links are forbidden for the duration. You will listen to her, and apply her data scrupulously. I will be doing the same. Mistress?'

Elg, tall and severe, stepped forward.

'Praetorian,' she said. 'Function is established. A hardline link to the Grand Borealis is ready. Our systems here are modest, for they have been established rapidly and needed to be portable, but Bhab can supply us with larger-scale acoustic data via the Sanctum listening watch. Due to the absolute secrecy of this undertaking, very few in the Grand Borealis are even aware of it. Only Master of Huscarls Archamus and my colleague Icaro have been read in. They will serve as data liaisons.'

Dorn nodded.

'I dislike secrecy intensely,' he said, turning back to the commanders. 'It is deceit, and it deserves no place among the honest and honourable doctrines of Fair War. Secrets are volatile and unstable. They are never stored safely. When they emerge, the mere fact of them can damage the friends and brothers around us.'

He paused, and looked down for a moment. He thought of the tactics he had chosen. The bitter choices. The Eternity Wall space port, dying already, no doubt, because he had elected to sacrifice it for this chance. He thought how he had kept that awful choice from almost everybody, most particularly his beloved brothers Jaghatai and Sanguinius. He had deceived and handled them both, either through psychological manipulation or a simple withholding. But he had weighed it, and found it necessary. Victory was the only goal, and he could not afford for either of them to be distracted, or to have them question him. They could not question what they did not know.

He thought of Sindermann, charged to gather up a history that would secure them the promise of a future. Dorn knew that very little of the old man's history would ever or *could*

ever be published or broadcast. Most of it would be sequestered and redacted forever.

And he thought of Vulkan. For a long time, only he and
the Sigillite had known that Vulkan was alive, and had
returned to Terra. Dorn had considered that an imperative
secret. Keeping it allowed Vulkan to pursue his very singular
defence of the Palace unhindered, free from any urging that
he should be deployed on the Palace fields. But Malcador, to
Dorn's dismay, had chosen to divulge the news of Vulkan's
presence to Sanguinius and the Khan, bringing them into a
circle of trust that Dorn had been certain excluded them. The
Sigillite had done this in front of him. To save face, and to
disguise any notion of dissembling, Dorn had been obliged
to feign shock.

He had thought the Khan and the Great Angel would see
through him in an instant, see his unpractised acting for what
it was.

But they had not.

The lies were becoming too easy. The dissembling too ordinary. Deceit had become a necessary tool in his arsenal, and
he despised it almost as much as the ones who had forced
him into it.

He became aware that he had stopped speaking. The
commanders were staring at him, ready but puzzled.

'Fair War,' he said. 'I have always prosecuted fair wars. I
have chosen honour. But this is not Fair War. It is foul. It is
unseemly and it is inhuman, and the very fact that brothers
have turned against us shows us that we cannot trust ourselves.
In this dark age, we must match our foe or be destroyed. We
must embellish our grand arsenal of honour, courage and fortitude with more unwholesome devices. The inevitable weapons
of surprise, deceit, entrapment and dishonesty. And we must,
I am sorry to say, set aside mercy and become merciless.'

He looked at the seven warriors.

'Questions?' he asked.

'Just an observation, great lord,' said Loken. 'If we destroy our enemies here, and end this, does it matter how?'

Sigismund and Garro both smiled quietly. So did Malcador, up on the dais. Haar snorted, amused, and turned the snort into a cough. Thane and Bel Sepatus scowled.

'Ordinarily, captain?' Dorn asked. 'Absolutely yes. Tonight, no. But I notice that you have chosen to sweep your own deceptions away. Or is this just more deceit?'

Loken glanced down at himself.

'I have always been a Luna Wolf, my lord,' he said. 'Loyal, to the death. I want them to see that as they die.'

'Hell, yes,' muttered Gallor.

Dorn stared at Loken, and nodded gently. 'Your livery, captain, once represented the best of us. I hope it will again. Anything else?'

'My lord,' said Sepatus. 'You are here, and committed to engage. We are told the good Archamus is participating from Bhab. My questions are... Who will be running the siege defence? Should my genesire not be informed?'

'I am running the siege, captain,' said Dorn. 'I have been from the beginning, at every hour, at every moment, wherever I go and whatever I do. This will be no different. And, like me, Archamus can multi-task. The Grand Borealis is efficient and well prepared. The tacticians and the War Court offer fulsome support, as they have since day one. My dear brother does not need to be informed yet. You know as well as I do how occupied he is at Gorgon Bar.'

'But,' Sepatus pressed, 'grace prevent it, if you should fall–'

'I won't,' said Dorn.

'My brother Bel Sepatus seems to doubt your prowess, my lord,' said Thane. There was some laughter from the line. 'But his concern is valid,' Thane went on, more sombre. 'You are the foundation of our defence. The architect of our fate. Is it wise to risk you by placing you at the forefront of a known flaw in this fortress?'

'Indeed,' said Sigismund. 'At a place where the very worst of our enemy is fully expected to stream in and unleash fury?'

'I have done my utmost to make this palace a true fortress,' said Dorn. 'I've built it from the ground up, diligently... some say obsessively... making sure that it is impenetrable and secure. But that is an impossible task. There will always be cracks, there will always be flaws. No fortress of mere stone and steel in our galaxy is truly impervious. So I must place myself directly before those cracks, and block them with my own flesh and fury.'

He gazed at them steadily.

'I am the fortress now,' he said.

Sindermann shivered. The hairs on his neck stood up.

'Now, each in turn,' Dorn said to his commanders, 'make your oaths of moment to me.'

'Here they come,' said Rann.

The assault force was driving out of the ruins of the third circuit wall. Columns of Iron Warriors, advancing shield-blocked, preparing for mass escalade. Motorised gun carriages and mobile artillery moved with them in escort, clattering over the rubble. They were already firing, hefting penetrator shells at the wall beside Katillon guntower. In the shadowy cover of the circuit ruins, heavy petraries were being prepared, and brutish, armoured siege towers were being rolled out behind the advancing legionaries.

'My lord?' Rann urged.

'I see it, Fafnir,' Sanguinius murmured. They were coming at Katillon, the site of their defeat the day before. They were coming at Katillon, because it was buckled, and wounded. Huge elements of the traitor host, beastkin and human wretches, were swarming out of the enemy line at six, no, *seven* different places, to harry and occupy the defenders' attention, and dilute any response to the main strike. Wall units were already beginning to chop them down in their hundreds.

He could see. But it was a blur.

'My lord?' said Rann, with greater urgency. Sanguinius leaned on the bulwark for a moment, both hands flat on the warm stone, to brace his body and wings. The pain had returned. The otherness flooded into his head like a caustic rip-surge.

'My lord, are you unwell?' Rann asked. Sanguinius rose upright.

'No,' he said. He was lying. The pain was as great as it had been at any point before. He breathed hard, and showed the calm face Rann and the others expected to see.

'Rann? Aimery? Lead repulse forces to receive and block the main strike,' he said. 'Katillon must hold. Lux? Stand in support, all your men. Halen, order blanket suppression fire from all wall deployments to curb the enthusiasm of the distraction charges. Have the guns of Katillon and Benthos target the war machines. I want those petraries smashed before they start to loose, and the siege towers ruined before they even brush the wall.'

Men started to move. Orders were yelled, trumpets sounded.

'My lord, will you come?' asked Khoradal.

'In a moment,' Sanguinius told his captain. 'I reckoned on two or three strikes. I'll hold here, and see if I'm correct. Otherwise, we commit too early.'

Another lie. A half-lie, but another one all the same. Sanguinius would stay put because it hurt too much to move. Khoradal Furio nodded, and moved off. Sanguinius turned and gazed out at the scene below.

He couldn't see it at all any more. The pain was like spikes driving into his brain. Butcher's Nails. *Oh, my brother! This is what it must feel like! This is how the Nails bite you! Unendurable!*

Pain blinded him to the unfolding mayhem of Gorgon Bar. He saw that other place again. Eternity space port. Monsalvant Gard. The barrier wall, its surface pocked and cratered like a slab of lunar surface.

He was standing outside, half a kilometre from the port, facing the Gard. He was walking towards it, crushing brittle rocks and dry skulls under his feet. A screaming host was close behind him.

He was Angron. He was in Angron's mind. He was seeing the world as Angron saw it, through a flecked and blotted red haze. Sanguinius had never been this close. His visions had brought him close before, but he had never actually intersected with one of his brothers' minds. Not this fully. He was inside Angron's brain. He was inside his pain. He was trapped inside his skull, and could smell the raw-blood meat-stink of the inside of his head.

And this was no vision, except to Sanguinius. This was now. This was happening *now*.

Niborran scrambled onto the parapet ledge below Tower Three of the barrier wall, and took the scope that Brohn offered.

'He's just out there,' Brohn said. 'Just… out there in the open.'

Niborran trained the scope down, and adjusted resolution. He could see the figure, standing alone on the strewn rubble of Western Freight, half a kilometre away. Even at that distance, he seemed immense. A hulking, hunch-shouldered ogre in spattered warplate. The huge, leathery pinions of a bat rose from his broad back. Red and gold. Blood red and soiled gold. Spoiled meat and dirty metal.

'Angron,' Cadwalder murmured. The Huscarl needed no scope to magnify the figure.

'What is he doing?' Brohn asked.

It wasn't clear. The primarch of the XII had advanced alone into the open ahead of his host. Niborran could see them massed in a great, dust-fogged swathe another half a kilometre behind their genesire. Angron was ignoring the portion of his force currently clamouring and ramming at the barrier gates to the west. He had held the remainder of his butcher-swarm back. He had walked into the open.

He had walked into the kill-zone.

'Is he mad?' asked Brohn.

'To do what he has done, and be what he has become, I would hope so,' said Cadwalder.

'Train all wall-mounts and batteries,' said Niborran.

'What?' said Brohn.

'Train the guns, Clem!' Niborran snarled. 'Did I stammer? He's walked into our fire field. Right into our kill field, as if we're nothing. I don't care what he is. Firing solution on all guns!'

Brohn, despite his near panic, wasn't idiot enough to ask for coordinates. It was a single figure, standing in the open. Around them, cued by Clem Brohn's frantic Hortcode instruction, weapon mounts began to traverse. Batteries panned. Gun-platforms adjusted on gyro-mounts. Loading systems rattled and buzzed.

'Weapons lock,' said Brohn.

Niborran stared through the scope. The intense magnification showed him the tattered, bloodstained rags flapping around Angron's filthy bulk, the massive set of the legs, the dents and notches in the gold plate, the scarring of war, the tattered lizard-wings, the excarnated skulls strung–

He lowered the scope quickly. He could see the figure well enough. He had no need of details.

Below them, Angron slowly raised a massive war-axe over his head on a tree-trunk arm. He was looking up at them.

'*Hear.*'

The word seemed to fall out of the sky like a thunderclap.

They all flinched, even Cadwalder. The Huscarl brought his bolter up in automatic threat response.

'Is… is he speaking to us?' Brohn whispered.

'*Hear. Hear me.*'

The words rolled around the rubble waste like the echo of an artillery salvo.

'*I make my offer once,*' Angron boomed, slow and leaden. '*According to the rites of this arena.*'

'Arena?' Niborran murmured. He looked at Cadwalder. 'What does he think this is?'

'*Your cause is hopeless,*' Angron intoned, wide echoes chasing each syllable. '*You face a foe that cannot be defeated. You are cut off, outnumbered, and defending a ruler too weak to be worthy of your loyalty.*'

'Clem?' Niborran whispered.

Brohn nodded.

'*My offer,*' Angron bawled. '*Give. Up.*'

There was a long silence, broken only by the stirring wind.

'*What is your answer?*' Angron demanded.

'This,' said Niborran.

Sanguinius winced as the entire south line of Monsalvant's barrier wall unloaded on him. A deluge bombardment, deafening, earth-shaking, a rain of heavy shells, main battery las and collimated plasma. He felt himself atomised. Shredded to molecules, and then those molecules incinerated.

There was no pain. There was no pain at all. A moment of pain-free serenity suspended him.

Sanguinius opened his eyes. He steadied his hand on the oh-so-solid, oh-so-real bulwark wall of Gorgon Bar. He saw the battle accelerating around him. The air full of shot and tracer fire, the Iron Warriors commencing their escalade at Katillon, siege belfries aflame, short of their target, firestorms choking the terrain below the fourth circuit wall.

It needed his attention immediately. Gorgon Bar needed the Great Angel.

But Sanguinius knew he had just felt Angron die. Sanguinius had been in his brother's mind as the guns of Monsalvant annihilated him. It was a moment, a moment of victory, but also grief. The death of a brother was no small thing. It was a momentous event that could only happen twenty times, and it had happened too much already.

And the worst of it, the heartbreaking part, was that in death, all the pain had finally gone. Sanguinius' poor, lost brother had finally found release.

Sanguinius steadied his breath. The oddest part, the most perplexing part of all, was that Angron's tortured mind had not been there. Sanguinius had shared his brother's space, and seen, as a vision, Angron's view of Monsalvant.

But that was not what Angron had been seeing at all. Angron's mind had been submerged in a vision all of its own. That was why his rage had stilled, briefly. That's why his berserk incoherence had gone, and some calm articulacy had briefly returned. A moment of lucidity. Angron had addressed the walls. He had issued his ritual challenge. He had seen Monsalvant's barrier wall as the arena walls of Nuceria, far off in the Ultima Segmentum; he had seen Monsalvant's defenders as the jeering of the Desh'ea populace. He had been Angron Thal'kyr again, Lord of the Red Sands, Child of the Mountain, railing at the braying audience of the pit.

He had been home again. He had gone home to die.

Sanguinius tried to understand what that meant. He tried to decipher what he had seen, Angron's dying vision locked inside his own. *Why that? Why there? Why Nuceria? My visions must have meaning! They must have purpose! Or are they simply heralds of my own impending madness? What truth am I supposed to learn from this?*

Sanguinius closed his eyes again, tight shut, ignoring the carnage of Gorgon Bar, and concentrated, trying to catch some fading trace of the vision that he could dissect and interpret. Nuceria. *Nuceria! There was a reason it had filled Angron's mind and stalled his rage. There was a reason it had been shown to him and, through him, to me.*

And I see it. I see it. The burned core of death, the charred corpse, the total extinction of–

The Lord of Baal gasped. He opened his eyes. The agony, so briefly relieved, nailed back into him. Raw life was bursting up. Rage was renewed. Fury reborn.

Sanguinius saw the smoking crater in the rubble wastes before Monsalvant. He saw the bombardment fume slowly clearing, the spats of fire still burning around the crater's lip. He saw charred scraps of exploded bone and half-cooked hunks of meat.

He saw them twitch and writhe. He saw broken, distorted panels of armour, splinters of pulverised ribs, and loose, fused vertebrae, clumping and wriggling, and locking back into place. He saw new sinew and muscle forming, re-stringing skeletal fragments, harnessing a frame, reforming a shape, sleeving it in flesh. He saw capillaries growing like delicate fern-fronds, in their millions, bringing the blood, delivering the blood to every new extremity.

Sanguinius saw incarnation.

He saw a massive fist pick up a re-wrought axe from the smoking base of the crater, a crater that had become a crucible.

He saw the mountainous bulk of a winged figure rising out of the crater.

It turned to face him. Their eyes locked. They gazed at one another, across all intervals of time and distance, as though they stood face to face.

Brother to brother.

Sanguinius looked into Angron's eyes.

Angron glared back at Sanguinius. He slowly raised his left hand, where new skin was yet to grow back over the oozing meat. He licked the blood from it.

'My blood for the Blood God,' *he said.*

'No,' said Brohn. 'No, that's… No, that's entirely not possible, it… No no no no no–'

Cadwalder took the man by the throat, and shook him.

'It's happening,' he hissed.

'It really is,' said Saul Niborran, gazing down at the wastes below.

Angron, Lord of the XII, Red Angel, daemon-prince and Eater of Worlds, lumbered clear of the burning crater. His physical mass now seemed colossal, a gore giant, flesh flayed and bleeding, golden battleplate burned clean and gleaming. He began to stride towards the barrier wall, each step shaking the ground. His pace accelerated. The long braids and plugs that trailed from the back of his scalp billowed behind him in a knotted, black-clotted mane. His hellish wings, larger than before, spread like rotting sailcloth. He raised his axe, and behind him the mass formations of the World Eaters roared, and followed his charge, a reverberating stampede that blocked the sky with dust across the horizon.

Angron opened his jaws, stretching the bloody, excoriated flesh of his distended face, revealing fangs so long and sharp they seemed capable of tearing out the galaxy's throat.

He howled. All coherence had fled from him, all words consumed in the bestial tumult of his berserk state.

He simply howled. A keening, savage, wordless noise. But its meaning was clear enough.

PART THREE

FOUR VICTORIES
(TO THE DEATH)

ONE

Dead lines
Trickster
Discord

'Something…' said Al-Nid Nazira, perplexed. 'My khan, lord, please come. Something has occurred.'

Shiban Khan turned from the work crews he was supervising. It was hot on the high platform, and the docking ring above them offered only partial shade. The crews, all civilians or port guild, were drenched in sweat as they toiled around the two Sysiphos-pattern tugs.

'That's the High Primary's concern, Nazira,' he said. 'We have our own duties to perform.'

Nazira, an Auxilia captain, a good and sober man, had been Shiban's chosen aide since the day Shiban had arrived at the port. He'd taken a liking to him at once, seeing the purposeful determination with which Nazira had attempted to bring order to the confusion and, needing reliable officers, Shiban had made him his second.

'My khan, you should see this,' Nazira called back.

Shiban put down the tools he had been using, and walked over to Nazira, picking his way between the heaps of surplus

components and fittings that the crews had already stripped
out of the tugs. The junk, trailing wires and unfastened brackets, littered the landing pad in the hard sunlight. Nazira stood
at the rail, staring down.

They were fifteen hundred metres up on the port's tertiary
landing pylon, still quite low down in terms of the pylon
structures, which soared above them into the sky, threaten-
ing to pierce the heavens. But it was still a long drop. The port
megastructure was spread below them like a large-scale map.
The sunlight was bright, rippled and tinted by the void fields
that still shielded the upper- and inter-orbit extents of the great
port. Down below, cloud banks of what looked like russet
smog drifted like dead leaves across the expanse of Western
Freight and the adjoining scarred landscape where the port's
Celestial City had once stood. Blacker cloud lingered to the
west, over the site of the Pons Solar.

'What's the matter?' Shiban asked.

Nazira pointed down.

'Look, there, and there,' he said. 'Those are serious
engagements.'

'Nazira, we know they're fighting down there–'

'No,' said Nazira. 'Before, it was focused on the gates of the
barrier wall. At the west. There. But it's spread. Increased. Just
now, there was a serious bombardment from the wall guns.
Look! Look, again!'

Shiban uncoupled his helm from his belt, and clamped it
on, bringing up visual enhancement and audio gain to his
visor. He enlarged a great belt of smoke and dust, the thick
line of the barrier wall, the towers, the main bulk of Monsalvant Gard. He saw numerous flashes: the sunlight glinting off
moving metal, and weapons fire, concentrated and intense.
Audio carried the distant boom and crack of it. Nazira was
right. The enemy was still mobbing the barrier gates, but a vast

horde, like something spilled and spreading from an insect hill, was swarming at the entire length of the southern line.

'I was right, wasn't I?' Nazira asked. 'It's worse, isn't it? It's escalated, in the last few minutes.'

It had. It looked disastrous. Shiban thought about lying, keeping Nazira in the dark a while longer, so he might work without worry. But Nazira was his comrade, his friend, and they were in this together.

'It's much worse,' Shiban said. 'The World Eaters have begun a mass-war assault to storm the wall.'

'Should we... should we go back down?' asked Nazira.

'There's no value in that,' said Shiban.

'Except honour?' Nazira suggested.

'We can honour our comrades more by trying to finish our task,' said Shiban. 'Our presence down there won't make the slightest difference, but several heavy grav-weapons might. How long?'

Nazira shrugged. He glanced at the work teams, toiling around the bulky, utilitarian craft.

'Another hour?' he ventured. 'Then we can ship them down to the surface-level platforms under their own power, and begin assembly. I don't know about the other crews.'

'Go and get them moving,' said Shiban. 'Don't alarm them, but get their motivation up. Let's see if we can take a few minutes off that hour. I'll worry about the other crews.'

Nazira nodded, and hurried back to join the working party. Shiban walked across the dock pad and into the deep shade of the massive docking ring. The pad's pylon side connected directly to the immense structure of the tertiary spire. There were four large hatches, the mouths of bulk freight elevators. An inspection plate had been removed from the wall between two of them, allowing access to the port power supply, and to hardline datacast and links. Spools of cables and tube connectors suckled at the inspection cavity and trailed away across the deck, like sleeping pythons, towards the parked tugs and labouring crews.

Shiban disconnected the hanging loop of the hardline cable from a voxcaster resting on the deck, and connected it to his suit system. He selected voice-to-Hortcode delivery.

'This is Shiban, work party six, tertiary pylon level forty. Monsalvant, respond.'

A crackle.

'Monsalvant, respond and report status.'

More static, like crumpling plastic film.

'Monsalvant, respond. Command cadre, respond. Tower Seven? Tower Six? Barrier gateway? This is Shiban, work party six. Respond and report status.'

The link answered with broken pops and spilled-acid hissing. He tried, in turn, the other work crews – teams like his own, deployed across tertiary and secondary pylons to scavenge parts and equipment and recover other useable craft. There were eighteen teams altogether.

None of them answered. Shiban hoped it was simply a problem with the hardline connection. But surely a hard-wired network couldn't have broken in multiple places?

He tried them again. Then he tried Monsalvant again.

Mistress Tacticae Katarin Elg entered the Saturnine forward command post, walked directly to her station, sat down, and put on her headset.

Her hands moved across the keypads, and the desk came to life, displays illuminating, screens lighting.

'Trickster, this is Trickster,' she said, with steady, declarative calm. 'Show Trickster live at this time. All kill teams report status, datacast only.'

Several responses crackled into her earpiece in quick

succession. As they came in, she marked them on the board with quick, haptic gestures, her eyes darting from screen to screen.

'This is Trickster, showing you as ready, kill teams. Standby.' She switched channels from datacast to hardlink.

'Trickster to wallguard vigil.'

'This is vigil, Trickster.'

'Trickster reads you, Captain Madius. Commence visual scanning.'

'Acknowledged, Trickster.'

She sat back briefly, though her hands continued to play across the keys.

'Kill teams report ready, my lord,' she said. 'Wallguard vigil is on active watch. We are live. Operation count has begun.'

Dorn nodded. The forward command post was a small gallery chamber near one of the deployment halls. It had probably once been a wine cellar, before all the basement levels had been seized, hollowed-out and fortified. Both long walls were lined with strategium desks, their screens and displays blinking in the gloom, illuminating the faces of the tacticians and operators who sat, back to back, manning the positions. There was a constant fidget of movement, of hands adjusting controls, a constant low murmur of voices as they spoke into their headsets, a constant crackling chatter of transmit responses.

'So noted, mistress,' said Dorn. 'Proceed.'

Elg acknowledged his go-order. Her face impassive, she turned back to her desk.

'Query hardline link to Grand Borealis?' she said.

'Hardline link standing by, mistress,' the operator at the desk beside her replied.

'Hardline link live, please,' she said.

'Hardline link is live,' said the operator.

'Trickster, this is Trickster,' she said. 'Acknowledge my signal, Grand Borealis.'

In the heart of the vast bustle of the Grand Borealis chamber, Archamus sat forward at his desk. He raised his left hand, and pointed to Mistress Icaro. She saw his gesture, handed back the dataslate she had been reviewing, and crossed to his station immediately. The Huscarl passed her a headset, and she put it on, standing at his shoulder.

'Grand Borealis,' said Archamus. 'Trickster, we hear you, you are live.'

'*Acknowledged, Grand Borealis,*' Elg's voice answered in their ears. '*Count has begun at this time. Trickster requests tracking evaluation.*'

'Standby, Trickster,' said Archamus.

Icaro stepped to the strategium station beside Archamus' console. She brought the display up, centred, enlarged and locked.

'Commencing tracking evaluation,' she said. 'Sifting all track, all seismic and all listening watch in target zone. Summary will be datacast by hardlink to you in twelve seconds, Trickster.'

'*Trickster, standing by.*'

Icaro and Archamus waited as the vast processors of Bhab Bastion diverted a small fragment of their tasking power to Icaro's specifics. It felt sly, uncomfortable. There was over a thousand personnel at work in the Borealis around them, operators at watch and vox-stations, War Court tacticians around display tables, marshals and lords militant at overwatch desks. A babble of voices and activity, the living brain and nervous system of the siege, monitoring and supervising thousands of separate battles and engagements, troop deployments, munition transfers, supply demands, aegis stability, received intelligence. Officers, servitors and despatch runners hurried to and fro; rubricators scurried past, arms laden with fresh reports; cartomancers adjusted the flag markers that throbbed and shifted gently on vast hololith displays.

None of them knew what Archamus and Icaro were doing. None had been briefed or read-in. None of them knew anything about the events unfolding leagues to the south of them in the Saturnine Quarter.

Archamus felt uneasy. Not even Vorst, at a nearby station, was aware. The Master of Huscarls drummed his fingers gently. Icaro glanced at his hand. Such a curious and tellingly human mannerism. She smiled.

'I'll stop,' said Archamus.

'Please don't, lord' she replied. 'It's good to know I'm not the only one feeling this tension.'

She looked at her board.

'First track results,' she said. 'Datacasting to you now, Trickster.'

'Thank you, Grand Borealis, standby,' said Elg. The data streamed onto her desk monitor. She gestured, and the haptic command threw it up on the post's main displays. 'Tracking seismic pulse,' she said.

'Seismic pulse confirmed, forty kilometres, spread,' agreed a nearby operator.

'Do we have target track?' asked Dorn.

'Analysing data product...' replied Elg. 'Negative. Seismic pulse reads as backwash vibration from the bombardments at Europa Wall section and Western Projection Wall section.'

'The distraction actions,' said Dorn.

'We presume they are distractions, lord,' said Elg.

'They're distractions,' said Dorn.

'They are intense enough to mask surface and sub-surface in the immediate zone,' said the operator.

'Are we blind?' asked Dorn.

'Washing them through separation filters, lord,' said Elg. 'But there may not be a signal to read yet.'

She glanced at him.

'If they're coming tonight,' she added. 'Or at all.'

Dorn didn't reply.

'Trickster, this is Trickster,' said Elg, returning to her screens. 'Datacast received, Grand Borealis. Initial results show negative track, repeat, negative track. Please proceed to supply tracking evaluation databursts at five-minute intervals from this mark.'

'Acknowledged, Trickster,' the link crackled.

Dorn turned from the quiet, ceaseless activity of the small room. Diamantis stood in the doorway.

'We're waiting,' Dorn said.

'Ninety-nine per cent of a soldier's life, lord,' said Diamantis.

That almost brought a smile to the Praetorian's face.

'Update me,' said Dorn. 'The sealing programme?'

'Magos Land reports ready,' said Diamantis. 'Some teething problems... A clogging issue with jet nozzles, or something.'

'That's not encouraging.'

'His processes have been conjured out of nothing in a matter of hours, lord,' said Diamantis. 'They have not been rigorously tested. But if he says it will work, I believe him. All of his staff, except for essential operation crews, have been evacuated from the site.'

'The Sigillite?'

'Already escorted back to the Upper Palatine, as per your instructions,' said Diamantis.

'Good,' said Dorn. 'He absolutely can't be here for this. Nowhere near.'

'He seemed disappointed, my lord,' said the Huscarl. 'Tetchy. He entirely supports the significance of what's happening here. I think he wanted to witness it for himself.'

'That's what we have the remembrancers for,' said Dorn.

'Interrogators,' said Diamantis.

Dorn looked at him, and raised an eyebrow. 'Really?' he asked. 'You want to correct me?'

'We can call them whatever you like, Praetorian,' said Diamantis.

Dorn grunted. 'Well, call them *in here*,' he said. 'The forward post is probably the best place for them.'

'So they can see what's happening?'

'So they don't get underfoot.'

Diamantis nodded, and stepped out into the hallway. He gestured to a pair of Hort Palatine guardsmen.

'Bring the interrogators through,' he said.

They stepped forward, bringing the boy, Therajomas, between them. The young man was clutching his slate. He looked as if he was about to shit himself with terror.

'Me?' he asked.

'In here,' said Diamantis. 'Observe. Record. Don't touch anything.'

The Huscarl paused.

'Where's the other one?' he asked the guards. 'Where's the old man Sindermann?'

'It's been a while, Garviel,' said Sindermann.

Loken straightened up.

'It has,' he replied. He held out his hand. Sindermann clasped the giant, armoured paw gingerly.

'There wasn't an opportunity to speak earlier,' said Sindermann. 'But I wanted to find you, before–'

'You've found me,' said Loken.

They were in deployment hall six, close to the assayed line of the flaw. The chamber was a brick cistern, a basement vault extended by servitor teams who had drilled out the subrock.

Behind Loken, his kill team was assembling, weapons ready. One hundred legionaries, most of them Imperial Fists. It was quiet, but for a few low conversations and the clack and snap of magazines slotting and power feeds connecting. There was a suspended hush that reminded Sindermann of a temple or place of worship, a congregation assembled in prayer. The closest equivalent these days, he reflected.

One wall of the chamber had been removed, and they could see through into the neighbouring deployment hall, hall seven. Sigismund and his kill team were prepping quietly there. Another hundred men, also Imperial Fists, but these marked with the blacks and charcoals of the Templar order.

The seven kill teams had been given call signs, as Sindermann understood it. Sigismund's was *Devotion*, Garro's was *Strife*, Haar's was *Black Dog*, Bel Sepatus' was *Brightest*, Gallor's was *Seventh*, and Thane's was *Helios*.

Loken's was *Naysmith*.

'It seems an age ago when I last saw you in those colours,' said Sindermann.

'A different age, Kyril,' said Loken.

'Quite so,' said Sindermann. 'You think of them as your true colours?'

'Always,' said Loken. 'But I am expecting them to provoke some psychological effect.'

'I'm sure,' said Sindermann. 'And your choice of call sign...'

'A word you taught me. I intend to disagree and challenge. The balance has gone, Kyril. We need naysmiths more than ever.'

'Do you think our Praetorian is correct?' asked Sindermann. 'That he's coming?'

'I think there's a high probability,' Loken replied. 'And if not my genesire, then the best spear-tip in the Legions, for an undertaking like this.'

'They don't exist any more,' said Sindermann.

'They do, as a twisted parody of that glory,' replied Loken. 'First Company. The Mournival. Abaddon.'

Sindermann sighed.

'Names that were always terrifying, no matter which side you were on,' the old man said.

'Back then, there *was* only one side. Are you here to make an account of this, Kyril? A remembrance? I was puzzled by your presence.'

'I am,' said Sindermann. 'Just a... twisted parody of the old order, to borrow your turn of phrase, but Lord Dorn has seen fit to reinstate us. To record the making of history as an act of faith in a future that–'

'You make the history, Kyril,' said Loken. 'I'm only here to make a mound of corpses.'

Sindermann paused awkwardly.

'If he *is* coming...' he began.

'Yes?'

'...what will you do, Garviel? He was your beloved master once, and–'

'Kill him,' said Loken. 'I'll kill him.'

Sindermann nodded. 'History tells us,' he said, 'that a culture may be in morbid decline when sons turn on their fathers...'

'My father turned on me,' said Loken. 'I don't need history to tell me anything.'

'There you are, damn it!'

Sindermann turned. Conroi-Captain Ahlborn was hurrying towards him, trailed by two Hort troopers in red body armour.

'I slipped my handlers,' Sindermann said to Loken, with a sly wink. Loken smiled a little.

'You don't find the things you're looking for if you don't break some rules,' Loken told him. 'You have to walk in a few dark places on your own.'

'You can't just wander around, sir,' Ahlborn was snapping

at Sindermann. 'Do this again, and we'll eject you. Come, please. There's a space reserved for you in the command post.'

Sindermann allowed himself to be walked away. He looked back at Loken.

'Find what you're looking for, Garviel,' he said. 'Wherever it is in those dark places.'

'I'll find it,' Loken called out after him. 'And illuminate it.'

They marched Sindermann out. Loken turned back to his preparation. He took up Rubio's sword, and resumed working the edge on a whetstone.

'I can find you a better sword than that old blade.' Sigismund had approached from the neighbouring hall.

'And chain it to my wrist like a World Eater?' asked Loken.

'Then it may never leave your hand, Garviel Loken,' said Sigismund. 'You never, ever have to put it down again.'

'This'll do,' said Loken. 'It's been with me a while, and it belonged to... someone.'

'It's a force weapon,' said Sigismund dubiously. 'A brother like you can't bring the best out of it.'

'It's still a blade,' said Loken. 'And its edge is good.'

They stood together, and looked at the two chambers, the quiet men assembled, braced to unleash hell.

'Are you set?' asked Sigismund.

'Yes. You?'

'Yes.'

'I liked your oath,' Sigismund said.

'The shortest one of them all,' said Loken.

'Yes,' said Sigismund. 'But a good one. I wish it had been mine.'

'Mistress Icaro?' Archamus said.

Icaro snapped out of her reverie at his prompt.

'The next tracking evaluation is due,' said Archamus. 'Trickster is waiting.'

'Of course,' she replied, resuming work. 'Commencing.'

It was the ninth evaluation she had run and sent. The processors whirred and chattered.

'Distracted?' Archamus asked as they waited.

'Just updates coming in on the main war maps,' she said. 'Colossi Gate and Gorgon Bar.'

'I saw them,' he replied.

'It looks as though they are intensifying rapidly,' she said. 'Intelligence paints swiftly deteriorating situations in both areas.'

'Both were predicted as key stress zones by the Praetorian,' said Archamus calmly. 'Hence his placement of the Khan and the Angel to command them. I'm watching them both. The War Court is watching them develop across a dozen desks. Reaction plans are in place in event of either becoming non-vi.'

'They're getting damn hot, Archamus.'

'They are. But we have work to attend to. Concentrate.'

'Track results complete,' she said.

'Trickster, this is Grand Borealis,' said Archamus. 'Datacasting to you now.'

Sindermann had arrived at the command post. It was his first look at it. It seemed cramped, crowded, busy, even though the only noise was the low murmur of operators talking.

Therajomas was cowering in a corner.

'Any news?' Sindermann asked.

Dorn raised a hand to silence him. He was staring at Mistress Elg. She was perched forward in her seat.

'Thank you, Grand Borealis. Standby,' Sindermann heard Elg say. The tactician deftly cast data onto the displays. 'Tracking seismic pulse,' she said.

'Seismic pulse confirmed, forty-one kilometres, spread,' said an operator. 'As before, backwash from Europa and Western Projection.'

'Do we have target track?' asked Dorn.

'Analysing...' replied Elg, concentrating on her screen, her hands twitching as they sculpted invisible data. 'Freeze there. One-seven-two. That's a new track. Scrub out the backwash. Clean it up.'

'Aye,' said the operator.

'Mistress Elg?' said Dorn.

'Wait please, lord,' Elg replied, without looking around.

'Seismic pulse confirmed,' said the operator. 'New track, new signal. In motion, inbound. Seismographic confirms, listening watch confirms, auspex confirms.'

'I have it,' said Elg. 'New track detected, my lord. Eight kilometres out from the Saturnine Wall, bearing one-seven-two. Inbound. Significant track, significant echo.'

'Sub-surface?' asked Dorn. 'How low?'

Sindermann knew that all expectations were of a major mining assault directly into the Saturnine fault. The flaw was a narrow seam of cavities and shale, viced between plains of bedrock, the only possible route that would submit to excavation or drilling.

'No, my lord, surface,' said Elg.

'Confirmed?'

'Confirming now.'

'Surface?' said Sindermann, frowning. 'What would—'

He shut up as soon as he saw the look that Ahlborn was giving him.

'I anticipated some surface assault,' said Dorn. 'They'll need to punch us hard, and keep the wall systems busy, no matter what they try and throw at us underground.'

'Surface track is confirmed,' Elg called out.

Dorn pulled a hardline vox-mic from its hook, the long cable slapping against his plate.

'Trickster, this is Trickster,' he said. 'Vigil, we have an inbound surface track. What are you showing?'

There seemed to be nothing but a cold, silent night.

The Saturnine Wall was a significant, south-facing section of the great Ultimate Wall, eleven hundred metres high and four hundred metres thick. It ran like a sea cliff for nearly thirty kilometres between the Europa and Western Projection sections. Though the light-shock and distant boom of the endless bombardments at those sections rippled through the chill air, at Oanis Tower, Saturnine's principal gun bastion, it was quiet. A pitch, storm-heavy darkness hung over the wall and the plains beyond. The air was sub-zero, and dropping with windchill. Hoar frost was forming on the sleek, black barrels of the macro-guns and the armoured shells of the casemates and turrets.

The voids, at optimal output, flickered and shimmered the night air, their skeins of charged particles occasionally conjuring aurorae colours that shifted and slid.

'Stand by, Trickster,' said Captain Madius.

The Imperial Fist, one of the newborn, new-made legionaries produced by accelerated recruitment to swell the Terran ranks, handed the link back to his waiting vox-officer, and hurried along the wall. He had been appointed wall master of the Saturnine stretch eight days previously.

'Come to alert,' he said to his sergeant as he passed him. He had five hundred Imperial Fists on the wall line, and two thousand soldiers of the Auxilia, not counting the hundreds of gun crews, loaders and technical support personnel.

Madius entered the wallguard fire control station at the junction of the main wall and Oanis Tower. The vigil officers and

gunnery masters were all on station, as they had been every
day and every night since the start of the siege.

'Hardlink!' Madius shouted as he walked in. An adjutant
ran to him with a cable, which Madius plugged into the jaw
of his helmet as he stepped onto the command plate.

'Visual?' Madius called out.

'Nothing, lord.'

'Auspex?'

'Nothing.'

'Full sweep, do it again,' said Madius. 'Increase depth, detector
field, ten points.'

'Ten points, aye,' replied a vigil officer. Madius watched the
phantom green patterns twitch and shift on the main grid.

'Auspex now showing track,' a vigil officer announced.
'Incomplete, obscure. Seven kilometres out, advancing, bearing
one-seven-two.'

Madius activated his hardlink. 'Trickster, Trickster, this is
vigil. Showing your track now, seven kilometres out, advancing, bearing one-seven-two, incomplete. Echo only, visual
scanning negative.'

'*Come to alert, Madius,*' the link crackled.

'Already done, lord,' Madius replied.

'*Full repulse order.*'

'Full repulse order acknowledged, Trickster,' said Madius.
'Wallguard! Full repulse, arm systems!'

The room stirred. Men started speaking urgently into their
vox-links. Amber runes began to flash silently over the hatch
frames and on the wall pillars. One by one, hololithic screens
blinked into life in the air, scrolling with preparatory target
data. Madius heard the whine of turrets realigning, the clatter
of hatches opening on casemates and down-wall gun-boxes.
He heard the rising thrum of power as reactors fast-fed power
to the primary energy weapon banks, and the ticking of vast

quantities of projectile munitions streaming out of the magazine chambers deep in the girth of the wall.

'*Vigil, this is Trickster. Do you have target visual?*'

'Negative, Trickster. Echo track only. Now... Six and a half kilometres out. We should be able to see something.'

'*You certainly should, vigil,*' the link sizzled.

'Auspex, I want definition,' Madius called out. 'Isolate that echo track. If we can't see it, let's hear it. Acoustic profile analysis. Is it tracks, infantry, engines? Boost audio.'

'Boosting audio, sir.'

Madius waited. A steady, muffled, *thump-thump-thump* like a cardiac beat echoed out of the speakers.

'Can we estimate mass from that echo?' he began to ask.

A scream tore through the chamber. It was so shrill, and so loud, glass panels shattered spontaneously. Consoles shorted out. Hololithic projector plates disintegrated into fragments. The noise suppression systems of those present wearing helmets kicked in automatically, saving them from the worst of it, but the personnel without helmets went into seizure. They collapsed across consoles, or onto the deck, blood running from their ruined ears, out of their noses, out of their tear ducts and the corners of their mouths.

The scream persisted for six seconds, until all the chamber speakers blew out in flurries of sparks and ruptured components.

'Vigil? Respond. Vigil, this is Trickster. Respond.'

Dorn waited.

'Hardline is down,' an operator reported.

'How is it down?' asked Dorn.

'Checking...' the operator said.

'Assessing all hardlinks and datacasts,' said Elg. 'Trickster, this is Trickster. All stations, send confirmation signal.'

Her desk buzzed and chattered.

'Datacast is intact to all kill teams and support, and hard-line to Grand Borealis is sound,' she reported. 'We have lost hardline link to the wallguard.'

'Fault?' asked Dorn.

'Unable to confirm, my lord,' Elg replied. 'Despatching repair crews immediately.'

'Get that link back up,' said Dorn.

'Stations!' Madius yelled. His head was still ringing. He could feel blood trickling inside his helm. Medicae were dragging the injured clear. Some were still screaming. Support staff were rushing in to take over their positions.

'Headgear! Noise reduction!' Madius ordered. 'What in Terra's name was that?'

'Acoustic event registered at two hundred and sixty-two deci-bels,' an officer said.

'No, Faltan, what in Terra's name *was* it?' Madius asked. He adjusted the cable plugged into his helmet. 'Vigil, this is vigil. Trickster, do you respond? Trickster, respond.'

'Hardline is blown, lord,' said one of the officers.

'Get it back up!' Madius barked.

'In work, lord.'

'Visual contact reported!' a gunnery master called out. 'Six kilometres out.'

'Show on screens!'

'Screens are down. Visual displays are down.'

Madius cursed. He strode out of the chamber, yanking the plug out of his helm and casting the cable aside. Outside, he ran to the wall's main bulwark. Space Marines were already in place, manning wall weapons, or braced with boltguns ready.

'Incoming!' Sergeant Kask reported, pointing.

Madius looked into the darkness, cycling the gain of his visor's optics.

The Donjon-class siege engine was an uncommon machine. Made by the Forge of Mars in the early years of the Great Crusade, its pattern had seen service in many theatres, though it had never been produced in significant numbers due to its bulk, cost of production, and cumbersome vulnerability on the field of war. Better doctrines, exploiting the fluid versatilities of the Legiones Astartes and the rapid aggression of the Titan engines, had consigned the Donjon to support and rear-line operations that it had not originally been designed to perform.

The Donjon engine was a quadruped, striding on a brace of the same motivator systems that propelled Warlord-class machines. The four massive legs supported a huge, flat-top carrier deck, a platform large enough for a squadron of aircraft or a full motorised company. The platform's rim bristled with heavy gun ports, and through-deck elevators were equipped with bulk machinery that could lift extending siege towers and scaling bridges to the highest battlements. But the Donjon was slow, painfully hard to manoeuvre, and its void systems were over-extended because of its mass, and prone to gapping.

First Captain Abaddon had procured three of the immense, rare beasts from the adepts of the Dark Mechanicum, and he had given them to the Phoenician Lord of the Emperor's Children.

The three behemoths trudged towards the Saturnine Wall, relentlessly advancing over the ragged, lifeless plain. At their heels came streams of armoured support: troop carriers, motorised mortars, wall-breaker gun carriages and assault belfry lifters. Range locked, the advancing giants began to fire. Plasma destructor mounts and inferno guns along the platform rims

started to retch and spit searing pulses and beams of annihilation. Mega-bolters shrilled as they unleashed blizzards of
explosive ordnance. Launch racks dispensed streams of darting
anti-void missiles. Bulk las-blasters pumped in their arrestor
frames as they kicked out giant spears of light.

The face of the Saturnine Wall around Oanis Tower lit up,
as the storm of incoming fire kissed the shields. Vast backflash
blinked as the voids struggled to absorb the bombardment.
The wall guns responded immediately, some systems keying
to automatic threat-registers, others manually commanded.
Casemates, gun-boxes in the tiered flank of the wall and
main wall-top batteries commenced a staggering onslaught
of defensive fire, raking and pummelling the forward voids
of the plodding, stoic giants.

Madius, waiting for the hardlink to be repaired, watched the
catastrophic exchange. It was his first time facing mass-scale
assault. It was his first time in any combat. Few in the Palace
had ever seen a Donjon stride into war. They were awe-
inspiring, leviathan machines, terrible in aspect.

But he had studied. He knew their weaknesses, and the
compounding vulnerabilities that meant they were seldom
used. It was all very impressive, but he was sure the wall's devastating firepower would crack their shields, and bring them all
down, burning and torn, well short of the ramparts.

The Phoenician had made some changes to the siege engines
he had been loaned.

His sound-wrights, inspired by acoustic nightmares whispered to them by the Neverborn, had masked the approach of
the bulk engines in sonic fields that had turned the air opaque,
and wrapped the Donjons in manufactured night from thirty
kilometres out. The profligate gossips of Slaanesh had blurted
secrets of noise-death to the disciples of the Kakophoni in
their dreams, and psycho-sonic weapons had been fashioned

and tuned, blasting their insanities from the foredecks of the siege engines, through gaping chromed vents, and broadcasting them on every frequency from infra to ultra. Already, they were generating a screaming aura ahead of the advance, a pattern of warped sound that made the air ring as though a giant tuning fork had been struck, and then the lingering note twisted into a distressing, atonal pitch that made blood shiver and tissue quake.

The screaming aura had been named the Sonance. It had already blown out Oanis' audio systems. It was shredding the vox. It was beginning to vibrate the wall's aegis envelope like a crystal glass set singing by a fingertip.

Laudatory vents, their sweeping gold mouths wide open like the blooms of pitcher plants, sang siren-calls of discord and despair. Amplifiers swelled dark, sub-vocal groans of bereavement and misery on infrasonic waves. The roar of the carnodon contains frequencies of less than twenty hertz, below the threshold of human hearing, but the effects are still felt. The consequence is paralysing terror, pinning the prey. The prattling tattle-tales of the Slaaneshi feverdreams had gibbered this secret to the Kakophoni too, and the Emperor's Children had made fluted auramite horns, which sounded a dirge that provoked cold-sweat, inescapable dread.

Madius shuddered. He was newborn and untried, but he was resolved. He couldn't understand why he was faltering. He turned, and saw that Auxilia units drawn up on the broad platform of the wall top were breaking and scattering, fleeing for the back steps and delivery ramps, dropping their weapons. Some had fallen, weeping.

'Stop them! Kask, stop them!' he yelled. 'Discipline! Line order!'

He felt a shockwave, a concussive rush of pressure. Sections of the aegis above them had failed, and collapsed. The voids were tearing like thin silk. Immediately, enemy fire penetrated.

Mega-bolter sprays raked the bulwark. Pulses of heavy las struck the alure, the fighting step and the rear parapet. Men were hurled into the air in geysers of flame. A plasma beam lanced in, and obliterated a gun turret entirely.

'Maintain barrage!' Madius yelled, but no one could hear him. The air was screaming around him. He ran towards the fire control station.

Approaching the wall, the striding Donjons dropped their voids. They began to take crippling damage immediately along their forward hulls, but it no longer mattered. They were less than a kilometre out. Launch units mounted on the platforms' decks began to fire, pitching drop pods into the air. Some were deflected by the shredding voids. Others were incinerated by the firmer sections of the shields. But many arced down onto the wall top, cratering the rockcrete as they impacted, claw legs dragging and gouging.

Some struck the face of the wall, and fell, but then clung on, their landing claws becoming bristled hooks and grotesque arachnid legs. They began to climb the sheer wall like mites, or haul themselves into the open maws of mid-tier gun-boxes.

Many plunged to the foot of the Saturnine Wall. They rolled on the broken waste of the foreland, righted themselves, then sprouted their Neverbred legs, and began to scuttle back up the wall like huntsman spiders.

Emperor's Children were emerging on the wall top, purple, gold, pink, black, screaming their death hymns, and blasting their weapons. The Imperial Fists turned from the wall, hammering bolter fire at the disgorging drop pods, cutting down the arriving enemy, and being cut down in turn.

Madius' boltgun was in his hand. He snapped off shots at nearby targets.

'Hardline! Hardline!' he yelled through the doorway of fire control.

'Still trying to re-establish the link!' a technician yelled back at him.

Sonic booms rolled across Oanis like thundercracks. Pockets of darkness popped open along the fighting platform, and figures dropped out of fissures that sound had warped and torn.

The champion elite of the III. Warriors too beautiful and ornamented to behold. They fell out of the warp fissures, which crumpled and closed behind them like the petals of black roses, then vanished like smoke, leaving only lingering snatches of choral plainsong behind them.

The figures fell, graceful, and landed on the wall on their feet, at a pace no quicker than a fast walk.

One dropped directly in the centre of the wide wall deck. It was larger than the rest, clad in a panoply of artificer armour, wrought in heliotrope and amaranthine, etched in gold. It landed in a crouch, its right hand clutching a slender, two-handed, single-edged blade.

Fulgrim rose slowly to his feet. His long white hair unwound, and ribboned out behind him in the night wind, like a pennant of shining satin.

He tipped his head back, beheld the devastation, and smiled.

In grinding darkness, they sat unspeaking, strapped in tightly, shaking with every jolt and scrape, as the assault drill's cutters gripped and cut and burrowed through the flaw's friable shale core. The only light was the red glow of the compartment's overheads. The roar of the tunnelling process was loud and harsh, a grating clatter and scrape as broken rock spoil was devoured, spat past them, and expelled.

Horus Aximand thought he could hear the breathing again, but it was just the men around him in the tight space. It was

claustrophobic, imprisoning. It reminded him too much of
the choking, pressing darkness he dreamed of all too often.

There was no vox. The rock was too thick. He wished he
could ask Abaddon for an update, but the First Captain was
aboard a separate drill.

Aximand glanced at Serac Lukash, his second. The man was
a newborn, freshly raised to the ranks of the Sons of Horus,
but from the set of his features, he was no doubt a son of
Horus. Not a son like Aximand. A son of Horus as he currently was.

'How long?' Aximand asked.

'Auspex estimates sixteen minutes to breakthrough, lord,'
Lukash replied.

'Get set,' said Aximand.

'Trickster, this is Trickster? Vigil, can you respond?'

Elg's patient repetition had become a near-mantra in the
command post.

'Still nothing, my lord,' she said. Red runes were blinking
on the station desk that monitored wall action. That said
enough. Though the link was down, Dorn knew that the
defence systems of the Saturnine Wall, from Oanis west, had
engaged with full force. They were repelling a major assault.

'Target tracks?' he asked.

'We are continuing to receive track evaluations from the
Grand Borealis, my lord,' Elg replied. 'Significant track patterns,
bulk mass. It could be engines at the wall line. We're certainly
reading drone tracks consistent with multiple tread vehicles.
And ripple-echoes from detonations.'

'But all at the surface?'

She nodded.

'No sub-surface tracks?' Dorn pressed.

'It's possible,' she replied. 'We are trying to separate the noise to determine that, but the surface track and accompanying acoustic is so considerable, it's masking any potential sub-surface pattern. To be honest, I don't understand the background noise level. Even bulk assault shouldn't–'

'My lord!' an operator called out. 'Hardline link re-established.'

Dorn snatched up the vox-mic.

'Vigil! This is Trickster! Make report!'

The voice on the other end was swallowed in a jumble of static and distortion.

'Vigil, repeat that!' Dorn snapped. He glanced at Elg. 'Amplify the signal!'

'–ster! Trickster, this is vigil!'

'Madius. What is going on?'

'Full assault, my lord. The Third Legion. Shields are ruptured. They are on the wall.'

'Vigil, what strength?' Dorn asked. 'Report the Third Legion strength.'

'Full Legion strength, my lord.'

Dorn looked at Sindermann, and then at Elg. Full Legion strength. The Emperor's Children were rumoured to have more than a hundred thousand legionaries in their ranks.

'Advise the Grand Borealis,' Dorn said to Elg. 'If Madius is correct, we will need to effect immediate recomposition of the battle sphere.'

His mind began to race. A full Legion force. What could they spare? What could they move? They were already stretched to snapping point. Nothing could be withdrawn from Colossi or Gorgon. The rest of the Anterior Barbican line was beset from Marmax south, expecting worse, and could not be diluted.

He'd already sacrificed the Eternity Wall space port to make this happen.

The vox in his hand crackled again.

'*Trickster, Trickster, can you hear me?*'

'This is Trickster, Madius.'

'*Trickster, he's here.*'

'Say again, vigil,' said Dorn.

'*He's here, my lord. The Phoenician.*'

TWO

The wounded tower
Potential prize or actual
Small weather

Katillon guntower had begun to collapse.

Weak from the grand assault the day before, it had been further wounded by the renewed brutality of the traitor assault. Sections of the upper platform and armoured mantling had shorn away, and many of the gun-boxes had become burning sockets. Fafnir Rann was certain that the entire structure would fall in the next ten or fifteen minutes, if the current intensity of assault was sustained.

If it fell, slumping and disintegrating under its own pummelled weight, it would tear down a segment of the fourth circuit wall.

And then the enemy would be in.

The Iron Warriors' mode of prosecution had been twin-headed, just as the Great Angel had expected. Two mass assaults – two determined escalades, sheltered under armoured sows and rolling belfries – were driving up either side of the tower, while petrary engines rained down destruction from a distance, and numberless subhuman hordes harried the entire length of the circuit wall to force a locked defence.

Rann admired it. He was a son of Dorn, an Imperial Fist, and siege war was their fundamental doctrine. This was how you broke a fortress down: prolonged erosion of the defensive lines, sustained and exhausting general assaults, and then surgical escalade, driving brute force against whatever part had revealed itself as vulnerable.

Ironic, that Katillon's structural weakness should have been the result of the defence's own savage thwarting of the foe the day before. They had, against all odds, broken back a storm force that should have overwhelmed the entire Bar, but Katillon had suffered in the numbing tumult.

It was no surprise. Rann had known from the start that the greatest test his Imperial Fists would face would be Perturabo's Legion, their only genuine rivals in this method of warfare. He hated them, but he appreciated their skill. In the heart of the fight, it seemed like mindless rampage, but it was ordered and purposeful, like a stonemason expertly applying the full force of his hammer and chisel against the one groove in a granite block that would split it.

He had, from his vantage, identified two of their leaders. Ormon Gundar and Bogdan Mortel, both chieftain warsmiths, both infamous from the Great Crusade for their deeds of sack and ruination.

He aimed to kill both of them.

They were the drivers of the assault. They had engineered the work thus far, and brought their forces through three circuit walls. Now they strained for the triumph, moving up from the backlines to join the assault they had masterminded, to taste glory first-hand. Take them down, and you killed the minds orchestrating the plan: you killed the brain, so the body flopped; you took the hammer and chisel to the granite. The Gorgon Bar garrison could not hope to match the invaders man for man, not even with the Lord of Baal at their side, and the Great Angel's lack of visibility was deeply troubling. The last time Rann had seen him, the Lord Sanguinius had seemed deathly sick, and tormented. If they lost him, if the Great Angel could not stand...

Rann shoved the thought from his mind. They were in the jaws of death, but if they took down the enemy host's conducting chieftains, the traitors might lose cohesion, and respite could still be won.

A fine enough theory. The practice was different. The onslaught was so intense, it had him fixed, fetching assaulter after assaulter off the parapet and ladders with his axes. It was trying to hold back an ocean surge that was about to pour over a sea wall. And Rann was not at full strength. He still carried the pain and wounds of the battle at the Lion's Gate space port. He did not know if he was capable of breaking out and executing the decisive action.

But the theory was sound. Just as Gundar and Mortel drove the enemy's attack, so too he could devise and drive others to execute.

Halen and his squads were a hundred metres away, as choked as he was. He saw them braced, heard them firing bolters on full-auto. An unthinkable expenditure of ammunition, utterly decried, except in extremis. Sepatus was gone, for reasons Rann did not understand. He hadn't seen the Great Angel in an hour. Furio, then, or Aimery, or Lux. Backed by the might of their bright blades, maybe he could...

Rann hacked a path along the fighting step, smashing Iron Warriors backwards off the shell-shot crenellations, kicking out ladders as they slammed against the stone. His squads flowed with him, covering the stretch, shields chipping as they took shots and deflected missiles. Emhon Lux was closest, leading his company in a defence of the balustrade, below Katillon's south side.

As he fought, Rann opened his vox.

'Lux!'

'Rann, good brother!'

'I am close!'

'I see you!'

'I need your sword with mine, brother! We take their chiefs!'

'In this? Fafnir, are you insane?' Lux replied. Then Rann heard him laugh. *'Where do we begin?'*

Rann buried both axes in the chest of a Cataphractii Terminator, wrenched them out one by one, and shouldered the corpse off the step.

'Katillon north side!' he yelled. 'Where their towers have drawn up! We'll use their own damn ramps to–'

A granite projectile, as large as a Land Raider, and launched by one of the Stor-Bezashk trebuchets, struck the upper side of Katillon guntower. Masonry spilled down in a vast cascade of floury dust. The entire south half of the wounded tower top caved in, and collapsed, raining stone and men and ragged scraps of gun-mount. The projectile had made no sound until its impact. The tower's collapse drowned everything in an awful, earthquake rumble.

Sundered stone fell across the south side wall, buckling the bulwark and parapet. An immense section of sliding tower hit the wall like a guillotine blade, exploded into fragments, and toppled sideways into the yards and glacis behind the wall, crushing hundreds waiting on the ramps. Another section slid forward and plunged in one piece down the face of the tower, wiping it clean of scaling Iron Warriors and siege belfry bridges. A rearing siege belfry, battered and mangled by the fall of stone, twisted, tilted and pitched backwards into the enemy host.

The enormous dust cloud lifted by the tower's collapse choked the air for hundreds of metres on the south side wall.

It rolled out slowly, leisurely, coating everything, blinding everyone. Stones and loose rubble were still pattering down. Rann struggled forward through the swirling dust. He came upon an Iron Warrior, who had been dropped to his hands and knees by a falling slab. He was trying to rise. Rann took his arm, hauled him to his feet, and then put an axe through his spine. In Fair War, you did not put a man down like a dog when he was fallen. You let him stand, no matter what kind of man he had become.

A few metres on, he found Lux. The petrary boulder that had decapitated Katillon, still entirely intact, had dropped onto the wall top. It had crushed Emhon Lux beneath it.

He was still alive. He lay on his back, his legs crushed under the rock. Stone dust caked his face and plate like fine powder, making the blood leaking from his mouth more livid. His eyes and mouth were wide open, in an attitude of surprise.

No time for words. Rann couldn't shift the rock, alone. He turned, as dark warriors of the IV came scrambling over the parapet in the haze, and began to swing at them, keeping them back from Lux's helpless form.

'Emhon! Emhon!' he yelled as he struck away shield and blade, and dug axe-edge into ceramite and bone. There were three on him now, four. Seven. Ten. 'Emhon, tell me! Where is the Great Angel? We need him now!'

The only answer, a wet gurgle from Lux's blood-flooded throat.

'Lux!' Rann roared. 'Where is Lord Sanguinius? *Where is the Great Angel?*'

Dorn had summoned the commanders of the *Helios* and *Devotion* kill teams. He spoke with them in the hall outside the command post. Thane listened, solemn. Sigismund took it as well as Dorn had expected him to.

'Are we abandoning this strategy?' Sigismund asked.

'No,' said Dorn. 'But we are obligated to adjust. Assemble your teams, and follow me to the wall top.'

'So the enemy has dismayed you?' Sigismund pressed.

'The enemy is the enemy,' said Dorn, not rising to Sigismund's scathing tone. 'We can continue here, waiting in expectation of a possibility, or we can move in response to an actuality. The wall is assaulted. The defenders need immediate reinforcement.'

'Do you believe this is the foe's design, my lord?' Thane asked. 'A full strike at the surface defence?'

'I do not,' said Dorn. 'It shows none of Perturabo's skill. It exploits nothing of the secret weakness that makes Saturnine the place to strike.'

'So the real strike is still coming?' Thane asked.

'I consider it likely.'

'Why, then we wait and hold!' Sigismund snapped. 'This is the very prize we–'

'Lose that tone, Sigismund,' said Dorn. 'I have told you my command. We either wait here for a possible prize, or we go aloft where a genuine one has manifested. Not the prize we expected or even hoped for, but a serious trophy none the less.'

'But–'

'But nothing,' said Dorn. 'Wall Master Madius reports that Fulgrim brings his entire host. Unchecked, they could break the Ultimate Wall. Is that something you'd allow?'

'No,' said Sigismund.

'Is Fulgrim… a distraction, lord?' asked Thane. 'You told us you anticipated a wall-face assault as a distraction?'

'If he is, he's a distraction bigger and bolder than anything we might have imagined,' Dorn replied. 'We make our best predictions. We adjust appropriately when we see reality unfold in actual time.'

'My lord,' said Thane. 'If your prediction was correct, and you must have believed it was to make all this preparedness… If you were right, and Lupercal or some comparable agency strikes here, what then?'

'Yes,' said Sigismund. 'What then?'

'Five kill teams remain,' said Dorn. 'I understand the balance, or I'd have taken all of you. Five kill teams. Five hundred men. Five hundred *good* men.'

'Good men,' Sigismund nodded. 'But good enough?'

'They are armed with surprise, Sigismund,' said Dorn. 'If they can't stop Lupercal with *that* potent weapon, then you being here is not going to make a difference.'

Sigismund looked away, swallowed fury creasing his face.

'But *you* being here would, Praetorian,' said Thane.

Dorn sighed. 'I have a choice, Maximus,' he said gently. 'Potential prize or actual. I must respond to real and present threats, not imagined ones. If Lupercal, or *whoever*, comes here, we will cut our cloth accordingly, and have this conversation again.'

'No doubt very quickly,' said Sigismund.

'No doubt.' Dorn looked at them. 'Get to your stations,' he said.

Diamantis entered the command post.

'I have operational command in the Praetorian's absence,' he said simply. Mistress Elg nodded. Arkhan Land had arrived from his laboratory post just a few minutes earlier.

'You?' Land asked. 'What, is everything scrapped then?'

'No,' said Diamantis. 'Are your systems ready?'

'People keep asking me that. Of course they are.'

'We need to monitor our readiness,' said Diamantis. Sindermann could tell how little the Huscarl cared for the magos. He seemed to find him even more aggravating than the interrogator order. 'You will advise of any sudden technical irregularities?' Diamantis added.

Land looked affronted. 'So long as you advise me of any sudden impending brutal death irregularities,' he replied. He stared at Elg. 'Is there really no sign of anything?' he asked.

'Mistress?' Diamantis asked.

'Still no target track or sub-surface echo,' she replied. 'We maintain systematic tracking as before.'

'Maybe I should tinker with your systems and improve your–' Land began.

'Just get to your station and be ready, please,' said Diamantis. Land glowered at him.

'The waiting,' Land said, 'is driving me mad.'

'Be thankful you only have the waiting to do that to you,' replied the Huscarl.

'Gentlemen,' said Sindermann, stepping forward, 'Lyclonus writes that a calm mind is the key to accomplishing–'

'Stick your books up your arse, history man,' said Land. He pushed past Sindermann, and strode away down the hall.

Sindermann glanced at Diamantis.

'I see what you mean,' he remarked.

The grinding of the Mantolith's drill head was incessant. Abaddon looked across at Urran Gauk, line captain of the Justaerin.

'Three more minutes,' he said.

'My lord,' one of the machine drivers called back. 'We are close to striking bedrock. We must–'

'Keep going,' Abaddon ordered. He looked back at Gauk. 'Three more minutes,' he repeated. 'Prepare.'

Abaddon, and every man in the rumbling machine, raised the snarling helms of their jet-black Terminator plate and locked them in place.

Loken paced. He spun Rubio's blade in his hand: two turns forward, one back, snap into grip, then two back and one forward.

'You'll wear it out,' said Leod Baldwin, his squad chief. Loken looked at the Imperial Fist.

'Can you practise too much?' he asked.

'Not as long as you can perform on the day,' replied Baldwin.

Loken looked past the waiting rows of his kill team. The deployment hall where Sigismund and his men had been preparing was empty, and had been for ten minutes.

'You think they've found better things to do?' Loken asked.

'What could be better than this?' Baldwin replied.

Ahriman and seven initiates of the Order of Ruin bowed to one knee in a semicircle as Magnus approached. Rolling mist, pungent with fyceline, drifted up from the ravished plains below Colossi. The fortress gate was a distant, marmoreal ghost.

'The summoned are refreshed from their onslaught,' Magnus observed, *'and the spirits of our enemy are worked thin by fear and doubt. Let's complete this rite of Ruin, oh my fair sons. The Pale Lord chides me, and I will not test his patience. He wishes to advance, and so, in my way, do I.'*

Ahriman rose. 'Colossi falls,' he said.

The others rose too. They turned as one to face the distant bulwarks of the Colossi Gate. Their eyes shone with the pitiless light of white stars.

Along the broken ridge on either side of them, the sorcerer-warriors of the Thousand Sons stepped up, cloaks and robes blowing out in the rising gale. A winding line of a hundred, five hundred, a thousand, following the contour of the ragged ridgeline, all murmuring the same soft litanies of overthrow.

The rain began, and turned into stinging sleet. The churned

ooze before them became sequinned with pools and puddles, every surface dancing and splashing in the pelt.

The ooze itself began to stir and lap, as though the mud was alive. Down by the bastion's wall, the horned and antlered daemons roused from their slumber, and rose to their feet.

Naranbaatar coughed up blood.

He spat, and wiped his mouth.

'Now they stir,' he said. 'Now they come.'

He had stripped off his helm, so his brother seers could mark his face with stripes of fire-ash and pigments. Flies were settling in the corners of his eyes and mouth.

'Marshal Agathe?' Raldoron called.

Her attention was lost. She was staring at the wall of the rooftop chamber. It was beginning to melt. Lime plaster was slipping down like mucus, and the exposed stone beneath was sponging into sludge.

'What is…' she stammered.

'The sons of Magnus focus their power upon us,' said Naranbaatar. 'They channel it through the warp beasts at our gates. Through them, what you think of as reality becomes fluid. It shapes to their will, like wet clay at the hands of a potter.'

Agathe looked around at the Stormseer.

'What shape do they want us?' she asked.

'Flat, I imagine,' he said patiently. 'Like a slab. Like a grave.'

'Lord Valdor and the Khan await,' said Raldoron. 'We must begin.'

'Yes,' she said. 'Yes.' She gathered herself. 'At once.'

She led them out of the chamber, trying to ignore the soft, squelching feel of the stone floor underfoot. The flies were even thicker in the access vault to the tower top. They swirled in a black blizzard. She could see maggots boiling from the stone walls and floor of the walk, as though it were rancid flesh. The men posted here were already dead, slumped, slack and cadaverous, strings of writhing larvae dripping from their hanging mouths, their eyes rotting in their skulls.

Agathe led the party on, resolute, walking ahead of Raldoron and the Stormseers, unchaining the gas shields and blast shutters. She had insisted on being part of this. She could feel her skin crawling, insects beneath her clothes. She could feel bruises blooming on her flesh.

She opened the last hatch, and took them once again onto the fighting platform at the top of Artemis Tower. This time, Raldoron did not ask her to go back. He understood her intent, and her determination to serve.

They stepped into swirling bacterial clouds, and a deluge of hail. The entire tower structure was being gnawed away, stone melting like ice, becoming putty, becoming sappy fluid. The bulwarks had already slumped, like soggy paper. Burr's head had washed away. They could hear the rising roar of the daemons below.

Raldoron held her back. The Stormseers advanced. They stood, Naranbaatar foremost, the other two behind him. They raised their staffs towards the thrashing sky. They began to chant, though the hail was too loud for her to hear the words. Where it fell, the hail made dimples in the jellifying stone.

Agathe knew nothing of magic, or whatever word they cared to call it. She didn't want to know. Magic was as far from Hatay-Antakya Hive as she ever wanted to travel. Magic was a place she decided she would never go again. But she had, as a career soldier, pledged her service to the Emperor, and to Terra. She had promised to give her life, or her death, as a marshal militant, and the Agathe family did not break their oaths. If this phantasmagoric nightmare had to be part of that service, so be it.

She knew nothing of magic, but the principles of this rite had been explained to her. Naranbaatar, who seemed remarkably kind and gentle for a Space Marine, a White Scars Space Marine at that, had set it out for her while he waited for his fellow seers to mix the pigments, select the correct charms and burn the proper herbs.

'Seers of the Storm are exactly that,' he had said. 'Our working is strong, stronger than most, but only under the wide sky. We call upon the elemental anima to aid us. But there is no wide sky here, no sky like the one we were born under, no open space that is our preference to make battle upon.

'So we are few. Just three of us here, at this hour. Weak, then. And the sons of Magnus Single-eye are strong and many. Their workings are fierce, and they draw upon the dark anima. They drink straight from the Neversea, so their power is not constrained or limited. They are boundless, because they have accepted power that we would never touch.'

'So how,' Agathe had asked, 'how in the name of hell can you do anything? You said you had a plan, an initiative. I took you to the tower top so you could assess whatever it is you assess for–'

Naranbaatar had raised his hand to quiet her. Ungloved, it was covered in threaded tattoos. She had been able to see them under the crawling skin of blowflies.

'High up is good,' he had said. 'We needed to smell the air.'

Agathe had stared at him through the smudged lenses of her gas hood.

'Are you shitting me, lord? *Smell the air?*'

And he had laughed.

'Yes, Aldana Agathe. The air. Listen, there is no wide sky here. The great sky that once overarched these mountains is gone, as gone as the mountains are gone. What sky there is,

is small, and it is closed. The void shields. The aegis of the
Palace. Everything is locked in and trapped, and this has been
so for months.

'There is still weather though,' he had said. 'Artificial weather
systems. What is the word?'

'Microclimates,' she had replied.

Naranbaatar had nodded. 'Microclimates. Weather systems
building and breeding under the shields, fed by smoke and
dust, and blood vapour, and piss-rain, and air, breathed a
billion times over, fed and stirred by impact winds and blast
concussion. Toxic weather, poisoned weather, spoiled weather.
Small weather.

'But weather, even so,' he had added. 'Trapped so tightly,
it is concentrated, compressed, furious with power it cannot
release. It is not the elemental anima we are accustomed to,
but it has an anima. You took us high up so that we could
smell the air, and know it, and learn its name and its pain.
And now we do. And now the sons of Magnus Single-eye are
breaking down the shields that trap it.'

'To get at us.'

'To get at us, they are setting the small weather free.'

Agathe huddled close to Raldoron, hail blitzing off them
both. Nothing seemed to be happening. They had been
ridiculous to expect anything to halt the–

A tiny spark blinked away from the tip of Naranbaatar's
raised staff. It was small, but so sudden it made her jump.
The spark, no bigger than a firefly, darted into the hail and
the cataclysmic sky.

The hail stopped, abruptly.

The lightning began.

Dazzling pillars of blue-white light, too fierce to see, shafted
straight down from the clouds. Four, five, six, there and gone
again; then another, two more. Each one made a noise like the

sky tearing. Each one hit the ground in front of the Colossi Gate with such force, the world shook.

The crack and boom of each discharge was like the concussion of a howitzer. The shock staggered them back. Raldoron steadied her.

She pushed forward. She wanted to see. Raldoron stopped her short of the platform edge, before she stepped too far and the liquescent edges of the roof gave out under her.

The lightning did not let up. Shaft after shaft ripped down, each one as thick as a bastion pier. The strikes were so bright they hurt her eyes, despite the lenses of her hood. Some flashed, there and gone. Others lingered, contorting and crackling, for long seconds before fading into after-image phantoms.

The seers were using the aegis. The White Scars Stormseers were using the broken envelope of the voids as a lid to focus and pressurise their power, and unleash the rage of what Naranbaatar had called 'small weather'.

They were amplifying their elemental gifts to match the overwhelmingly more potent talents of the Thousand Sons.

Below Colossi, in the blast zone, the Neverborn were writhing. Some had fallen, spasming, suffused with electrical discharge. Others were being pinned to the mud by coruscating spears of lightning. Others were howling and stumbling back towards the enemy lines, their flesh and antlers burning with corposant.

Their will was broken. They were freshly birthed into the realspace of Terra, with all its thrilling new textures and flavours, but it had stung them. They were recoiling from the unexpected pain.

For now.

'Once the shields are gone,' said Raldoron, 'this is not a trick the seers will be able to duplicate. So let us make the most of it.'

Agathe nodded. She keyed her vox.

'Open the sortie gates,' she said. 'Unleash.'

The sally ports and iris shutters of Colossi bastion opened. Bright missiles raced out, some passing the gates before they were fully wide. The missiles were gold and red blurs.

They accelerated.

It was Constantin Valdor's turn to ride out. He led the pursuit prosecution. His voidbike flared ahead of the rushing Legio Custodes Kataphraktoi of Agamatus Squadron. Gyrfalcon jetbikes screamed as they chased his vehicle, hounds baying at the heels of the hunt master.

The Khan could not sit by watching at such a moment. He led his own riders out in a murderous wave behind Valdor's formation.

Valdor and his Custodians killed from the saddle, running down the limping, fleeing Neverborn, swinging their guardian spears, one-handed, to hack them through the legs and back as they passed. Hamstrings sliced, spines snapped. Agathe's observation had been correct: the Custodians, more than any other warriors, possessed some numinous quality that could render true harm to the Neverborn.

Valdor gripped his spear tight, jaw set, racing into the kills. He braced his mind. The Emperor had gifted him with one of the most potent weapons in the arsenals of the Palace, but the spear carried a price. Each blow he struck with it taught him something of the things he killed. Each spear thrust brought knowledge that increased his understanding of the Primordial Annihilator. The golden spear made him a better warrior, but its precious lessons were hard to bear, even for him.

Now he learned from raw Neverborn.

He steeled himself, and struck anyway.

Daemons fell, hobbled, screaming, sprawling and clawing in

the mud. Gilded riders banked, turned, and came again, raining execution strikes with spear blades, thrusting with lances, or
raking fallen bodies with their lastrum cannons. Some Custodians dismounted, and strode pitilessly towards their crippled
prey. They hefted their gleaming spears with both hands, raised
them above their heads, and brought them down.

The Neverborn could not die, but their new flesh-forms had
been traumatised by the Stormseers' battle-magic. The Custodians' blows, impelled by the will of the Emperor, which blessed
them and flowed through their limbs, cut daemon-flesh apart,
and broke giant bones. Black blood splashed up, like welled
oil. The Neverborn shrieked and shrivelled as the meat forms
they had dressed in to visit the mortal plane failed them, and
were destroyed.

Closing in behind Valdor's squadrons, the Khan slowed
his voidbike. He stared at the surgical slaughter as he coasted
past. There was something surreal, something inhuman about
the scene: gleaming jetbikes, masterpieces of artifice, hovering on idle as their riders – noble giants of wrought gold,
majestic in aspect – stood upon the smouldering field and
calmly, with flat effect, thrashed blows down on the pathetic,
mangled carcasses of giant beasts, shredding, chopping and
dismembering them into smaller and smaller parts, long past
the instant of their deaths. Beautiful, gleaming gods mechani-
cally butchered their helpless foe, reducing them to scraps in
clinical acts of unconditional degradation as apocalyptic lightning split the sky above them.

It was complete. It was macabre. It was victory, but it didn't
look like the one Jaghatai had wished for. It was unsettlingly
obdurate and detached, an almost ritual deed of obliteration
that seemed unworthy of the demigod Custodians, as though
they were indifferently rendering meat for some sacrificial
tribute.

But it *was* victory. That was the word that mattered. The Khan turned in his saddle, raised his dao, and flicked the blade in a gesture of command.

Jaghatai Khan and his riders swept past Valdor's extermination, and gunned for the ridge, accelerating, their weapons thundering as they came into range.

The winding line of the Thousand Sons vanished into the air as they drew near, leaving nothing but fumes of acrid mist that spiralled and whirled in the wakes of the White Scars bikes.

'A strange turn,' murmured Ahriman, slowing his breath to normal. He rose to his feet. 'Colossi holds.'

Magnus made no reply.

'The Pale King will be displeased,' Ahriman said.

'Damn him and his damned soul,' Magnus whispered. *'He must learn the patience of Perturabo, regroup his cowering Legion, and make new plans. The siege is ours to win. Time stands with us, and we will outlast Colossi.'*

'So, do we rally and assist him with–'

'Let him prove himself,' said Magnus. *'Let him show Lupercal what he can do. We sapped their spirit, wore them down–'*

'But we failed to close,' said Ahriman. 'Dorn will see this as a victory.'

'Dorn can continue to delude himself,' said the Crimson King. *'Let Jaghatai and Constantin celebrate. It will be their last chance. This was no failure, my son. I got what I came for.'*

He walked away, down the wind-scoured steps of broken Corbenic.

Ahriman followed. There were preparations to make.

Katarin Elg sat up straight, and peered at her display.

'Confirm that track,' she said.

'Confirmed,' said the operator beside her.

'What do you have?' Diamantis asked, stepping forward.

'Target track,' she replied. 'We have just managed to tease it out of the acoustic backwash. It's a faint echo, barely visible against whatever fury is hammering against the wall.'

She looked at him.

'Confirmed sub-surface target track, Huscarl,' she said. 'Approaching rapidly. Trajectory predicts zone mortalis Gamma.'

Diamantis activated his datacast.

'This is Trickster, this is Trickster,' he said. 'Alert kill team *Naysmith*. Incoming target echo confirmed. Expected, vicinal Mortalis Gamma. Deploy!'

The Mantolith juddered hard as it ate its way out of the flaw's shale and met unyielding bedrock.

'Lord, we can go no further,' one of the drivers protested.

'Full stop!' Abaddon ordered.

The drivers threw levers, and the drills died with a whine. The massive vehicle, inclined at a thirty degree angle, shuddered to a halt.

Abaddon's spearhead unstrapped and rose, braced upright on the sloping deck. The magi in the rear section were bringing the internal systems to power. A deep hum began to build.

'Set homer beacons,' Abaddon ordered, his voice a crackle through his visor speakers.

Each Terminator voice-activated the unit under his chestplate.

'Weapons up, weapons set,' he said. There was an answering clatter of metal.

'I'll say this once,' Abaddon growled. 'Let us illuminate. Lupercal!'

'Lupercal!' the men answered.

Abaddon turned his head, and looked at the lead magos in the rear of the craft. He waited. The Mechanicum adept nodded.

'Brace for teleport,' said Abaddon.

THREE

The zones mortalis

The Termite carrier erupted into the open air. It breached the underground chamber at the intersection of the floor and the west wall, rupturing flagstones and strewing bricks and ashlar blocks as the wall face split around its bulk. Its huge whirring drill and bore-heads, caked with taupe shale from the slurry of the flaw, slowly droned to a halt.

There was a moment's quiet. Nothing stirred, except the retarding whirr of the deactivated drilling gear and the slither of settling stones and brick fragments. Dust drifted in the gloomy air.

The armoured hatches of the half-buried craft slammed open. Dark figures deployed with fast, rehearsed grace. Cthonae Reaver Squad, Sons of Horus, the tactical elite of 18th Company. Tybalt Marr led them, flanked by his assault captain, Xan Ekosa. They spread out, weapons raised, stalking across the chamber.

Marr, a veteran company captain, one of the Lupercal's very best, had been proving his combat ability since the Great

Crusade, since the time of the Legion's old name. He was proud to stand among the Warmaster's finest sons. He scanned the scene, using his visor display to compare an auspex review of the location against old, archive maps of the Palace that First Captain Abaddon had supplied.

'Basement vault, Canasaw House, Saturnine District,' he voxed.

'Verified,' Ekosa voxed back, making his own visor-read. 'Plan is not a precise match to stored schematic, my captain.'

'Stored schematics are old, Ekosa.'

'Look there,' said Ekosa. 'It's been extended. Built out. The archway widened and banked out.'

'Dorn has spent years fortifying–'

'That brickwork is new,' said Ekosa. 'He fortified *every* basement?'

'He's nothing if not thorough,' replied Marr. He raised his left fist, and made two quick gestures. Cthonae fanned forward.

Assault formation. Achieve the surface. Secure. Connect with other units as they emerge. The First Captain's orders had been clear. Maybe they were the first up? It didn't matter. There was honour in being first in, and honour in this action. No time to pause. A spearhead stayed in motion. That was the enshrined doctrine, and Marr had used it enough times to know that it worked.

They had the razor edge of secrecy on their side.

But Ekosa was right. That brickwork was fresh. There was something off about this place…

'Locate surface,' he voxed. 'Fast progress to street access. Secure location.'

'Lupercal!' Ekosa snapped back.

The squad moved again, weapons up.

The first bolter shell hit Xan Ekosa square in the face-plate, and annihilated his head. His body was still on its way down when the full barrage began. Bolter and las-fire, bracketing them from three different directions, howled out of the darkness.

Tybalt Marr started to shoot, bracing against his boltgun as it shook, full-auto. He didn't know what he was firing at. Men either side of him were shooting too, yelling. The chamber flickered with fast-strobing muzzle flash. Bodies crashed over, ripped apart from multiple angles. Blood sprayed the walls and floor. Gouts of it splashed the vaulted ceiling. Shards of fractured armour scattered and bounced like strewn coins.

Cthonae Reaver Squad, pride of the 18th, was rendered extinct in slightly less than fourteen seconds.

Silence.

Smoke billowed in the chamber's cold air. It wreathed across the heaped and twisted bodies. Blood gurgled and dripped from exploded black plate.

The kill team emerged from the shadows, guns low and ready. They walked forward.

'Headshots to every one,' ordered Loken. 'No exceptions. I don't care if they look dead. Baldwin? Clean out that tunneller with a flamer, then blow its motivators.'

'Yes, captain.'

Loken walked among the dead. *Cthonae, the 18th. So this is where that proud legacy ends.* Behind him, single shots began to ring out as his men picked through the corpses, pressing bolt pistols to each helmet in turn.

He found Marr. He was on his back. Gunfire had blown out his right hip, and severed his right arm at the elbow. A bolt-round had hit his neck and torn his helmet off. It had taken a substantial portion of his head with it. His last breaths bubbled through blood. He gazed up, stupefied, with his one remaining eye.

He saw a Luna Wolf standing over him. A death dream,

surely, a flash of the past flitting across his vision as he fell away. The last thing he would see. The thing he wanted to see.

'Garviel…?' he wheezed, bloody foam clotting his mangled lips.

Loken crouched down.

'To the death, Tybalt,' he said. He put his bolter in Marr's mouth, and pulled the trigger.

'*Naysmith* reports force annihilation, zone mortalis Gamma,' said Elg calmly. 'Kills confirmed. Vehicle disabled. No losses.'

Diamantis picked up the vox-mic. '*Naysmith*, this is Trickster,' he said. 'Declare contact.'

'*Sixteenth*,' the vox hissed back. '*Cthonae Reaver and the company captain.*'

'Acknowledged, *Naysmith*. Stand by.'

Sindermann watched the Huscarl. Diamantis was impassive. The XVI. The Praetorian had been right. The Sons of Horus themselves.

'Tracking?' Diamantis said.

'Stand by…' Elg replied, then very rapidly added, 'Confirmed sub-surface track, approaching rapidly. Trajectory predicts zone mortalis Delta. Two additional confirmed sub-surface tracks. Trajectory predicts zone mortalis Alpha. Additional track, predict mortalis Beta. All running.'

Before she had finished speaking, Diamantis had activated his link and begun speaking over her.

'This is Trickster, this is Trickster, alert kill team *Black Dog*. Incoming target echo, expected, vicinal Mortalis Delta. Deploy! Alert kill team *Strife*. Incoming, two targets, expected, vicinal Mortalis Alpha. Deploy! Alert kill team *Seventh*. Incoming target, expected, vicinal Mortalis Beta. Deploy!'

It was all so frighteningly calm. Fascinated, Sindermann watched the post's war board. The moment she had acquired the first target, Elg had punched up a hololith display of the entire Saturnine operation. He'd been astonished at the scale of it. The chart showed, as a milky ghost, the ragged spur of the flaw, the only drill-navigable part of the subcrust. It ran like a jerk of lightning across the screen, a pale river locked in impervious bedrock. Over that ran a schematic of the basement levels, almost three kilometres of interlocking, built-out and conjoined cellars, linked by tunnels and clearance channels. A considerable area of Saturnine District had been seized, and the basements opened and connected to cover every part of the flaw that rose to within breaching distance of the surface. All the chambers directly over the flaw had been marked as zones mortalis, and ciphered Alpha through Sigma. These were the killing floors, blocked out, reinforced, and girt with inward-facing glacis, redans and other retrenchments. Adjoining those, but not overlapping the flaw itself, were the deployment halls, one through seven, the munition stores, the support chambers, an infirmary, the command post, and Land's manufactory lab. Beyond these were sealable causeways, and secondary chambers for fall-back. On top of the schematic plans lay another graphic overlay, showing the intricate system of ducts and pipes that connected Land's lab to various locations along the fault.

It seemed so simple, so ruthlessly logical. The only places where infiltrators could emerge were directly inside the zones mortalis, where kill teams would be waiting for them.

I suppose, thought Sindermann, *it all depends on how many units try to get in.*

And who they are.

'Confirmed sub-surface track,' Elg called out. 'Trajectory predicts zone mortalis Theta. Additional, confirmed sub-surface track. Trajectory predicts zone mortalis Rho. All running.'

Diamantis was already relaying.

'This is Trickster, this is Trickster, alert kill team *Brightest*.

Incoming target echo, expected, vicinal Mortalis Theta. Deploy! Alert kill team *Naysmith*. Incoming target, expected, vicinal Mortalis Rho. Deploy!'

The power hum rose, and then fell away again, querulously.

'Try it again!' Abaddon snapped.

'Lord First Captain, that will overload the grid,' the lead magos began to explain.

'Again!' Abaddon demanded.

'We are right up against the bedrock, lord,' replied the magos, 'because you drove us so deep. The mineral density of the lithified structure is denying us a secure teleport lock. We have attempted transfer six times. Without due cooling time, or an immediate repositioning of this vehicle, another attempt will burn the grid out.'

Abaddon took a step towards the Mechanicum elder.

'Don't make him come to you,' Gauk warned. 'Do it again.'

The trained guns of kill team *Strife* greeted Arnok Assault of the 25th in Mortalis Alpha, and cut them to ribbons. The slaughtered Space Marines had no cover. Their bodies slammed back against the hull of their Terrax-pattern Termite, blown open and ruined.

'Consolidate!' Nathaniel Garro told his subordinate, Gercault, as he reloaded his bolt pistol. 'Trickster said two.'

The Imperial Fist nodded. He sent a squad to sanction-check *Strife*'s first set of kills, and they fanned out under the low vault of Mortalis Alpha.

'This is *Strife*,' Garro voxed. 'Alpha clear. Target one extinct.'

'*Acknowledged, Strife. Second target expected, vicinal, immediate.*'

'Understood, Trickster.'

Garro crouched. He put his left hand down, palm flat, on the flagstones. Behind him, several confirmation shots boomed out.

'Quiet!' Garro called.

He shifted his palm. A vibration, very faint. A tremble.

Garro raised his hand, and pointed.

'West quarter,' he said.

'Move,' ordered Gercault, repositioning the fire-teams. They could hear the approaching rumble now. Men braced, bringing up their weapons to ready.

The second Termite, the big Plutona-pattern, ploughed up through the floor in the very corner of the chamber. Its spinning drill heads flung out scraps of crushed flagstone. Dust spewed out.

It had overshot. The tunnelling head gnawed into the wall, spraying brick, and within seconds, the huge machine had dragged half of itself through into Mortalis Eta.

Gercault's sections hammered the stern hatches as soon as they opened into Alpha, mowing down the Sons of Horus as they emerged. Bodies dropped. Some legionaries fell back inside the machine, trying to use the hull as cover so they could return shots. The first enemy shots of the action were fired.

Garro was already running, two squads at his back. As Gercault prosecuted the rear hatches, Garro crossed under the connecting arch to tackle the forward hatches in Eta.

Black-clad legionaries were jumping clear, the machine's drill heads still spinning. Thedra Destroyer Squads, of the 18th. They ripped out bursts of gunfire at Garro as his men appeared. The Imperial Fist beside him sprawled, gutshot. Garro dropped behind one of the rockcrete firing walls Dorn had erected, and returned fire. He hit one of Thedra. The impact of the rounds from Garro's Paragon gun hurled the ruptured body back into the drill heads, which vaporised it in a crunching blitz of red fog.

'Heavy!' Garro yelled. He had men shooting from the firing

wall, and enemy fire exploding against the wall face and off the ceiling.

His Murder section arrived, lugging the support weapons. Mathane opened up with his lascannon across the low wall, tearing las-bolts the size of machetes at Thedra. Orontis emptied the saddle mags of his arm-slung autocannon, riddling the kill-site with high-rate fire and punching hundreds of holes in the Plutona's hull.

In Alpha, Gercault's squads had scoured the rear section, and tossed fragmentation bombs into the back hatches. The contained blast drove flame and grit out of the fore-hatches in Eta, staggering the last of Thedra's Destroyers forward. Orontis cut them down, dead casings spewing out of his cannon's ejector like sea-spray.

He ceased fire, and tilted the rotary barrels up. Smoke boiled from the muzzle, and the cyclic motor purred to a standstill.

'Consolidate!' Garro ordered.

In Mortalis Delta, Endryd Haar stopped punching the Sons of Horus legionary with his power fist, paused, then decided on one more for luck. The traitor had died several punches ago, so it was more about venting grievance.

Haar tossed the mangled body aside. It hit the stone floor like a sack of broken glass.

'Well?' he rumbled.

'Kills confirmed,' the Blackshield's squad chief told him. They had met a Plutona coming in, and opened fire before it had even begun to unhatch, cracking it open like a meal-can to scoop out the contents.

'*Black Dog* to Trickster,' Haar said. 'This one's done. Delta is cleared. Where now?'

'*Stand by*, Black Dog. *Deploy to Mortalis Epsilon. Incoming target echoes, expected, vicinal.*'

'Understood,' he replied. 'Move, lucky brothers!' Haar said, turning his massive bulk to face his squad. 'More welcoming to do.'

The Mantolith had come to a dead halt.

'On your feet,' ordered Falkus Kibre. His men unlocked and rose. In the rear section, the tech-magi were achieving grid power. The vehicle throbbed with the hum.

'Set homer beacons,' Kibre ordered. Each Terminator voice-activated his unit. Kibre, the Widowmaker, had the honour of commanding the Justaerin Elite sections, a role he had conducted since the years of crusade. But for this undertaking, First Captain Abaddon had claimed that right, and Kibre, a brother of the Mournival, and Abaddon's loyal subordinate, had given them up without a murmur. Kibre had taken the notorious Catulan Reaver squads instead. The Catulan were just as exemplary and just as efficient, though Kibre, a Justaerin man, was loath to confess that out loud. The two elite sections vied for supremacy and battle honours. That was why there were two elites in the First Company: competition bred performance. Another of Abaddon's simple but brilliant war doctrines. *One elite smacks of hubris, and risks resting on its laurels*, he had said. *Two elites provoke each other and strive for ever finer glory. Like rival brothers. Like Dorn and Perturabo.*

'Weapons up, weapons set,' Kibre ordered. DeRall, the Catulan's vicious chief, relayed the order fiercely.

'The Emperor must die, Catulan,' Kibre announced. 'Let us be bringers of despair. Lupercal!'

'Lupercal!' the men answered.

Kibre nodded to the lead magos in the rear of the craft.

'Brace for teleport,' he said.

The compartment filled with light.

'Confirmed sub-surface tracks, approaching rapidly,' said Elg, matter of fact. 'Three, repeat, three tracks, inbound. Awaiting trajectory plots.'

Diamantis waited, his face grim.

'Come on...' he murmured.

'*Naysmith* reports force annihilation, zone mortalis Rho,' said Elg, watching the data-feed. 'Forty kills confirmed. Vehicle disabled. No losses. *Seventh* reports force annihilation, zone mortalis Beta. Twenty-five kills confirmed. Vehicle disabled. Gallor reports two casualties, minor. *Brightest* deployed, Theta, still awaiting contact.'

'Mistress!'

She looked at the operator beside her. He was staring at his plate, trying to parse a fresh block of readings.

'Make your report, please,' she said.

'Teleport flare!' the operator cried. 'Teleport flare detected!'

'Trickster, this is Trickster,' said Elg immediately, 'All kill teams. Incoming material transfer detected. Stand ready. Repeat, stand ready.'

'Track it!' Diamantis snapped at the operator.

'Stand by...' the operator replied, fear in his voice. 'Plot is refracting... Plot locked! Zone mortalis Alpha!'

'*Strife!*' Diamantis yelled. 'Teleport flare, Mortalis Alpha! They're on you!'

Catulan Reaver section manifested in Mortalis Alpha with a savage bang of displaced air, and started shooting before the flare of the teleport had subsided. Kibre couldn't assess the full situation, but he could see Imperial Fists in front of him, and the dead hulks of two tunnellers embedded in the stone.

Catulan advanced at a walking pace in their black Terminator plate, sowing fire at the loyalist squads. Garro's kill team buckled and fell under the almost point-blank assault from behind them. Twin-bolters and lascannons shredded the Imperial Fists' unprotected formation, splintering yellow ceramite and spattering hunks of meat. Gercault tried to turn. Kibre's bolter shells blew out his face, throat and chest.

'The hell is this?' DeRall yelled over the link.

'Illuminate them,' Kibre replied.

'They were expecting us!' DeRall cried.

'Shut up and kill,' growled Kibre.

But the Catulan chief was right, and Kibre knew it. Their undertaking had been made at the highest level of confidence. No one was supposed to know. They were supposed to be deploying into empty cellars and forgotten undercrofts.

Not face to face with a VII strike force. The chamber was crawling with shit-scum Imperial Fists! Fifty, sixty or more.

Many were dead already. That was something.

'Reap them, Catulan,' Kibre voxed, firing continually, his Terminator plate vibrating with the discharge. 'Make a space.'

They were compromised. There was no doubt. The Imperial Fists he was killing had taken out two of their infiltration vehicles. How many Sons of Horus had they butchered? *I have to clear the chamber,* Kibre thought. *Secure it. Work out what the hell is going on, find out what we've lost...*

...decide what the hell we do.

The thought had barely formed before Kibre realised that Catulan was taking hits from the flank.

Garro, still securing Eta, had heard Trickster's warning. He brought his fire squads back through the connecting arch into Alpha in time to see the flare fading, and Catulan slaughtering his men.

He had partial cover from the arch and a short firing wall. His Murder section took the fore, spraying the striding Terminators with their heavy weapons.

Tactical Dreadnought suits and Cataphractii warplate were hard to kill. Murder had the firepower, but they were outnumbered by the pack of monstrous Sons of Horus. As soon as the first of Catulan started falling, exo-plate gouged open by cannon and heavy las, spurting blood and clouds of sparks from open wounds, the Terminators swung about, and started to bombard Garro's position.

The torrential gunfire ripped at the firing wall, the flagstones, and the arch. Stone chips scattered like chaff, and the air filmed with a thick haze of brick dust, which made the flicking bolts of las more luminous. DeRall tracked the pulses of Mathane's lascannon as though they were tracers, and hammered his twin-bolters at the source. Garro was in cover beside Mathane when the Imperial Fist blew apart.

Garro and the men around him took shrapnel. A triangular shard of yellow ceramite stabbed into Garro's faceplate just below his left eye, and wedged there. He and his men maintained fire, but the beasts of Catulan Reaver were more numerous and more heavily plated.

Garro's cover was crumbling. What was left of *Strife* kill team, less than a third, was being driven back into Eta.

'*Strife* reports Catulan Reaver section, zone mortalis Alpha,' said Elg. 'Taking heavy losses. Extending back into Eta. I am showing forty-eight casualties, fatalities.'

'Forty-eight?' Ahlborn murmured.

'Catulan Reaver,' said Sindermann. 'A name to conjure dread since the formation of the Sixteenth.' Therajomas pushed past them, and bolted for the door. They heard him vomiting in the hallway.

'This is Trickster,' said Diamantis evenly. '*Naysmith, Seventh, Black Dog*. Urgent support needed, Alpha. Apprise me if you are task-completed and can assist. Repeat, urgent support needed, Mortalis Alpha.'

'We were tasked to Iota, lord!' Leod Baldwin cried.

'Iota can wait,' replied Loken. He had broken into a run. 'Alpha is closer.'

Baldwin knew the Luna Wolf was right, and he could hear the echoes of heavy weapons fire rolling down the hallway already. But his Lord Dorn had set out clear protocols for the operation. They had to obey the rules of defence, as dictated by Trickster, or risk losing prosecution control of the zones.

'*Naysmith*, move! With me!' Loken yelled.

'I cannot allow this,' said Baldwin. 'Loken, we are ordered to Mortalis Iota! We–'

'The Iota track is still minutes out,' Loken replied, not slowing down. 'Catulan is at Alpha! *Catulan Reaver*! Garro's men are being decimated!'

'Team *Seventh* has reported response,' Baldwin insisted.

'We're closer,' was Loken's only answer.

The hallway was broad and almost straight. Ahead, to the right, it passed the access arch into the as-yet virginal zone mortalis Mu. Baldwin realised there was no arguing with Garviel Loken. He wondered if he should follow, or shoot the man for dereliction. He looked back at the legionaries behind them.

'Form into squads, then!' Baldwin yelled at them. 'You're Imperial Fists, *Naysmith*, show some damned order! By squad, advance on my lead. Follow the insane Wolf bastard!'

Running ahead, Loken sensed the flare before the wave of it washed in. He came up sharp, his boots scraping on the stone.

'Teleport!' he yelled at the men behind him.

Air pressure bulged, and then burst down the length of the hallway. In a rush of sudden radiance, black-plated figures popped into reality, one by one, in rapid succession, all the way along the hallway ahead of him.

A full section. Vincor Tactical, First Company, Sons of Horus. Loken was barely six metres from the section leader, face to face.

The leader was a hulking giant. He looked at Loken as though bemused, as though he recognised him of old, and not from the anachronistic livery of the Luna Wolves. It was something deeper, and more personal.

'*Loken*,' wheezed Tormageddon.

His voice was a clotted corruption of Tarik Torgaddon's. He had a chainfist on his left hand, and a chainsword in his right.

Both began to rev.

Loken swung his chainsword up, and drew Rubio's blade.

'What is the damned delay?' demanded Horus Aximand. The Plutona was wallowing and rolling, like a ship in a heavy swell. The motivators groaned as they fought for purchase.

'We have bored into a cavity, lord,' one of the drivers said. 'An air pocket. The halite and shale of the flaw have subsided and–'

'So?'

'We've lost primary traction. There is nothing to grip.'

Aximand growled. 'How far short?' he asked. 'How far down are we?'

'Auspex shows us forty metres below the target subfloor, my lord.'

Aximand gripped the overhead rail to steady himself. The confinement was plaguing him. Buried so deep, and now helpless. He felt as though he were being crushed by the weight of the whole Palace.

'Full reverse,' he said. 'Get traction, and come at it again.'

The drivers threw the machine into reverse. The Plutona lurched, swam, and then seemed to grab some semblance of grip.

'Now!' barked Aximand.

The drivers wrenched the motivators into forward process, and the machine lurched again. Then it began to grind forward. Aximand could hear the drill heads start to chew again, pushing spoil back over the hull in rattling streams.

He smiled. They were moving. Not long now–

Massive impacts resounded through the hull, as though a giant had decided to batter them with a hammer. For a moment, Aximand thought they were taking fire. The compartment skin above his head buckled under extreme force.

Then they started to roll violently. Aximand, the only man standing and not strapped in, was thrown hard. Internal lighting failed. There was a noise like an avalanche, a tide of rock raining down. The Plutona shook.

The onslaught stopped.

Emergency lighting kicked in. The craft was on its side. The motivators had died. Aximand clambered to his feet.

'What happened?' he demanded.

One of the drivers was unconscious and lolling in his restraints, his head gashed open. The other was blearily checking gauges.

'Rockfall, lord,' he said. 'Our drills tore loose the unstable edge of the cavity, and it collapsed on us.'

Aximand stared at the wall that had now become the ceiling. Their motivators were dead. Thousands of tonnes of rock had subsided onto them.

The Plutona-patterns, unlike the big Mantoliths, carried no onboard teleport grids.

In the constricting darkness, he could hear his own breathing, shallow, fast. He realised, with revulsion and outrage, that he understood his old, oppressive dream. The sound of breathing in the darkness was him. It was now.

This metal box was going to be his tomb.

'Reading a sinkhole collapse,' announced one of the post's operators.

'Location?' asked Elg quickly.

'Beneath Theta and Pi,' replied the operator. 'Target track to that vicinal has just dropped off the board.'

'A major subsidence,' Elg told Diamantis. 'This was a concern. Pockets of the flaw are stress-weak. The scale and speed of the enemy's tunnelling was liable to cause collapse sooner or later.' She looked at the Huscarl. 'Magos Land should begin,' she advised.

'Too soon, mistress,' replied Diamantis. 'I won't make that call yet. The idea was to trap as many of them as possible. There are… how many confirmed tracks?'

'Sixteen incoming, lord,' replied an operator, 'all now within the flaw, all inbound in the next fourteen minutes.'

'Sixteen tracks,' said Diamantis to Elg. 'That could be two or three company strengths. I won't abandon this snare with so much game still to catch.'

'You speak as a warrior, Huscarl, counting victory in blood spilled,' replied Elg. 'As a senior of the War Court, I count victory as units lost and enemy strengths extinguished. You do not have to kill them all with your own hands, Diamantis. Magos Land's lockcrete will seal them all in the flaw forever. There would be no escape.'

'I require confirmation kills,' replied Diamantis. 'You are presuming Magos Land's process will perform to required parameters.'

'It had better,' said Elg. 'Let me put it another way, lord. Subsidence has now begun. It will propagate rapidly. If Magos

Land is not permitted to seal and bind the flaw now, there could be a catastrophic sink event. It could even fracture the Ultimate Wall at Saturnine. At the very least, the flaw would be wide open, and too large to refill or close. There would be a hole in the side of the Sanctum Imperialis.'

Diamantis hesitated. He picked up the vox-mic.

'This is Trickster,' he said. 'Land, you are ordered to commence.'

Garro's team had expended almost all of its munitions. Catulan Reaver were pushing what was left of them back into Eta. The arch and firing wall had been chewed away by hurricanes of gunfire, and the vault air was boiling with dust.

They were going to have to fall back through Eta entirely, and try to make a new stand at the choke point where Eta met the secondary clearance causeway. Garro instructed them so. The men began to move.

Garro glanced back.

The sound of the approaching gunfire had suddenly altered, and changed pattern. The roar of new salvos was overlaying the Catulan fire.

'*Garro! You still alive?*'

He heard Gallor's voice break over the vox.

'Gallor?'

'Seventh *at your side,*' Gallor replied.

Kill team *Seventh* had entered Alpha through one of the two causeway arches. Fronted by Gallor's heavy squad, all Imperial Fists Cataphractii, they were scything into the Catulan from the rear. Falkus Kibre tried to draw his exposed men aside and use the other arch as a hold point. Reavers were being blown off their feet, or chopped apart by squealing beams of plasma.

Kill team *Black Dog* entered through the second arch. Haar roared orders, and his mix of Blackshields and Imperial Fists laid down pitiless enfilading fire.

The glory, and the story, of Catulan Reaver section ended in seconds. The combined guns of *Black Dog* and *Seventh* reduced them to pulp. Two Terminators tried to fight their way through the second arch. Haar's squad chief felled one with a power axe. The Riven Hound put the other's head into the wall with his power fist.

Garro and his few survivors, ammunition spent, were pulling back across Eta to get clear of the crossfire's brutal collateral spill. Orontis slammed his last saddle mag onto his autocannon, and provided them with retreating cover.

Garro heard Gallor yell.

'Garro! Coming at you!'

Kibre, DeRall and one remaining Catulan Terminator had fled towards the ruined Eta arch. Orontis met them coming in, and split DeRall in half with his cannon, but the Terminator put his power sword through Orontis' neck. Kibre pushed past them both, ion maul lit, munitions loads empty.

Garro rushed him head-on, *Libertas* drawn. They slammed off each other. Garro, smaller and lighter, evaded two lethal swings of Kibre's mace. His ancient sword sliced Kibre's belly-plate wide open. Blood blurted down the Widowmaker's thigh. Kibre swung again, the mace burning the air. His exo-plate alone out-matched Garro, but Kibre's body was amplified terribly by the warp. Garro ducked, and tried to grapple, blocking Kibre's arm, and trying to keep the sizzling mace at bay.

Then the Terminator who had ended Orontis rushed him.

Garro broke away in time to out-step him, dancing outside the downswing of the Terminator's power sword. Garro checked, crossed, and swung the broadsword down with both hands.

The blade did not slow or drag. It cut through the Terminator from right shoulder to left hip in one stroke. The severed halves of the Catulan Terminator crashed onto the flagstones.

Kibre's mace took Garro off his feet.

Garro cartwheeled, and landed hard, his pauldron splintered. *Libertas* had been knocked out of his grip. The sword had landed two metres from him, tip down, the blade buried a third of its length deep in the stone floor.

Garro struggled to recover, to get back up.

Kibre thumped towards him. He glanced at the sword, quivering in the ground. He'd seen what it could do. Kibre needed everything he could get.

He grabbed it to pull it free. It would not budge. He pulled harder, applying the full might of his amplified body and amplified plate.

Libertas would not come free.

A plated heel smashed Kibre in the face, and staggered him back-wards.

Garro was on his feet again. His kick had creased Kibre's faceplate. Kibre ran at him.

Garro slid the sword out of the stone with no effort at all. The blade came up, and impaled Kibre through the chest.

Falkus Kibre rocked. Garro wrenched the blade out of him, and hacked, splitting Falkus Kibre through the chin, the sternum and the groin.

Torn open, Kibre sank to his knees. Glossy black organs bulged and spilled out of him, carried by a rush of fluid as dark as promethium. He had not been Falkus Kibre in any organic sense for a long time. Whatever invisible, aetheric thing had been nesting in him shrieked and fled, leaving its ruined host body behind.

'Throne of Terra,' Garro murmured. 'You poor bastard…'

Garro swung, quickly, surely, and struck off Falkus Kibre's gasping head.

They had cut their way out of the dead Termite. Aximand

and Lukash led Haemora Destroyer section up a great slope of halide waste in twilight darkness. It felt as though they were route marching some arctic escarpment at night. Open blackness encased them. The blue-white halide crust crunched beneath their feet and looked, in their visor view, as lambent as nocturnal snow. Every few minutes, there was a rumble of further collapses and rockslides from the deep cavity behind them.

Aximand tried the vox, but it was as dead as before. He was lost beneath the earth with fifty warriors whose high purpose was nullified.

'We are climbing,' said Lukash. He checked his auspex. 'Another two hundred metres will bring us close to the point where the damned Mechanicum was supposed to deliver us.'

'Lord captain!' one of the Destroyers called out. He was crouching, examining something.

'What?' asked Aximand.

'A flagstone,' the legionary said, holding up a chunk of shaped rock.

'Wonderful, Sackur. That's the very thing we've come all this way to find.'

'My lord, it has clearly tumbled down,' the man replied. He pointed. The Haemora was right. There was a long, scattered trickle of dark rock marking the halide ahead, a dark smear almost a hundred metres long.

A flagstone. *Part of a sundered floor.*

Aximand slapped the man across the pauldron.

'Good boy,' he said. 'Haemora, with me!'

They scrunched their way up the slope at double time, following the dark smear of spoil, which was starkly visible against the glowing white halide. More pieces of flag, and some bricks. Aximand's visor detected a rise in background luminosity.

There was a hole in the night sky, because the night sky

was the underside of the subfloor. Pale light shafted down, revealing the base of a sinkhole. Tonnes of masonry formed steep piles that climbed from the halide bank to the sagging hole. The bottom of some ancient cellar had caved in during the landslip.

'A way in,' said Lukash.

'A way in,' Aximand agreed. Now fate was *finally* smiling his way.

'Fire-team formation,' he ordered. 'Lukash, lead the way. Let's get up there, secure that chamber, and locate our brothers.'

'Lupercal!' Lukash rasped.

'For him indeed,' Aximand agreed.

Veterans all, Haemora moved quickly. Weapons ready, and with purpose, they began to clamber up the slump of broken stonework towards the light.

Bel Sepatus had kept his right hand raised, index finger extended, for nearly five minutes, maintaining, with that simple and commanding gesture, total silence. His elite squad, the exo-plated Paladins of Katechon, needed no greater urging to do this than their Keruvim sire's slightest word, but Sepatus wasn't sure about the others in kill team *Brightest*. Imperial Fists, a dozen Space Marines from shattered Legions and a squad of ill-mannered Blackshields. Not the brigade he would have chosen, for he would have selected exclusively from the high orders of the Blood Angels, but the one he had been given. The Praetorian had commanded him, and the Great Angel had approved that command. This was the Saturnine gambit, one that had astonished Sepatus with its daring. It promised unprecedented glory, the glory Sanguinius had said would be waiting for Bel Sepatus wherever he walked.

Sepatus had not expected the first step towards that glory to be half an hour standing in an empty cellar, nor another forty minutes watching a hole in that cellar floor that had yawned open after some tectonic shudder. The datacast from Trickster spoke of pitiless executions taking place elsewhere in the zones, but zone mortalis Theta had offered nothing but a cursed hole and a slow waft of settling dust.

Except now.

Sepatus heard a minute skitter of rock. Then another. His auspex began to scroll contact icons across his visor: amber runes and place markers that grew red as they came closer.

He saw every man in the kill team around him tense, their visors showing them the same thing. Their weapons came up ready.

Sepatus reset his in-visor tally. The kill-counter, a small set of digits in the bottom left of his view, was logging one hundred and seventy-eight. He had left it running throughout the days of action at Gorgon Bar.

He thought of the Bar. He prayed that it still held.

His tally sat at zero.

Rocks scraped. The icons glowed as red as blood.

Something stirred in the hole. A black helm. A bound-up topknot crest.

A Son of Horus.

Sepatus swept his right hand down.

The kill team unleashed.

A blizzard of death poured down the hole, more lethal than the torrent of falling slabs that had opened it. Las-fire, bolter rounds, the twitch of yellow plasma beams, two searing exhalations of furnace-wrath from a flamer.

Lukash was the first to die, his head and shoulders shot away. The leading squad of Haemora perished in the same fashion, their bodies tumbling, bringing loose rocks with them, and corpses and loose rocks alike struck down the squads behind, sprawling and sliding them, and making them easy targets for the weapons blasting down through the hole in the sky. Ten dead, sixteen, twenty-seven, thirty-one…

Aximand stumbled down the halide slope, staring in dismay as Haemora Destroyer section met destruction first-hand.

'Cease!' Sepatus yelled, and leapt feet first into the hole before anyone could advise him otherwise. The Katechon followed him, blades drawn.

Sepatus landed hard in the blue gloom, sliding and skidding on the steep and loose incline. The air was wreathed in smoke, and black-plated bodies lay tangled on the scree. A few remained alive, struggling to move clear of the sinkhole base.

He would not permit them to leave.

Sepatus fired his jump pack, and fell upon them, his longsword rending armour and flesh. The Katechon, magnificent in their gold and cochineal-red warplate, arrived at his side, but there was no more killing left. The last of the gleaming black corpses lay on the halide slope, streaking the crystal white with streams of crimson.

Sepatus turned.

'Clear, lord?' asked his second.

The Paladin-captain scanned the area rapidly. His tally counter rested at seven. Forty-three other Sons of Horus lay dead on the sinkhole slope.

Fifty total. A full section strength.

'My lord?' pressed his second.

'One more,' said Sepatus, looking around. 'Fifty men. One leader. Where is the leader?'

There was no clear track. The long halide slope and the darkness seemed empty.

'*Brightest*, this is *Brightest*,' said Sepatus. 'Trickster, are you there?'

'*Acknowledged,* Brightest.'

'Zone Theta is clear. Enemy eradicated. One possible evader, attempting egress through the subfloor collapse. I am pursuing.'

'*Negative,* Brightest. *You're needed in the zones. And sealing has begun. If you remain below the subfloor, you will be engulfed.*'

'Acknowledged, Trickster,' Sepatus replied. 'Back above!' he said to his men. He followed them towards the spoil slope.

He took one last, frustrated look back.

Aximand moved through the darkness along the crest of the vast halide slope. His breathing was ragged… *breathing in the dark…*

He wrenched off his helmet, and sucked in cold air.

They were all dead. The whole thing, the whole operation, it was lost.

He was lost.

He considered picking his way back down to the wrecked Termite. It was buckled scrap, and he'd killed the Mechanicum crew for their incompetence, but from its position he could work backwards, perhaps find the cored tunnel his vehicle had bored through the flaw, and follow it back outside.

A long walk. A long, long walk, but better than his other options.

He started to slither down the slope, scurfing up flurries of crystal.

He heard a sound. Lapping. A river flowing. *How could there be–*

He saw the river below him. A river of viscous grey ooze, flowing like magma. It was rising with extraordinary speed. He edged towards it. It stank. A synthetic, a polymer or some industrial form of 'crete. Liquid rockcrete, or something like it. It was filling the cavity. The loyalist bastards were sealing the flaw.

That was no way to die. Sealed eternally in rockcrete like a fly in resin, *alive*? That was his *entire* nightmare.

He scrambled back up the slowly vanishing slope. There had to be another choice.

The massive river of liquid rockcrete was disturbing the precarious structure of the cavity. He saw outcrops of halide sagging or being carried over into the flow. Rockfalls slumped down the cavity walls, the tumbling boulders squirting gloopy sprays as they vanished into the river.

More landslides. More sinkholes. *If more of the subfloor gave way...*

Aximand moved higher, as high as he could go.

The Plutona drivers had advised Lev Goshen that they were two minutes from the target point, but those two minutes seemed to have stretched. The craft was floundering. It felt as if they were in the belly of a dying fish that was too weak to swim against a current. Everything swayed and pitched. The screeched roar of the drill heads had become a muffled splutter. The motivators were straining, finding nothing to bite. It sounded as though they were gurgling uselessly through mud instead of rock.

'We're moving backwards,' said Goshen. 'How can we be moving backwards?'

'My lord–' said a tech-priest.

'Tell me!' Goshen snapped.

'The indicator systems, lord, they show we are submerged,' the magos said.

'In what?'

'A flow of viscous fluid,' said one of the drivers.

'Like what?' Goshen demanded. 'Magma? Mud?'

'Sensors read an artificial substance,' the magos said. He had come to the prow to work at a cramped technical station beside the helm positions. His dentritic fingers had conjoined with the stations ports, and he was reading data off the inside of eyelids that had been sutured shut. 'Analysing structure, composition, properties...'

'I don't need a scholam thesis, you turd,' said Goshen. 'I require immediate delivery to the target vector.'

'That is not possible,' said the magos. 'We are immobilised.'

'Don't tell me what's possible,' warned the captain of the 25th Company.

'We are immobilised,' replied the Mechanicum adept. 'We are suspended in a body of composite material similar to liquid-form rockcrete. Our motivators and drill heads cannot gain traction. It is fast-setting.'

'Get us free!'

'That is no longer possible, my lord.'

'Then open the damn hatches–'

'We will flood. We are submerged. I refer you to my earlier answer.'

Goshen tried to think of another question, another demand he could make. He couldn't think of anything. The walls of the compartment seemed very tight suddenly. He was enclosed with fifty battle-ready Space Marines and a Mechanicum crew. Craft capacity. There was barely enough room to move as it was.

The Plutona had stopped moving. The silence was the worst thing Goshen had ever heard.

'How long?' he asked eventually.

'How long for what, lord?'

'Until it sets?'

'It is already setting, my lord.'

'Then... when it's set, when it's solid, we can dig our way through it.'

The magos turned to look at him with stitched-up eyes.

'The material is inside our farings, our drill cases and our engine assemblies,' he said. 'It is set solid, so those things are solid, like rock. The beautiful mechanisms will never run again. The material has not penetrated this compartment, because this compartment is a sealed unit. We cannot open the hatches. We cannot dig out. We will never move again.'

And no one can dig us out, and no one is coming, and almost no one knows we're even here…

Lev Goshen couldn't process what he was being told. He sat down in his arrestor seat. He started with the basics.

'How long?' he asked.

'Lord?'

'Will our power last?'

'One hundred and ninety-six days,' said the magos.

'Air?'

'With recirculation, and given your gene-bred biology,' said the magos, 'effectively indefinitely.'

Goshen nodded.

'How long do your kind live?' the magos asked.

'Why?' asked Goshen.

'Because that is how long you will be here,' said the magos.

Tormageddon, saying nothing, fought Loken backwards into the empty arena of zone mortalis Mu. Outside the fortified archway, *Naysmith* kill team was meeting Vincor Tactical head to head, exchanging torrents of heavy fire along the length of the hallway.

Through his link, Loken could hear scattered scraps of frantic vox: cries of pain and death, Leod Baldwin rallying the men, fragments of tactical exchange.

But Loken had no time to listen, or concentrate on the words, or offer orders of his own.

Tormageddon was fast. His huge, daemon-bloated frame

looked ponderous, but he threw blows with unnatural speed. Twice already, his whirring chain weapons had almost torn Loken open.

Loken read the fight as it began to flow, and saw that his only advantage was accuracy. Tormageddon was all force, but his angles of attack were awkward and relatively clumsy, as though some immortal power was channelling its entire strength through a body that was too mortal to cope with it.

Like a primarch, Loken thought, *trying to fit his hand into a legionary's gauntlet.*

Loken kept moving, swinging his long-pattern chainsword and Rubio's dead blade in a furious rhythm to deflect blows and block strikes. Tormageddon pressed in relentlessly. When their chainswords met, teeth sheared off in a screech of sparks.

The ruined Sons of Horus legionary was an empty husk. His strength, prodigious in its magnitude, flowed from a warp-seated spring. Tormageddon wasn't poor Tarik, or even Grael. He wasn't a man, or a gene-son. He wasn't even a he, he was an *it*, and *it* was a slab of mindless muscle and meat, animated by aetheric powers unaccustomed to physical nuance. It was a sheer killing strength locked in an unfamiliar form, and that form was broken and slow-witted. Whatever sentience lingered in Tormageddon's shell, it was too dull, too damaged to guide its power, too wasted to draw on decades of honed skill, too burned out to do anything except drive strike after strike after strike.

But it was more than capable of killing him.

Loken had put down World Eaters less berserk, and Night Lords less energetic. Tormageddon was more tireless than Iron Warriors he had slain, more rapid than Emperor's Children he had duelled. It was blunt trauma like a Salamander's warhammer, cold fury like an Iron Hand's mind, seething rage like a Wolf of Fenris, zealous hatred like a Bearer of Words. It was the terror of the shining Angels, it was the unknowability of their darker cousins, it was the invincibility of Ultramar, it was the swift death of Deliverance.

It could not be trusted, like a Son of the Hydra; it could not be bargained with, like a sorcerer of Prospero; it was rotting inside, like Mortarion's wights.

Like a rider of the Khan's pack, it was in constant motion.

And like an Imperial Fist, it could not be pushed back.

It was an Angel of Death.

But it was not a Luna Wolf.

Loken tried to force it into errors. He was spurred by an overwhelming desire to purge the beast he was fighting. It was more intense than his urge to survive. The fire of his vengeance had guttered out. With the others, like Marr, Loken had shown only cold rage, and he had delivered it with clinical ferocity. Revenge, revenge upon the Sons of Horus for the sins of Horus. That urge was all Loken had known for a long time, it was what he had become, and the Saturnine ruse had finally given him a chance to fulfil it.

Then Tormageddon had spoken his name with Tarik's voice. One word.

Loken knew he couldn't save Tarik, or in any way bring him back, but he wanted to honour him. He wanted to honour Tarik, and Nero Vipus, and Iacton, and all the other beloved brothers who had been betrayed by heresy and lost to horror. He wanted to release the pitiful traces of Tarik Torgaddon from their enslavement, and lay them to rest.

Grant Tarik absolution. Give his soul peace from torment. Cast the daemon out, back into hell, and free the abused bones and defiled flesh. In memory of the Luna Wolves, Loken would wrest this Astartes corpse back for burial. He would not allow it to remain the cadaver-puppet of some repellant corpse-god.

He ducked a whirring blow, blocked a purring blade, sidestepped, turned, denying brute power, and using Tormageddon's lack of spatial awareness against it. He forced it into overstretch, lured it into overstep, drew its reach too long and skewed its balance.

His chainsword locked with Tormageddon's, both screaming as they sheared and mangled into each other. Loken took his chance, and thrust straight in under Tormageddon's blocked guard.

Rubio's dead blade struck the dead centre of Tormageddon's chestplate.

And slid aside.

It left nothing more than a chipped dent. Even with all his force behind it, Loken hadn't been able to penetrate. Every shred of his skill had won Loken that split-second chance. Every ounce of his strength had not been enough to make it count.

Tormageddon smashed Loken backwards, and tore the sword block aside. Loken tried to keep his guard, but their locked chainswords had become hopelessly enmeshed, and all he managed to do was tear the weapons out of both their grips. Tormageddon hit him again, and Loken went down.

He tried to rise.

The beast grabbed him by the head, and picked him up off the ground.

Tormageddon's screeching chainfist was clamped around Loken's helmet, shredding its plating, buckling his visor, and shaving flakes of ceramite and steel into the air as it began to squeeze. Loken flailed, choking on his own throat seal, feeling the neck rings mangle and snap, the crumpling faceplate crushing in against his cheeks and teeth, the vicing pressure increasing to burst his skull.

I will not die this way. He wanted to scream that into

death's face, but he couldn't even move his mouth inside the compressing helm. He willed it instead, in fury, and stabbed.

And fell.

He sprawled, blind. He could hear the angry crackling of the fused chainswords nearby. He tore the broken pieces of his ruined helmet off, spitting blood. The bones of his skull felt impacted.

Tormageddon lay flat on its back, Rubio's old sword impaled through its heart. The dead, dull blade was pulsing with a fading flicker of pale light. Trace veins of energy, like cobwebs made of miniature lightning, played across the palm and fingers of Loken's hand, the hand he had used to drive home the blow.

The little flickering traceries of light died away, and vanished as he stared at them.

He got up, flexing his aching jaw. Blood dripped from his nose. He wrenched Rubio's sword out of the corpse. The blade was dead and cold again, as dead and cold as the Mournival Son at his feet.

Tormageddon was lifeless. The infernal power that had inhabited the legionary corpse was extinguished, or had fled, the broken vessel abandoned.

Loken wanted to gather the body up and carry it to a bier where it could lie in silence, but the fight beyond Mu's archway was still raging.

He left the killing floor.

The fierce contest between *Naysmith* and Tormageddon's Vincor Tactical had rolled to the far end of the hallway. Baldwin had driven hard, pushing Vincor backwards into Mortalis Omicron, but it had been at a cost. The hallway, scorched and peppered with blast holes, was strewn with dead, friend and foe.

Loken hurried to join his own rearguard. He paused to scoop

up a chainsword from one of the fallen Imperial Fists, thanking the dead man for the gift, and promising to use it well.

At the mouth of Omicron, the slaughter was almost done. Gallor had brought *Seventh* in through another assault door, and the two kill teams had pincered Vincor between them in the open space. The fight had turned into blunt execution.

Leod Baldwin had been wounded, but was still on his feet.

'Good work,' Loken told him. 'Get to the infirmary.'

'When we're finished,' Baldwin replied.

Loken walked through the smoke to greet Gallor.

'How are we faring?' Loken asked as they clasped hands quickly.

'Quite the tally,' Gallor replied. 'Feels like we've gutted the best part of two companies between us all. *Brightest* and *Black Dog* are still engaged.'

'*Strife?*'

'Took a mauling,' said Gallor. 'Garro and the bits of *Strife* that made it through went with Haar's mob.'

They both turned at the sound of a long, drawn-out rumble.

'That keeps happening,' said Gallor. 'Trickster says the place is caving in. The undermining has turned some of the zones into sinkholes. But that Land fellow is pouring his concoction in, so I'm told.'

'They're sealing the flaw?'

Gallor nodded. 'Any bastards that haven't shown their heads yet will be trapped. Some justice.'

Loken realised his vox had been torn out with his helmet.

'Raise Trickster,' he said to Gallor. 'Ask them if they have any more work for us.'

'Trickster? This is *Seventh*, with *Naysmith*,' Gallor said into his link. 'Requesting target tracks.'

* * *

'Acknowledged, *Seventh*,' said Elg. 'Stand by.'

'Any tracks remaining?' Diamantis asked her.

'Nothing on sweep, or Grand Borealis acoustics,' she replied. 'Magos Land's efforts may have entombed any extant infiltration units.'

'Maintain tracking pattern,' said the Huscarl.

'Of course,' she replied.

'Some may yet break through,' said Diamantis. 'Land's process will be effective, but it will take time to pump sufficient material into the fault.'

'The magos estimated six hours and forty-three minutes to achieve full seal,' she said.

'He was that precise?' asked Diamantis.

Elg smiled. 'He gave it in seconds too, but I thought that was superfluous.'

'So how long now?' Diamantis asked.

'Flow has been running for two hours and seven minutes, lord,' said an operator.

Diamantis stepped back, and ran a hand across his cropped hair.

'Any word from the wall?' he asked.

'The hardline is down again,' said an operator.

Diamantis scowled.

'Surely we'd know, lord,' said Sindermann.

'Know what?' Diamantis asked him.

'If...' Sindermann began. 'If our efforts here have been to no avail. If we were doomed by other means...'

'Diamantis?'

The Huscarl looked back at Elg. She was frowning at a side monitor.

'What, mistress?'

'According to these readings, the sealant flow has stopped,'

she said. 'Level register has not altered in the last four minutes. The pumps have shut down.'

'Clogged nozzles?' said Ahlborn.

Diamantis ignored him, and took the mic from the hook.
'This is Trickster,' he said. 'Magos, report status.'

He waited.

'Magos, this is Trickster. Report your running status. We
show you stopped. What is the situation?'

He looked at Elg.

'No response,' he said.

'If there's a technical issue, he's probably working on it,'
suggested Sindermann.

'Or he's lost in some mathematical puzzle, and isn't paying
attention,' said Diamantis.

'I'll go and see to it, lord' said Ahlborn.

Arkhan Land perched at the very edge of his work stool. On
his bench, his artificimian cowered, wide-eyed, in the small
cage Diamantis had permitted Land to bring.

'I suppose,' Land said, 'you're going to kill me?'

'I might,' said Horus Aximand. 'I might just do that.'

'You killed everybody else,' said Land.

Aximand glanced down at the blood-soaked bodies of Land's
team.

'I did,' he agreed. He pointed *Mourn-it-All*'s tip at Land. 'I
have had a miserable day, in my defence,' he said. 'I had to
scramble up through a filthy, stinking hole in the ground. I
didn't know where I was. All I knew was that everything –
everything – was ruined. I had to take that out on somebody.
These idiots were the first somebodies I found.'

'Also,' said Land carefully, 'there's a war on. And they were
enemy personnel.'

'Well yes, obviously, that too,' said Little Horus.

'But you let me live?'

'They were servitors and adepts,' said Aximand. 'You're clearly a magos of some sort. In charge of all this.'

He gestured with his free hand at the 'this': the bulk tanks and pumping rigs around them.

'I needed you alive to shut it down,' he said. 'Because this filth is part of the reason everything's ruined. You did *do* that, didn't you?'

'You watched me.'

'It's definitely shut down?'

'The pumps are off,' said Land. 'I suppose I'm surplus to requirements now?'

'No,' said Aximand, stepping closer to him. 'You're smart. In charge of this area. You're going to show me the way out.'

'Out?'

'Of here. Into the Palace.'

'And then what?'

'I haven't decided,' said Aximand.

'You're alone,' said Land. 'What could you do, alone, in the Sanctum Imperialis?'

'A lot of damage,' said Aximand. 'An incredible amount of damage. One man is hard to find. Hard to stop. I could complete the mission.'

'A one-man spear-tip?'

Aximand glared at him. 'Have you any idea who I am?' he asked.

'Horus Aximand, Mournival, Sons of Horus,' replied Land. 'Called Little Horus. Not the Horus we were hoping for.'

Aximand snatched up his sword. Then he lowered *Mourn-it-All* slowly.

'Clever,' he said, smiling. 'You're trying to goad me. Force me into killing you so I can't coerce your help.'

Land shrugged. 'Speaking as someone who has been on his

own for most of his life,' he said, 'doing his best to wage a one-man war to set things right, I can tell you, Horus Aximand, your chances aren't good. You need allies. Friends. Comrades. No one man will turn this. No one man will win it. That's what I've found.'

'Oh, you're right,' said Aximand. 'But luckily, I've got you. Get on your feet. Show me the way. Open the locks and the secure access. Lead me out of here, and take me into the Palace.'

Land sat back. He folded his arms. He looked Aximand in the eyes.

'No,' Land said. 'Sorry.'

'Wrong answer,' said Aximand, pressing the tip of his blade against Land's throat.

The bolter shell hit Aximand in the left shoulder, shredding his pauldron and hurling him backwards.

'Land! Get out of the damn way!' Diamantis yelled, advancing down the walkway between the sealant tanks, bolt pistol aimed.

Land threw himself sideways. The Huscarl fired again, but the bolt went wide, and tore up deck plates. Aximand rolled, his shoulder smoking, and fired his bolter in reply.

The shell detonated against Diamantis' left hip, and slammed him into the side of a store-tank. Aximand got up and ran in the opposite direction, ducking in among the lab's pump systems.

Down on one knee, blood leaking from his wound, Diamantis grimaced, and aimed again.

'No!' Land yelled, running to him. 'No more!'

'He's–' Diamantis began.

'Blast away with those things in here, and you'll hit something critical!' Land exclaimed. 'Blow out a pump, Huscarl, and we'll never seal the fault!' He tried to help Diamantis to his feet.

'Get me to the link,' the Huscarl growled.

'You couldn't take him down with one shot?' Land asked.

'You were in the way!'

'I thought you were supposed to be good?'

'You were in the damn way!'

Diamantis grunted with pain as he reached the desk, and leaned his weight on it. He grabbed the vox.

'This is Trickster! This is Trickster!' he yelled. 'Traitor Astartes loose in the operation area! I repeat, Traitor Astartes loose. He was in the pump lab, now moving! One of the damn Sons–'

'Mournival,' said Land. 'Aximand.'

'–one of the Mournival!' Diamantis spat into the mic. 'Response urgent! Target is not, I repeat, not contained in the zones mortalis! He is at large in the support areas!'

He put the mic down, wincing in pain.

'You're bleeding quite a lot,' said Land.

'I know.'

'I think your whole hip is–'

'I am aware, magos.'

'How did you know?' asked Land.

Diamantis looked at him. 'The pumps had stopped,' he said with effort. 'I thought I'd come in person and find out what you were playing at myself.'

'Ah,' said Land.

'He forced you to shut them off?'

Land nodded. 'He had a sword, which he was clearly prepared to use–'

Diamantis glared at him, breathing hard to control his body's response to pain and blood loss. 'So turn them on again!' he barked.

'Yes! That! Of course!' Land ran to the main system station. He started hauling back the heavy levers of power switches. There was a churning, sloshing noise from the row of tanks, and the pumps began to rumble again, one by one.

'I hope the nozzles haven't clogged…' Land remarked.

Every breath an effort, Diamantis snatched up the mic again with a bloody hand.

'This is Trickster,' he said. 'I repeat advisory. Traitor Astartes loose in the operation and support areas. Target is Mournival. I repeat, Traitor Astartes loose. Vicinal pump lab, now moving. Someone respond *now*!'

Gallor listened to his earpiece carefully.

'There's one loose,' he reported. 'One got through the zones. Loose in operations and support. Trickster says it's one of the Mournival.'

Loken was already moving.

'Spread out,' Gallor yelled to the kill teams. 'Systematic search, chamber to chamber! Find him!'

Two Termite wrecks smouldered in Mortalis Kappa, surrounded by the corpses of the Sons of Horus they had tried to deliver. Haar left his men checking for survivors, and walked through the arch into Mortalis Lambda, where another Termite wreck lay surrounded by a ring of black-armoured dead. Garro was standing with Bel Sepatus. The two kill squads, along with Garro's remnants, had combined to meet the three simultaneous incursions.

They had been mercilessly precise.

'One hundred and seventy-five kills,' said Haar with a grin. 'Biggest haul yet, and only nine of ours lost. You know, I wish I was able to see the dismay on their damn faces as they stepped into your sights.' He paused. 'What?' he asked.

Sepatus was listening to his link.

'There's a stray one,' Garro said to Haar. 'Got through into operations. Trickster is assigning a kill team.'

'Just one?' rumbled the Riven Hound.

'Mournival,' said Garro.

'Even so,' Haar said. 'He can't get far. He might as well be dead already.'

Sepatus looked at them. 'I have requested we be permitted to deploy and join the hunt,' he said.

'And?' asked Haar. 'I fancy getting some Mournival red on my fist. I hear they make the effort worthwhile.'

Garro snorted.

'I am waiting for Trickster to give the word,' said Sepatus, glancing at them both with a lofty air. 'If the main board remains clear of target tracks for another five minutes—'

The bang of decompression drowned out his next words. They were bathed in frosty light.

Sons of Horus snapped solid out of the air all around them, in the midst of the two kill teams, throughout Kappa and Lambda.

Cataphractii. First Company. One hundred brothers of the infamous Justaerin Terminator section, the most feared and notorious warrior elite of the XVI.

One hundred warriors, and First Captain Abaddon.

Havoc ignited.

FOUR

Oanis burning
Just us and the monsters
Brother against brother

Below the burning walls of Oanis guntower, Fulgrim smiled. His teeth gleamed in the firelight. His long white hair blew out in the night wind, dancing like the vast tongues of flames above him.

'*You're very young,*' he said.

He crouched beside the Imperial Fist sprawled on the wall top.

'*Very young. New to this,*' he whispered.

Madius was trying to crawl. His bones were as broken as his warplate. He had lost his helm somewhere, and his face was drenched in blood. Every shaking move took supreme effort, every centimetre he dragged himself through the slick of his own blood was a triumph of will.

'*Are you trying to escape?*' Fulgrim asked. He tutted. '*I don't think you're supposed to do that. Your father doesn't like it. You're supposed to stand and fight. But then, you* are *new. Maybe no one's had time to tell you the rules.*'

The Phoenician looked around. Across the broad top of the Saturnine Wall, his children were massacring the wallguard garrison. Still more of his children were arriving through the void breach, via drop pods, or scaling the bulwarks from wall-base deployments. The Sonance had shut down. The guns of the Saturnine Wall, still firing, had begun to disintegrate the vulnerable Donjons, destroying all the beautiful instruments they carried. The siege engines were collapsing in vast fire clouds that lit up the face of the wall like sunrise. It was a shame, but the carriers and the instruments had finished their performance anyway. The III Legion were in. They had claimed a rampart of the Ultimate Wall.

'*I'll tell you this,*' said Fulgrim gently. '*Even if you could run, and you can't with those poor legs of yours, mind, I don't think you could escape. There's no sanctuary here.*' He glanced at the Palace beyond them. '*Soon, there won't be any sanctuary anywhere,*' he added.

He looked down at the Imperial Fist again. Madius was still crawling, gasping and straining with each tiny movement he managed to make.

'*Poor frightened child,*' Fulgrim said. '*There, there.*' His face darkened. '*Oh, I see,*' he said. '*You're not trying to escape. You're trying to reach that.*'

He glanced at the chipped gladius that lay a metre or so in front of the young captain. Madius' bloody fingers were clawing towards it.

Fulgrim stood up. '*You don't want that,*' he said. '*I've got a much nicer one.*'

He drew his long, single-edged sword, and took it in a two-handed grip.

'*See?*' he said.

He raised his arms to strike.

Something hit him. Something cannoned into him, and staggered him backwards. Something hacked at him. Something was *hurting* him.

Fulgrim wrenched backwards. Sigismund kept swinging, his powerblade scoring and cracking Fulgrim's beautiful armour.

'Get off!' Fulgrim exclaimed. *'Get away from me!'* He was three times the Templar's size. He kicked out, like a man kicking at an aggressive dog, and knocked Sigismund backwards. Sigismund rolled, and came back to his feet. He swung his blade, two-handed, into Fulgrim's thigh.

The Phoenician shrieked, more in indignation than pain. The shriek was attuned across strange pitches, and it shivered the stones of the wall. He snatched Sigismund up by the throat with one hand. The blade, still bound to Sigismund's wrist by its chains, pulled out of the wound. Choking, Sigismund grabbed the dangling blade, and struck repeatedly at the giant holding him. He lopped off a lock of the Phoenician's hair. Then he cut his lip.

Fulgrim shrieked again, and flung Sigismund away. The Templar sailed five metres, hit the wall of Oanis Tower, and dropped onto the platform.

'How dare you!' Fulgrim yelled, striding towards where Sigismund lay. He staunched his split lip with one hand, and spun his long sword in the other.

'Sigismund's courage sometimes outstrips his abilities.'

Fulgrim stopped. He turned. He smiled with blood-pinked teeth.

Rogal Dorn glared back at him. He flexed his grip on his raised greatsword.

'Mine doesn't,' said Dorn.

When Sanguinius rose above them, it was as a wonder. They had all truly thought he had abandoned them. He seemed to shine like a star, his wings unfurled.

Rann thought of the moment, which now seemed years past, but had only been days before, when the Great Angel

had come to them at the Bar's outworks, and driven back the
traitor engines. Rann had believed he would never see a greater
deed, not if he lived ten thousand years.

This simpler deed seemed greater.

And it was not a triumph of arms, a single-handed assault
on a belching Titan machine. He was just appearing when
they had believed he had gone, soaring like an eagle when
they thought he had flown from them.

Their hearts lifted with him. Their tired spirits rose.

'The Great Angel is with us!' Rann yelled. 'The Great Angel
is with us!'

They were all yelling. Every loyal warrior on the fourth circuit wall.

Against iron and steel and fire and smoke, most things
cannot stand. Hope seems weak, and effort overwhelmed. A
symbol rallies men against the dark. It shields hope from the
fire, and armours effort against iron. A flag, a standard raised,
a ray of light, a banner held aloft, a winged figure ascending,
alive with light. At burning, crippled Gorgon Bar, the sons
of Terra knew they could not die, for the Angel Sanguinius
flew above them, and he, like his father, could never, *ever* die.

The savage rhythm of war changed in an instant. Khoradal
Furio, at the head of his host, reclaimed the overrun extent
north of shattered Katillon, and blunted one prong of the
traitors' thrust. Rann, with Halen and Aimery and both of
their brigades, drove in through Katillon's lower floors, stones
tumbling from the trembling tower, and stormed the ramps
of the siege belfries the foe had drawn up to storm their wall.
They broke the Iron Warriors back down the shafts and ladders
of their scaling towers, and heaped them dead upon the earth
in piles seven deep. They burst out of the wall-foot ditch in
a counterstrike that cracked the iron perseverance of the IV,
fractured their mettle, and scattered them towards the third

circuit ruins, leaving tower frames and broken petraries and upturned sows behind them, the instruments of their cruel warfare discarded in flight.

A scouring began, chasing the traitor host towards the third circuit. Sparks flurried like autumn leaves across the banks of enemy dead.

'Brother Fafnir.'

Sanguinius descended to him, spear in hand.

'We thought you'd gone,' said Rann, his axes wet. 'Our wounds seemed so deep, and close to killing us.'

'Wounds heal,' said the Great Angel. 'I was wounded.'

'Lord?'

'My mind,' said Sanguinius, 'beset by scenes of horror that brought me to my knees. I'm sorry. I could not fight or fathom them, or see light anywhere.'

He looked down at Rann.

'Fear not, though we still have much to fear,' he said. 'The horror is real, and looms upon us. Our greatest tests await us. I saw such cruelty being done, Fafnir, such atrocities... My brother Angron, rage incarnate... A totality of violence...' He sighed. 'Angron has done things no man should see or speak of. Things that history would best forget. But in the pitchest depths of his foul darkness, I saw something. I think I was supposed to. I think that's why I was made to endure such abominable visions of heresy. So I could see.'

'See what, lord?' Rann asked.

'Hope,' said Sanguinius. 'There is still hope. Know that. Tell everyone. Hold it close to your heart.'

'I will,' said Rann. 'But these visions–'

'Fled now, brother,' said Sanguinius. 'Gone for good, I hope. The mysteries have passed, and the truth has shown its face. There are no more masks, illusions or disguises. No more veils, no more lies. It's just us and the monsters, eye to eye.'

He took up his spear.

'So,' he said. 'Ormon Gundar and Bogdan Mortel?'

'Key warsmiths, both of them,' said Rann, 'the architects of ruin who seek to bring down Gorgon Bar.'

'Emhon told me their names as I carried him to the Apothecaries,' said Sanguinius. 'He said you had marked them. That to hold the Bar a little longer, they must be foremost on our list of foes.'

'They are,' said Rann. 'But they have fled behind the third circuit to recompose their host. I cannot reach them–'

'I can,' said Sanguinius. 'Rann, what say you we win third circuit back?'

Madius beheld it all. Propped up against a broken pillar, he watched his Praetorian's wrath unleashed.

'Your pretty wall is broken, Rogal!' Fulgrim declared. He lashed his blade into Dorn's shield, and drew splinters. *'Your famous fortress is undone! It–'*

Dorn's blow knocked the next words out of his mouth. Fulgrim stumbled. Dorn's greatsword tore into his ribs. Fulgrim struck back, but found only shield again.

'You are a man in a broken tower!' Fulgrim taunted, and spat out blood. *'You stand so* **proud,** *and so* **defiant,** *ignoring the fact the tower is falling around you! It will–'*

Another blow. Fulgrim staggered away, then spun, head lowered, hair billowing, keeping his distance. Dorn lunged anyway, driving his shield into body and face. Fulgrim threw him off, and leapt aside.

'So silent, Rogal,' he crooned. *'No words of denial? No pleading for me to change my foolish ways and come back to you? You can tell me it's not too late. You can promise me sweet forgiveness–'*

Dorn blocked into him, broke his guard with his shield,

buried his blade in Fulgrim's shoulder meat, then body-smashed him across the platform.

'Deeds are my words,' Dorn said.

Fulgrim nodded, and spat blood again.

'Always,' he agreed, licking blood off his teeth. *'You were never the wit. Never one for fine conversation. Just hard at work and–'*

Dorn broke his guard again with another lunge, carving a chunk of plate from Fulgrim's flank. Fulgrim surged, and hammered out nine rapid blows, each one a master kill-stroke. Dorn blocked each one. Their blades flew, ringing against each other, drawing sparks.

Fulgrim danced backwards. Dorn advanced.

Fulgrim wiped his mouth with the back of his hand, and smeared blood across his cheek.

'Are you really not going to try and convince me,' asked Fulgrim, *'that I have made a mistake? Talk me back into the fold, where I can make amends?'*

Dorn surged, and threw two rapid blows that Fulgrim only blocked with effort.

'No,' said Dorn.

He struck again, a low slice that Fulgrim parried, then a high back-cut that tore through Fulgrim's gorget, and scattered broken rings of golden mail.

'I'm just going to kill you,' said Dorn.

The Phoenician growled, and charged two steps. Dorn met his first slash with his shield, and countered his second with his blade. A third, he parried; a fourth, he turned aside in a squealing slide of steel that threw off sparks.

Fulgrim backed off, arms spread, circling.

'Are you, now?' Fulgrim said. *'How bold. How empty. Look around.'*

Dorn's glare remained fixed on Fulgrim. He feinted a

step, a bait Fulgrim took, then rammed the Phoenician with his shield, and hammered two blows into his ribs with his pommel before they broke contact again.

'I said look around!' Fulgrim snapped. Blood was streaming from his wounds, rolling down his gashed armour. Some had got in his hair. He tossed his sword from hand to hand, then seized the grip with both, and hacked down at Dorn. Dorn blocked with a raised shield, turned out, and raked his blade deep across Fulgrim's chest. Fulgrim stumbled clear.

'Look around! Look around!' Fulgrim screeched. *'See what's happening, **Rogal** dolt! Your tower is tumbling down! No more running to daddy crying, "Look! Look what I've built!" It took you years to make this, and in one night, I roll down upon you, crack your shield and build a foothold–'*

Dorn stamped at him, and they traded four swift blows that chimed like bells.

'Look?' said Dorn. His gaze did not shift from Fulgrim's face. 'I don't have to. I see it all.'

'All what?' snarled Fulgrim. He swung. Dorn turned the blade aside.

'I see your siege machines burning at the foot of the wall,' said Dorn. 'I see your sonic weapons silenced. I see your host, foolishly committed in its entirety, pouring into a run of wall that can be held by a force a tenth that size.'

Their blades flashed and rang again. Dorn lost a chunk of shield. Fulgrim took a laceration to the shoulder.

'And *is* held by a force a tenth that size,' said Dorn calmly. 'Imperial Fists, now bolstered by the two hundred Legiones Astartes veterans I brought with me. Two hundred veterans who are skilled in every doctrine of war. Who have rallied this garrison and this wall stretch, and are now slaughtering the vanguard you so wantonly committed. They thank you for giving them such a wealth of bodies to reap. You have no foothold.'

'*I have!*' Fulgrim roared. He smashed his blade at Dorn, a series of furious strokes. Dorn parried them away. Only one got through, and gouged his shoulder guard.

'No,' said Dorn, as they circled again. 'You're a fine fighter, but a poor strategist. You committed everything against a gap that could be held. You've burned the cream of your host for nothing. Made them cannon fodder. Nine thousand dead and counting. I know, Fulgrim. I know everything.'

'*You know nothing!*' Fulgrim cried. He railed in, and his gleaming blade sliced the flesh above Dorn's right eye. Dorn caved his ribs with the edge of his shield, punched him in the face with his sword's guard and kicked him backwards.

'You've let yourself be used as a distraction,' said Dorn, keeping his gaze on his adversary, ignoring the blood pouring down his face. 'You've let your host be decimated. For nothing. The Saturnine ruse – I know about that too – has failed. Perturabo played his move, and lost his piece. You're just a pawn. Was it the Lord of Iron who fooled you into this? Lupercal? Abaddon? You must have been willing. Were you getting bored with it? The spear-tip is broken. You're holding a gate for no one. You're just an idiot standing on a wall.'

Fulgrim's eyes widened very slightly.

'*It failed?*' he whispered.

Dorn lunged. Fulgrim leapt back. Dorn sliced, and Fulgrim capered clear.

'I'm not trapped here' said Dorn. 'I'm not under siege today. You are. And that's why I'm going to kill you.'

The Praetorian swung. Fulgrim parried. Dorn followed in, and the greatsword tore Fulgrim's cheek open. The Phoenician stabbed frantically, splitting armour, and lacerating Dorn's side. Dorn struck out, and severed Fulgrim's left wrist so the hand was left hanging by a shred of flesh.

Dorn drove the entire length of his blade through Fulgrim's belly.

They stood for a moment as though embracing, the length of Dorn's sword spearing out from Fulgrim's spine, steam rising from the blade.

Fulgrim rested his bloody cheek on Dorn's shoulder, and sighed.

Dorn ripped the sword out, and stepped clear.

'*Well,*' whispered Fulgrim, blood spattering out of his mouth. '*What a mess.*' He straightened up, gore running from his torn face and broken plate. '*It really failed, then? The Mournival plan?*' he asked.

'It did. They are all dead.'

'*Oh.*' Fulgrim smiled as much as his butchered face would allow. Teeth were visible through the slash in his cheek. '*You do fine work,*' he said.

'I wanted a scalp,' said Dorn. 'I wanted his head. Lupercal. But you came instead. A Traitor primarch. I'll make do with you.'

'*All these things you know,*' said Fulgrim. '*So very able and informed. But there are things you don't.*'

'Name one,' said Dorn.

'*One,*' said Fulgrim. '*I can't die.*'

He stared at Dorn. His wounds closed, the skin re-knitting without a scar. His dangling hand re-fused. His armour fixed itself and regained its lustre. His blood dried up, and blew away as dust.

'*Two,*' he said. '*I am sick of all of this. All of it. The others can find a way to grind you down and bring your fortress low. I cannot die, but I feel the pain, and I won't take any more of it.*'

He sheathed his blade. His form began to grow, stretching its dimensions with an unearthly inner light. His legs fused like flowing wax, and he became, from the waist down, a gigantic serpent. The thick loops of his snaking lower body coiled out across the stonework, scales gleaming like mother-of-pearl. He rose up, his lammia-form towering over the Praetorian. There were scales around his eyes and cheek, and his tongue was forked.

Dorn stared back up. He did not take a step backwards, but his eyes narrowed and his grip on his sword tightened. There were no words for the impossibility of what he was seeing with his own eyes.

'Three,' Fulgrim said, no longer smiling. *'I hope our father burns when the time comes. I hope Lupercal turns Him into a screaming corpse. But you won't see that, Rogal. You're the one who dies here.'*

The Phoenician turned, and his huge form glided away towards the parapet. He surged off the edge. Black rose petals opened in the air, swallowed him, and vanished.

Dorn turned slowly.

They had formed a ring around him. Eidolon, Von Kalda, Lecus Phodion, Jarkon Darol, Quine Mylossar, Nuno DeDonna and fifty other gleaming warriors of the Emperor's Children elite guard.

Dorn shook out his shoulders, and raised his sword and shield.

'Try me,' he said.

They rushed him.

The battle in Kappa and Lambda zones never left the limits of those joined killing chambers. It lasted thirteen minutes. It was close, tight-packed, immediate, with no cover and no room for evasion: the Justaerin, regarded as the most mercilessly able of the Sons of Horus, a legacy that had been remarkable even in the time of the Luna Wolves, against the Praetorian's two hand-picked kill teams.

There was no quarter. No limit. No hope that any of them would walk away unscathed. The kill teams fought for Terra, and for honour, driven by a deep hatred and long-held yearning for vengeance against those who had betrayed them. Abaddon and the Justaerin personified that.

The Justaerin and their First Captain abandoned any dreams of glory or famous victory within nanoseconds of arriving. They could plainly see their gambit had failed. The loyalists had outplayed them, and were waiting for them. The exhilarating promise of their ruse had evaporated.

They fought for nothing more complicated than survival.

Mutually assured surprise. Mutually assured destruction. An instantaneous orgy of raw and savage killing.

There was no range of any sort. Warriors found themselves pressed together, face to face. Weapons blazed anyway, in circumstances that the doctrines of any Legion, no matter their methodology, would have ruled for close-quarter combat. Bolters roared, point-blank, detonating men whose physical debris injured those around them like shrapnel. Plasma weapons and bulk lasers blasted against plate, their scorching beams passing through two or more bodies at a time. Assault cannons were pressed to faces or the sides of heads, and fired. An entire quarter of Kappa was filled with fire, as a flamer gouted in the thick of a throng. Space Marines died standing up, Cataphractii plate locked out, frozen like smashed statues. Space Marines died explosively, burst apart with such force only scraps of them remained.

The Justaerin quickly tried to dominate through the brute power of their Terminator exo-plate, swinging demolishing fists and scything blades at anything and everything, overpowering and smashing legionaries in more conventional suits of warplate. Heads crushed, limbs snapped, bodies tore. Some warriors died from three or even four simultaneous blows from as many opponents.

But the kill teams had the likes of Garro among them, with *Libertas*, which could cut anything, and Haar, whose size and power fist wrecked Terminator panoply like foil. They had Bel Sepatus, and his avenging Katechon Paladins, who did not flinch, and who had longed for a worthy combat.

Bel Sepatus, in the thick of everything, believed he had found the glory his genesire had predicted. He killed two Justaerin Terminators in the first second and a half with the gleaming edge of *Parousia*.

Abaddon killed with astonishing speed and meticulous efficiency. For the first minute of the fight, he merely tried to centre his thoughts and reconcile the sudden reverse of fortune. For the next three, he began to believe the Justaerin *could* prevail. They were the Justaerin, after all. They were the best of the best, Angels of Death beyond compare. They had never failed. They had never been overcome. There was no stage of war on which they could not triumph. He began to calculate the logistics: how they would break out, where they would go, how they would secure, what the next step would be. Into the Palace, into the Sanctum Imperialis. Divide up, run terror strikes to damage the citadel. Conduct solo missions. It would take time for Dorn and Valdor to run them all to ground in a maze like the Palatine. Perhaps the original spearhead mission *was* doomed, for none of them could reach the Throne Room alone, but there were other plans they could improvise. Other targets. The Sigillite. Valdor. Dorn. Bhab and the Grand Bastion.

By the fourth minute, he had decided on the aegis. There was no question. *That* should be their target. They would break clear, leaving this rabble dead in their wake, and bring the aegis down. That would be enough. That would end the Siege of Terra. The Palace would be open to bombardment from the fleet. Great Lupercal would raze it from orbit. The *Vengeful*

Spirit would send down monumental beams of high energy, and annihilate the Palatine and the Throne within.

In the fifth minute, Urran Gauk was decapitated by one of the Katechon. Abaddon quickly hacked the killer apart, but the loss was psychological. His schemes seemed to recede, like ghosts, like dreams departing at sunrise. His vision of the Palatine bombarded and ablaze grew distant, and smaller, and out of reach.

In the sixth minute, killing without pause, Abaddon began to re-evaluate. The skill and tenacity, the rationally brilliant approach to warfare that had carried him every step of his long career, and made him First Captain of the finest company in the finest Legion, the first among firsts, a name taken seriously by even primarch genesires, centred him like an axis. They were cornered. They were trapped. They were being killed by the dozen. Not even the Justaerin, not even *they*, could prevail. Loyalist reinforcements would be coming. Even if they killed every last bastard in the chambers, their hope was dashed.

He voxed retreat to his surviving men. *Activate homing beacons and get out. Pull back to the Mantolith. Retreat now.*

Yes, the Sons of Horus were not above that. They were wise warriors, not fools. They knew to read the flow of a fight and act accordingly. They were no good to anyone dead. Damn the Imperial Fists and their simplistic 'no backward step'. Only a *fool* never took a backward step. The Sons of Horus were more like the barbarian White Scars. Those heathen primitives got *that* much right, at least. 'Withdraw to advance'. There was always another day, and that other day might bring victory instead. If you stood your ground like a yellow-armoured fool, you couldn't live to see it.

By the seventh minute, Abaddon realised he was going to die.

They had sent the homing signal repeatedly. Once every three seconds, standard protocol. *Extraction ordered, urgent.*

No flare had come.

Their signal might have been blocked. The Mantolith might have withdrawn from teleport range. No, the damn thing's grid had jammed. That was it. Abaddon could picture it, the filthy tech-adept scum, frantically scurrying around the Termite cabin, trying to repair a burned-out grid, his beacon signal flashing on their consoles. The teleport had failed so many damn times on the approach. The magi had blamed it on bedrock, on energy obstruction, on everything but themselves.

It was their own shoddy, miserable incompetence. They'd barely managed to get Abaddon and his men to the target. Now the inadequate bastards couldn't get them back out.

In the eighth minute, Abaddon decided that if he ever got out, if he *did* manage that somehow, he would track down Eyet-*Good-For-Nothing*-One-Tag, and kill her. He would kill her and her whole shitting linked unity at the Epta war-stead for their ineptitude. He would hack off their hands and feet, and load them into a teleport grid, and transfer them, unprotected, into hard vacuum. Or the heart of a star. Or on an unset, diffuse pattern so the organic drizzle of their remains rained down over multiple sites at once.

By the ninth minute, bleeding from a dozen wounds, two of them critical, he had resolved to kill the Lord of Iron too. *If* he got out. In that *dream* of escape. He would find the great Perturabo and kill him. This had been *his* great idea. Perturabo had seen the flaw, the Saturnine fault. He had toyed with it, cooed over it, revealed it to Abaddon furtively, like some pornographic image. He had gulled Abaddon into this. He'd *used* the First Captain, with his reputation, and his authority, and his unrivalled connections. He had *used* Abaddon to make this happen. Perturabo, damn his soul, had played First Captain Ezekyle Abaddon like a fool. He had tempted him with glory, made him feel smart and noticed, preened his ego.

Made him feel like it was all *his* big, clever idea. The bastard
had even made Abaddon *beg* him to let him do it. The Lord
of Iron, *lord of shit*, had *manipulated* Abaddon into using his
influence to draw resources from the Sons of Horus, coerce
the Emperor's Children into playing along, broker the help of
the Mechanicum. He'd made Abaddon do all the work and
take the credit, so if it failed – *if it failed* – if it failed like it
was failing *now*, Abaddon would be to blame.

Perturabo had deniability if it turned to shit. Perturabo
could claim ignorance if *three companies* of the Sons of Horus,
including the elite, not to *mention* how damn many of the
Emperor's Children, failed to return.

In death, Abaddon would be blamed for the disaster, and
his memory dishonoured. In death, he would be disgraced.
Called overreaching. Called 'that fool Abaddon'.

Abaddon would find the Lord of Iron, in that dream
escape from this hell-pit. He would annihilate those damned
war-tometa with meltas. He would face Perturabo, and tear
his skull off his spine, and ram the haft of *Forgebreaker* down
the stump of his neck, and *keep* ramming it until the bastard's
body split like a rotten gourd.

In the tenth minute, Abaddon arrived at a point of calm. Of
serenity. He accepted his onrushing death, which was surely only
seconds away. It had become a game, a contest, like the old practice cages. How many of them could he kill before he was bested?
Some? Most? *All?* Some were fine warriors. Sepatus, he was *magnificent*. Haar was a brute, but an interesting challenge. Garro…
Abaddon fancied his own chances in an even match, but the
man's sword was a piece of work, and so was Garro's skill with it.

He realised, as he killed, and killed, and *killed*, that he owed
the Lord of Iron a genuine debt of gratitude. Abaddon was a
warrior. He'd always been a warrior. It was his life. His purpose. He excelled at it. The warp was a distraction. It was just

another weapon. Those who knelt before it and pledged their worship, treating it like some kind of *god*, they were fools. All of them. Magnus. Lorgar. Fulgrim. Fools. Horus was a fool. The warp was *nothing*.

Being a warrior was everything. It defined him. The skill of combat. The lessons of defeat. The joy of triumph. *That* was his sacrament. Let them worship their false gods and giggling abominations. *This* was what he had wanted. The chance to fight, like a man, not a daemon. The chance to take the Palace, and claim Terra, the *old-fashioned* way. By force of arms.

He had wanted to win as a warrior. Perturabo had let him try. He owed the Lord of Iron thanks for that.

This was *everything*, he realised, as he entered the eleventh minute, with almost everyone dead. This moment. Its simplicity. Skill and courage, tested to the limit, for no other reason, to serve no *grand plan* or *devious ruse*… just tested for the sake of skill and courage.

This moment was his life in its purest form. His life distilled. He fought Katechon, and Imperial Fists, and Blackshields, and Cataphractii Terminators, and Tactical Space Marines, for no other principle than to find out who was best. There were no sides. No good or bad. No rebel cause or loyalist alliance. No Warmaster. No Emperor. No point to *anything* outside the broken, blood-smeared walls of the killing chamber.

Just war. Only war. The binary test of the galaxy, that you passed in triumph, or failed in glory.

Death, rushing closer, was *immaterial*.

How many could he take? How many more times could he prove his prowess?

He was Abaddon. Let them come. Let them *all* come. Find *more*, and bring them too. Bring anyone. Bring *everyone*.

He would take them. Or he would die. Either way. It didn't matter any more.

In the twelfth minute, Nathaniel Garro reached him, cleaving through one last Justaerin to close with him. They duelled, blade into blade, munitions long since exhausted. Garro was good. His sword was remarkable. He dealt Abaddon two wounds that would have killed lesser men. He drove Abaddon back, boxing him against the chamber's ancient wall. Good tactics, but a mistake. When Abaddon pivoted, it was Garro who found himself boxed, *his* back to the stone. Abaddon threw a punch that smashed Garro against the wall. The man slumped, dazed, chestplate cracked. Abaddon swung to finish him.

Bel Sepatus blocked his descending blade. Sepatus. Now, a *proper* test. A dance of equals that carried them into the thirteenth and final minute of the fight. Their blades clashed and parried with such speed. It was *joyful*. The Blood Angel was amazing. The deftness of his skill, the precision of his strokes, the intensity of his address. Sepatus produced nuanced swordplay that Abaddon could barely turn back. There were skills here to learn, tricks to appreciate and copy. And the Kheruvim's attack was absolute. A *miraculous* degree of murderous focus.

Abaddon was sorry to kill him.

His blade cut Sepatus in half.

The Riven Hound slammed Abaddon into the wall. Bricks shattered. Abaddon felt bones break and organs rupture. Haar was size and brute strength. There was no skill to speak of. Just beautiful fury, like one of Russ' pack-dogs, or Angron's thug Khârn. A wall of strength that crushed *everything* before it. The Blackshield had him by the throat. Haar took six or seven of Abaddon's kill-thrusts in the belly and chest, and refused to die. Just *refused*. His strength seemed to grow as the blood wept out of him. Haar's power fist, like a siege ram, hammered at Abaddon's head until his helmet broke and deformed, and Abaddon's face was a mess of gore.

One more like *that*. One more and it's done.

But Haar was a dead weight, pinning him to the wall. Abaddon's blade had found Haar's throat and slid in, up into the brain, and out through the back of the Riven Hound's head.

Abaddon couldn't move. He could barely *see*. Endryd Haar's dead mass was slumped against him, crushing him against the wall. Abaddon tried to get free. There wasn't time.

Garro was back on his feet. That sword of his, *gleaming*.

Garro raised it.

This was it then. One downward slash from a sword whose edge cut everything. This was it.

Abaddon wanted it to never end. Ever. *Ever*.

The end came anyway.

Garro lowered *Libertas*.

'No!' he yelled. 'No!' He punched the wall.

Haar's enormous corpse shifted and fell away as the teleport flare faded.

'My lord!' the Mechanicum adepts cried. 'My lord!'

They carried him to the arrestor seats, and tried to peel the bloody visor of his helm away without taking his face with it.

All the other seats in the Mantolith's compartment were empty.

'We tried,' a magos said. 'The grid… We had to reposition the Termite to fire the grid again. It took time. I am sorry.'

Abaddon murmured something.

'What is he saying?' the magos asked.

'We are returning,' one of the others told Abaddon eagerly. 'Full rate. The motivators are running. We are exiting the fault, lord, ahead of the enemy's attempt to seal it. The medicae will be waiting for you.'

Abaddon's mouth stirred again.

'My lord?' the magos asked, leaning in to hear.

'Let me go back...' Abaddon whispered. He was weeping. 'Let me go *back*...'

They tested him. Eidolon was the worst by far. The howling lord commander fractured Dorn's warplate with his polyphonic screams. His blade pierced the Praetorian twice. Eidolon had the strength of a primarch.

Dorn had slain sixteen of the killers. They were on him two or three at a time, raking and jabbing. Dorn's shield, already shredded, was hooked away by one of Quine Mylossar's chrome sabres. Mylossar's blade reach was extreme. Dorn knew he had to kill him fast, so he could concentrate on the others.

Mylossar's head came spinning off in a shower of peacock feathers. The squirts of blood from his severed neck shot metres into the air.

Sigismund said nothing, turning from Mylossar's toppling form to smash his blade into Janvar Kell. As Kell collapsed, the Templar yelled a war cry, but it had no words. It was just a howl of defiance. He despatched the champion Jarkon Darol with two hacking blows.

The Praetorian and the Templar slotted back to back, covering each other's guard, turning together to drive away the circle of killers. They deflected cuts and thrusts, snapped golden spears and endured the keening, concussing screams.

'To the glory of Him on Earth!' Dorn roared.

'To the death!' Sigismund shouted.

They smashed the gaudy, lethal champions of the III down, one by one: Von Kalda, who bellowed an adult's death scream from his child's face; Illarus, who crawled on all fours for several seconds, searching for his severed head; Symmomus, whose body split apart as Dorn caught him; Zeneb Zenar, who fell to his knees, and tried to hold his sheared body together

with both arms; Lecus Phodion, the vexillarius, who was sent
cartwheeling away in a welter of blood.

When Eidolon surged in again, Sigismund charged him out
of the circle, knocking men aside. The two fought like furies
along the edge of the wall, both possessed, but only one a
daemon. When Eidolon, gleeful, rammed his sword through
Sigismund's collarbone, Sigismund snarled, seized the bare
blade impaling him, and used his bodyweight to tear it out
of Eidolon's grip.

Eidolon looked appalled as Sigismund came on, the sword
wedged through his shoulder. He scrambled backwards. The
Templar's chained blade ripped Eidolon's pink plate open.
Blood like quicksilver, like liquid chrome, sprayed out and
dappled Sigismund's armour.

Eidolon screamed. Sigismund kicked him over the ledge.
The lord commander's flailing body plunged away, eleven
hundred metres down into the burning darkness below the
Saturnine Wall.

By then, Dorn had felled another nine with his greatsword.
Their bodies lay around him like the ransacked contents of a
jewel box. Nuno DeDonna, famed for his cunning, tried to
slip in behind Dorn as the Praetorian fought off two others.

Maximus Thane broke DeDonna's back with his hammer,
then mashed his head into the wall top for good measure.

The wallguard, a mix of Imperial Fists and Auxilia troops
led by members of the kill teams *Devotion* and *Helios*, had
cleared the lower galleries, and driven the Emperor's Children out of the wall, either into the night or into the arms of
death. Below, the ravaged host of the III Legion, perhaps in
answer to some petulant summons from their fleeing lord,
began to withdraw. They left some eighteen thousand of their
dead behind.

The last to die were on the wall top, as Thane's garrison

scoured out the last pockets of resistance beneath the burning flanks of Oanis guntower. Bohemond was with them, trudging and snarling, blitzing fire from his gun-pods to mow down the last few of the killer elite that menaced his beloved Praetorian lord.

There was cheering when the voids flared back into life overhead, their breach repaired. Weary, bloodied men lined the wall under the aurora shimmer, shouting the war cry of the VII defiantly at the night beyond the wall. A few last confirmation shots echoed around the battlement.

Dorn crouched beside the broken form of the newblood Madius.

'The Apothecaries are coming, my son,' he told him.

'Did we win, my lord?' Madius asked.

'This is what victory feels like, wall master,' said Dorn. 'I'll make damn sure you live long enough to get used to it.'

'What did we win, Praetorian?' asked the captain through a film of his own blood.

'The day,' Dorn replied.

When Loken found him, he was still looking for a way out.

He had reached the lower levels of the emptied Saturnine mansions, expending all the ammunition he carried to cut down any of the Hort Palatine or *Seventh* or *Naysmith* kill teams who got in his way. A long way to come, all on his own, through fierce opposition.

But then, he *was* Mournival.

He was picking his way along a gloomy gallery, half-lit by the dull glow of the solar lamps that lit rows of hydroponic tanks full of dead plants, searching for a door, a window.

Aximand turned as Loken approached. The sight of the armour and the face made him breathe hard.

'You're a dream!' said Little Horus.

'No,' said Loken.

'A nightmare!'

'That, perhaps,' said Loken.

'You should be dead!'

'I decided to live,' said Loken. 'So that you and your kind could die.'

Aximand drew *Mourn-it-All*.

'All these years, you've been coming after me!' he spat.

Loken shook his head. His chainsword purred in one hand. Rubio's blade crackled in the other. 'Not you particularly,' said Loken. 'Just all of you.'

'No, *me*!' cried Aximand. 'You've *always* been there! I know it!'

'That's probably just your guilt,' said Loken.

They flew at each other, blades arcing in the soft light. Edges clashed. The rapid impacts echoed in the empty gallery. Aximand parried both of Loken's blades. He hadn't lost his touch. He sliced at Loken. Loken ducked, swung out, braced his chainsword to block *Mourn-it-All*, and thrust with Rubio's blade.

Aximand darted out of reach, springing on his toes, mobile. He lunged again. Loken drove *Mourn-it-All* aside.

'I wanted Abaddon,' said Loken. 'I wanted Lupercal. Those were the names at the head of my list.'

'Well, you got me,' Aximand sneered.

'You always were the wrong Horus,' said Loken.

Aximand screeched in rage, and lunged.

Rubio's blade, lit from within, parried *Mourn-it-All* away.

The chainsword rammed through Aximand's sternum, and speared out between his shoulder blades. Loken lifted him on the revving blade, and held him there, quivering. Aximand uttered a long, slow, oddly modulated scream, as the cycling blades chewed up his internal organs. A torrent of blood pumped out of his mouth, down his chin and chest, pulsing with the tempo of the whirring chain.

He dropped *Mourn-it-All*.

Holding him fast, Loken raised Rubio's blade, and sliced his head off with one fluid execution stroke.

In the gloom, the sound of slow breathing that had haunted Little Horus Aximand ceased, forever.

FIVE

Totality

The wall that had held them at bay was falling. The wrath of Khârn's master, Angron, the Red Angel, had brought it down, into the dirt. The port was open.

The rest would be swift. It would be totality, as his master desired.

Khârn, hound of war, First Captain of the World Eaters, prepared himself. Warriors surged forward in a great, blind torrent on either side of him, bellowing in incoherent triumph as they saw the wall collapse. Most were so far gone in their feral lust that they did not understand what they were attacking. They didn't know it was a space port. They didn't know it had significant strategic value. Like their primarch lord, they didn't care.

A thick wall had halted them. Now the thick wall was gone. They could move again, and plough onwards into the next place, where there would be more things to kill.

Where they could make new libations for the Thirsty God.

Khârn had forced himself, with some effort, to retain a

slightly greater measure of reason and coherence than his brothers. Someone had to keep the destructive swarm of the World Eaters pointing in the right direction, and moving with something vaguely resembling a purpose. Once Terra fell, he could give in entirely, and submit to the sublime and eternal fury.

Khârn yearned to do that.

Until then, someone had to think, at least a little.

The World Eaters host poured ahead of him. Through his visor display, Khârn saw the poverty of the port's defences. A curtain wall, a bastion gard. Nothing like the meat-body resistance he had expected. It was a space port. Surely Dorn would have wanted it defended at all costs? Where were the Space Marines? The Blood Angels, the Imperial Fists... even the slippery White Scars, so hard to catch?

Maybe Dorn was slipping? Maybe the so-called loyalists were closer to the end than Perturabo thought? Perhaps *Great Dorn* no longer had the forces to stage an adequate defence?

Disappointing.

His visor showed him target icons, though. A decent number. A moderate challenge to fill an afternoon. How many of them would be his?

He considered, for a moment, resetting his tally counter. The number, a long one now, throbbed in the bottom left of his visor display. Most Astartes-pattern warplate had this function. Some called it a kill-counter. It had its uses, for making swift tactical assessments during a prosecution or an engagement. Khârn had never really bothered with it. His kind of warfare had little use for such fripperies. He'd just left it running, unmonitored.

It had been running since the first day of his career. When the number started to get quite large, he had become fascinated by it. The counter held a fetishistic interest now, a simple reminder of his advancing, unmatched progress. He wasn't superstitious like some legionaries, but it seemed unreasonable to reset it. He wanted, privately, to see how high it could get. Did it ever reach a number it couldn't surpass? Roll back over to zero and start again? Did it have a limit?

It might, but Khârn believed he didn't.

No, resetting it to zero would be unreasonable, and he was still, just, a warrior capable of reason.

Time to move. He shuddered as he let the Nails do their work. The berserk cloud descended upon him and scorched him with its exquisite agonies.

Surrendering to the rage, he raised his axe, and began to run with the others.

Shiban Khan could hear the freight elevators rattling and banging. It wasn't the elevator systems ascending. It was something in the shafts. Something clawing its way up the shafts.

The World Eaters were swarming in. The World Eaters…

If the World Eaters were in the pylon, then it was already too late. Nazira had been right. While they had been focused up here on the platform, catastrophe had swept over the curtain wall and Monsalvant Gard. He should have been down there. He should have been down there with the rest. He was a White Scars Space Marine. He would have stopped a few of them, at least.

But now…

The hatches of the freight elevators rattled and shook. The things coming up the shaft were getting close. How long did they have left?

He walked towards the work crew. They had almost finished stripping out one of the tugs. He'd told them to concentrate on one. One finished in time was better than two finished too late. The crew members looked at him. They'd all heard the noises echoing up the elevator shafts. They were soaked in sweat, caked in dirt. They were too tired to show their fear, except in their eyes.

'What do we do?' Nazira asked.

'Is this one ready?' Shiban asked.

Nazira nodded.

'Then I need a pilot to help me get it down to the base pads,' he said.

'Still?' one of the crew asked.

'We worked hard,' said Shiban. 'You worked hard. If it can still do some good, yes. So I need a pilot.'

A woman in a torn flight suit raised her hand. Her name, Shiban believed, was Marin. He hadn't had long enough to learn all their names.

'I'll do it, khan,' she said.

'Thank you,' said Shiban. 'I know it's a lot to ask. Marin, correct?'

'Nerie,' the woman said. 'That's Marin there.'

'My apologies. You base-norm humans all look alike to me.'

That made them laugh. All of them. Despite their fear.

'The rest of you,' said Shiban, 'thank you for your efforts. Get aboard the other tug. All of you. Get higher up the pylon, a higher platform. Use the tug to keep ahead of them. Once you get the chance, run low, and try to get clear of the port area. It's not much, but that's the best chance.'

The team members looked at each other.

'Leave?' asked one.

'If you can,' said Shiban. 'There are no longer other options.'

Behind him, the elevator shutters rattled and shook in their frames.

'So please, hurry,' said Shiban.

'I'm staying,' said Nazira.

'No–'

'I'm staying, khan, like it or not.'

Shiban stared at Nazira. Captain Al-Nid Nazira wasn't going to be told no. That's why Shiban had picked him.

Shiban nodded. 'Very well,' he said. 'Nazira, get these good people on that tug, and get them clear. Nerie? Get this one running.'

The team began to move.

Shiban turned back to face the freight elevators.

He put on his helm.

He unclamped his boltgun, and checked the load.

'Let's run, you and me, boy,' Piers said.

They could hear a wave of carnage sweeping into the cage-ways and cargo ramps. Mass weapons fire was close and intense. The boom of the defence grid system was continuous. And they could hear screaming. So much screaming. A maelstrom of noise. It was War roaring out its one-word howl again, Hari thought, the way it had done down by the Pons Solar.

But this was different. Piers had been scared then, but he was *different* scared now.

'Where do we run?' Hari asked him. 'I thought… I thought the whole point was there was nowhere to run to.'

'I'll think of something,' said the old grenadier. 'Work me old magic. You mark my words. Mythrus will show me the way. Have a little faith, boy. Eh? Have a little faith.'

Willem Kordy (33rd Pan-Pac Lift Mobile) and Joseph Baako Monday (18th Regiment, Nordafrik Resistance Army) chose firing positions down the side of the ramps behind the cage-ways. Clouds of burning debris were spilling off the cargo tracks. The ground was shaking.

The ramps afforded them some cover, and gave them a good angle on anything that came through the gate onto the cage-way approach. Willem had brought all the ammo he could carry, and they'd shared it with the rest. About forty people, a patchwork of different units, covering the cage-way access.

Joseph glanced at his friend. They were both trembling.

'Do you want to run, my friend?' Joseph asked.

'Nah,' said Willem. 'Not again. Bad habit. Didn't we learn that already?'

Joseph chuckled. 'After the last port fell,' he replied.

'After the last port,' Willem agreed. 'Come on, think about it. The Praetorian. He won't let two ports fall, will he? I mean, that's why he sent the old man to us.'

'The Lord High Primary?'

'Yeah, him. I like him. Spoke to me personal. He knows what he's doing.'

Joseph stared at his friend's face. He thought about the story of the convoy, and the other one about the banner. Miracles do happen. He thought about Lord Diaz on the bridge.

He clearly remembered what Willem had said, that day; the day Lord Diaz had found them in the rubble. *If I break, or you break, then everyone will break, one by one. If I stand, and you stand, we die, but we are standing. We don't have to know what we do, or how little it is. That's why we came here. That's what He needs from us.*

'We all know what we're doing,' said Joseph.

A gritty blast ripped across the mouth of the cage-ways. One of the freightyard gates, ferrosteel and eight metres square, cart-wheeled through the air like a sheet of paper, and smashed into the cage railings.

'Here we go,' said Willem.

'I can no longer raise Custodian Tsutomu,' said Cadwalder. The Huscarl had to raise his voice above the deluge of noise simply to be heard. 'The hardlink's burned.'

He turned to look at Saul Niborran.

'I'm sorry, lord,' Cadwalder said.

Niborran shook his head. He was busy reloading his rifle and his handgun. They had used up almost every mag just getting back across the Gard approach. Those things wouldn't die. They just… They wouldn't die. You hit them with everything, the full force of the defence network, and–

There was no defence network any more. Nothing responded to Niborran's Hortcodes. The towers were dead, the emplacements burning.

Niborran got up. With a few quick gestures, the deft handmarks of a veteran squad chief, he signalled troopers to their places at the embankment wall and open doorways.

Then he joined Cadwalder.

'My lord–' the Huscarl began.

'Don't say it, Huscarl,' said Niborran, with a sad smile. 'You might enjoy saying it, but I won't enjoy hearing it.'

'What, my lord?'

'Some variation of "I told you so". Or "I tried to warn you",' replied Niborran. He adjusted the strap of his lasrifle. 'You did. I decided I knew better. This is my decision. There. That's an end of it.'

'I… would not enjoy saying that,' said Cadwalder.

'Well, it doesn't need to be said at all now,' said Niborran. 'But this does, Cadwalder. I'm very sorry.'

'For what, general?'

'You,' said the old general, 'are only here because of me. I'm sorry about that.'

Cadwalder stared at him, though his expression was invisible behind his visor.

'I made a decision too,' Cadwalder replied. 'It was my own. I chose to step forward onto the deck of a Stormbird, and not step backwards off its ramp. What I was going to say, my lord, was *stay behind me*. They are closing very rapidly. My visor is crowded with contact icons. They are accelerating. Please, stay behind me.'

'Like hell,' said Niborran. 'None of that. I'm not your Praetorian, and you're not my bodyguard. I'm Niborran, of the Saturnine Ordos, and I have zone command here. I'm not getting behind anybody.'

He looked up at the Huscarl.

'Right here, right now, Cadwalder, you and me, we're the same.'

They stood in the mouth of the gate, side by side, human and transhuman, and began to fire as the World Eaters swept in.

Shiban could hear them clearly. Hear their claws scraping on metal. Despite the rising whine of the tug's thrusters behind him, he could hear the scaling hooks and talons shredding their way up the elevator shafts.

'Go!' he instructed.

'Come on!' Nazira yelled.

Shiban looked over his shoulder. The stripped-down tug was stirring on the pad, eager to lift. Through the beak canopy, he could see Nerie at the helm, holding the powerful tug's urge to rise in check a moment longer. Nazira was half-hanging out of the open side hatch, beckoning to Shiban frantically.

'Come on, damn it!' Nazira yelled.

'Go,' Shiban repeated. He looked back at the elevator bank. Two of the hatches were beginning to buckle, battered and savaged from inside. He raised his bolter, and took aim.

One hatch shredded out onto the platform, then two more. The World Eaters, thrashing and jockeying to be first, spilled out, clawing and striking each other like disputing alpha rivals in an animal pack.

Shiban's first burst dropped one. Another burst felled the

second. A third burst threw a charging World Eater off the edge of the platform.

Too many. Too many. And it took several bolts to stop even one of them.

'Khan! Come on!' Nazira yelled.

The tug still hadn't left the pad, though Nerie had it hovering now, drifting on a scream of thrust. Nazira was still in the open hatch.

'Now!' he was yelling.

No backward step. That was Shiban's Tachseer's mantra. No backward step. He prided himself on that. But Nazira was risking his life. And maybe they could still put the tug's grav-systems to work. Kill many more of these monsters than he could with his last mag-loads of shells.

Shiban blasted on full-auto, obliterating the nearest three World Eaters in a blitz of blood and armour fragments. More were rushing him, pouring out of the torn elevator hatches.

Shiban turned, ran.

Nerie began to pull away. The tug was two metres up and swinging sideways on the pad when Shiban, leaping at full stretch, clamped his hands around the hatch rail.

The tug cleared the pad. Shiban hung for a moment, his legs dangling over empty air. The clawing, howling World Eaters reached the edge of the platform, packing in and raging up at the tug that had just – and only just – escaped their clutches. They gathered with such an enraged frenzy that several at the platform lip tottered and plunged, pushed off by the frantic surge of those behind them.

Nerie tried to keep the tug level. Nazira tried to haul Shiban into the cabin. Shiban Khan tried to hold on.

On the landing platform below them, the World Eaters, driven into even deeper frenzy at being cheated of their prey, started to shoot.

Bolter fire went wide, then bolt shells began to slam into the tug's hull, blowing out panels and side fairings in thumps of flame. Shiban, clinging on, saw mangled debris tumbling away below him. The tug began to yaw badly, trailing a thin plume of dirty smoke. Shiban exerted maximum effort and, despite the torque generated by their ugly, slewing track, managed to haul most of himself over the frame of the side hatch.

More shots hit them. Dull bangs against the hull. Loud booming explosions all around him, sprays of plastek and metal fragments. Al-Nid Nazira fell past him out of the open hatch.

Shiban tried to catch him, but he wasn't fast enough.

And Nazira was already dead. A bolt-round had hit him. The inside of the cabin was painted with his blood. Shiban watched his friend's exploded corpse drop towards the port's ground docks far below.

The tug was spinning even more severely. Shiban had to crumple metal to maintain his grip.

'Nerie!' he yelled. 'Nerie! Stabilise us!'

The spin grew worse. Everything outside – the sky, the docks, the pylon and the soaring face of the great Eternity Wall that enclosed the north-eastern side of the port and gave it its name – *everything* whirled past. A rotating panorama, the view from a demented carnival ride.

'Nerie!'

Shiban clawed forward. Nerie was dead in her seat, slack across the helm. She'd been destroyed by a bolt-round. She'd been dead since the shooting began.

The world whirled.

Shiban lunged forward to get a hand on the helm controls.

The impassive face of the Eternity Wall met him coming the other way.

* * *

If stories ever have ends, then this story ends here. It ends with
the totality of Angron's wrath.

I think, though it is not my field of specialisation, that some
stories end, but others carry on. They are eternal. They secretly
carry on after the story appears to be finished, continuing in
silence. These stories do not talk. They are never heard. I think
my story may be like that.

If I could, I would ask the young man, the historian boy.
Stories are his field, so he may know something of these secret
stories that continue on after words end.

But I do not think I will get that chance. I think the boy
is already dead.

And I think my story ends here too. Soon.

I would have liked to tell it to someone. Share it. But that
sort of connection is something I have never been allowed.

Here are the things I would have said.

I am fighting to the end in a battle that cannot be won. I am
fighting to the end in a battle that I knew could not be won
before it even began. I have done this, not because I am brave,
or because I am foolish, but because it was the only thing to
do. If we give up on the doomed, we give up on ourselves.

My presence, the curse of my company, has kept the doomed
souls alive a little longer than fortune had planned. I have not
driven off the daemons or the night, for they are too strong for
even me to banish. But I have held them at bay for a while. I
have made the daemons wary.

And I have killed. I have killed many, many World Eaters.

I have killed Ekelot of the Devourers and Centurion Bri
Boret at the curtain gate. I have killed Centurion Huk Manoux
on the curtain wall parapet. Barbis Red Butcher, Herhak of
the Caedere, Menkelen Burning Gaze: those I killed at the
foot of Tower Two. Vorse and Jurok of the Devourers: those
I killed in Western Freight, with Tsutomu at my side. I killed

Muratus Attvus in the cage-ways. I killed Uttara Khon of III
Destroyers and Skalder in the cage-ways, because they had
killed Tsutomu. It took sixteen of them to kill the Custodian,
all at once. I could only avenge myself on two.

I killed Sahvakarus the Culler in the second yards. I killed
Drukuun in the gully by the fitting shops. I killed Malmanov
of the Caedere and Khat Khadda of II Triari beside the
ground-side landing pads.

I have just killed Resulka Red Tatter.

I have killed or driven off a host of Neverborn beastkin.
My curse is a weapon.

At the Eternity Wall space port, late in a very long life, I have
discovered to my joy that my presence, the curse of my company, can also be a blessing. This is new to me, and unfamiliar.
I have fought to protect these people, who cannot see me, but
the mystery of me – for it appears it can be a mystery as well
as a curse – has inspired them. The fact of my absence is a
place they cannot explain, so they have filled it with stories
and ideas, and those stories and ideas have given them strength
and hope and courage.

I never planned for that. I did not set out to do it. It simply
happened.

These are strange times.

I will confess, now, because no one is listening, that this has
been the greatest accomplishment of my life. It is completely
unexpected. My whole life, I have stood apart, and wherever
I have gone, I have spread only fear and discomfort. But here,
briefly and unexpectedly, I have affected people in another
way. I have been an unlikely conduit for strength and unity.
I have been a mystery that has compelled them to stand up
and believe, not cower and shrink in fear.

I have been able to touch them.

This is my fortune. It is all I have ever wanted.

I wish it could continue, but it will not. As I have said, this is a story that is reaching its end.

So I stand, and I kill. I kill as many of the foe as I can before the end comes.

As I pass across the battlefield, my sword in my hand, I see the ruination that the uglier face of fortune has wrought. I see things that should be noted down for history, so that they can be remembered. But they will not be. The young man, if he is not already dead, will not survive this blizzard of destruction. So his story ends here too.

But I see things that I would have made him mark down on his dataslate, if he had been able to hear me. The names of the dead. The manner of their deaths. Custodian Tsutomu, and ninety-six others, in the cage-ways. Oxana Pell (Hort Borograd K), and three others, at Tower One. Getty Orheg (16th Arctic Hort) and fifty others, at the curtain wall. Bailee Grosser (Third Helvet), and twenty-six others, in Western Freight. Militant Colonel Auxilia Clement Brohn and forty-two others, at the guard gate. Ennie Carnet (Fourth Australis Mechanised) and one hundred and sixty-four others, between the curtain wall and Tower Two. Pasha Cavaner (11th Heavy Janissar), and sixteen others, in the second yards. Willem Kordy (33rd Pan-Pac Lift Mobile) and Joseph Baako Monday (18th Regiment, Nordafrik Resistance Army), on the cargo ramps behind the cage-ways.

Those two died together, as they began, fighting for each other. They would not leave each other's sides when the World Eaters came. There is a bond stronger than steel to be found in the calamity of combat.

I wish I knew the names and stories of the ones I have called the others. I do not. And even if I did, there would not be enough time left to tell them all. There are so many. So very many.

And totality is here.

I cross the open quad below Tower Four to meet it. World Eaters come, crushing and scattering the mutilated remains of the dead. They crush everything underfoot: rubble, girders, flak-board, wreckage, bones, helmets, broken weapons, lives, the few effects the troopers were allowed to bring, the picts of loved ones, the little uniform kits of needle and thread, the trinkets and charms, the battered dataslates some of them carried.

I wonder if, in time to come, any of these things will be found. Will these battlefields be picked over, and the relics of our last day retrieved? Will they be mended and fixed back together, like a broken cup, and put on display in some museum of memorial? Will the dataslates be read? The bones buried?

Will they wonder who we were?

Will they care? Will anything we did or said here matter to them?

Only fortune knows.

The World Eaters come. I kill Goret Foulmaw with a clean blow. I make Centurion Cisaka Warhand shiver and recoil, then take off his head. I kill Mahog Dearth of VI Destroyers by impalement. I gut Haskor Blood Smoke, and then Nurtot of II Triari. I cut the spine of Karakull White Butcher.

I see Khârn coming. Khârn, First Captain. He is a true giant. My null curse does not even slow him down, or give him pause.

I raise my sword, *Veracity*.

I speak in Khârn's language.

I

The quad was washed with blood. Khârn's rage was deeper than he had ever allowed it to be before. The Blood God drinks deep.

A flicker. Khârn noticed the long number of his tally count had suddenly risen by one.

A moment of confusion. He did not remember making another kill. He did not see anything. But his axe is spitting blood.

The rage makes everything a blur. The number did not matter. It never had.

The flicker of confusion passed as the Nails bit, and the fury deepened.

He moved on.

Piers returned to the yard where they had raised the battle banner, him and the boy. They had propped it up, wedging the poles with sandbags and fuel drums, so it could flutter in the wind. There He was, the Emperor Ascendant, the Big Man, in His sunburst, looking down at him.

They had raised it up, him and the boy, him and Hari, then they had gone back to round up others to stand with them, others to crowd around the banner in defiance. Show their good faith. Rally around it, and protect it, so that He would see them and protect them.

But there were no others. And the boy, he hadn't come back.

Piers felt bad about that. He'd seen it all. Hardened to horror, was Olly Piers. Nothing got to him.

But some losses were oddly hard to take.

The old grenadier straightened his shako, and sniffed, and rubbed his eyes. *Stupid old bastard. You've seen worse.*

He could hear it coming. Like a storm in the high Uplands. He heaved up *Old Bess*, and checked her charge. 'Don't let me down,' he muttered to the caliver.

He stood before the banner. Right before it. No other place to stand. If the boy had been there, he'd have stood at Piers' side. Of course he would have. The others would have too. They all would have–

It had arrived. *Shitting shit. Look at that, boy. The size of god. It's got wings! Wings like a daemon-bat...* Each slow step towards Piers a little earthquake. The drone of the axe.

Piers didn't budge.

So that's what a primarch looks like. Shitting ball-bags. The Lord of the Eaters. Big as hell itself.

If the boy had been there, he'd have asked Piers if he was afraid. Because he always asked such stupid questions. But Piers would have answered him. He'd have said 'no'.

Because he always lied.

'Come on, then,' Piers cried, 'and see what happens!'

The winged monster snorted. Its berserk pace had slowed. It plodded forward, as though it was curious, puzzled by the little man, and his little gun, and his ragged banner. It snorted, a great bellows snort like a bull. Liquid drooled from its lips.

Piers aimed *Old Bess*.

'Come on then,' he yelled. 'Show me what all the fuss is about!'

Come on now. Don't let me down. Come on now, spirit of Myth-rus, I'm right here. Your loyal bloody soldier, Olly Piers. That's Olympos Piers to you, fickle mistress of war. I'm your chosen one. You know me. Come on, now. Don't keep me waiting. Come on, war-lady, come on, Dame Death, you useless bitch, wherever you are, send your old soldier some grace, for shit's sake. I know I ask a lot, but you've only got one bloody job. Come on, now. Come on. I'm asking you nice.

Angron, the Red Angel, started to charge. The yard shook. The banner shivered.

Olly Piers fired *Old Bess*, beam after beam, dead centre. *Bloody shitting centre mass, you big ugly bastard!*

'Upland Tercio, hooo!' he screamed. 'Throne of Terra! Throne of Terra!'

Bathed in blood, Angron raised his fists to the sky, flexed

his arms, spread his gigantic wings, and let out a roar so loud, the burning guntowers of Monsalvant Gard shook.

And the banner, soaked in sprays of blood, slipped from its broken pole and fluttered to the ground.

THE TWENTY-SIXTH
OF QUINTUS

'After the torchlight red on sweaty faces
After the frosty silence in the gardens
After the agony in stony places
The shouting and the crying
Prison and palace and reverberation
Of thunder of spring over distant mountains
He who was living is now dead
We who were living are now dying.'

– from the Terran vision-cycle
The Waste Land, early M2

Battles lost, battles won. Gains made, losses weathered. In the heart of an endless galaxy endlessly ablaze, there was a small space of darkness and silence, and in that space, laid out before Him, was the simple wood and bone surface of an old regicide board. The ancient game, the game of kings, of conquest. He had mastered it before He could walk.

It had come to this. One tiny fold of darkness and silence, and the old game. The tension of the silence was almost unbearable, even for Him. There were so few pieces left on His side, so many in the ranks facing Him.

Move followed by move, each one judged with infinite precision, calculating the multiplicity of consequences that followed the adjustment of even one minor playing piece. Not just this move, but where it would lead, moves plotted ten or twenty or even a hundred in advance, weighing every possible outcome.

His opponent, invisible in the darkness on the other side of the board, was no fool. He had not raised fools.

The last few moves had been to His advantage, desperate strategies that exploited His few meagre pieces to their limit. But they had paid off. He had taken several of His opponent's carved-bone pieces off the board. He had blocked ploys and out-stepped stratagems. He had averted looming defeat, but only briefly. Victory was no closer. All He was doing was postponing His opponent's inexorable advance.

His opponent had so many more pieces to play. The warp kept placing fresh pieces on the board as quickly as His plays removed them.

He had imagined, in the end, the Inner War would be apocalyptic, the aetheric web shaking and screaming in convulsion, roaring like a stoked furnace.

But it was not. It was rigid silence, with just the occasional soft click of a bone piece moved across old wood. It took His whole mind to focus, every thought bent towards each move. He hoped, He trusted, that in the Palace around Him, His few remaining sons could play their part and keep the Real War at bay, just a little longer, by whatever means they could.

He had so few pieces left. It was a miracle He had kept the game alive for so long. Soon they would be face to face, no moves left to play, no pieces left, no board. Just Him and His adversary, one against one.

In the grim darkness, a hand reached out to make the next move.

He heard the invisible darkness chuckle to itself.

'You didn't have to come to me, face to face,' said Rogal Dorn.

'I wanted to,' replied Sanguinius.

Dorn's Huscarls had escorted the Lord of Baal to the War Room adjoining the Grand Borealis, a private command cabinet away from the noise and murmur of the vast chamber. It was wise to do so: the Great Angel was a distraction wherever he went. An awed and fascinated hush had travelled with Sanguinius as Vorst and the men escorted him across the Grand Borealis, operators and War Court seniors glancing around from their vital work.

Besides, Dorn wanted privacy. More and more these days, it seemed.

The Praetorian nodded to the Huscarls, and they stepped out, closing the tall panelled doors of the marble War Room behind them.

'I just needed a situational report from the zone commanders,' said Dorn. 'Personal evaluation, not what I can read on the feed. Hardlink would have sufficed.'

'Well, I can make the report gladly,' said Sanguinius. Dorn, in his grey overcloak and his father's robe, had sat down at the cabinet desk. The Angel, his armour glorious, but marked and scuffed with the toil of war, stood as though at attention before him, a general making report to his warlord.

'Gorgon Bar is firm, Praetorian,' he said. 'We are holding it to the third circuit wall, a regain from earlier loss, after some argument. The enemy is in disarray behind the second circuit line, attempting to recompose after the sudden loss of their field leaders. With reinforcement, I believe the Bar's garrison could reclaim the second circuit, though I doubt reinforcement will become available. As things stand, I am confident Gorgon Bar will hold robustly for another two weeks minimum.'

The Angel eased slightly. He looked at Dorn, and continued in a less formal tone.

'That's why I came,' he said. 'The stability permits me an hour or two's grace away, and Rann can hold the line. His fire is undiminished.'

Dorn nodded. 'Satisfactory, then,' he said. 'But that's not why you came in person.'

He gestured to a seat.

Sanguinius looked at the gilded chairs nearby: chairs for War Court generals and lords militant, waiting like nursery furniture beside the two or three larger thrones made for demigods. All came here, in their turn, for discourse in the private office of Terra's warlord. There were no seats built for Space Marines. The legionaries always stood.

Sanguinius sat down, flexing his hands on the lacquered arm rests of the throne he had chosen, as though impressed by the scrollwork and the gaping lion heads.

'It's not,' he admitted. 'A private matter, in fact.'

'So I imagined,' said Dorn. 'I had heard reports, brother. Nothing official. Concerns for your health. Just tell me directly–'

'Oh no,' said Sanguinius. 'I am entirely well. Entirely well. Weary from the struggle, but aren't we all?' He looked around. 'Is the Great Khan joining us? I thought he might.'

Dorn shook his head.

'By link?'

'Too busy for "chatter", so he said in his message,' Dorn replied with a touch of disdain. 'But he's blocked them squarely at Colossi. I think "too intent" is what he means. Fiercely readying his Legion, no doubt, to make a run at Lion's Gate space port.'

'We do need a port,' Sanguinius said. He leant forward earnestly. 'The word from Eternity Wall Port is bleak. An atrocity, and a wounding loss.'

Dorn didn't comment. Some shadow seemed to pass across his face for a moment. Sanguinius noticed it, but chose not to remark. He stared at the patterns in the gleaming marble floor instead, pensive.

'Angron is...' he began. 'Rogal, he is beyond words. I can no longer contain the horror of him in language. We have much to fear from him. He is a force now, not a once-brother.'

'He's a monster,' Dorn replied, with flat affect.

'Each is, in his own way,' replied the Angel. 'It pains me to think so, but that's the way of our world. It's just us and the monsters.'

Dorn leaned back in his chair, and rubbed his jaw with the heel of his hand.

'Jaghatai can have his run,' he said, as though he was allowing something he had any power to prevent. 'With all my heart, I hope there soon comes a time when we need a port again. Anyway, it could be days or weeks away before he gets the chance. The Pale King is driven back, but he controls the approach and holds the field. The Khan of Khans will have to deal with him, and he is not easily dealt with.'

'But you,' said Sanguinius, 'I understand you have made a gain. A decent one. Archamus was tight-lipped, but there's word of a good fight that went in our favour. They say you took the field in person.'

Dorn rose to his feet and wandered to the wall displays to check some passing data.

'I had hoped for more, but yes,' he replied. 'An engagement at Saturnine. Three full companies of the Sons of Horus destroyed, including the First. The Mournival annihilated.'

'Are you… joking?' Sanguinius began.

Dorn shook his head. 'That's not the half. We repelled the Phoenician from the wall there. The Phoenician and his entire Legion. Fulgrim is now a true monster too. I shudder at the thought of his transformation. I merely fought. He… he took brutal losses. I didn't close to kill him, despite my efforts, but I think… I think he's done. I think he's broken, and quit the siege, and taken his damn children with him. The monsters are one fewer.'

Sanguinius tilted his head, quizzical. He laughed in astonishment.

'You tell me that, brother…' he said, 'all of *that*, and yet you preface it with the words "I had hoped for more"? What more could there be?'

'So much,' said Dorn, expression grim. 'For a moment, there seemed a chance to take Lupercal himself. But no. I was denied.'

Sanguinius rose to his feet, arms wide, wings rippling.

'Fulgrim's departure is a great prize, still!' he cried. 'Great Terra! Rogal? This is a victory for us. For you.'

Dorn nodded. 'And I mark it as such,' he admitted. He looked at his brother ruefully. 'You know the real irony? Fulgrim could have taken the wall. The power he has, the Legion strength. The unimaginable *daemon gifts*. He cut the wall wide open, brother, wide open. But for a… a stroke of fortune, I held it closed. Fulgrim got deeper, and faster, than *any* of them so far. Excess was his undoing, as ever. The brazen confidence of over-strength. He threw his whole damn Legion into a space too small.'

Dorn shook his head. He smiled at the Angel sadly.

'I tell you this plainly, brother,' he said. 'If the Warmaster or the Lord of Iron had ever managed to harness him, he would have won this for them in a matter of days. He could have been their greatest weapon.'

'Some of us are hard to control,' said Sanguinius.

'Some of us always have been.'

'Gifted beyond belief, yet wayward,' the Angel remarked. 'So too Angron. The World Eaters, like the Emperor's Children, as you say, could win this outright. But they are wild, and will not be commanded. They do as they will, capricious as storms. Sometimes their actions benefit Horus Lupercal, and sometimes, thank every star in heaven, us. They are wasted assets.'

They stared at each other for a moment.

'Well,' said Sanguinius. 'Rogal, you've surprised me with word of triumph. I thought I was going to be the one bearing better news. That's why I came. To tell you in person.'

'You have my full attention,' said Dorn. 'Speak this better news. I long to hear of something other than death.'

'At Gorgon Bar, during the fight there,' said the Angel, 'I... I came into possession of some intelligence. I won't say how, not yet.'

'A secret? From me?'

'Please, trust me.'

Dorn shrugged. 'I can do no less, brother, without damning myself, so...'

'The intelligence is genuine,' said Sanguinius. 'Confirmed. Nuceria is destroyed.'

The Praetorian frowned. 'It's dead. It's *been* dead for–'

'No,' said Sanguinius. 'Destroyed, not razed. Eradicated. Exterminated by fleet action. There is only one thing that could have done that. The moment I learned of it, my hope was renewed.'

Dorn stared at him. 'They're coming?' he breathed.

'They are coming at last,' Sanguinius nodded. 'Roboute. The Lion. The others are finally coming.'

'What's it about this time?' Land asked. He was wearing heavy protective gloves, and they were plastered with lockcrete residue that was starting to harden. The chamber air stank of industrial chemicals.

'Get your things,' said Maximus Thane.

'My things are here, because I'm working here,' Land replied. 'As I am sure you can readily see.' His artificimian chittered a scathing threat display at the Imperial Fists officer from the cluttered laboratory bench. 'Your Praetorian charged me, *me*, in *person*, to assist with the war effort. I think you were there. Have you taken a blow to the head since? I am doing the Praetorian's work, as I was asked to do.'

'You are, magos.' said Thane.

'Uhm… technoarchaeologist. Or "sir". "Sir" is perhaps easier and more appropriate. "Good sir", even.'

Thane grunted.

'Yes, sir,' he said, as though the honorific was a supreme hurdle to overcome. 'You are doing the Praetorian's work. For which all of Terra is grateful, I'm sure. You'll just be doing it somewhere else.'

'It'll take days to dismantle and transport this apparatus!' Land snorted.

'Someone else will do that,' said Thane.

'No, I will. I need it. To develop the defensive potential of lockcrete, I–'

'Someone else will do that too.'

'I… Wow. Wow. Bring them in. I want to meet this exceptional genius,' said Land.

'I am ordered to take you back to Munition Manufactory Two-Two-Six, where you were being so useful before. Armament production is the priority now.'

'No, no,' said Land, trying to pull the gloves off. 'I've moved on from that.'

'Strange to tell, our war has not,' said Thane. 'Get your things. You've been awarded official clearance to work at MM-Two-Two-Six, which I appreciate will come as a shock.'

Land shot him a withering look.

'So… get your things, *sir*,' said Thane.

Land sighed. He peeled off the crusted, thickening gloves, and dropped them into a disposal container.

'Oh,' said Thane, as he waited, 'that brother of the Ninth you were asking about. Zephon? As a gesture of… Anyway, I pulled some strings, and located him for you.'

'Good. Where is he?' asked Land.

'Now?' asked Thane. 'The stasis core at Bhab. He was killed in action at Gorgon Bar a few days ago.'

Keeler heard the footsteps. The clink of keys. The echo of plated boots striking their way along the cell block of the Blackstone. She got up off her cot, and waited for her cell door to open.

The footsteps passed by.

'Amon?' she called. 'Custodian?'

Amon Tauromachian heard her, but ignored her. He continued along the cell block in the darkness, and drew open the door of Fo's cell.

'Alone today?' asked the little prisoner. 'That's a bad sign. You've come to kill me, haven't you? You've thought about what I said, and now you think I'm too dangerous to live. A quiet execution in a cell. But you don't want her to see, because she likes you.'

Amon tossed him a dataslate.

'Write it down,' he said.

'Write… what?'

'You know.'

Fo picked up the slate, and frowned. 'It's not as simple as that…'

'Write it down.'

'I need a laboratory,' said Fo. 'Dedicated bio-technical apparatus. Access to all data archives. Time to plan it precisely, so I can verify my process. It's not just something you jot down.'

'Just the basics,' said Amon. 'The principles. The fundamental elements. The details can come later. Write it down. *All* of it.'

The cubicle was small and simple. Candlelit, a smell of lapping powder in the air. Enough room for a simple cot, a repair unit and the warplate rack. Sindermann had to stand in the doorway. Every now and then, the distant boom of a casemate trembled the floor, and made dust skitter down from the ceiling.

'Did it bring you any satisfaction?' Sindermann asked.

'Not really,' Loken replied. He had laid out his blades on the cot: three of them now, the Imperial Fist's chainsword, Rubio's old gladius, and the other one. 'You?'

'No,' said Sindermann. 'I recorded a detailed account, which I'm sure will never be seen or read. Which is, to my mind, a strange use of history. But I'm not the one deciding history. Just watching it pass.'

Loken nodded. He was working his new blade. *Mourn-it-All* had a frosty gleam.

'Will you use that?' Sindermann asked.

'A good weapon is a good weapon, Kyril,' Loken replied.

'But three swords? Garviel, I hesitate to point out the number of hands you have...'

Loken looked at the old man. 'And I hesitate to point out the number of enemies there are,' he replied. He put the sword down and picked up another, then fished a whetstone from the oiled box.

'What will you do now?' Sindermann asked.

'Go back to the wall,' said Loken.

'Aren't you tired of it?'

'That's not an option,' Loken said.

He ran the whetstone along the blade. Then he stopped, and looked at his old mentor.

'I learned things, Kyril,' Loken said. 'On the killing floors. They were things I thought I already knew, but I didn't really. Not fully. I saw exactly what our enemy has made our brothers into. The weapons he has fashioned out of them. And I saw that the Emperor has done the same.'

'The same?' asked Sindermann.

'In a way. A different way, I suppose. I understand my place. Just like the Sons of Horus are conduits for Lupercal's twisted power, I've become a conduit for His will.'

'What do you mean?' Sindermann asked. 'You always were.'

Loken held Rubio's sword up to the light, and examined its edge.

'Not like this,' he said.

The sun rose over the Guelb er Richât. Clear light. A sky of cornflower blue. Good desert winds.

Good sailing weather. A propitious day to cast off and begin a voyage, even in a desert.

The neck-bells of the stock clunked as the grazers trotted down the ridge away from the approaching figures.

She had used her sunstone to confirm the readings of John's torque-tum.

'How accurate do we think this is?' John asked her.

'In leagues or weeks?' Erda replied.

John sighed. 'But we think he's there?' he asked.

'By every means I know,' she said, 'that's where he's gone. I have consulted the sun, the stars, the cards, the Red Thread and the black mirrors. The cards were the most insistent, others were more reluctant to commit to an answer. But they all agreed. Ollanius is there, two weeks away from now.'

'Right then,' said John. 'I'd best go and get him.' He took out the wraithbone shears, checked his pockets, and kissed Erda on the cheek.

She looked at him, puzzled.

'I don't know why I did that either,' John said. He glanced over his shoulder. 'Are you coming, or what?'

Leetu nodded. 'If it's that important,' the legionary said.

'I will keep safe until you return to me,' Erda told Leetu.

'Just saying, I'm the one who'll need keeping safe,' said John. He looked at Erda. 'Right. See you later.'

'Or before,' she replied.

* * *

Niora Su-Kassen turned in her command seat. She lowered the slate an ensign had passed to her.

'No, Master of Auspex,' she whispered. Most of the personnel on the vast bridge looked around at her. *Phalanx* had been on silent operation for months, with scarcely a word spoken anywhere on the vast fortress-ship. Silence within, as silent as the void without. That a vessel of their magnitude had to operate so stealthily spoke of the potential harm that awaited them everywhere in the Solar Spheres.

The sound of a human voice, even a whisper, shocked almost every one of the five hundred crew and staff present.

The officer standing on the tier of the deck below her shrugged awkwardly. Grand Terran Admiral (Acting) Su-Kassen rose to her feet.

'Use words,' she instructed.

'Trace confirmed, my lady,' he whispered back.

Su-Kassen looked up at the immense oriel and arched ports that spilled light across the bridge chamber. The stained glass had been tinted to reduce the soft brilliance of Saturn's rings, the radiant plains of light and colour beneath which they sheltered. Mighty *Phalanx*, and the rest of the Solar fleet it dwarfed, including the massive flagship *Imperator Somnium*, were in turn dwarfed by the Saturnine expanse. Its mass, and radiation bands, and magnetic fields, concealed them all like a sheltering father.

Since the ravages of the Solar War, she had moved the remnants of the Imperial fleet in from the system edge, creeping into traitor-held space, evading enemy eyes. It was a desperately risky gambit, but it put them closer to strike range, or closer to a rescue run if such an unthinkable thing became necessary. All the while, they were watching for any sign that the reinforcement and relief they had been hoping for had finally arrived.

'We hold–' Su-Kassen said, then stopped and cleared her throat. Talking was so unfamiliar, even whispering. 'We hold, away from all Terran navigation lanes, civilian or military. I chose the vector personally. We are to evade the eyes and ears of the traitor fleets for as long as we can. Or until He calls for us. Any contact signal could make us vulnerable.'

'Agreed, admiral,' whispered the officer. 'But the trace profile–'

'Show me full detail.'

The Master of Auspex motioned to one of his subordinates. Data rolled across Su-Kassen's command station's primary repeater screen.

'Definitely a fleet,' she murmured. 'In military formation. Aetheric wash suggests it's just made translation beyond the system rim.'

'They haven't seen us, lady,' hissed the Master of Watch.

'Those ship profiles are unmistakable,' whispered the Master of Auspex.

Su-Kassen looked at the Officer of Vox. 'Hailing channel,' she said. 'Tight beam, direct.'

'Aye, lady. Done.'

'This is–' she started to say. *No. No identifiers. Keep it simple.* 'You are in our gun sphere. Identify yourself.'

'Incoming visual.'

'Display it,' said Su-Kassen.

'Display, aye.'

An image unfurled, at giant proportions, cast above the vault of the main bridge by hololithic plates.

A face. Black armour. *Unmistakable* black armour.

'I am Corswain of the Dark Angels,' the vox-speakers crackled. *'We come to stand with Terra.'*

ACKNOWLEDGEMENTS

The author would like to thank the 'High Lords' – Nick Kyme, Guy Haley, Chris Wraight, John French, Gav Thorpe and Aaron Dembski-Bowden – for efforts above and beyond the call, and also the *High Lords Emeritus*, Graham McNeill and Jim Swallow. Thank you all for your help and patience.

Serious thanks too to Jacob Youngs (honorary High Lord) and Karen Miksza, Nik Abnett and Jess Woo for first reading and copy edit brilliance, Rachel Harrison for skillfully negotiating art and maps, and to everyone, great and small, Primarch or lasman, who has contributed to the myth of the Horus Heresy over the years.

ABOUT THE AUTHOR

Dan Abnett has written over fifty novels, including
Anarch, the latest instalment in the acclaimed
Gaunt's Ghosts series. He has also written the
Ravenor, Eisenhorn and Bequin books, the most
recent of which is *Penitent*. For the Horus Heresy, he
is the author of the Siege of Terra novel *Saturnine*,
as well as *Horus Rising*, *Legion*, *The Unremembered
Empire*, *Know No Fear* and *Prospero Burns*, the last
two of which were both *New York Times* bestsellers.
He also scripted *Macragge's Honour*, the first Horus
Heresy graphic novel, as well as numerous Black
Library audio dramas. Many of his short stories
have been collected into the volume *Lord of the Dark
Millennium*. He lives and works in Maidstone, Kent.

YOUR
NEXT READ

MORTIS
by John French

After a series of victories, the Imperial forces are on the back foot once more. The power of Chaos is rising, the Traitors gain ground, and all hope seems lost. Can Terra endure?